PRAISE FOR THE ROSE OF YORK NOVELS

"A deftly written, reader-engaging, thoroughly entertaining, and enthusiastically recommended historical novel that documents its author as a gifted literary talent." —*Midwest Book Review*

"This admirable historical novel belongs on the shelf of all true Ricardians next to *The Daughter of Time*."
—*The Historical Novels Review*

"A perfect ten!" —*Romance Reviews Today*

"[E]xtraordinary . . . will breathe glorious life into an era of history that's dark [and] tumultuous." —*Heartstrings Reviews*

Lady
OF THE
Roses

SANDRA WORTH

BERKLEY BOOKS, NEW YORK

THE BERKLEY PUBLISHING GROUP
Published by the Penguin Group
Penguin Group (USA) Inc.
375 Hudson Street, New York, New York 10014, USA
Penguin Group (Canada), 90 Eglinton Avenue East, Suite 700, Toronto, Ontario M4P 2Y3, Canada
(a division of Pearson Penguin Canada Inc.)
Penguin Books Ltd., 80 Strand, London WC2R 0RL, England
Penguin Group Ireland, 25 St. Stephen's Green, Dublin 2, Ireland (a division of Penguin Books Ltd.)
Penguin Group (Australia), 250 Camberwell Road, Camberwell, Victoria 3124, Australia
(a division of Pearson Australia Group Pty. Ltd.)
Penguin Books India Pvt. Ltd., 11 Community Centre, Panchsheel Park, New Delhi—110 017, India
Penguin Group (NZ), 67 Apollo Drive, Rosedale, North Shore 0632, New Zealand
(a division of Pearson New Zealand Ltd.)
Penguin Books (South Africa) (Pty.) Ltd., 24 Sturdee Avenue, Rosebank, Johannesburg 2196, South Africa

Penguin Books Ltd., Registered Offices: 80 Strand, London WC2R 0RL, England

This is an original publication of The Berkley Publishing Group.

This is a work of fiction. Names, characters, places, and incidents either are the product of the author's imagination or are used fictitiously, and any resemblance to actual persons, living or dead, business establishments, events, or locales is entirely coincidental. The publisher does not have any control over and does not assume any responsibility for author or third-party websites or their content.

First edition: January 2008

Library of Congress Cataloging-in-Publication Data

Worth, Sandra.
    Lady of the roses / Sandra Worth.—1st ed.
        p. cm.
    Includes bibliographical references.
    ISBN 978-0-425-21914-0
    1. Great Britain—History—Wars of the Roses, 1455–1485—Fiction. 2. Margaret, of Anjou, Queen, consort of Henry VI, King of England, 1430–1482—Fiction. I. Title.
    PS3623.O775L34 2007
    813'.6—dc22

                                                                                            2007037416

PRINTED IN THE UNITED STATES OF AMERICA

10 9 8 7 6 5 4 3

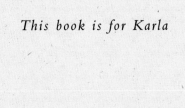

This book is for Karla

ACKNOWLEDGMENTS

I wish to thank my agent, Irene Kraas, for her confidence in me, and my editor, Jackie Cantor, for the meticulous attention she gave this book. I am also indebted to noted graphologist Florence Graving, whose expertise gave me insights into the character of many of these historical figures.

THE HOUSES OF
York, Lancaster, and Neville, 1399 to 1476

EDWARD III

Black Prince

Lionel, Duke of Clarence

John of Gaunt*, Duke of Lancaster

Edmund*, Duke of York

Thomas, Duke of Gloucester

RICHARD II

Anne Mortimer — *m* — Richard, Earl of Cambridge

HENRY IV

HENRY V

Joan Beaufort — *m* — Ralph Neville, Earl of Westmoreland

Henry Stafford, Duke of Buckingham

HENRY VI — *m* — Marguerite d'Anjou

Richard, Earl of Salisbury

Cecily Neville — *m* — Richard, Duke of York

Thomas Neville

John Neville, Lord Montagu

George Neville, Archbishop of York

Richard Neville, Earl of Warwick

issue

Isabelle

Anne

Anne, Duchess of Exeter

EDWARD IV

Edmund, Earl of Rutland

Elizabeth (Liza), D. of Suffolk

Margaret, D. of Burgundy

George, D. of Clarence

Richard, D. of Gloucester

Edward, Prince of Wales

*For simplification of this chart, John and Edmund are shown as if they have traded birth order.
Broken lines denote a missing generation.

Chart by David Major

THE HOUSE OF
Neville

Ralph Neville, — m — Joan Beaufort,
Earl of Westmoreland Countess of Westmoreland
b. circa 1364 *b. 1379*

Richard Neville, — m — Alice Montagu,
Earl of Salisbury Countess of Salisbury
b. 1400 *b. 1405*

- Richard Neville, Earl of Warwick *b. 1428*
- Thomas Neville *b. 1429*
- John Neville, Lord Montagu *b. 1431* — m — Isobel Ingoldesthorpe *b. circa 1440*
- George Neville, Archbishop of York *b. 1433*

Richard Neville, Earl of Warwick *b. 1428* — m — Anne Beauchamp, Countess of Warwick

1. Isabelle *b. circa 1452* — m — George, Duke of Clarence *b. 1450*
2. Anne *b. circa 1454* — m — Richard, Duke of Gloucester KING RICHARD III *b. circa 1452*

John Neville, Lord Montagu *b. 1431* — m — Isobel Ingoldesthorpe *b. circa 1440*

1. Anne
2. Isabelle
3. Elizabeth
4. John *(died at birth)*
5. Margaret
6. George *b. 1465*
7. Lucy*

*Ancestor of President Franklin Delano Roosevelt and Sir Winston Churchill by her second husband, Sir Anthony Browne

THE HOUSE OF
Lancaster

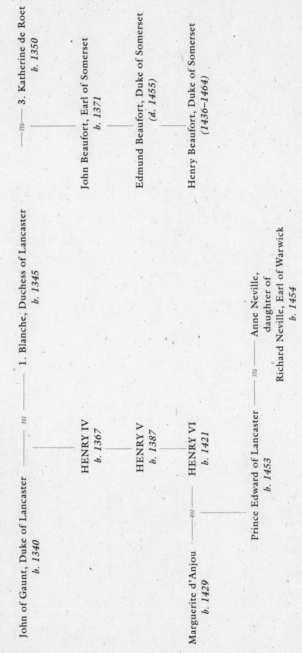

John of Gaunt, Duke of Lancaster
b. 1340

m

1. Blanche, Duchess of Lancaster
b. 1345

m —— 3. Katherine de Roet
b. 1350

HENRY IV
b. 1367

John Beaufort, Earl of Somerset
b. 1371

HENRY V
b. 1387

Edmund Beaufort, Duke of Somerset
(d. 1455)

Marguerite d'Anjou
b. 1429

m

HENRY VI
b. 1421

Henry Beaufort, Duke of Somerset
(1430–1464)

Prince Edward of Lancaster
b. 1453

m

Anne Neville,
daughter of
Richard Neville, Earl of Warwick
b. 1454

LADY OF THE ROSES

Prologue

"MY LADY."

The familiar voice startled me. Unexpected and too gentle, it seemed to prepare the listener for ill tidings. I glanced up, the fear at my heart stopping my breath. Tom Gower, my husband's squire, stood at the threshold of the small chamber, and the expression on his face did nothing to ease the cold that had begun to spread through my body. The cloak I darned slipped from my fingers, and I rose from my chair with difficulty, a hand on the armrest to steady my legs. Then he stepped forward, and I saw that he held a missive. Relief flooded me. I wanted to cry out with joy! *God be praised, he had not come to give me dread tidings of battle, but to deliver the missive my beloved lord had sent!* The smile I gave him as he approached to do his obeisance was so broad, I felt my cheeks would surely crack.

"Tom, dear Tom . . . rise, I pray you. For a moment, I thought— No, pay no heed to what I thought—" Still smiling, I took John's letter from him greedily and held it close to my heart. Then I realized that Tom had not returned my smile and that his face remained as pale and grave as that cold moment when I had first heard his voice. "Tom . . . how goes the war for the Lancastrians?"

He hesitated before he replied. "I know not, my lady. I dressed my lord the marquess in his armor, then he bade me leave him ere the battle started. To bring you this missive . . . and this ring." He reached inside his doublet. As I watched him fumble for the ring, I saw that his fingers were stiff, as if he moved them with difficulty. When I looked at his face, I knew that he kept something from me.

I took the velvet pouch he offered, and removed the ring, feeling as I did so that I stood outside myself, looking down on the scene from high above. In the fading light of day, the stone, dark blue like my husband's eyes, twinkled with the same light I had seen in John's. The world suddenly went very quiet, and there rose before me the vision of a fifteen-year-old girl seated at a window, watching the sun set over the world, her heart breaking with loneliness. She had bartered with the Fates that day for her destiny, and the Fates had listened and granted what she had asked.

That girl was me. Seeking a gift, I had offered a promise, and the time had come to fulfill that promise. However dark the shadows now, I have never forgotten that I am the most fortunate of women. Of storms and sorrow I have known my share, but I have also been blessed with a love such as few are given, a love that dazzled my life with its radiant light as the sun warms and bedazzles the earth. The glory of that love will dry the tears, as it always has, for love transcends all things, even time . . . even death. I regret nothing.

Regaining my composure, I raised my head and looked at Gower. "You have had a long journey," I managed, thankful my voice did not waver. "Tell the cook to prepare you the best meal we can offer, and get rest. . . ." In spite of myself, tears stung my eyes and my lips trembled. I turned away and heard Gower's footsteps echo down the hall as he left.

LANCASTRIAN
ENGLAND

1456–1461

One

JUNE 1456

AMID LIGHTNING, THUNDER, AND THE PELTING
rain of a summer storm, a castle appeared in the distance, as if in
answer to my prayers. "There!" I cried, unable to restrain my great
relief. "We can take refuge there, can't we, Sœur Madeleine?"

With the wind whipping her cloak around her, Sœur Madeleine turned her small, plump bulk in her saddle and, ignoring the
young man-at-arms, Guy, directed herself to the squire accompa-
nying us on our journey. "Master Giles, you know this place that
is so curious?" she inquired. Her English was so heavily laden with
the accent of her native Anjou that if I didn't listen carefully, she
seemed to be speaking French. But she was right about the castle.
Set in an open emerald field instead of high on a hill, and more like
a magnificent country mansion inviting to guests than a fortress
designed to repel enemies, it made a strange sight with its hexago-
nal redbrick towers, large windows, and tall, narrow frame.

"I believe it belongs to Lord Ralph Cromwell, Sister," replied
Master Giles, his horse's hooves sucking in and out of the sticky,

mud-mired road. "I heard he built a castle of red brick in Lincoln-shire called Tattershall."

"And this lord . . . which is his allegiance, the Red Rose or the White?"

Master Giles threw Sœur Madeleine a small, sardonic laugh. "No man can be sure, Sister—'tis said Lord Cromwell changes color with the wind. He was King Henry's lord chancellor back in the thirties, but a few years ago he quarreled with the Lancastrians and wed his niece to a Yorkist lord. After the Battle of St. Albans, I heard he quarreled with the Yorkists and now considers himself a loyal Lancastrian adherent of the queen's."

Sœur Madeleine gave a horrified gasp. "Such a man is a traitor! In France we would know what to do with him."

From what I could see of Master Giles's face, hidden between his collar and his sodden wool hat, I could tell his thoughts: This was England, and a good thing too. Even the French queen who had wed our King Henry couldn't change that.

"Perhaps we should not stop," Sœur Madeleine said suddenly, pulling up so sharply her horse almost lost its footing in a muddy puddle and snorted in protest. "*Mon dieu*, he may have changed back to York, and I will not take 'ospitality from a traitor!"

Master Giles and Guy rested their gazes on me, and their ex-pressions told me I was the only one who could avert this setback. If we passed up this castle, we had no assurance of finding a hamlet with lodging for the night, and might well find ourselves sleeping under a tree. Wet and shivering with cold in the stinging rain, I too had been excited at the thought of a hot meal and a change of clothes. Now all stood in jeopardy. Fond as I was of Sœur Mad-eleine, she could be quite impractical. Fortunately, thanks to the kindly, almost maternal interest she had taken in me during the few weeks we had known one another, I had been able to use my influence with her for the benefit of our entire little party on the long journey from Marrick Priory in Yorkshire down to London. I took a breath before I spoke.

"Sœur Madeleine, Lord Jesus said that sinners who find the true way are saved, so if this Yorkist lord who strayed from the Red

Rose has now returned to the righteous fold of Lancaster, then God will forgive him—and surely we should, too?"

Sœur Madeleine turned her face up to Heaven, as if to weigh the strength of both God's forgiveness and the storm. "*Alors, mon enfant*, you 'ave much wisdom for your fifteen years—there can be no other reason why God has put this place into our path in weather so formidable. He must intend us to stay here for the night, *chère* Isabelle." As if to seal her approval, she gave my name an extra flourish so that it sounded French.

Losing no time, Master Giles spurred his horse and sped in the direction of the castle. I knew he had rushed off so that Sœur Madeleine couldn't change her mind again, and I galloped my palfrey after him as best I could on the muddy highway. Guy, the young man-at-arms whose horse pulled my coffer, followed too, but, slowed by the small cart he dragged, his horse kept floundering in the deep puddles and he was the last to reach the castle gate.

As I drew alongside Master Giles, someone peered from the watchtower and the cry came down, "Who goes there?"

"The queen's ward, Lady Isobel Ingoldesthorpe, and her guardian, Sister Madeleine of Marrick Priory. We seek refuge for the night," Master Giles said, his face dripping with rain as he looked up.

The portcullis creaked open. I cantered my palfrey into the shelter of the castle gateway and dismounted with Master Giles's help. The porter came out of the guardhouse, and I smiled my thanks.

"You're fortunate, my good people," he said. "You'll find safe haven here with my lord Cromwell, whether ye be Lancastrian or Yorkist."

"You have Yorkists sheltering here this night?" Sœur Madeleine exclaimed.

A crash of thunder drowned out the man's reply to this dangerous question, and I seized the chance to distract everyone by pretending to faint. Sœur Madeleine and the porter rushed to my aid.

"Breathe deeply, my dear," advised Sœur Madeleine. I did as she suggested.

"Good that you came when you did," said the porter. "The young lady is in need of rest, and the storm is worsening."

As if Heaven decided to help us, the rumbling grew louder and the driving rain poured faster as he spoke. But Sœur Madeleine returned to the subject of Lord Cromwell.

"Is your lord the same Lord Cromwell who served King Henry and our gracious queen Marguerite d'Anjou as chancellor?" asked Sœur Madeleine, her tone less demanding now. I held my breath.

"The same," he replied. "So, where are you headed?" he asked pleasantly, handing the horses over to two young, damp boy helpers.

"To court, sir," Sœur Madeleine said with a haughty look. "I am Sœur Madeleine of the Benedictine Order of the Abbey Notre-Dame de Wisques, and my charge here is Lady Isobel Ingoldesthorpe, ward of Queen Marguerite d'Anjou. Her father was the loyal Lancastrian knight Sir Edmund Ingoldesthorpe of Newmarket, Cambridgeshire, and her mother was the true Lancastrian Lady Joan Tiptoft of Cambridgeshire, both deceased, God rest their souls." She made the sign of the cross, pursed her lips, and lifted her chin in challenge.

I gave the porter a quick smile to melt the coldness of Sœur Madeleine's reply and bowed my head to hide my thoughts. Contrary to what Sister had just said, my father was no dyed-in-the-wool Lancastrian. In order to avoid fighting for the Lancastrians, he had spent most of his adult life not answering the king's many summonses, then explaining his actions and paying for expensive pardons. *"A corrupt lot!"* was how he'd described the French queen and her favorites, who ruled the land during King Henry's frequent illnesses. But such talk was treasonous, and he had been careful not to let anyone suspect his Yorkist sympathies. I forced back the memory and, throwing off my wet hood, shook out my hair. I noticed that the porter's gaze went to my face and lingered there. Sœur Madeleine noticed too. "You are bold, sir," she snapped. "I hope your lord has better manners than you."

The man flushed in apology. "Aye, Sister, have no fear. He is a true knight and well he knows how to treat a lady. Pray, follow me."

LORD CROMWELL, A GENIAL MAN WITH HAIR THE color of frost, came to greet us as soon as we were announced in the great hall, where he had been in conversation with the chamberlain while servants rushed around busily preparing for a grand feast. Some covered the long tables with white cloths; arranged fruit bowls and dishes for salt; and laid out pewter bowls, steel knives, silver spoons, and cups. Others positioned iron candelabras, replaced burned-out candles, and secured torches into the wall brackets, while still others swept up refuse, bone fragments, dog excrement, and stale rushes. Wooden barrels brimming with fragrant rose petals, hyssop, and sweet fennel had been carted up from the cellar and waited nearby, ready to be scattered over the clean floor. Clearly, Lord Cromwell had spared no expense.

"Gracious sister—my dear young lady—we bid thee both a hearty welcome!" he boomed as he kissed my hand and bowed to Sœur Madeleine. "You have timed your visit well, not only to shelter from the inclement weather—aye, not only for that!—but for the banquet planned for the evening, a very special banquet, I might add. My niece Lady Maude Neville is arriving shortly with her husband and an entourage of young friends who shall be delighted to meet you, dear Lady Isobel. No doubt you will have much to discuss together—you know, those matters that absorb maidens so completely—*young men!*" He gave me a wink that brought a smile to my face and a frown to Sœur Madeleine's. "There will be music, and dancing, and a troubadour to entertain us, and flame throwers—you must get rest and refresh yourselves so you can enjoy the merriment!"

We were ushered to our chamber, a pleasant room high on the third floor, overlooking the inner court, where my coffer had already been set. In spite of the rain, the room greeted us as cheerfully as its owner had. At one end, the redbrick wall provided a bright backdrop for the gold bed curtains and coverlet, and at the other a large window threw light over a colorful tapestry that covered nearly all the brick. Two servants entered, bearing a jug of wine, a platter of cheese, tall goblets, and a silver basin of water for washing, which they set on a high chest. One lit the candelabra while another took our wet, mud-splashed cloaks and hung them to dry in the garderobe before he left. As I watched the door shut behind him, excitement overwhelmed me and I rushed to my coffer to retrieve my most beautiful dress, as yet unworn.

"*Isabelle*," Sœur Madeleine announced sternly.

I knew what that tone meant. I turned slowly, my heart sinking in my breast.

"We are not attending the banquet. You have no need to change."

"May I ask why, Sœur Madeleine?" I inquired in a small voice.

"Did you not hear his niece's name? She is a Neville."

"Not all branches of the Neville family support the Duke of York. Many are Lancastrian."

"*Peut-être*, but I take no chances with you, Isabelle. We will 'ave supper in our room and go to bed early so we can be ready for tomorrow's voyage. Now 'elp me out of my gown before I die of the cold."

Her resolute expression left no room for hope and I knew entreaty was useless. I swallowed my disappointment and slowly closed my coffer. "Aye, Sœur Madeleine."

Untying the cloth belt that secured her gown, Sister removed her rosary from around her waist and pressed it to her lips before setting it down on the chest. I unfastened the brooch that secured her veil; took off her white crown band, wimple, coif, and the soft white cotton cloth underneath; folded everything; laid them neatly aside; and helped her out of her pleated white habit, which made up the outer garb of the Benedictine Order. I hung it to dry on a peg in the garderobe. After aiding her into the high bed, I brought her a goblet filled with wine, which she quickly emptied, and some cheese, which she waved away. In her simple cotton shift, with her thin gray hair exposed and the blanket drawn up to her shoulders, she no longer seemed plump and robust, but old and frail. Seized with compassion, I refilled her goblet and mopped her brow with a towel dipped in the perfumed water from the silver basin. I ran my brush of boar bristles gently over her pink scalp and wispy hair. "Is this better, Sœur Madeleine?" I asked.

She sighed with pleasure. *"Oui, mon enfant,"* she said softly, and closed her eyes.

I crossed to the window. Guests had begun arriving, and their laughter drifted up to me in my bower, piercing my heart. I'd been in a nunnery for the past eight months, and I longed for the company of young people, and for laughter, and music, and dance—all that I'd missed since my father's death.

"Isabelle, sing for me," said Sœur Madeleine abruptly.

I went to the coffer and removed my small wooden lyre. It had served me well at the convent, since it was not loud, and even at night I had been able to drown my loneliness in its sweet notes. I carried it to the window seat and opened the window. The air, cool and damp, brushed my cheek. The violent storm had lifted, and the wind had chased away the clouds and ushered in what promised to be a lovely July sunset. A pale purple hue stained the east now, and in the west the few clouds that remained had turned to peach, casting a glow over the village, where a few lights already twinkled. But in the months since my father's death, I had found that nature's beauty, far from soothing the ache of my spirit, summoned an inexplicable sadness from within my depths.

I missed my mother and my father, and I had no sisters or brothers. I was on my way to court to be married, but while my heart yearned for the kind of love that troubadours sang about and wordsmiths described in their lovely manuscripts—the kind of love my mother and father must have had for one another, since he never wed again after her death—I knew love would likely not be my portion. Marriages were made for lands and wealth, not love, and few young women with lands to offer a husband could hope that fortune would bestow on them a love match. Even royalty married for alliances and trade agreements, and my future lay in the hands of the Lancastrian Queen Marguerite d'Anjou, wed at fifteen to a mad king. What pity would she have for me? Her interest lay only in my wardship and marriage, because the wardship paid her a fair annual income, and my marriage would fetch a goodly profit for her purse.

I didn't know why the world was made so bitterly, but in this it played favorites, and I—foolishly, I suppose—dared to hope I'd be one of the rare and fortunate few who would find Fortune's favor. In the meanwhile I longed for small joys, like the banquet that I might have attended tonight, where I could laugh and be with young men my own age, and feel the lightness of life.

I bowed my head with an acute sense of loss and plucked the chords of the latest lament to sweep the land. Raising my voice in song, I poured my heart into the words, and the haunting melody so encompassed me that I heard my own tears in the music. . . .

> *Will I never feel the sun before clouds gather?*
> *Will my heart never dance before it dies?*
> *Will I never know your love, beloved?*
> *You are lost to me, lost to me. . . .*

I lifted my gaze to Heaven. The sky was awash with color. As I sang, the clouds turned to gold and deepened into rose. A lone bird soared high above, free to roam where it willed. I followed it with my eyes and my words until it faded from my sight. The sky changed again, and now, like fire, the rose glow caught the earth, bathing all the world in tender beauty. I don't know what came over me, but of a sudden I was swept with an indescribable yearning I could neither define nor understand. Yet I knew instinctively that the only potion that could banish the emptiness, that could break the loneliness, was that elusive thing the wordsmiths called love. I brought the song to a close, bent my head, and closed my eyes. Silent words fell from my heart, and, bartering with the Fates, I sought a gift and made a promise.

"Isabelle."

I blinked. It took me a moment to reorient myself. "Aye, Sœur Madeleine?"

"We can go to the banquet, if you wish it."

Disbelief left me speechless, incredulous. My mind spun with bewilderment, and when at last her words registered, I laughed in sheer joy. I laughed at the sky, at the clouds, at the servants taking the horses from the guests arriving in the courtyard below. I threw my arms up and laughed, and I twirled from the window seat, laughing. I clasped my hands together to my lips in prayer, and I murmured *thank you* to Heaven, half laughing, half crying, and twirled again. Then I looked at Sœur Madeleine. A tender smile hovered on her face as she watched me.

I rushed to her side, and, taking her hand to my lips, I kissed the wrinkled skin. "Thank you, dear Sœur Madeleine."

She blushed. *"C'est rien,"* she murmured. " 'Tis nothing. But if we are to go, I daresay we had better hurry, *ma petite."*

I ran to my coffer and rummaged for my new gown: a rich lavender silk and silver-tissue sarcenet, embroidered with tiny silver leaves, which I had never had occasion to wear before. The high-waisted gown, with its low neckline trimmed with miniver, fell in voluminous folds into a train at the back, and it shimmered like moonlight as I took it out of the coffer.

"You must be very careful, Isabelle," Sœur Madeleine said as she helped me into the magnificent dress and arranged my long hair loosely around me.

"Why?" I replied, half-drunk in my joy.

"You are too beautiful, with your swan neck and so big eyes, and I fear there are Yorkists at the banquet. Rapists and murderers, all of them."

"Not all, surely?" I said, teasing in my delirium. I wondered if Sœur Madeleine had drunk too much wine. She had never complimented me before, and why should she, when my eyes were not blue, but brown, and my hair not gold, but dark as chestnuts? If only I had a mirror! But mirrors were forbidden at the priory, for, as the nuns kept reminding us, the only eyes that mattered were the eyes of God. "I saw some Yorkists once," I said gaily, "and they didn't look like rapists or murderers."

Sœur Madeleine gave a shocked cry, and for a moment I feared

I had made a disastrous mistake that would cost me the banquet. But she said only, "*Mon dieu*, what is the world coming to?"

"I found them attractive, as a matter of fact," I giggled. I was drunk, surely, or I would never have dared to make such an admission.

She gaped at me. "I should report you to the queen!"

I bent down and kissed her forehead with a smile. Bending came naturally to me, for though I was a head shorter than most men, I was taller than most women. "But you won't, will you?" I laughed, not comprehending what made me so bold.

"*Mon enfant*, you are impossible. I don't know why I let you 'ave your way with me, but to tell you true, I love you like my own. Maybe because your dark hair and eyes, they remind me of—" She broke off, seemed to catch herself, and added, "Of Anjou." She fell silent, in reverie.

I, too, returned to reverie. But the scene that came to me made me giggle aloud.

"What do you find so amusing?"

"Nothing," I lied, wiping the grin from my face with effort. I had never confided my secret memory to anyone, and certainly I had no intention of sharing it with Sœur Madeleine, no matter how drunk on joy I might be. In the previous spring, I had gone north to Yorkshire to visit friends, and we had been returning to Wensleydale after a day's outing picnicking in a meadow filled with wildflowers. Singing and laughing, we rolled along in our cart, the sun shining brightly on the pear orchards shedding their blossoms over us. At a turn of the River Ure some distance yet from the manor, the woods parted, and two young men suddenly emerged from the river. Caught by surprise, they stood naked as babes for a moment before they quickly covered themselves as we passed—but one covered his face instead of his manly parts. My friends and I burst into sidesplitting laughter and strained to see more as our two bodyguards cursed and the driver whipped the horses and barreled past. That sight, our first ever of a naked man, kept us in merriment for weeks.

But in these months I hadn't forgotten the one who had covered his face, and sometimes I even saw him in my dreams, though only fleetingly, as I had in life.

"Listen to me, *mon enfant*," Sœur Madeleine said, taking me by my shoulders. She seemed suddenly grave, and I grew fearful. "You are young, romantic, but you must be realist. Love has little place in life. A young girl who is Lancastrian must wed with a Lancastrian. If she has no wealth, she must wed for wealth, old, ugly, and toothless though he be; and if she has some land like you, she must wed for more. To love is to open oneself to pain, and in this world filled with troubles, there is trouble enough without love to worsen matters. 'Tis best to see all Yorkists as rapists and murderers. Do you understand, Isabelle? Do you?"

It suddenly occurred to me that old people were filled with empty warnings about life, and I felt a rush of relief. I could dismiss her words like a faint rumble of thunder that had moved far away and no longer touched us. "Aye, Sœur Madeleine, I understand," I said to please her, my mood as bright as ever.

Two

The Dance, 1456

AT THE FIRST CALL OF THE SUPPER HORN, I CROSSED the castle courtyard with Sœur Madeleine beneath a violet sky set with a solitary star, and wound my way up the stairwell to the great hall, trailed by my fellow guests. The hum of conversation grew louder the higher we went, until a raucous din told us we had reached the passageway to the chamber. Crowds thronged the entry, some engaging in conversation, others of low rank waiting to be seated. Heads turned as I passed, and I couldn't help but take pleasure in my gorgeous gown and the bows and admiring glances that followed me.

Though privy to the banquet preparations earlier, I was taken aback by the splendor of the hall. A heavy scent of roses wafted up from the scattered petals on the floor, and the room danced with light from the many flaring torches and the candles flickering on the tables and in the deep recesses of the windows. Behind the dais where Lord Cromwell would sit, a fire blazed in the enormous stone hearth bearing his coat of arms. Silver, pewter, and the panes of glass in the windows reflected the flames so that even the banners and tapestries decorating the paneled room twinkled with jeweled lights.

Across the hall, a few knights and ladies were already at the tables below the windows, and the chamberlain led us to them. We passed Master Giles and Guy, seated with other heralds, squires, clerks, scriveners, and their wives at a lower table below the salt, reserved for commoners, bare of fruit and silver, and set with wooden bowls and cups instead of pewter and horn. They gave us a bow as we passed, and the admiration in their eyes lightened my step. Arriving at our table, I noted with delight that we had been seated next to the dais. With a crosscurrent of greeting, and a nod from Sœur Madeleine, I slipped in first, next to a burly knight with a florid complexion who stood to give a courtly bow. Sœur Madeleine took the end of the bench, and her lips remained pursed as she inclined her head to the knight in greeting, so I gave him a little smile, which I was soon to regret.

Other knights and ladies, clergy, and those of rank came to join us at our table, and with each placement, the ruddy knight edged closer to me, forcing me to slide toward Sister until all space was exhausted and any further movement in that direction would have either pushed Sister off the end of the bench or alerted her to the knight's antics and guaranteed a scene. Faced with this choice, I suffered in silence and tried to ignore his thigh and shoulders pressing into mine, and his bold glances that raked my bodice.

A sudden flourish of trumpets stilled the buzz of conversation. Like everyone else, I hastened to rise, adding to the rustle of silk that rippled through the hall.

Gazing around at his guests with a broad smile of welcome on his rosy face, and followed by an entourage of lords and ladies, Lord Cromwell entered, a pleasant-looking, fair-haired young lady on his arm whom I took to be his niece, Lady Maude. Though I had been to banquets now and again with my father, I had become accustomed to the stark regimen and drabness of the nunnery, and I couldn't help but stare spellbound at the colorful group entering the hall, their gorgeous velvets and gold cloths aglitter with gems.

Then I noticed the hound at the rear of the procession. It pranced with an air of hauteur and bore such a lordly expression that I almost laughed aloud. I glanced at its owner, and a wave of recognition flowed through me. But how did I know this knight? And if I had once seen him, how could I have forgotten such a face?

Save for the hound at his heels, he walked alone at the end of the group, lean, broad-shouldered, and taller than the others, his tawny head brilliant in the candlelight, his eyes scanning the crowd as if he searched for someone. Somehow I knew it was a maiden, and a strange pain twisted my heart. For one so tall, he bore himself with grace, and there was about him an unmistakable air of knightly nobility, from the fine straight nose and square jaw down to the high boots he wore in lieu of the courtier's pointed-toe shoes. Despite his fashionable attire of green velvet embroidered with rich gold thread, his sun-bronzed complexion and muscular thighs spoke of a man who spent more time riding in the sun than drinking at feasts. A voice spoke in my head: *Ah, yes,* it said. *Whoever she is that he searches for, surely she is the most fortunate of women.* At that moment he turned his head and caught my stare. The hint of a smile touched his generous mouth, and his cheeks creased, flashing dimples. My breath caught in my throat. I knew his smile was not intended for me, yet I blushed furiously and hastily dropped my lids.

Lord Cromwell took his place at the center of the dais and gave a speech of welcome. As he spoke, I thought I felt the green knight's gaze on me, but I made a resolute effort not to let my glance stray to the dais, where he sat. Instead I occupied myself by counting the beauties present in the hall . . . at least four, and their heads shone like spun gold at the tables. I stole a glance down at my own hair. Though it was thick, shiny, and long almost to my waist, it fell straight as a Roman road behind me and in the candlelight seemed as dark as raven's feathers. A sense of my own inadequacy swept me. If I had been given to envy, it would have engulfed me now, but as I sat admiring the fair ones, there was only acceptance tinged with regret that I couldn't count myself a beauty like them, for beauty would have drawn his eye to me. No, the young knight couldn't have noticed me; it was just me, wishing it were so. *Wishing* . . .

My father's oft-repeated words echoed in my mind: *Be content, and remember, there are always those who have more than you, and always those who have less.* I decided to count my blessings: I had asked to come to the feast, and here I was, and I would enjoy myself to the hilt.

After grace, servants poured rose water into the small basins set out for hand washing. I dipped my fingers into mine and held them out to a passing servant to be dried with a linen cloth. When everyone had washed, the basins were removed, and the pantler distributed bread, butter, and pig fat while the butler and his boy helpers poured jugs of wine and beer. Sister quickly downed her cup and accepted a refill.

"Bah!" said the knight at my elbow, startling me. Setting down his wine cup, he spat on the floor and wiped his mouth with the back of his hand. "Wine's sour and smacks of pitch! Can our lord not afford better?"

"Where have you had better?" came the reply from someone down the table. "Tell us, and we'll go there!" A chorus of laughter met this remark.

"You are quite mistaken, monsieur—this wine is excellent. Very fine indeed," announced Sœur Madeleine, tipping her cup for a longer draught. "As it comes from Bordeaux, there can be no question about that."

I took a sip. The wine did taste of pitch, but at the priory it had been worse: so greasy, flat, and muddy with sediment that I always closed my eyes and filtered it with my clenched teeth when I drank. Sister was truthful: Compared to that wine, this was very fine.

The knight acknowledged Sister's remark with a "humph" that left no doubt where he stood on the matter, and turned his attention to the fresh herring pie that had just been placed on his trencher, seasoned with ginger, pepper, and cinnamon. I caught his garlic breath as he reached across me to dip into the salt, and lost my appetite.

"What, you don't eat?" he asked with his mouth full, tearing a piece of bread for himself and spreading it with a thick layer of the pig fat. "A young lady like you should not lack appetite for life!" He gave me a wink and dug his thigh into mine again. I felt myself redden to the roots of my hair.

"*Oui, mon enfant*, eat," Sister chimed in. "You are too slender as it is. *Mange, ma petite.*" Then she tapped me on the knee and said, "You are causing some interest across the hall. Do not encourage them, Isabelle."

I glanced in the direction she indicated. A table of young men were indeed eyeing me, and when they found my gaze on them, a curly-haired young fellow picked up his goblet and toasted me with a drink. In no way did he resemble the young lord on the dais, and I glanced down. "Aye, Sœur Madeleine," I said, and realized my voice was tinged with melancholy.

Obediently I ignored the young men and nibbled my bread while the ruddy knight beside me gave a belch and picked his teeth with a dirty fingernail. The thought came to me that he was probably married, and at that moment I made a vow never to give my consent to a match by the queen, unless I felt some affection for her choice, no matter how much pressure she brought to bear. A nunnery would be preferable. . . . My eyes stole wistfully to the knight at the dais. How splendid he was! He was laughing at a joke someone had made, and it made no sense to me that my heart should twist again with the yearning I had felt when I'd watched the beauty of the sunset.

Having no one else to turn to, I decided to make the best of the evening. "Do you know who they are that sit at the High Table?" I asked the ruddy old knight, prepared to view the food he chewed in exchange for information.

"Indeed I do!" he replied, munching. "The lady next to Lord Cromwell is his niece, Lady Maude, and she's wed to the dark-haired knight seated on her right. His name is Sir Thomas Neville. And see there . . . that's his younger brother Sir John Neville, sitting on Lord Cromwell's left."

At the name "Neville" I threw Sister a nervous glance. Fortunately the crowd in the hall had grown rowdy, and Sister was so engrossed in her capon and wine that this information failed to reach her. Although she drank heavily, her cup remained filled; I realized suddenly that a varlet hovered nearby, constantly pouring as though she were born royal. I gave this no more thought, rejoicing instead that I could feast on information without her reprimand, despite my rapidly declining spirits.

Though I had an uncle who had been created an earl, the Nevilles were of the blood royal and counted many a lord, earl, and duchess among their number. Their climb to power had begun in the twelfth century through the marriage bed, when Robert Fitzmaldred wed the heiress of Henry de Neville from Neuville in Calvados and their children took the mother's name.

Family feuds in successive generations made bitter foes of the two branches of Nevilles, driving one to champion the White Rose of York, and the other the Red Rose of Lancaster. The successes of the Yorkist Nevilles also brought them into clashes with yet another powerful clan—the Percies. Long a law unto themselves in Northumberland, the Percies resented the steady erosion of power and wealth to these Nevilles, whom they viewed as upstarts. Yet through all the troubles, Fortune kept her smile fixed firmly on the Yorkist Nevilles, and the marriage bed, where they had made their richest conquests, continued to bless them. Through his wife, Nan Beauchamp, whom he had wed at the age of eight, Richard Neville, the eldest of the four sons of the Earl of Salisbury, had recently been created Earl of Warwick, the premier earl of the land.

"You are very knowledgeable," I said, warming a little to the knight. His uncouth manners and sideways glances into my bosom no longer offended me, since he had proved so helpful. "Can you tell me more?" I leaned close so that the raucous bursts of laughter from our companions along the table as they exchanged court gossip would not deprive me of a word.

"That young man beside Lady Maude is quite a knight, *pardieu!* Now there's a tale—"

I glanced at Sir John Neville. He had tilted his chair back and was engaged in conversation with Lady Maude behind Lord

Cromwell's back. I looked away before he could notice me. A question was throbbing for an answer.

"These Nevilles, are they from the Yorkist or the Lancastrian branch?" I asked as casually as I could manage. So that the ruddy knight would not see in my eyes what the answer meant to me, I occupied myself by picking up a piece of the grilled hare now on my plate and making a show of swirling it around the spicy mustard sauce. But he surprised me by laughing; an uproarious, belly-shaking laugh that occupied him for quite a spell. I watched him curiously.

"You are an innocent one, aren't you?" Still laughing, he turned to the others down the table. "She wants to know whether these Nevilles are Yorkist or Lancastrian!"

"I've been in a nunnery, sir." I felt myself blush as I tried to explain my ignorance.

"Then you do have a good deal to learn, and lucky the man to teach you!" he guffawed.

The ladies smiled, and a few of the men snorted with laughter. One, who turned out to be Lord Cromwell's seneschal, took pity on me and said, "They are *the* Yorkists, my lady."

I turned back to the ruddy knight, and he picked up where he had left off. "Indeed, each time King Henry slips into madness— excuse me, *illness*—the queen and Richard, Duke of York, vie to rule the land as Protector of the Realm. Sometimes York has the upper hand, sometimes the queen. But no matter—these Nevilles have stood staunchly by York through thick and thin since the very start of the troubles. . . . Aye, I see you're beginning to understand. They are sons of the Earl of Salisbury and brothers to the Earl of Warwick."

I felt as though someone had struck me a reeling blow, and I must have blanched, because faintly, as if through a wall, I heard him say, "Are you all right, Lady Isobel?"

I nodded. " 'Tis merely . . . the hare is tough." I laid the morsel down on my trencher and swallowed on my tight throat. "Pray continue."

"Well, here's a tale for you. . . . There are the Nevilles, and there are the Percies, and the two clans hate one another, right—you know that much, eh? Good. Now, see Lady Maude there . . . she's the heiress to the Cromwell lands and estates, which include several former Percy estates confiscated from them by Henry IV for treason back in early 1400. So when she married Sir Thomas Neville right here in this castle two years ago, that meant the Nevilles would one day lay claim to several strongholds that had once belonged to the Percies. Seems that Lord Egremont, a hot-tempered younger son of the Earl of Northumberland who's landless himself—and such a rowdy fellow that no heiress will marry him!—didn't take too kindly to the idea of Percy lands falling into Neville hands, no matter that the properties in question had been confiscated more than fifty years ago. So Egremont lay in wait for the bridal party at Stamford Bridge. They say that it was thanks to the younger son, Sir John—who's as valiant a soldier as you'll find anywhere—that the Nevilles—taken by surprise, mind you, and with a much smaller army—routed the Percies! Though he's a third son and but twenty-five years of age, his father, the Earl of Salisbury, puts great store in his counsel. Aye, lady, I'd fight with Sir John Neville any day . . . that is, if Lord Cromwell gives the word. I'm in his service."

"I see." A vegetable course of peas and onions in saffron had been cleared away untouched, and now I stared down at the figs on my dessert plate, beautifully served with almonds and rose petals, and decorated with powdered sugar. I picked one up and tried to swallow. I couldn't understand what was wrong with me. The banquet I'd wept to miss had ended in sorry disappointment, and I found myself wishing the evening over.

But Sister was not ready to leave. Turning to me, she gave a clap and said as gaily as any child, "The flame throwers are here, Isabelle!" She pointed to two bare-chested young men, with beads around their necks, entering the hall amidst a fanfare of trumpets from the minstrels' gallery. They juggled the fire with a display of rare skill and ended their performance by devouring the flames. Raising their extinguished torches high in victory, they turned to receive the hearty applause and silver coins that rained down on them. Next came a troubadour with his gittern to sing a lewd tale

about a fishmonger's cheating wife, full of ribaldry, followed by a
lament of Elaine's doomed love for Sir Lancelot, brimming with
sad sighs, tears, and desire. All I could think of was the lord with
the creases around his smile. Now I was glad of the ruddy knight's
company, and I tried to focus on him so that I would not look at
the one who sat high to my left on the dais, so far above me.

At last the troubadour gave a bow and said, "Thus ends my tale.
God save all this fair company—amen!" The minstrels in the gallery broke into loud chords, and the floor cleared for dancing. The
passionate Celtic rhythm they played on their harp, rebec, pipes,
and lutes spoke of love in every note, but I sat stiffly on my bench,
determined not to feel the music. Lords and ladies rose to dance,
and the ruddy knight slapped the table.

"Ho, my dear lady! 'Tis time for some revelry—let us—"

He broke off in midspeech. I turned in the direction in which
he gazed, to find myself staring straight into Sir John Neville's dark
blue eyes. The breath went out of me.

"Lady Isobel, may I have the honor of this dance?" he said, his
voice resonant, touched with the accent of the North.

He knew my name! My lips parted in search of air. I rose mutely.
He bowed to Sœur Madeleine, and she stood to let me out, though
reluctantly, weaving slightly. She was clearly displeased, but I ignored her frown and gave him my hand. With a touch that was
light yet commanding, he led me to the center of the hall. We
took our positions along with other dancers on the rose-petaled
floor, and in time to the exotic beat that evoked something of the
wild moors, we moved together: a small step to the side, forward
three steps, back two, and a hop. I barely knew what I was doing.
His eyes scorched mine, and I could not look away. We reversed
the sequence, parted from one another with a step, and drew back
together again. I felt the movement of his breath, and with it the
candles blurred, the walls of the room receded, and the other dancers faded into oblivion. There was only him and me in all the
world, and music, and a fiery wind beneath my feet sweeping me
forward, sweeping me back. He knelt, and slowly I circled him,
feeling as if I moved in a dream, my hand never leaving his, his eyes

never leaving mine. He came to his feet, took his turn. Time hung suspended, and I stood helplessly as he passed around me, igniting my burning heart into flame.

We moved forward a double step, back one, gave a hop, and took another small step to the side. We danced palm to palm, face-to-face, in slow and perfect harmony, first in one direction, then the other, and we were two halves of a circle spinning together in eternity, spinning, spinning. . . . The melody filled all the air, leaving none for me to breathe, and I could not draw my eyes away from his; I could not move my hand from his. I never, ever wanted to leave, never wanted the dance to end, never wanted to return to the barren world I had known.

But end it did. Suddenly and with a clash of cymbals, we were paused in place, locked in one another's gaze, breathing in unison as the notes quivered into silence. The song was over; the world had stopped spinning. All my strength was focused on recovery, but my heart pounded so violently against my ribs that I knew my heaving bosom betrayed my emotion. A sick giddiness born of shame, heat, and excitement made me falter, and I raised a hand to my brow.

"My lady," he said, steadying me by the elbow. "It seems we must seek some air. The warmth in here is suffocating."

I nodded, the corners of my mouth lifting. And then I remembered Sister. She would never permit me to leave the room with anyone, especially not a knight. Especially not a Neville.

"But—" I said, turning to the front of the room where Sister sat.

"We shall request permission, as is seemly," he said, but his tone held a smile.

When we reached Sœur Madeleine, I realized why. She no longer sat on the bench but in a tapestried chair set off to the corner, and her head lolled to one side as she slept, snoring loudly. A wineglass lay lightly in one hand, engulfed in the folds of her skirts. Having spilled its last drops on her knees, it bobbed up and down with each heavy breath, like a ship at sea.

I suppressed my laughter and glanced at him.

"It seems Sœur Madeleine is in no condition to deny us permission, my lady," he said, his eyes twinkling and a grin revealing his irresistible dimples. He put out his hand to me. I seized it most undecorously. The fact that I remembered the hovering varlet and realized that unholy temptation had deliberately been set into Sister's path made not a berry's worth of difference to me.

The air was fresh, the night beautiful, and the small walled garden profuse with blooms that sparkled with raindrops. Music drifted from the open windows of the great hall as we passed a server with a tray of oranges, and a group of courtiers and maidens around a smooth stone fountain, laughing amidst the roses.

"They tell me you are Lancastrian," he said.

"They tell me you are Yorkist. And that all Yorkists are rapists and murderers," I replied, stealing a wry look at him from beneath my lashes as we strolled.

He laughed, a hearty, wonderful laugh that creased his cheeks and flashed his dimples to my delight. A light twinkled in his dark blue eyes. "Don't believe everything you hear. There are a few exceptions."

I glanced down at the hound that strutted happily at his heels. "And what is he, Yorkist or Lancastrian, do you know?"

"Yorkist. But sometimes he forgets and licks a Lancastrian." He mocked a grave countenance but a corner of his mouth twitched.

I smiled, suffused with happiness as we talked. "Is he always with you?"

"Always, except when there is danger, as in a battle . . . or at a dance. Then he watches from the tent—or from under the table. . . . He has more sense than I do, you see." He looked into my eyes, and even in the starlight I felt the fire that had singed me when we danced together.

I tore my eyes from his.

"Northumbria is very beautiful. I was there once," I said, dropping my gaze.

"Cambridgeshire is even lovelier. I should like to visit more frequently."

I shot him a glance. His mouth had curved, as though he knew I had caught his meaning. I blushed again, feeling my cheeks as red as poppies, and I was grateful for the night that shielded me with its darkness.

We strolled deep into the garden. Here, no torches blazed to light the way, and there were no prying eyes, except those of the silver stars that sparkled over us. The music faded, and only the chirping of crickets broke the silence of the night. I was acutely aware of his nearness, and a burning tension flooded me, making me ache for his touch.

He said, "I never had the honor of meeting your father—God rest his soul—but I know your uncle. The Earl of Worcester is a devout and scholarly man."

I relaxed a little at the turn of the conversation. "Aye, that he is. He has a great love of learning, and taught me the pleasure of manuscripts at a young age."

"What have you read?"

"Ovid, Christine de Pisan, Euripides, Socrates, Homer, and Plato . . . and—"

"Whoa!" he laughed. "That is a mouthful, but no less than I would expect from the niece of such a man. I'm afraid I have not had the pleasure of reading at any great length, unless you count *De Rei Militari*."

His reference to the great manual of military strategy saddened me, for it revealed something I would not have guessed from his demeanor. The troubles of the present weighed heavily on this knight despite his light banter, and I sensed that his carefree exterior masked the deep and thoughtful nature of a man given to reflection. My heart took a perilous leap toward him.

"Did you know we are related, Lady Isobel? Your uncle, the Earl of Worcester, was once wed to my sister Cecily—God rest her soul."

I looked at him with disbelief. I had no knowledge of this.

"Indeed, it was many years ago, when he was Lord Tiptoft and not yet Earl of Worcester. My sister was his first wife. They were married but a few months before she died."

I mumbled my regrets, still startled by the revelation. "No one ever told me," I explained. "I only remember my aunt Elizabeth. She died when I was young."

He gave me a small smile. "Elizabeth Greyndour was his second wife. You were but a babe when he was wed to my sister, and
I daresay that being related to a Yorkist is not something to boast
about these days."

I did not reply, as that could not be denied, and in any case I still
struggled with this bond of marriage between our families—and
the hope it had sparked in my breast.

"Your uncle is deputy in Ireland now, so I understand. How is
he doing, have you heard?" he asked.

"Aye, well," I said, more brightly than I had expected. My heart
had assimilated the knowledge he'd given me, and joy was cours-
ing through me now. "He has written that he plans to make a pilgrimage to Jerusalem when he gets back from Ireland, and perhaps
spend time in Padua, studying Scripture, Latin, and Greek."

"Indeed, he expressed that to me before he left last year. . . .
I believe he has an interest in translating Ovid from the Latin."
Abruptly, he demanded, "How old are you?"

When I hesitated, he grinned. "If you're concerned about
Rufus here, I can assure you he won't tell anyone."

I couldn't help myself; my spirits were so light that I pealed with
laughter. "Fifteen," I said finally.

"Is it true you're a ward of Marguerite d'Anjou?"

I could not have foreseen the effect this question would have
on me. In one swift blow it reminded me that Nevilles were not
welcome at court and ripped from me the cocoon of fantasy I had
woven around myself. I came to my senses suddenly and violently.
Maybe the fresh air had cleared my head; maybe it was the shock of
my feelings, which had been as wanton as any tavern girl's; maybe
just the rest of my father's words coming back to me again: *Aim
not too high; ask not too much. The greatest griefs are those we cause ourselves.* . . . But all at once I recognized how rash and foolish I had
been. The marriage that once bound our families had passed into
history and was a thread long since severed. Times had changed,
and hatred had solidified. The marriage meant nothing, changed
nothing. The divide between us remained as wide as a stormy
sea. This knight belonged to one of the most powerful families in

Christendom and was a foe to the queen who owned me. How could I be sure that he didn't toy with me for his own amusement, thinking in some way to humiliate the queen he loathed? Even if that were not so, why should his attributes matter when he remained as unattainable to me as the stars above my head? I had forgotten my place, and reached too high, and asked for the impossible, and the gods had answered by sending me fire. I had to get out while there was still hope of recovery. My nurse was right. I was reckless, foolish, and wild. When would I ever learn?

"My lord, 'tis true that I am a ward of the queen. We should not be here, and well you know it. I ask that you return me to my guardian, and that we forget we ever met." My words fell like stones from my lips.

A strange, bewildered expression came into his eyes, and for a moment he didn't move. Then he drew himself up to his full height and said in a stranger's voice that sent an arrow straight to my heart, "Indeed, you are right, my lady. Pray, accept my apologies. I shall take you back forthwith." He put out his elbow stiffly, and I rested my hand on his sleeve as lightly as if I were touching a hot iron, and we turned and went back through the damp garden to the hall that we should never have left.

I didn't sleep that night but lay awake in the long darkness, weeping silently into my pillow, listening to Sister's snores and counting the church bells that tolled at the end of every hour. Never would I forget the exquisite, piercing sweetness of the dance we had together, but time would heal this woe, and life would continue. I knew that because the books had told me so.

Morning broke sunny and beautiful, but the bright song of the lark wounded me anew and wrapped me in a cocoon of anguish. He didn't break fast with us, and I heard that he had ridden off before cock's crow. I had no stomach for food, and I wouldn't have nibbled at the slice of bread if Sœur Madeleine hadn't forced me. We stood in the courtyard watching the groomsmen saddle our horses, and I heard the barking of the hounds with a wretchedness of mind I'd never known before. As bells rang for Prime, we set out on our way and the castle gate clanged shut behind us. The redbrick castle grew smaller the farther we rode, and our fellow travelers fewer. The cluster of timber houses around the castle gave way to a straggle of cottages, fields, and barns, and finally opened out into the lonely moors. As I gazed at the tall grasses and flowers basking in the sun, the quiet of this world after the bustle and noise of the castle sent anguish pouring through me, and I felt as bereft as if I rode in a wasteland. My palfrey's hooves rang out on the road, *clippity-clop, clippity-clop*, and their steady pounding rose to a thunder in my ears. Unable to help myself, I slowed my pace and, dropping behind the others, gazed back past the summer heather to where Tattershall Castle lay.

"Last night you couldn't stop laughing and dancing, and now you are as silent as a mouse with a cat near," Sœur Madeleine said, turning in her saddle. "What is the matter, *ma chérie*?"

I couldn't reply. I felt as though I would never speak again. Tears lay on my heart and blinded my eyes. My palfrey caught up with hers, and I bowed my head so that she wouldn't see my face.

Sœur Madeleine reached out and pressed my hand. "You are young, my little one," she said quietly. "Someday another will come and make you forget."

I raised my head and looked at her then, feeling that it was the first time I had ever truly seen her.

Three

IN DRENCHING RAIN, I RAN DOWN A HILLSIDE OF rocks and thorns, unable to stop. I didn't know where I was going, only that I had to escape the creature pursuing me. Swept with sheer black fright, I threw a glance behind me, my heart pounding and blood surging in my ears, but in the darkness I saw nothing. *Where is refuge? Where shelter?* If this thing caught me, my fate would be unspeakable! The horror of the thought lent wings to my feet, but now the ground grew thick with mud, impeding the way. Gnarled branches twisted out from nowhere and gained ferocious life, sighing and grasping at me as I fled past in the darkness. I choked back my screams and kept running, tripping and nearly falling several times. All around me, loud sobbing cries and pitiful moans rent the air and sent panic rioting through me. I covered my ears so I would not hear them. Suddenly I could go no farther. Something blocked my path, yet strangely I felt comfort, not fear. A flower glimmered before my eyes, and I saw that it was a white rose. Aware that the noises had ceased, I uncovered my ears, and the rose floated into my hands. I marveled at its iridescent beauty, which held a strange, almost ethereal quality. Then I lifted my eyes. Sir John Neville smiled down at me. I was engulfed in warmth, and my lips parted with joy and wonder, but in my surprise I dropped the flower. Sir John bent to pick it up for me, but when he stood again, he was a stranger, standing in shadow, and I could not make out his face. The stranger handed me the flower, only now the rose was red, not white. I didn't want to take it, but it sprang into my hands, and I saw that blood dripped from its petals. It was blood that colored the white rose red! I dropped the flower and backed away, screaming in horror—

I awoke to find myself sitting upright in bed, drenched in sweat, my heart pounding.

"My poor child, you've had a bad dream, but the fever has broken at last. You will soon be well." Sœur Madeleine removed her hand from my damp brow. Turning behind her as she sat on the edge of my bed, she dipped a cloth into a basin of water held by a young girl and wiped my face. I flinched, for it was cold. My vision, which sleep had blurred, began to clear. I looked around. There was little to see, only the stone wall of a castle bedchamber, a window, and a coffer. "How long have I been sick? Where are we?" I asked.

"We are at court, in Westminster. You fell off your horse and have been unconscious for two days."

"I don't remember arriving here."

" 'Tis because you were already ill and burning with fever. I had great fear for you, child."

I frowned, straining to recall the journey, but there was nothing in my head except a dull pounding. Then all at once remembrance flooded me. "Aye, it's come back to me now," I murmured softly. With memory had come the ache of leaving Sir John Neville at Tattershall Castle. I laid my head back on my pillow, dimly aware that Sœur Madeleine was speaking.

"Isabelle, this is Margery. She'll be taking care of you in my absence, child. I leave for Kenilworth Abbey and shall be gone several days. I shall check on you when I'm back." She patted my hand,

and the girl curtseyed. I gave them a nod, too weary to speak, and closed my eyes.

The trip from Lincolnshire to Westminster had been exceptionally arduous, perhaps due to the unseasonable heat. Beneath leaden skies that oppressed land and folk alike, we had passed friars; peddlers whose toes stuck through the rags that wrapped their feet; itinerant workers; merchants with their wares; women sagging beneath the weight of the milk jugs they carried on their heads; and farmers headed to market, dragging their carts laden with hay, leeks, and apples. Many looked as weary and low-spirited as I had felt. Unable to bear the prospect of entering a house now emptied of my father's loving presence, we did not stop at his manor in Burrough Green, though Cambridgeshire lay on the path to London. Instead we spent the night at an abbey on the outskirts of town, where I shared a pallet with Sister. Her rolling snores, my own coughing spells, and the fleas and bedbugs that infested our lumpy straw mattress had kept me awake, and, as I had done since leaving Tattershall, I counted the church bells that tolled through the night and struggled to keep thoughts of Sir John Neville at bay.

For the last two days of our journey, I had subsisted on a few swallows of bread and wine. It became clear to me that I had caught the ague, but as the remedy for the sickness was to swallow a spider wrapped in a raisin, I made no mention of my fever in case Sister decided to cure me, and I grew progressively fainter. Then, strangely, the world retreated from me into silence and mist. Sister spoke to Master Giles and Guy, merchants greeted us as they passed, beggars put out their bowls to us from the roadside and called for alms, but their words didn't reach me. By the time London's crenellated city walls drew into view across the fields, my legs were in an agony of cramping and I had difficulty sitting upright on my palfrey. My head swam, and though my stomach lay empty, we had to stop twice before we reached Bishopsgate, so I could retch. Nor did it help to arrive in the city. The sights and smells of London sent my stomach churning anew as we passed butcher shops where clouds of flies banqueted on meat hung to dry, and rode down gloomy streets where the air was choked out by the upper stories of merchants' houses projecting over the narrow streets, blotting out sun and sky. In these dingy, filthy streets, pigs roamed freely, digging in refuse piles that emitted a stench worse than the dung heaps we had passed on the country roads.

All the while, as I rode and struggled to remain erect in the saddle, the world continued its uncanny silence. Mercers and customers argued in the streets; whirling wheels raised dust in the roadways; and blacksmiths hammered in their shops, fire spitting from the steel they forged, all without a sound. When we finally arrived at Westminster, the large palace courtyard teemed with crowds as mute as if they were etched in an illuminated manuscript. Grim-faced retainers strode purposefully across the court, hands clenched on the hilts of their swords; messengers galloped in and out, bearing missives to and from the far reaches of the kingdom. All unfolded dimly and without sound.

I turned to Sister and saw her talking to the porter in the castle bailey, and I saw the porter nod and point to one of the towers near the river. My head spun, light faded from the day, and the last thing I remembered as the ground rushed up to meet me was the startled look in their eyes as they turned to me.

I gave a soft sigh.

"Is there anything I can do for ye, m'lady?" the girl asked.

I shook my head, murmured my thanks, and closed my eyes. I must have fallen asleep, for it was dark when I opened them again. I pushed myself up into a sitting position. By the light of a single candle on the small bedside table, I made out the girl's form as she sat dozing against the wall. Her eyes flew open when I stirred.

"M'lady, you're awake!" She came and knelt beside me. Squeezing out excess moisture from the cloth in the washbasin, she wiped my face. "Your color is much better, m'lady. May I fetch you something to eat—some bread or broth?"

I declined the offer. My stomach was still queasy.

"A gift came for you while you were sleeping," she said, moving to the coffer in a shadowy corner of the room. She picked up something and brought it to me. "Someone else has been concerned for you, too. . . . They sent you this."

I cried out and shrank back, repelled by the sight. *A red rose.* The girl frowned in puzzlement. " 'Tis only a rose, m'lady. It was left outside the door, with this." She slipped a letter from her bosom and gave it to me. There was no seal. I opened it to find a rhyme carefully scratched out in black ink. I bent my head to read, hope stirring in my breast with each line.

Take thou this rose, O Rose,
Since love's own flower 'tis,
And by this rose
Thy lover captive is,
And has been, since that fair night
At Tattershall Castle.

Joy exploded in my breast, and I felt the brightness of my own smile. I scoured the missive wildly, checking for a signature, but there was none. "Did you see who brought it?" I cried.

"I only saw his back as he left the flower. He is young and well built." The girl smiled at me, and I smiled back, my heart soaring. *Sir John Neville.*

The rose was exquisite, in full and perfect bloom. *The dream was an omen of good, not evil,* I thought. I buried my face in the soft petals and lay back on my pillow, inhaling the flower's lovely perfume, the sick feeling in my stomach suddenly gone. Bathed in its scent, I softly hummed the melody of the dance to myself as I drifted off to sleep once more, the song a lullaby for my heart.

Sustained by the knowledge that the visitor had to have been Sir John, I poured my energies into getting well. When Sœur Madeleine returned, she was pleased to find me recovered, and I, for my part, was delighted to see her again, for I had grown fond of her over these many weeks. "Sœur Madeleine, I don't want you to go back north," I pleaded as she dressed me for my first outing from the bedchamber. "Pray, ask the queen to let you stay with me."

"Dear one, I'm needed back at the priory. No doubt the queen will appoint a gentlewoman for you when you have your audience."

"When will that be?" A stab of panic came and went at the thought of an audience with the fearsome Marguerite d'Anjou.

"Whenever the queen can find time for such small matters. She is busy running the realm now that the king is ill again, so it may be a while. You will have to be patient."

"The king is ill?" I inquired.

"Aye, he needs rest. State affairs have proved too onerous a burden of late." She knelt down and busied herself with the hem of my gown. I had the feeling this was a subject she had no wish to discuss.

Unwilling to cause her discomfort with any more questions, I said, "Then I shall pray for his recovery, Sœur Madeleine."

She nodded her approval.

Ill was the word Sœur Madeleine had used, but over the next few days, as I strolled through the gardens of Westminster Palace and ate in its halls, stealing wistful looks at my rose, I brooded over the open secret of the king's madness. He was shut up in the royal apartments so no one would see that he sat silently all day, unable to speak, staring at the ground, not comprehending a single thought. But in a castle, light falls into the darkest corners, and secrets never remain secrets for long.

When the queen's royal infant, Prince Edward, had been presented to his father for his blessing, Henry had glanced at the boy and cast down his eyes, saying nothing. It was spoken in hushed tones that Edward had been sired by the late Edmund Beaufort, Duke of Somerset. He could always be found at the queen's side until his death at the Battle of St. Albans, which had taken place in May 1455, a year before I'd met Sir John Neville. In this battle, fought between the Yorkist party headed by Richard Plantagenet, Duke of York, and the queen's party, headed by Edmund Beaufort, the Nevilles had sided with York, and it was by a Neville that Somerset had been slain.

The horn sounded the dinner hour. Securing Sir John Neville's rose to my bodice with my brooch, I abandoned the garden seat where I had been watching the sunset and reliving the ecstasy of the evening at Tattershall. The flower had wilted since he had delivered it to my sickroom, but to me it was still the most beautiful rose in the garden.

I made my way to the great hall reluctantly. Sœur Madeleine was still away, and I dreaded eating alone in the great hall. At the priory I had made few friends, for the girls were wont to cast me long looks and whisper behind my back, jabbing each other in the elbow when I passed. One who had befriended me—a girl named Alice—had given me the reason.

"They think you beautiful and wish to punish you for it," she had said.

"But why?" I asked, stunned by this revelation.

"I suppose it's because they think your beauty gives you the right to be loved, and to be happy."

"But *why*, when my hair is dark and my eyes brown, and my lips so full?" I persisted.

Alice had laughed. "You have no idea, have you?"

I'd shaken my head.

" 'Tis what I like best about you," she'd replied.

Alice had died of the plague the following year, when she turned fifteen. I felt a squeezing hurt and whispered a prayer for her soul, as I always did when I thought of her.

I crossed the circle of green and headed to the keep. I had become accustomed to the loneliness, and my reception here at court matched my experience at the priory. I sighed softly. *It'll probably take far longer to find a friend here, if indeed a friend can ever be found in such a place.*

But the Fates proved kind. Though on my left I was seated next to an old man who put his hand to his ear and grunted, "Hah—what's that?" each time I spoke to him, until I abandoned all effort at conversation, to my delight I found myself with pleasant company on the right. She was a young woman, clearly gentle-born, and still unmarried at twenty-five. She chattered amiably, telling me about herself and asking questions of me in a refreshing manner devoid of artifice. Her name was Ursula Malory, and she had red hair. *Like Alice,* I thought. Blue-eyed and of middling height, with a bright smile and nicely drawn features, she would have been considered fair but for her freckles and a crossed look to her eyes.

"You are slender as a cypress tree, m'lady, yet you're not gaunt. On the contrary, you're well covered—well covered indeed!" Ursula Malory grinned, throwing a glance at my bosom while I blushed and tried to pull up my bodice. " 'Tis all in the way God makes us, I suppose, though I wish He had seen fit to move things around on me—to give me more on top, you know, less in the girth, so I wouldn't resemble an old hen."

I was about to protest, but she stopped me with a wave of the hand. "Tish-tish, all's well. When I was younger, I did on occasion cut back my portions, but my body didn't wish to shrink. So I decided to accept my shape and enjoy my food! Like you, my lady—" With that, she scooped up a handful of spitted boar and cabbage in a slice of bread, dipped the mixture as I had done in the small wooden bowl of sweet sauce we shared, and munched happily, matching me bite for bite, for I had always enjoyed good appetite, except at Tattershall Castle.

I banished the memory and focused on Ursula Malory. Plump and merry, she had an endearing quality that brought to mind not a hen, as she thought, but a colorful bird with fluffed-up feathers. I liked her more with every word. I gave her a wide smile, charmed by her warmth and by a disposition bright as her hair. She told me that her father, Sir Thomas Malory, had fought against Joan of Arc during the wars in France and had been a member of parliament in the early fifties.

"My father was also a member of parliament. He, too, fought in France at the same time," I offered, between sips of leek soup. "I wonder if they knew each other."

"Surely they did. We must ask them the next time we see them."

"My father is dead," I said softly. " 'Tis a year now."

Ursula rested her hand on mine. "I'm sorry." After a brief silence, she spoke again. "Why are you at court, my lady?"

I felt the change of subject was a deliberate effort to get my mind off my sadness. Gratitude flooded me as I struggled to recover my composure. "I'm a ward of the queen's. I've been brought here from the nunnery to find a husband. What about you, Ursula?"

"A ward of the queen?" she exclaimed. "Ta-dee-da! Then I must mind my manners."

I laughed.

"I'm here to find a position," she replied. "Though my father is a knight, he has no means. I have no dower for marriage, and I need to maintain my keep."

Barely able to contain my excitement, I said, "Then you need look no further, Ursula! I am seeking a gentlewoman companion."

Her face lit up. "But nothing can be this easy . . . except maybe in my father's tales."

"Fortune has indeed smiled on us this night," I replied, marveling. A varlet cleared away our dishes and another brought a dessert of cinnamon apple pudding with almonds and raisins. It was so good, I requested a second helping. "So your father is a wordsmith? What does he write about?"

"Mostly love and knightly feats of arms over damsels who look like you," she said.

I was too startled by this to offer any objection. We giggled through the evening, and the next morning, when Sœur Madeleine returned, I lost no time introducing Ursula. She gave us her approval and a promise to do what she could to expedite my audience with the queen so that Ursula could begin drawing payment. Here Sister proved greatly successful: The day of my audience arrived less than a week later, far earlier than I expected. Suddenly I was filled with dread.

"But, Sœur Madeleine, what should I say to the queen? What should I do?" I asked with panic as she and Ursula assisted me into my most prized gown, the lavish lavender and silver tissue, trimmed with miniver, that I had worn when I met Sir John Neville.

"Be yourself, *ma chérie*. Be yourself, and you will melt the hearts."

Her words failed to reassure me. I already knew Marguerite d'Anjou was not easily charmed. "Will you come with me?"

"I regret not. I have many matters to attend, but Ursula can accompany you," she said.

I gave Ursula a nervous smile as she twined daisies into my hair, which hung loose down my back. Sœur Madeleine smiled with approval, for that was Queen Marguerite's emblem. "Her hair is so thick, it can take more, Ursula," she advised before she left.

The great bell on the abbey's clock tower struck the hour of three. My stomach tightened. The time had come to head for the White Chamber and my audience with the queen. Ursula stood back to assess her handiwork.

"I don't rightly believe I have ever seen anyone as fair as you. Your eyes are like gems weighted down with lashes. . . . Your skin, 'tis fine as alabaster, and your hair pours down around you like heavy silk, as richly dark and glossy as the feathers of the black swan. You are lovely, m'lady," she said without a trace of envy as she helped me into my woolen cloak.

Ursula's kind nature touched me deeply, and I gave her a long embrace. With my hood up and my head down to protect the flowers in my hair against the wind, we crossed the inner ward and took the river path to the stately keep. It pleased me greatly that I turned heads along the way, for I needed reassurance. The day held the nip of approaching autumn, and a strong wind blew, ruffling the dark river with waves, but there was no rain. The cool weather was a relief against the recent unrelenting heat of summer, and as a result, the Thames was crowded with a profusion of gilded barges. There was much bustle of both nature and business, as swans glided past, gulls mewed and dove for fish, and boats pulled up to the barge landing, unloading men and goods.

We reached the keep and took the worn tower steps up to the audience chamber, but the sentry standing guard at the anteroom stopped Ursula. "Only those with appointments may enter."

I was about to protest, but as Ursula removed my cloak, she leaned close and whispered, "Chin up, bosom up—and all will be well!" She drew back, a grin on her face, and I went in laughing.

At once I saw why the sentry had refused Ursula entry. The small alcove was filled to overflowing with people who hoped to see the queen. I gave my name to the clerk who stood at a high desk near the door, and cast about for a place. The closest bench

was occupied by a group of nuns whispering prayers on their ro-
saries, no doubt beseeching God for His help in getting the ben-
efices they sought. Near them a weary-looking knight and his lady
spoke together in hushed tones of a problem with the dues on their
manor. By the leaded windows on the opposite wall, a group of
black-gowned clerics conversed about the weather. A messenger
from Anjou sat in a nearby corner, wearing the cross of Lorraine.
The place beside him lay empty, and I claimed it.

My seat was situated directly opposite the entrance to the audience chamber, and soon the door opened to let out a beautiful
young lord and his retainers. Golden hair flowed from beneath the
lord's jewel-studded velvet cap, but though his face had the grace
of proportion, I thought him too womanly and without appeal. A
deferential silence fell as he swept past, broken only by the swish of
fabric as everyone stood and bowed.

"Who was that, sir?" I whispered to the messenger from Anjou.

"The Earl of Wiltshire, *ma dame*," he replied. Then, as if realizing I was a newcomer to court and needed clarification, he added,
"James Butler, Earl of Wiltshire and of Ormond."

I gave him a smile to express my thanks. I had heard of this earl
before, in an inn where we had stayed on the journey to Westminster. Wiltshire was one of the names mentioned as a possible father
to the queen's young son. The door stood open to the audience
chamber, and I turned my gaze on the queen. Young, beautiful,
and sparkling with jewels, Marguerite d'Anjou sat on her throne
chair, engaged in conversation with an opulently dressed, handsome fair-haired lord in a furred cloak who stood beside her on
the dais. Even from the distance, I could tell from his relaxed stance
and the way she looked up at him that their relationship was a close
one.

"And who is the lord with the queen, sir?"

"That, *ma dame*, is Henry Beaufort, Duke of Somerset," he said
with great reverence.

I nodded my thanks. This name required no explanation, for
even I knew that twenty-three-year-old Somerset, who had suc-
ceeded his late father, Edmund, to the dukedom, was the most

powerful lord in the land—king in all but name. His late father, Edmund of Somerset, had arranged Marguerite's marriage to King Henry. In gratitude, she had taken him to her bosom—and, it was widely rumored, to her bed.

Clearly the queen had a high regard for the son as well, since he was always at her side and she never went against his will as she did with her husband, King Henry. Castle gossip had revealed that once, when King Henry was freshly recovered from a bout of madness, he saw a traitor's torso impaled on a pike and inquired after it. Informed that it was a human part, he had expressed horror at the practice of quartering a human being and demanded that the torso be taken down and given a decent Christian burial. Naturally, the practice continued. King Henry never knew his wishes were ignored, for he soon returned to the confines of his madness. Everyone had laughed openly at the tale, but none dared laugh at Somerset, except secretly. "I wager the queen's son was sired by a Somerset," I had heard someone snicker behind a tavern wall, his tongue no doubt loosened by drink. "But whether Edmund or Henry, father or son, it scarcely matters now, does it?"

I did not have to wait long to see the queen. My name was called immediately after the messenger from Anjou, who bore a missive from the queen's father, the much-loved poet-king René of Anjou, known as "René the Good."

Weak-kneed, my heart pounding, I walked up the long aisle leading to the queen on the dais, aware of her gaze on me, trying not to notice the sour-faced clerics dotting the benches on both sides or the courtiers who stood together in clumps, undressing me with their eyes as they whispered behind their hands. Then I remembered Ursula's advice, and a wide smile came to my lips. Lifting my chin high, I inhaled deeply and drew back my shoulders. The walk to the throne chair no longer seemed so arduous, and I reached it soon enough. Sinking low to the floor, I dropped my head into the silvery folds of my gown and curtseyed before the queen.

"You may rise," Marguerite d'Anjou said in a voice accented with the throaty sweetness of her native land.

The queen, though petite, was no less formidable up close. Drenched in jewels, she glinted dangerously, and the eyes she fixed on me, green as the pears of Anjou, held warning. A gold and ruby circlet sat on her dark blond hair, which was braided and twirled into pearl nets on either side of a face that was a trifle short and broad, with a jaw too square for a woman. Yet she might still have passed for fair had her skin had not been flawed by marks left by the pox, which she had caught on her journey to England as a young princess of fifteen—my age now. As I stood before her, I thought I saw a softening in her hard look, and I dared to widen my smile once more. Then Somerset's laugh drew my attention to him.

"This one will start a bidding war, my queen."

Marguerite d'Anjou grinned. "Indeed, 'Enri, she will fetch a pretty purse for the royal treasury, of that I am certain."

They were assessing me as if they were a pair of butchers buying the cow they would slaughter for the night's dinner. My smile faded, and I dropped my gaze to hide my anger. I took an immediate dislike to Somerset.

Marguerite d'Anjou may have recognized her lack of manners, for she leaned forward gently in her throne and said, "Child, do you have French blood?"

I was taken aback at this question. "Not that I am aware, my liege."

"You have a French look, my dear—does she not, Monsieur Brézé?"

I turned to the lord she addressed: the great French naval hero Pierre de Brézé, the seneschal of Normandy, whom Sœur Madeleine had pointed out to me proudly one night at dinner. He stood to my right, close to the dais, opulently swathed in furs, jewels, and velvet according to the French fashion. I curtseyed to him, and he threw me a charming smile.

"Well could you be from Her Grace's beloved Anjou, for Anjou is reputed to produce the most exquisitely beautiful women in the world," he said, flourishing a most elegant bow.

I inclined my head in thanks. Brézé was rumored to love the

queen, and indeed, the adoring eyes he turned on her confirmed it to me.

"*Grand merci, Monsieur Brézé*," the queen said sweetly. Then, all business again, she addressed me. "Never mind, I have heard good report about you from Sœur Madeleine. That will suffice." The queen fell silent, appraising me with her sharp eyes. "Lady Isobel Ingoldesthorpe, 'tis your wish to be wed and not to enter a nunnery, is that correct?"

I blushed. "Aye, my queen. Except—except . . ."

She waited coldly.

I found my tongue. "Except that I would have as husband a man of my choice."

Her eyebrows shot up. She exchanged a glance with Somerset and returned her eyes to me. "The law is on your side. Only with your consent shall you be married." A pause. "Is there anything else you would ask of me?"

"My queen, I would like to engage the services of Ursula Malory, daughter of your faithful servant Sir Thomas Malory, as my gentlewoman."

She leaned back in her chair, and Somerset whispered something to her in French. She gave him a reply before turning her attention back to me. "Sœur Madeleine has spoken of your desire. It seems Malory's loyalty is not as assured as you seem to believe, but I approve his daughter's position on one condition." She beckoned me to approach. I drew near, and she bent down to whisper, "That you report to me anything unusual that comes to your ears about her father's activities. These are troubled times."

So this was court. A nest of spies intriguing against one another under the guise of friendship. "Aye, my liege," I murmured. Marguerite d'Anjou gestured dismissively to indicate that my interview was over. I curtseyed again and made my escape past the leering faces of the courtiers and the dour looks of the clerics. As I approached the entry, a guard threw the door open for me. Feeling as if stones had been lifted from my shoulders, I swept through the antechamber like the breeze, eager to take the good tidings to Ursula. I thought I heard my name called behind me in the passageway, but I ignored it in my rush to the garden, tearing through doorways and down the narrow, winding stairs of the keep. I had not gone three steps in the sunshine when someone called my name again. This time I turned.

The young man looked familiar, and I knitted my brows together, trying to place him. He came rushing up to me, breathless.

"William Norris, Esquire, at your service, my lady. I am thankful indeed to find you recovered from your bout of illness, Lady Isobel," he said, sweeping his hat into a deep, courtly bow. "I see you don't remember me. We met at Tattershall Castle—well, not exactly met, since I was never given the chance to request a dance that evening." He waited expectantly.

My mind raced through the memories of that precious night, trying to find a match for this brown-eyed youth with the thick, curly brown hair who stood looking at me so hopefully.

"Perhaps this will help?" He withdrew a scarlet rose from beneath his cape. "My lady, 'tis the mate to the one I sent you in your sickroom."

A gull mewed on the river, a bargeman slammed into the landing with a loud oath, and the knowledge washed over me in a violent flood: This was the young man who had lifted his glass to me from across the room at Tattershall Castle. Gazing up at Sir John Neville that evening, I had turned on this squire unseeing eyes blinded by looking too long into the sun.

Four

SEPTEMBER 1456

IT WAS THE END OF SUMMER.

In my tiny chamber, I abandoned the manuscript of Chaucer that I was reading and, standing on my bed, I gazed listlessly out the high window. Fingering my mother's crucifix, which I wore at my throat, I watched a deluge of rain drench the palace grounds. My sixteenth birthday, on Lammas Day, the first of August, had come and gone, marked by scant ceremony. The queen had sent me a silver plate of candied rose petals and gingerbread cakes, tied with a silk ribbon, while a gathering of ladies accompanied by a royal minstrel had sung to me in the great hall and then departed, laughing. It was a kind gesture, to be sure. But I didn't know these women, and I recalled with aching pain, as if from a fragment in a dream, a childhood memory of my mother's warm and loving embrace as she crowned me with rosebuds and twirled me around, laughing, and of my father's face, shining with tenderness as he watched me and sang, "A posy, a posy for my fair little damsel—"

I drew my cloak close around my shoulders. With September

had come a raw wind that blew through the palace halls, hissing softly through the cracks in the walls and furling the tapestries. It was not merely the weather that depressed me.

Though I had prayed much and said little to anyone during these weeks since my arrival, I had learned a great deal about state affairs, and certain issues that had seemed meaningless at the priory now took on great significance in light of my feelings for Sir John Neville. The queen hated Richard, Duke of York, and lived for his destruction. At the heart of their conflict lay York's superior claim to the throne by birth, which the queen saw as a threat to her, and on York's part it was the mismanagement of the affairs of the realm by the queen's favorites. York could do nothing about his birth, and Marguerite was unwilling to give up her favorites. It all seemed so hopeless. . . .

Below me, across the thinning grass, messengers passed to and fro on foot, striding urgently on palace business. Their grave faces tightened the knot in my stomach. I thought of King Henry, whom the queen had sent to Coventry to be nursed back to health away from the pressures of court. When in possession of his faculties, King Henry VI had served as peacemaker between the queen and the Duke of York, but his void always unleashed a bitter duel between them. With the help of young Henry of Somerset, and that of his late father, Edmund, before him, the queen had hatched two plots to murder York but failed both times. Her greatest achievement had come in 1450, when she banished York to Ireland. Even there she failed: York turned his exile into triumph by settling old quarrels at the Irish court, maintaining order, and offering justice. His rule, the best Ireland had ever known, won the hearts of the Irish to the cause of York, so the queen recalled him—and tried to murder him on the way back.

During these weeks, I also received an education in the perils of life at court as I learned more about the reckless and violent men around the queen. Dalliances and amours abounded, and wary of competition, the women threw me hard looks as they swished past in their gaudy damascenes, with their noses lifted in disdain, while the men paid me bold and unwelcome attention.

As a result, I dared not befriend anyone, lest they proved false, or worse—dangerous. Half-hidden hatreds and jealousies charged the air, and I watched as many a person was dispatched to the Tower for a carelessly spoken word. Fearful of joining their ranks, I kept very much to myself. Never was I as lonely as in those early days at court, facing an uncertain future, my heart filled with thoughts of the one I could not have, and with no company save Ursula and, on rare occasions, Sœur Madeleine.

Abruptly, one day in mid-September, the king reappeared at court. Although he didn't attend council meetings, he was frequently seen at mealtime, sitting meekly on his throne, as demure as a damsel. Initially, during these appearances, he gazed at his queen with lackluster eyes, then turned and stared at the ground, seemingly oblivious of what went on around him. As I learned, the queen had brought him back to court before he was completely well in order to rid herself of the Duke of York, who was about to take over the reins of government.

Gradually, however, I witnessed a change in King Henry. His expression turned cheerful and gentle, and he smiled kindly at everyone who approached. As he became more the man he had been, he gave out an impression of great goodness. Although still a prisoner of the darkness of his mind and feeble in his will, he struck me as a compassionate figure. The queen, always so austere and proud with others, also changed in his presence, exuding a solicitous and maternal side, so that the king's eyes, when they alighted on her, shone with affection and implicit trust. One night, in our chamber, I mentioned this to Ursula, with whom I'd come to share a deepening friendship.

"Aye, such trust," Ursula whispered, glancing around our empty room before she spoke, "that he cheerfully allows himself to be pillaged into debt."

"Hush!" I said fearfully. " 'Tis treason what you speak, Ursula!"

"Then I've just put my life in your hands."

Indeed, court seethed with turmoil and traps, and I was reminded of that fact when the queen sent for me one evening after supper. A fat cleric round as an egg was leaving as I approached, attended by two hooded monk manservants who followed after him, heads bowed. I did not see him at first, for he was cloaked in shadow as he glided noiselessly through the hall, and his sudden greeting, coming forth from darkness, jolted me. I recoiled with a cry.

"Ah, my child, forgive me for startling you. The queen is free now, and you may enter." He gave a wave toward the queen's apartments, scrutinizing me in a manner I found most unpleasant. Nor did his fish eyes soften his demeanor as he murmured, *"Benedicite,"* in dismissal. I curtseyed, gave my thanks, and hurried away greatly discomforted, for there was something sinister about the man.

The queen paced to and fro in her chamber, dictating to her scrivener, who was perched at a high desk near the window. With a wave, she indicated that I should take a seat and wait.

"—and cease your threats on the life of our bailiff of the lordship of Hertingfordbury and leave our other tenants in peace there, or you shall know our displeasure to your peril, Edmund Pyrcan, squire—" she continued, gesticulating with her hands in the French manner as she spoke. She paused and, exhaling sharply, picked up a sheaf of papers. Leafing through them, she selected one. "Ah, here it is—from the abbess of the convent of Stratford le Bow. Direct this letter to our masters of horse, aveners, purveyors, and other officers of our stable, and sign it from me, as usual. They are to be commanded not to take any belongings of this abbey, nor to lodge there, nor even to pass through the town, for we are granting the abbess our full protection, and they violate our order at their peril. . . ." She put that down and picked up another letter. "Ah, here is a more pleasant matter—*l'amour*—" Her voice held a wistful note. "Affairs of the heart interest me, and I much enjoy the arranging of marriages," she said, turning to me. " 'Tis one of my happier duties. . . ."

"To our well-loved John de Vere, Earl of Oxford," she dictated. "As you well know, we have Elizabeth Clere in our service, and she has confided to us her affection and regard for a certain young man in your service, by the name of Thomas Denys, so we are writing to you to implore you earnestly to do what you can to persuade the young man to readily agree to this proposal. You may undertake to inform him that we shall be generous to them both, if he will agree to the match. We ask you to do your best in this matter, as we shall do for you in the future. May the Holy Trinity keep you—and so on." She waved her hand at her clerk and turned to me. "Lady Ingoldesthorpe. Here, come and sit with me for a while, until my other ladies arrive."

I curtseyed and settled myself on the low cushion she indicated, as close to the fire as I could get. The storm that had descended over London earlier that morning had intensified, and now the wind howled. The silk curtains draping the walls moved with the drafts that blew in through the spaces in the stone, and I shivered. The queen must have felt the cold draft too, for she went to warm her hands at the fire. She stood there for a time, her face turned to the window. Then she gave a soft sigh and took her seat. "How I miss the sun of Anjou. England is always so dreary. Naught but rain, and cold most miserable."

"Maybe spring will come early," I offered.

"You will find that London is as unpleasant in spring as it is in winter. For that, no doubt, we owe a debt to its citizens. They are an ungrateful lot. *Mordi*, grumbling and complaining are all we hear! They are never content, no matter what we do for them. I shall make sure we are not here in the spring."

Just then the creak of a door and a rustle of silk drew my attention to the entry. There stood a young woman of surpassing beauty. She carried herself with a bearing more regal than the queen herself, and her loveliness lit up the room like a torch. Her complexion was ivory, and her shining hair, which streamed down her back, glimmered with a faint silver halo. If any feature could be criticized, it was perhaps her green eyes, which were small, not large, and held a sly expression. The girl, perhaps two or three years older than myself, drew to the queen's side and whispered in her ear. I caught a few words of French, and the name Edward, and understood that the queen was anxious about her little prince. The three-year-old child nursed a cold, and she had sent the girl to check on him.

The queen nodded. *"Bien . . . bien."* She turned to me. "Lady Isobel Ingoldesthorpe, have you met Elizabeth Woodville? She is also a newcomer to court. Her mother, the Duchess of Bedford, is French. From Luxemburg."

I murmured the niceties and gave Elizabeth a smile. She responded with a feeble nod and looked away as soon as the queen had turned her attention back to me. I was struck by her rudeness. Even the girls at the nunnery hid their dislike of one another beneath a mask of civility. *"Alors,* Isabelle, are you happy with us here at court?" the queen inquired.

"Aye, my queen. Everyone has been most gracious."

She laughed. "Indeed, you have attracted a fair amount of attention, just as we expected."

"My lady?"

"Eh bien, you have had three suitors already for your hand in marriage, one for each month you have been here. Only Elizabeth can match that tally, but she is not my ward, and so it does me no good." She threw a warm smile in Elizabeth's direction, which Elizabeth returned with one of her own, as dazzling as sunlight.

Stunned at the news, I stared at the queen.

She patted my hand kindly. *"Vraiment,* perhaps you didn't know? I thought everyone knew everything that happened at court before it happened, but not this time, I see. In any case, the suitors are of no import. You were not informed, because they offered too low a price." She bent near and lowered her voice. "You will fetch a great sum for the royal treasury, my dear. For that you should be proud."

I didn't know how to respond to this, so I mumbled my thanks.

"It must sound quite banal to you, so fresh from the nunnery, this talk of money, but you should regard it as performing a great duty to the king. God knows, I myself was happy to bring him a treaty of peace. I was fifteen, you know, when I arrived on these shores, quite alone."

Not a treaty, but a truce, I corrected mentally, promptly chastising myself for the disloyal thought. "Aye, my queen," I murmured. Fifteen was too young to be married off to someone you had never seen, sent off to a foreign country, and torn from family, friends, and all that had been familiar and dear to the heart.

She threw me a glance. "Are you sure you have no French blood, like Elizabeth?"

I shook my head.

"*D'accord*, I suppose you need not be French to be beautiful . . . or lonely."

My heart went out to her, for I had a sudden appreciation of her plight. She was a woman thwarted at every turn: an outsider who could never belong, a woman married but with no husband, and no love, and no true hope of happiness, except her child. The smile I gave her must have shown my sympathy, for she gave my hand a squeeze. "There is something about you *très charmante*. I think we shall be friends, Isabelle, don't you agree, Elizabeth?"

At these words, Elizabeth turned her bright green eyes on me for the first time, and her full gaze held warning. I knew then that she regarded me an interloper and would protect at all costs what she viewed as her territory.

"I have made a decision!" Queen Marguerite announced suddenly. "You shall be my lady-in-waiting, Isabelle. Just like Elizabeth."

"WE HAVE AN HOUR BEFORE SUPPER," URSULA said kindly, placing a gentle arm around my shoulder. "Shall we seek out a wisewoman? Perhaps she can bring you comfort with good tidings."

Gazing at her from my bed, where I had been playing my lyre and dwelling on thoughts of Sir John Neville, I shook my head sadly. "I have no faith in prophecy, Ursula. If my fortune is good, I shall hope too much and be fearful lest it proves wrong. If I get a bad fortune, I shall dread my future. 'Tis best to keep away from wisewomen."

"Then what say you to a stroll along the river to see the sunset?"

Perhaps Ursula was right, and fresh air would banish my melancholy. In any case, I was to take up my duties as the queen's lady-in-waiting when she returned from Kent, where she had gone to attend the trial of a group of rebels. Soon enough I would have little free time to spend as I wished.

We took the path down to the riverbank. The palace grounds were quiet, and we met few people along the way. The rains had ceased, and the late September wind swept through the gardens, rustling the autumn leaves that still clung to the trees and stirring the sweet, damp smell of evening. Turning a corner, we stepped through an arched stone gate. Abruptly the palace walls gave way to the sky, offering up a sunset without boundary. The Thames was dotted with gilded private barges, and its rippling currents caught the crimsons and golds of the sky, which soaked the water, dazzling my eyes.

"God has surely designed His seas and rivers as mirrors to catch and reflect His glory," I whispered to Ursula as we stood arm in arm, the water lapping gently about the privy stairs. Ursula nodded and squeezed my hand.

A haughty voice interrupted our reverie. "My lady Isobel. What a pleasant surprise."

I turned to find Henry Beaufort, Duke of Somerset, staring at me with a rakish expression. A warning spasm of alarm erupted within me. "My lord Somerset," I said, suppressing my aversion and dropping into a curtsey. I had not forgiven Somerset for the way he had assessed me when we first met, and since then I'd learned much about him that I did not like. Here before me stood a degenerate young man from whom the world withheld nothing, breeding in him few scruples, little integrity, and a robust appetite for the sins of the flesh. No doubt he had vanquished many women in his career, for he had good looks and a certain charm that came from the power he wielded.

Somerset dismissed his entourage with a wave. Then, with a flourish of the hand, he indicated that we should stroll together. Ursula stepped aside.

"I am pleased to have such delightful company on an evening as fine as this. How do you find court, my lady Isobel?"

"Quite different from the abbey, my lord."

He gave a loud laugh that sounded almost like a snort. "Indeed, indeed . . . That is an ambiguous reply worthy of a statesman, my lady. But what does it mean? Does it bode well or bode ill? That is the question."

I threw him a smile. "It bodes whatever pleases you, Your Grace."

"Aha! Another statesmanlike answer to confound me. You are a clever one."

We strolled in silence for a while. Then he halted abruptly and turned to face me. "I should be gratified if you would sup with me in my private apartment tomorrow evening," he said.

I felt heat rise to my cheeks. Clearly accustomed to overly easy conquests, he was propositioning me like a common harlot! "I would have to first obtain the queen's permission. As you may recall, I am her ward."

It was his turn to color, but he recovered quickly. "Then perhaps you will join me for song and a cup of wine at the fountain instead?"

"My lord Somerset, you know that is not possible."

"Anything is possible . . . if you will it."

"My lord, that is indeed true for you, powerful as you are. But for me it must be by the queen's will, not mine," I said.

A silence fell. He took my hand into his own. " 'Tis a harmless thing, to sing together. You do not need the queen's permission for that. Will you not relent?"

I looked down at the hand that gripped mine. It was broad of palm and short in the fingers, and I found it crude and unattractive. "Only if the queen commands it, Your Grace."

Something in my tone must have betrayed my inner feelings, for his eyes took on a dark glint. After an interval he said stiffly, "You are indeed unversed in the ways of court, or you would know not to trifle with me. I always have my way . . . in the end." He turned his back and strode angrily toward his waiting retinue on the riverbank.

I was about to call out that, according to rumor, he certainly had his way with the queen. But I caught myself just in time. Unnerved by the challenge I had nearly uttered, I watched his receding back on an unsteady breath, my nurse's words echoing in my head: *She's a wild thing, and reckless; she must be tamed for her own good.* I had to do what I could to avoid Somerset in the future. He was a complex man, and a dangerous one. The power and rage I sensed in him made for a lethal mix, and I dared not trust myself to play the demure damsel.

A FEW DAYS AFTER MY MEETING WITH SOMERSET, great whisperings ebbed and flowed through the halls and passageways as giant waves sweep an ocean, but neither Ursula nor I could make any sense of the fragments we overheard. Then, with a leap of the heart, I caught the names of the Duke of York and the Earl of Salisbury. Realization struck me. Bursting with excitement, I seized Ursula from among a group of ladies in an alcove where a silk merchant was showing off his bolts of fabric, and rushed her off to our chamber, forcing myself not to run the distance. Ursula kept throwing me puzzled glances along the way, but I dared not whisper a word of my discovery until we were safe behind locked doors.

"The Duke of York and Sir John Neville's father, Richard Neville, Earl of Salisbury, are coming to court to attend the queen's council meeting! Salisbury will be accompanied by his eldest son and namesake, Richard Neville, and—"

"The famous Earl of Warwick?" Ursula interrupted with wide eyes. "The handsomest, most valiant knight alive?"

"Aye," I said impatiently. "And—"

"The Earl of Warwick was responsible for the Lancastrian defeat at the Battle of St. Albans! There's talk that he killed Edmund, Duke of Somerset, himself! Did you know Somerset's vowed revenge on the Yorkists—"

I grabbed Ursula by the shoulders. "With him comes his brother, Sir John Neville!"

Ursula gave up her starry thoughts of Warwick and stared at me. "Sir John Neville? Oh, my dear Isobel . . . my poor Isobel. It can't do you any good to see him again!"

"Whether or not that's true, I have to see him—I have to know—" I turned away in confusion. *Know what?* "I have to know if he's forgotten me, Ursula."

"And if he has, what then? There's only grief in that."

"There's only grief now! Maybe *knowing* he doesn't care will serve to cure me."

Ursula threw me a look of pity.

Other information about the Nevilles—far more urgent than I could ever imagine—came to me from an unexpected source that same day.

"My lady Isobel!"

Strolling in the garden, all my thoughts on Sir John's visit, I looked up, disoriented for a moment. William Norris was hurrying through the crowded palace walk to reach my side. "Greetings, my fair lady . . ."

I gave him a smile, and we walked together in genial conversation. I was glad of his company, for his talk of the weather and the upcoming tournament helped deter thoughts of Sir John, if only for a brief space. William was squire to Humphrey Stafford, Duke of Buckingham, brother-by-marriage to both the Duke of York and to the Lancastrian Earl of Northumberland. Though he stood related closely to both York and Lancaster, Buckingham's loyalty to Henry VI was so well-known that his men provided the royal bodyguard. Yet he had acquired the nickname "Peacemaker" for his continuing efforts to bring unity to the queen and the Duke of York. For this, I found myself as grateful to William personally as to good Duke Humphrey. The young man, who by sheer chance had become entangled in my memories of Tattershall Castle merely by being present at a critical moment in my life, now embodied my sole connection to Sir John Neville and even my hopes for peace between the Red Rose and the White. It seemed strange to me, but I felt close to Sir John in his presence, though I was also thankful that William would never know the reason why his company pleased me so well.

"—Sir John Neville?"

"Forgive me, what did you say?" I asked, jolted out of my reverie.

"Do you have an interest in Sir John Neville?" he repeated, watching me closely.

"That is a curious question," I replied, stunned, stalling for an answer.

"You danced with him at Tattershall Castle, and you strolled with him in the garden. I need to know if you return his interest."

I felt myself turn crimson. "You are being presumptuous—"

"Then you would not be upset if something happened to him?" He watched me carefully.

I steeled myself to remain calm and said as coldly as I could manage, "Sir John Neville is of the White Rose, and I am of the Red. Of course it is of no import to me what happens to him." In spite of myself, the words burned my lips. I threw him a sidelong glance as we strolled again. "What do you know? You owe me an explanation for your impertinence."

"I am glad you have no feelings for him, my lady. Though I am only a humble squire without hope of ever winning you, my wish is only for your happiness." He drew a deep breath. "The queen has no intention of letting the Nevilles arrive in London safely. I thought you might care, and am heartened that you don't."

My heart pounded wildly in my chest. "How did this knowledge come to you?"

"Duke Humphrey is most concerned and would send them a warning, but he fears there is nothing he can do." He paused then, and stole a glance at me. "The queen suspects as much and has put him and his retinue under watch."

"Including you?"

"Including me."

"Then it is in God's hands, isn't it?" I was amazed that my voice held no tremor even as my heart thundered in my ears and my mind rampaged violently in a thousand directions.

Five

AMBUSH, 1456

AS I HURRIED ALONG THE HEDGE WALK BACK TO my chamber, my head down and my mind spinning, I bumped into someone and turned to murmur my apologies.

"Ah, 'tis the beauty from Cambridgeshire," Henry, Duke of Somerset, said to his companion as he halted in his steps to give me a leisurely look, his former animosity seemingly forgotten. "Your apology is accepted, my lady, but only if you do penance by tolerating my company for a few moments."

"Aye, Your Grace." I gave a curtsey and dropped my lids.

"And where are you going in such a hurry, my lady? Not to some tête-à-tête, I hope?"

"No, my lord. Merely to my chamber. I am feeling unwell."

"That does not please me, yet it pleases me immensely that no engagement of any import impels you."

I lifted my eyes to his face, lest my reluctance to look at him be taken for rudeness.

"They make the roses fair in Cambridgeshire, don't they, Egremont?" he said to the man beside him.

I was seized with an instant aversion to Somerset's companion, Thomas Percy, Lord Egremont. From a narrow face dominated by a long nose that gave him the appearance of a rat, he stood leering at me with strange opaque eyes, a gap-toothed smile on his lips. He was a man ten years older than Somerset, and, like Somerset, he had lost his father, Henry, Earl of Northumberland, at the Battle of St. Albans. No doubt their shared loss had drawn them close, despite their age difference.

"They do indeed," Egremont replied. He bent to kiss my hand, and I felt the touch of the oily, unkempt hair that hung to his shoulders. I tensed, forcing myself not to recoil. "How about a private supper in your chamber, where I can also join you?" he said to Somerset in a tone that left his meaning clear.

"There will be no supper, Egremont. This is not merely any lady, and certainly not one to be ill-used by you. She is the niece of John Tiptoft, Earl of Worcester, and she has my protection as well as the queen's." He threw Egremont a wry glance, and Egremont retreated a step, palms up in a mock gesture of submission. I thought it clever of Somerset to present himself before his friend as such a chivalrous knight, when he had attempted the very same insulting ploy with me only the evening before. My back stiffened.

"You can rest assured that I will be in touch, my lady," Somerset said, kissing my hand, an amused expression in his eyes at the secret we shared.

Taking a moment to catch my breath and recover, I watched him leave. I hated his arrogant swagger. Ursula appeared at my side. "Be careful, my lady," she whispered, leaning close as we walked back to the palace. "He fancies you, but the queen fancies him, and people are beginning to gossip."

I nodded. Aye, court was full of traps.

We passed through the Temple Gardens and took the tower steps up to the second floor. When we neared the passageway to our chamber, Ursula left me to use the privy. Alone in our room,

I shut the door. I knew what I had to do, but how to do it—that was the question. My head pounding, I leaned against the door and forced myself to draw long, steady breaths. I needed to sort through what I had learned from Norris, and make plans. My eye fell on my coffer. I threw back its carved wood lid and rummaged through my clothes. I pulled out Sœur Madeleine's old habit, which she had left behind when Ursula assumed her duties. I had been intending to return it, but now I found my procrastination fortuitous. I could disguise myself.

But the questions whirling through my head turned up no answers, only more questions: I had to warn Sir John, but where was he, and how would I get there? Could I go alone? Could I tell Ursula? No doubt she'd been instructed to spy on me, as I'd been told to spy on her. An attempt to warn the queen's enemies was treason by any measure, so was it safe—or even fair—to involve Ursula?

If I didn't involve her, could I manage the journey alone? Travel was always hazardous and not something to be undertaken lightly, even for short distances. The approaches to and from the city were beset by brawlers, ruffians, and robbers who indulged themselves with rape and plunder. For these, a lone traveler made prey, and people always sought to join a party of horse. Even two women together provided more security than one traveling sole. But if I didn't confide in Ursula, she would be concerned when I disappeared. My absence would be reported to the queen, and then what excuse would I give?

I sank down on the bed and stared at the habit crumpled in my lap, as if it could give me the answers I sought. I shut my eyes on a breath. No, I could not succeed in the venture by myself, and failure was too terrible to consider. I had to tell Ursula.

Surely she would help me! As I had learned, her own father, Sir Thomas Malory, was no rabid Lancastrian . . . like my own father . . . perhaps like Duke Humphrey. The good duke had wanted to warn York, but his hands were tied. *Maybe I can help him untie them.*

Ursula's footsteps sounded in the passageway. I braced myself. The door creaked open, and Ursula appeared. "What is the matter, lady dear? What do you with that?" Her eyes went to the nun's habit I gripped tightly to me.

Slowly I rose to my feet.

THOUGH I OFFERED URSULA A CHANCE TO RE-main aloof from my plot to save Sir John Neville, she fell in with my plans immediately. With her help I dressed as a nun and set out for Duke Humphrey's chambers at first light. He was in his private quarters when I entered his antechamber and gave his clerk a false name. The man looked at me haughtily, with disdain. "The duke does not grant audiences at this hour."

"I'm not here to plead for alms or a bequest. My business is of an urgent and most private nature. I need to see the duke quickly and alone." I slipped the clerk a gold noble from beneath my sleeve. He stared at the coin in bewilderment for a long moment before pocketing it. When he looked at me again, his expression had changed.

"Pray, wait here. I shall get the message to him."

I watched him disappear into the duke's chamber, and the man-at-arms at the door turned to look at me more intently, aware of something out of the ordinary. I gave him my back and bowed my head so he couldn't see my face. Fortunately the clerk emerged a short moment later and ushered me into a small private chapel attached to the ducal bedchamber. He held the door open for me and swept back the red velvet curtain. The chapel was tiny, with a long, narrow window to one side, overlooking the courtyard, which was filled with the bustle of palace business, the clatter of horses' hooves, and the rumble of carts rolling in and out. A medley of voices drifted to me from below: children laughing, mothers scolding, men calling to one another. At the altar, I bowed my head in silent prayer for the success of my plan, until footsteps made me turn.

Duke Humphrey was a silver-haired man of tall stature, with a fighter's physique and observant eyes of a clear gray hue. He lost no time getting to the point.

"Sister—if sister you are—tell me what brings you here in such unusual fashion, and be quick about it. Pressing business awaits me."

"My lord duke, I am no nun, as you have discerned, and I shall be quick indeed. No business is more pressing than life and death."

"Speak, then."

After informing him of my true identity and the ties that made us kin by virtue of my uncle the Earl of Worcester's first marriage to Cecily Neville, niece to his wife, Anne Neville, Duchess of Buckingham, I made my request. He remained silent a long while, turning the matter over in his mind. Then he walked over to the window and gazed out, hands clasped behind his back. Finally he turned to me.

"What you ask is treason."

"What I ask is your help in preventing needless bloodshed that will have drastic consequences for us all, including the queen."

"It is still treason."

"The king would not see it that way. He has made it clear that he condemns ambush and murder and all such evil practices, has he not?"

He mulled my words. "You speak persuasively." I did not flinch beneath his direct gaze. At length, he said, "As I am loyal to the king, I will help, but information is all I can offer, no escort. We are watched."

"I know."

"You shall need to make haste. There is no time to be lost. I hope it is not already too late."

ARMED WITH A MAP, URSULA AND I RODE HARD for Barnet, ahead of the point of ambush. Exhausted by the journey, we rested our horses in Camden Town and approached an old alehouse in the village square, just past the churchyard, near the town hall and the stocks. Between the wood seller's shop and the glassmaker I caught sight of a butcher slaughtering a lamb. As the animal's throat was cut and blood gushed from his neck, his front legs collapsed beneath him and he sank down to his knees, a stunned look on his face. I turned away, a sick feeling churning my stomach. Surely men had died this same way.

The alehouse was dark, unventilated, and dingy, and though the shutters stood open, the place smelled of soot and sweat. Three customers sat at one of the greasy tables, chattering. We crossed the beaten earth floor and took our seats. Another man entered to make them four.

"Ho, Charlie!" one of the customers greeted him. "How goes the rat-catchin' business?"

The one called Charlie grinned broadly. "My pocket's ajingle with silver. The plague in London's got everyone afraid, so they're willin' to pay large to catch them rats."

"Then I daresay ye can afford to buy us a pint, eh?"

"Why would I do that? There's only so much where this came from, and I gots to keep my own belly filled."

The chorus of groans and affectionate swearing that met this refusal ceased abruptly when a large painted woman passed the door, towering over a toad-faced fellow on her arm. The woman's laughter floated behind her, and the stairs creaked beneath their weight as they mounted the steps. The three men and one woman at the table guffawed and put their heads together.

"That Nellie, she gets good business from the parish clerk— that's twice in one week, if I know how to count!" exclaimed one of the men.

"You should have so much life in you," said the woman.

Ursula, clad in a nun's habit given us by the good duke, turned around and gave them a cold stare. I suppressed the laughter in my throat. Chastened, the man who had spoken swallowed his beer, set a farthing on the table for the alewife, tipped his hat to us, and left. The woman fell mute and dropped her lids. No one said a word while we drank our beer and ate our cabbage, though they exchanged smiles and stole amused glances at us when the plank boards above our heads began to groan. I listened, fascinated, wondering exactly what the parish clerk and his painted woman did to shake the floor in such a manner.

"Eat up, child!" Ursula said sharply. I realized I had begun to smile at my own thoughts, and I bowed my head sharply to hide the laughter bubbling in my throat. When we were done, Ursula left to use the privy out back, and I waited for her outside by a climbing rose tree that rambled across the tavern window, its foliage thick despite the approach of winter. Thinking us gone, the patrons spoke freely now, and their conversation drifted through the open window.

"Did ye hear the latest? Trouble's a brewin' for sure," the rat catcher said. "The queen's sacked the Duke of York and turned out all his ministers. She's ordered him back to Ireland. Now the queen and her favorites are free to loot the land again, God help us all."

"How do ye know?" the woman asked.

"A peddler told me. Just came from London hisself. I gave him a pint for the news."

"Nah, York's no fool. God bless 'im, he won't go," said the other man. "He knows what the Frenchwoman's up to—the last time she exiled him to Ireland, she tried to murder him on the way there, and on the way back, too. An' he made such a success of himself in Ireland, they say Irish hearts are all for York now. . . . Nah, she daren't send him back. I hear he's on his way to London to give his refusal in person."

"What I want to know is, who's the father of the queen's son, Prince Edward?" the woman said. "Sure as cockles it ain't Holy Harry, I'll wager my tail on it. . . . That man's a monk—and a saint too, God bless 'im."

"*Everyone* knows it wasn't Holy Harry, woman! We're not stupid—it's clear as day why you make your wager. You make it to lose it!" The rat catcher chuckled. "In truth, you're yowlin' for us to leap on your tail—admit it now."

"God break your withered neck, I never had a taste for aged meat," she replied.

The rat catcher gave a boisterous laugh. "My money's on Somerset," he said in a different tone. "Father or son."

"There's no knowin' if it was Somerset or Suffolk," the other man said. "Might have been either one. Or might have been Wilt-shire. Maybe the queen doesn't know herself. All anyone can be sure is that it wasn't King Harry. Why, when they showed him the babe, he was as surprised as everyone else—" The man broke off with a snicker. " 'Must be the child of the Holy Ghost!'—that's what he said!"

Everyone howled with laughter.

"Goes to show that just because he's mad don't mean he's a fool," the woman snorted.

They all broke into another round of laughter, but their words only deepened my anxiety. As we galloped our horses toward Bar-net, I contemplated what I'd heard in the alehouse and wondered what lay ahead for the realm, and for my own hopes and dreams. Fixing my gaze on the passing church spires that disappeared into the gray clouds, I whispered many a silent prayer to God for mercy on England, and on Sir John Neville.

At last, the rude beacon tower of Barnet's Hadley Church ap-peared over the rolling hills. We rode hard for it, my heart beating erratically. At the churchyard, we dropped from our saddles, tied our palfreys to the wood post, and followed the beaten path, which was lined with tombstones, up to the church porch. We creaked the door open and entered. A dim light fell from the high window into the darkness, and my eyes took a moment to adjust. Then I saw the priest. He had his back to us as he bent over some flowers at the altar.

"Father!" I called out, rushing up the aisle. "Pray, forgive us this intrusion, but we are here seeking the Earl of Warwick and his party on a matter of the greatest urgency. Can you direct us to him by the shortest possible route?"

The priest straightened at this rude interruption, and when he saw our appearance, the pearls of sweat on our brows, the stains on our habits, he frowned deeply. "Sisters, you are a disgrace to your nunnery. What is the meaning of this—"

"Father, we heartily regret our unseemly conduct, but lives hang in the balance, and much else as well. Pray, tell us where they are!"

It took several precious moments of arguments and the evidence of the Duke of Buckingham's missive bearing his seal, but, finally persuaded of the urgency of our mission, the priest led us outside. "They've only just arrived. They're staying there, in town, and if you stand here, you can almost see the two-story building, behind the pasture with the horses, where they lodge for the night—" He pointed it out to us and gave us a shortcut to the inn. We mounted our palfreys and took off at a gallop.

DUSK WAS FALLING AS WE RODE INTO BARNET. Torches had been lit in the village square, and men milled around with their horses, so preoccupied with their preparations that they barely noticed us. I fingered the pouch where I kept Duke Humphrey's missive. It assured us of entry, and the thought gave me comfort as I drew up to a man-at-arms.

"We have urgent business with Sir John Neville," I told him breathlessly. "Pray, take us to him immediately." My heart pounded as I spoke Sir John's name.

"I can show you his quarters, Sisters."

He led us to a slender, two-story gabled building packed with soldiers. A sentry blocked our way. "They're here to see Sir John Neville. Claim it's urgent," our man said.

"Says who?" the soldier demanded, his eyes scouring us.

I handed him Buckingham's missive. "Make haste—lives are at stake!" I exclaimed as he turned it over slowly in his hands. It occurred to me that he couldn't read, but after giving us another penetrating look, he returned the missive to me and called for someone to take us upstairs. A ruddy blond lad about my age answered the command.

"Follow him, Sisters," the sentry said. The boy took the stairs two by two, and we rushed after him, Ursula in the lead.

I saw John before he realized we were there, and the sudden violent constriction in my heart stopped the breath in my lungs. He stood at a table, his wolfhound at his feet, his tawny head bent over a large map he was examining with a group of men, and his voice reached me, resonant with depth and authority. I froze in my steps. He looked up then and saw us. His eyebrows furrowed in confusion. The dog came to its feet and barked.

Three long months had passed since Tattershall Castle, every month feeling like a year, and though I would remember every detail of that night to my dying day, the realization struck me forcefully that Sir John must have forgotten. Even disguised as I was, to have him not know me was bitter. Bracing myself with the certainty of his indifference to me, I lifted my chin and followed the others into the chamber. A silence fell. The youth and Ursula turned to me.

"My lords," I said, "we are sent by the Duke of Buckingham to warn you of an ambush prepared for you by Henry, Duke of Somerset, and Lord Egremont. They have come in force. The details are here in this missive, sent you by good Duke Humphrey, who wishes conciliation and to avoid bloodshed." I held out the rolled parchment to John, and only then did I realize that I had been addressing him the entire time, and that his eyes had never left mine.

He knew me!

The dazed look of incredulity on his face gave way to awe, and his generous mouth broke into a broad smile, creasing his cheeks and dazzling me with his dimples. Joy sent a smile as wide as his to my own lips, and a surge of warmth flooded my whole body. The faces around us—the candles, the walls—blurred and receded, just as they had on the night of the dance, and again there was only the two of us in all the world, dancing to the music, the gorgeous, melodious music that was filled with fiery flowers falling from Heaven. I felt John willing me to him, and I had to fight the need that impelled me closer.

A man's voice broke the magic holding me in its spell, and I realized Sir John Neville had made no move to take the missive I held out to him. "Well, then, let us see what welcome they have designed for us!" The man snatched the roll from me, broke the seal, and unfurled it. I turned my head and looked at him, feeling myself awaken as if from a dream. He was a large man, tall and strong, with broad shoulders and thick brown hair, dressed opulently in heavy scarlet velvet embroidered with the emblem of the ragged staff in rich silver and gold. Such a grand presence could only belong to John's brother, Richard Neville, Earl of Warwick, the most famous knight alive, admired and beloved by the common people, and clearly by Ursula, too, for she gazed at him utterly mesmerized.

I returned my attention to John. He stood quite still, staring at me with a grin on his face. Even his hound seemed to wear a cheerful look as he wagged his tail. *No wonder he so enchanted me at Tattershall Castle,* I thought; *he smiles even as he stands in the thick of danger.*

Warwick spoke at last. "We owe these good nuns our lives. Had they not risked theirs to get this warning to us, we would have been done for, I can assure you." He passed the missive across the table to an older man in his fifties. This must be Richard Neville, Earl of Salisbury, father to Warwick and John, and brother-by-marriage to yet another Richard in the Yorkist group—Richard, Duke of York. The years had turned his thick hair a startling hue of purest silver and etched his face with lines, but otherwise they had left few marks. With Salisbury's compelling blue eyes, firm features, and a physique that spoke of power and ageless strength, it was clear to me where John derived his good looks. His father was the handsomest man I'd ever seen.

"Indeed," Salisbury said, passing the missive to the next man. "I have no need to read further. Dick is quite right. They outnumber us three to one."

"Those cowards Somerset and Egremont—ambush and murder are all they know. They've not fought fair once in their miserable lives." Warwick spoke with a note of disgust that heightened the nasal quality of his voice.

"Never mind, son, we'll foil them by plotting another route to London," Salisbury replied. "Now, let us not keep these good sisters here any longer. They are tired, no doubt, and ready for supper and a bed for the night. Someone show them to the dining hall—"

"Aye, Father, I will," John said, perhaps with a trifle too much enthusiasm.

His father raised an inquiring eyebrow as he watched his son lead us out.

WE WERE HOUSED IN A SMALL ROOM AT AN INN across the street. John gave the innkeeper strict instructions on making us as comfortable as possible. Then, turning to me, he said, "Sister, may I have a word with you alone?"

Ignoring the shocked expression on the innkeeper's face and Ursula's knowing smile, I nodded my head and clasped my palms at my chest in proper nunlike fashion, as I had seen Sœur Madeleine do many times. Then I led the way into the small parlor at the end of the hall.

As soon as we were out of their sight, he seized my hand. I felt the contact like a burn, and my legs went so weak, I had to lean against the trestle table in order to keep upright. His hound settled comfortably on the reed mat and laid his head on his paws to watch us.

"My dearest lady Isobel, you cannot know what the sight of you means to me!" he said in a low tone. The touch of his hand was suddenly unbearable in its tenderness, and I had to force myself to concentrate on his words. "Ever since we met, I haven't been able to get you out of my mind. But I thought you didn't care—that there was no hope for me. By coming here tonight, you've changed everything. . . . Tell me I'm not wrong in believing you return my affection."

"My lord, I cannot deny what I feel. But I fear you are wrong—there is no hope for us."

"Why, Isobel? How can there not be hope for us when we love one another?"

Love one another. My knees shook, and my hand trembled in his. Tears stung my eyes. "My dear lord, can you not see—how can you not see? Our love is doomed! You are a Neville, and I am the queen's ward. She would never grant us permission to wed. So it matters not that I love you—because the world is as it is, and we cannot remake it to fit our desires."

"You are wrong, Isobel!" He seized me by my shoulders. "We shall remake it. I will not let you go, queen or no queen!"

My pulse swam; I could barely breathe. " 'Tis not merely the queen," I managed. "Have you forgotten your father? He must approve, and why would he? I am the daughter of a Lancastrian knight, now firm in the grip of the queen herself. This is madness!" I tried to pull myself from him, but he tightened his hold.

"You don't know my father. He will support us. He understands love. He cares for my happiness."

"Oh, my lord, I want to believe, but I can't! I won't let myself hope. It only leads to sorrow."

"Isobel," John said in a different tone, one as firm and resolute as when he had spoken to the men gathered over the maps. "Take heart, and believe, as I believe. *It will be.* You'll see."

I shut my eyes as I struggled to compose myself. A tear escaped and rolled down my cheek. "Now I must go," I heard him say. "God keep you, Isobel, my love. I'll see you in London."

Six

OCTOBER 1456

WE FOLLOWED A DIFFERENT ROUTE BACK TO LON-
don. My head was so filled with thoughts of John that I barely noticed the quacking geese and herds of bleating sheep that forced us
to halt as they crossed the road, or our fellow travelers, merchants
and farmers bearing their wares to market, beside us in the dismal rain. Here and there we passed a knight or noble lady with
a retinue, and though I risked little chance of being recognized, I
bowed my head until they passed. I felt as if I were borne back to
Westminster in a cloud, so unnoticed were the puddles, ruts, and
difficulties of the journey that had overwhelmed me only a few
months earlier. Soon we were picking our way through London's
airless streets back to Westminster in time for supper, no one the
wiser. In our chamber, we removed our travel-stained habits and
bundled them into the bottom of my coffer.

"I don't see any need to get word to good Duke Humphrey," I
said, thinking aloud as I shut the lid. "He'll know soon enough of our
success." Somehow the quiet of our room seemed unbearable after

the danger and the excitement of our mission. I knew I should be tired, but I didn't feel it; I felt exhilarated. Kicking off my leather slippers, I sang the melody of the dance at Tattershall Castle and danced, circling and dipping, twirling my arms and moving my body languorously. Ursula watched, a look in her eyes I had not seen there before.

"You dance so beautifully, my dear lady. You make me think of a creature from an enchanted forest, a nymph . . . so lissome, so graceful."

I blushed. "You are kind, Ursula. Always generous with your praise."

" 'Tis not flattery. 'Tis truth."

I sat down on the edge of the bed in my shift, my head filled with thoughts of John as I had left him. "John should have arrived at the Erber by now," I said, referring to the Salisbury residence in Dowgate. "I wonder what he's doing."

"Thinking of you." She chuckled.

I grinned. Ursula had a way of getting to the heart of things. "Tomorrow he'll come to the council meeting at Westminster and I'll see him again," I said dreamily. The thought sent a rush of heat through me, and I realized that time, far from healing my feelings for John, had inflamed them. "I don't understand it, Ursula, but I ache all over when I think of him. I know 'tis this thing called 'love,' but I don't know how or why. . . . Do you?"

"Love has confounded wiser heads than yours, dear Isobel. 'Tis in all my father's writings, this mystery. . . . At least you have tasted it and know what it is. 'Tis a blessing, I suppose, though I wouldn't want it for myself."

"Have you never been in love, Ursula?"

"Can't say that I have. There was a boy once. I thought he was nice enough. But I never felt as you do now—'consumed,' I'd call it. Happy and unhappy at the same time."

"Consumed, aye, as by fire . . . and when I saw John there in that room—oh, Ursula! It was as if my whole being took flight and soared into his. And when I can't see him, 'tis misery indeed. . . . If I get to wed him, I vow it won't matter if we're rich or poor, live long or short—I shall never ask for more!"

"That is a rash vow," Ursula replied, crossing herself against the Devil. "I pray that you do marry, that you live long, and that you live happy—" She shook herself, as if to shed a thought, and then she said, "But these are great riches indeed, and it falls to few in this world to wed the one they love. You would be blessed indeed to have your heart's desire."

"Do you think it will ever be any different? That the world will ever change?"

"I daresay it will, but what comfort in that? 'Tis the now that counts. . . . Here's something that matters. What you wear tonight—" She rose and went to my four gowns hanging on pegs in the corner of the room. "When I went to fetch water, I heard from Agatha the cook that there's to be dancing in the great hall. The queen is back from Kent, and the castle is celebrating her return. So you shall have to dress." She flipped through my gowns. "Not the lavender, 'tis too elegant and royal . . . Not the green, 'tis not festive enough . . . Aha! The claret velvet—" She drew it out from among the others and held it up for my inspection. Dusted with tiny crystals, the high-waisted gown had tight fitted sleeves and a plunging neckline trimmed with fox that was filled in with fine silver embroidery across the bosom to match the design on the broad belt.

I fingered the fur. "But fox is not in fashion, Ursula," I said.

"It will be, m'dear, once you wear it," she replied jauntily. "Lavender was not the rage until you chose it for your audience with the queen, and how many parti-colored gowns of black and silver were there before the ladies saw you in one? They copy everything you wear—have you not noticed? They've even stopped curling their hair, hoping to have it drape behind them like a heavy satin train as yours does. But in that they must fail, for no one else has such thick, glossy hair as you."

"Oh, Ursula," I said, giving her a light kiss on the cheek. "You're so good to me."

"Aye, claret velvet tonight, and your hair loose, dusted with crystals and pearls." She paused to study me for a moment. "There's one thing I'll never understand. How can you eat so much and remain as slender as you do?"

I looked down at myself. It was true that I enjoyed a good appetite.

" 'Tis unjust, my dear . . . absolutely unjust," she sighed.

Ursula must have done an exceptionally splendid job of dressing me, for I attracted more than my customary share of attention as I took my seat in the great hall, between two young knights. They vied for my attention throughout the evening so that supper became an occasion of marked gaiety for me. After we had finished eating, a lion from the Tower menagerie performed for us by leaping through rings of fire as he was led around the hall by a Gypsy man, to the *oohs* and *aahs* of the crowd. Minstrels arrived in the gallery, and the hall filled with music. Jewels dazzled as noble lords and ladies rose to dance. I danced with both knights, and another came to claim a rondel, and then several more followed. Finally weary, I would have refused any more requests, but no sooner had I found my seat again than Somerset appeared before me.

"My lady?" He bowed.

I rose stiffly and gave him my hand, touching his so lightly, it might have rested on air.

"You look particularly lovely this evening," he said as he led me to the center of the hall. "But, then, you seem to gain in beauty even as we gaze. Like a rose opening to the sun."

"You are mistaken, my lord," I said as we moved to the music. "Perhaps you have partaken too much of the fine wine served tonight."

" 'Tis not just my opinion, but that of many others. I am indeed fortunate to have partnered with you, for it seems half the hall wishes to dance with you."

"There is a shortage of ladies this evening, Your Grace."

"You are too modest." He twirled me under his arm and I passed with ease around him, for he was a surprisingly graceful dancer despite his height and powerful build. "Are you enjoying the entertainment?"

" 'Tis royal enough," I replied noncommittally, passing under his arm in the opposite direction.

"You should. The festivities are for you, by my command."

"Not for the queen?"

Aware he'd been reckless enough with his comments, he did not reply.

As innocently as I could manage, I said, "You have been absent from court recently. I hope you were not indisposed?"

One corner of his mouth lifted, and he gave a small laugh. "Not indisposed, and gone merely for a day. I had urgent business to attend out of town."

Aye, ambush and murder, I thought. "I trust it went well?"

"Not as well as I had hoped. So you missed me? That is encouraging."

As I danced, my glance moved across the hall and caught the queen. She was watching us. "My lord, the queen's eyes are on you. And there's nothing encouraging in them."

He stiffened. Silently I rejoiced. In his fear of the queen lay my only protection, for I knew without a doubt that had I not been her ward, and had he not been her lover, the rake would have ravished me long before this. "I suggest we end this dance, as I am feeling quite dizzy of a sudden, Your Grace."

He escorted me back to my seat. "Fear not, my lady," he said under his breath as we parted between a bow and a curtsey. "There will be other chances."

Late that night a page came to our door to inform me that the queen had summoned me to her apartments. It was after Vespers, and Ursula and I were both preparing for bed, but I dressed quickly, with some apprehension.

"What would the queen wish with me at this late hour?" I fretted.

"Maybe 'tis nothing, merely a whim," she said, hoping to comfort me.

"I hope it's not jealousy over Somerset. I shall tell her the truth, then. Mayhap she'll restrain him, and I shall be done with the matter." Absorbed by my thoughts, I turned left out of my chamber and left again into the short, narrow passageway that opened into the main corridor. The hall was silent, empty, and dark, lit only by a single torch. I hurried along, but I never reached the main corridor, for Somerset leapt out of the shadows. Taken by surprise, I shrank back with a gasp. I didn't like the look on his face.

Suppressing my fear, I lifted my chin. "My lord Somerset, pray let me pass. The queen has sent for me."

He didn't move. "It wasn't the queen who sent for you, Isobel." He bent his face down to my lips, and I smelled his wine-soaked breath.

"My lord!" I cried, pushing him away.

"Isobel, you grow lovelier every day. Court agrees with you. Come, my sweet, why do you play coy? I swear your mouth is made for love."

"I understand you not, my lord."

"I think you do."

In a tone of ice, I said, "My lord, your attention is most unwelcome. Surely you do not wish me to tell the queen that you accosted me thus? It would place you in a most difficult position. Now . . . let go of my arm."

He removed his hand. "Isobel, let's stop these games. Be truthful with yourself. You have a passion for life. You dine with appetite, dance with exuberance—wait until you know of love! And let me be the one to teach you, my beauty! I vow you shall not tire of it—we're made for one another, Isobel. Though you play the proper damsel, you're as reckless and wild as I am, and you desire me as much as I desire you."

"Pray, my lord, if we must be truthful, let me speak plain. There may be many at court who desire you, but I am not one of them."

His soft expression vanished; his eyes narrowed and he gave a laugh, mean, harsh, full of menace. "That will change when you are wed to a man three times your age with rotten teeth who farts as he sticks his prick into you—"

"You have a foul way with words, my lord."

"Perhaps, but you agreed we would speak plain. After you have tasted him, you'll be only too glad to rush into my arms, I warrant."

"I shall refuse my consent to such a match. The queen has given her word that I may do so, and it is my legal right."

He laughed. "Ah, my dear little innocent from the priory, take heed. When the price is right, there are ways to acquire a maiden's consent . . . rape, for example, and the humiliation of being with child—a bastard, no less."

"You wouldn't—you couldn't do such a thing—"

"That, and more, if I pleased. You see, my dear lady Isobel, I don't need your consent. I can take you now, if I choose to—"

I backed away.

"But I won't, unless I am driven to it." His eyes fixed on my bosom. "I have no wish to see such a beautiful body as yours wasted by childbearing. Therefore, I shall be patient awhile longer. I would rather have you panting for me."

"That day will never come!"

"Heed my words, Isobel. As to the match, I lie not. There is indeed such a man lusting for you. At the moment, I am all that stands between you and marriage to the old lout. You see, I have advised the queen that his price is too low, but a few choice words from me and she will relent, I assure you. You would have no choice but to accept, my lovely lady Isobel."

I stared at him, unable to breathe.

"Give it thought, Isobel," he hissed in my ear. "Him or me. Which will it be?"

"Neither," I replied, seething. "I'll tell the queen I have changed my mind and wish to enter a nunnery."

He threw me an indulgent smile. "She dreams of riches when she looks at you. Do you think she would agree to rob her own purse?"

"Even a queen can't refuse God," I said with more conviction than I felt.

He burst into uncontrollable laughter. "You have much to learn about the world, Isobel." Bowing low, still laughing, he left me. I stood alone in the shadowy hallway, shivering, his laughter echoing in my ears.

CHURCH BELLS TOLLED THE HOURS OF THE NIGHT. I heard every chime, and every breath Ursula took as she lay on the pallet on the floor. Slowly the gray, fitful light of morning broke the heavy darkness. A rooster crowed; birds burst into song; the castle stirred. Ursula opened her eyes. She sat up, startled.

"Lady dear, what are you doing sitting on your bed in your gown? Did you not sleep? What happened with the queen?"

"I never saw the queen, Ursula."

I related the events of the night. She seized my hand. "You must seek Sir John Neville as soon as he gets here. Go break fast in the hall. I'll stand watch in the courtyard and get word to you as soon as he arrives. Do you have a token I can give him, if I get the chance?"

I unclasped my mother's ruby crucifix from around my neck. "Take this! I wore it when I saw him in Barnet."

Halfway through breakfast, Ursula approached my bench and gave me a curtsey, her eyes alight. I excused myself to those at the table and followed her into the garden, my heart hammering. "Where is he?" I whispered. "What did he say? Did you give him my token?"

"Aye, indeed. He noticed me the minute he rode into the court-yard, and his eyes told me to approach. The groom took his horse, and he went to the fountain and pretended to adjust his boot. I bent to pat his hound and slipped him your cross. He knew it right away. As he took it, he gave me instructions to have you meet him in St. Paul's at the hour of nine."

"Did anyone see you?"

"I don't think so. There was such bustle and comings and go-ings. We were both very discreet."

"That's only forty-five minutes from now! We'll just make it if we hurry, Ursula!"

HE STOOD BETWEEN THE ALTAR AND A SIDE CHAN-try, near a bank of candle offerings, his hound beside him. His eyes found me the moment I entered the nave. I hurried to him, and we hid behind a marble pillar in the chantry, protected from prying eyes. Ursula remained a distance away, out of earshot. He took me into his arms, and a melting sweetness poured through me as his lips met mine.

"My love, what is so urgent that we must chance this meeting?" he asked, taking my hands into his own.

I recounted the events with Somerset. The hound watched us, ears moving as if he followed the tale of the night's doings.

"God damn that fool!" John muttered. He grabbed a side rail as he considered the problem. Strangely, his anger served as a comfort to me. Somehow I knew that if anyone could set things right, it was he, even against such impossible odds. At last he spoke. "I don't believe you are in any great danger at the moment. Somerset is rash, but not rash enough to damage the queen's property—for that is what you are, Isobel. And he knows, along with the rest of us, what high store she puts on her property. Therein lies safety for you. No—more likely, he'll try to push the match for vengeance's sake. We need to stall for time."

A match? Marriage to someone else? I shut my eyes at the horrible specter. John cupped my chin in his hand and tilted my face to his. "Isobel," he whispered. I opened my eyes. A smile played on his generous mouth. "Beloved, now listen to my news. 'Tis good— nay, splendid—news! I have spoken to my father. He approves our match and will do all he can to see us wed!"

A cry of joy escaped my lips. I offered him my mouth and clung to him with reckless abandon. After the melting tenderness of our kiss, he broke our embrace and looked at me gravely. "But there's something you must do, and there's no time to be lost. Write your uncle the Earl of Worcester before he leaves Ireland, and ask for his help facilitating our way with the queen. He stands high in her favor. Marguerite has newly appointed him her papal ambassador to Rome. She will listen to him. My father will speak to her before he returns to the North. No doubt she will refuse at first, but it will seed the thought and speed our way in the end."

A commotion drew our attention to the entry as the massive door creaked open. John's hound leapt to his feet. A group of men entered and someone shouted, but I couldn't make out the words or see him clearly, for he stood in shadow with the light behind him.

But when the church door slammed shut, he strode forth and came into view. I gasped. It was Somerset, and he had brought men with him. "I know you're here!" he was yelling. "Show yourself, knave!"

I looked at John helplessly. Spies were everywhere at court! John took me by the arms and placed me gently behind him. He stepped out from behind the pillar and moved into the open. "I'm here, Somerset," he called. "I see you come well protected. Do you fear an ambush in God's house, or come to give one?"

Somerset swung around and marched up with angry strides as John's hound gave a low growl. When Somerset caught sight of me standing behind John's shoulder, his lips thinned with a cold smile. "Tish-tish, toying with the queen's jewels, are you? 'Tis a danger-ous game you play, Neville."

"No more than you. But my intentions are honorable, while yours are not. The queen will appreciate the difference."

Somerset's grin faded. "More fool you, if you think there's any way in hell Marguerite will accept you." He sneered.

"We'll see about that."

I marveled at John's composure. He had assumed a princely stance, his head held high, one leg forward, a hand on the hilt of his sword. The thought came to me that he exuded the righteous-ness and inherent nobility of his motto—*Honor, Loyalty, Love*—and were it a thousand years ago, here would stand a knight of Arthur's court, just so. If I had not known it before, I knew it then—I loved him with all of my heart, to the death and forever afterward, into eternity.

"Curse you, fiend!" Somerset drew his sword. A gasp sounded around the church, and a crowd gathered.

"How dare you defile this house of God!" someone yelled. Other angry voices arose, and soon Somerset and his men were surrounded by a rabble of furious citizens, one voice drowning out another: "Lay down your sword before we tear it from you!" "We're sick of you and your fights in our streets!" "Take your confounded feuds back to the palace!" "Out, out with you!" The crowd picked up these words and chanted with one voice, "Out with you! Out, out!" The outraged citizenry had turned into a mob, and Somerset did not fail to note its ominous tone. He paled and lowered the sword in his hand. Many a lord had died at the hands of a mob such as this, including his father's friend William de la Pole, Duke of Suffolk, whose head had been sawed off by a sailor with a rusty sword as Suffolk tried to flee England aboard ship.

A priest pushed through the throng and addressed Somerset. "Best you return to the palace, my lord. Do not tarry, I pray you."

Somerset flashed John an angry look. "We'll finish this later," he hissed as he sheathed his weapon. Cautiously he backed down the nave, surrounded by his men.

The ancient doors were pulled open, flooding the area with daylight. Framed in the entrance, Somerset stood for a moment, a black specter darkened by the light. A fleeting instant later, he was gone. The church doors clanged shut with a thunderous roar that reverberated in my ears. Unaware that I'd been holding my breath, I exhaled deeply.

The eyes of the crowd turned to us, as did the priest.

"I thank you most humbly," John said.

The priest, short and stout, looked up into John's face. "I can see you are made from a different mettle from your adversary. We can only pray that such as he do not inherit our world, for then there is but little hope for us all. What name do you have, that we may pray for you, my lord?"

"I am Sir John Neville, son of the Earl of Salisbury and brother to the Earl of Warwick."

At this a loud cheer resounded through the nave of St. Paul's. "A Warwick! A Warwick!" the citizenry cried. "God bless Warwick! God bless the House of York!"

The priest waited for the cheers to subside. "You have our prayers, my lord. May God save the Earl of Warwick, the most illustrious knight alive, and his noble brother, Sir John Neville." Amid another round of cheers, the priest stepped aside and the crowd parted for us, their faces struck with awe. To their applause and blessings, John and I walked down the aisle arm in arm. I dared not look at his face, for pride had so flooded my heart that it had broken its boundaries and wetted my cheeks as tears.

I took leave of him on the steps of St. Paul's. He returned my ruby cross and galloped back to Westminster to attend his audience with the queen. With a small escort provided by the citizenry, Ursula and I returned to the palace.

"I HAVE DECIDED 'TIS TIME YOU WERE WED," THE queen said, pacing back and forth before me like a caged lioness. Somerset stood in the background, his eyes watching me, sultry with desire. "We are negotiating now," the queen continued, "and may have an announcement for you shortly."

"May I ask who I am to wed, my queen?"

She checked her steps and looked at me. "You will be informed in good time." She nodded her dismissal. I saw a warning cloud settle on the queen's features as she turned to Somerset, and I realized this display was for his benefit.

Ursula was waiting for me in the antechamber to the royal apartments where Marguerite's ladies wiled away their time, some chattering, some embroidering, others merely awaiting her instructions. With Ursula's help I dragged myself to my room.

"Bring me paper and pen, Ursula. 'Tis urgent. Go quickly!" I found myself whispering, though we were alone. After only a few months, I had picked up the habit of the court: that it was prudent to keep one's own counsel, and failing that, to speak in whispers if words had to be uttered at all.

When Ursula returned, I stood on the bed and rested the paper and ink pot on the uncomfortably high window ledge as I wrote. Privacy was too important, and nowhere else in the palace would I find it.

My dear and much beloved uncle,

   I greet thee well and pray all is good with thee. As my missive regards a matter of utmost urgency to my happiness, I shall dispense with my frivolous news and get to the heart of the matter. Uncle, I wish to wed, but I fear my choice will not meet with the queen's approval unless you champion me. Sir John Neville, son of your former brother-by-marriage, the Earl of Salisbury, wishes to wed me, and I him, with all my heart. You know well the quality of this family, and so I shall say no more on that subject. Sir John and I are aware of the difficulties of our situation, and I am sure that in your wisdom you would advise us to forget each other. But I beg of you to remember what love is! We are lost to wisdom. You have always spoken to me of the beauty of love, and now life has graced me with true knowledge and removed wisdom from all thought and action. You yourself have not wed again since the death of your illustrious lady, and so I believe your heart can feel for us. All my joy and happiness in this world resides in Sir John Neville. I implore you to remember love, and to support my cause, for I feel my very life depends upon it.

Your loving niece,
Isobel

I dispatched the missive to my uncle in Ireland where he was serving as Lord Deputy, and then went to the chapel to pray for its safe delivery before he left. By mealtime, palace whispers reached me that the council meeting had resolved nothing with the queen, and the Nevilles had departed for the North. By the next afternoon I learned why the queen had called me to her solar to inform me that she was arranging a match for me. As I embroidered a portion of tapestry assigned to me, so engrossed in my thoughts was I that it took me time to realize I was seated next to Elizabeth Woodville. She gave me a wily smile when she caught my eye.

"Is all well?" she inquired, as if she well knew it was not. She raised her eyebrows.

"I have been feeling a trifle dizzy. I expect it's this close work."

"Then I shall distract you by telling you a humorous tale."

I waited.

"The queen had a visitor yesterday. He asked for your hand for his son."

I felt myself pale. She threw me a slanted, feline glance and, clearly amused by my reaction, continued. "It was a great jest. . . . If you look around, you'll see the whole court laughing about it."

I let my glance move swiftly across the room. She was right. Everyone seemed to be eyeing me, and their lips twitched with suppressed laughter.

"Don't you wish to know who it was?"

I laid down my tapestry. "Pray, Elizabeth, be kind and tell me."

The corners of her mouth lifted in triumph. "It was the Earl of Salisbury, asking for your hand in marriage to his son, Sir John Neville."

My head swam. I closed my eyes, conscious of the tittering around me.

"Do you know the queen's reaction? She laughed him out of the room. Everyone laughed. Somerset laughed loudest of all."

I opened my eyes at this last remark. "Dear Elizabeth, I beg your indulgence. I need to lie down. I feel most unwell of a sudden."

With what dignity I could muster, my head clouded and my legs trembling, I left the great hall, followed by the snickering of the queen's women. In the antechamber, as soon as Ursula caught sight of me, she put away her father's manuscript, which she had been reading, and came to my side. She pressed herself close so that I leaned into her as we walked, giving me succor without anyone seeing her do so.

I did not see the queen the next day, since I had pleaded ill health, but she sent for me that evening. I went to her in the royal solar, anxiety tearing at me. When I saw she was alone, unattended by her ladies and Somerset, a wave of relief swept me.

"Your Grace," I said, sinking low into my curtsey, for I had learned that Queen Marguerite placed great store in such exaggerated tokens of respect.

"You may rise." She waved me to a seat beside her and scrutinized me with her green eyes for an agonizingly long moment. At last she spoke. "The requests for your hand have been coming in remarkably fast and furiously. . . . Now, it seems, the Earl of Salisbury would have you as bride for his son Sir John Neville."

She fell silent, her eyes not wavering from my face. I knew

she wanted my reaction, but I dared not give it, so I said nothing, though I felt myself redden horribly.

"So you know this already?"

"Aye, my lady queen. Elizabeth Woodville told me of it."

"Did she also inform you of our reaction?"

"She did."

"What say you?"

I was on treacherous ground, and I knew it. "I don't know what to say, my liege," I replied softly.

"You can begin by telling me how this came about, since evidently you and Sir John Neville have met before."

"It was at Lord Cromwell's castle, on my way down to Westminster with Sœur Madeleine, my queen. Sir John was present with his brother Sir Thomas. There was a feast. Sir John asked me to dance. . . ." My heart quickened at the memory and I saw him again, gazing at me and holding out his hand; I saw myself take it and move with him to the dance floor; I felt my feet lighten, my being soar. . . .

I fell silent and dropped my gaze to my hands.

She rose from her chair with an angry swish of her silk gown. "He is a Yorkist!" The accusing harshness in the queen's tone brought me back to reality with the sharpness of a dagger thrust. I threw myself at her feet.

"My lady, he may be a Neville, but he is also an honorable knight and well he knows his duty to the king! But where the heart leads, can we command it not go? I have tried, my queen. But reason is no weapon against love!"

The stiffness left Queen Marguerite. She let herself down heavily into her chair. "My father said that once . . . in a love note to my mother. He is a rhyme maker, you know. . . ." Her eyes took on a faraway expression. Her thoughts had drifted across the sea, to a place in memory reserved only for her.

"'I went to bed early one night,'" I quoted from King René's manuscript, "'tired and preoccupied with musings about love. Then— was it a vision, a dream?—Love himself suddenly appeared before me, taking the heart from my breast and handing it to Desire. . . .'"

"You have read my father's tales?" she asked with great surprise.

"I have committed them to memory, my lady. Your royal father writes beautiful rhyme and shows tender wisdom about matters of the heart."

"Rise, my child. Take a seat." The queen reached out her hand to me and drew me to my feet. "I believe in love. 'Tis a wondrous thing, not to be lightly dismissed. 'Tis why I spend so much time arranging matches. It pleases me to see love rewarded, to make others happy."

I looked at her and knew my eyes had widened with hope. But her next words shattered it as a sword shatters glass.

"But this can never be."

I hid my face and bit my lips to keep back my tears.

Seven

YULE, 1456

I KEPT TO MY BED FOR DAYS. TEARS I COULD NOT shed before the queen flowed copiously now, drenching my pillow. How could I marry someone for whom I had no regard, now that I had tasted love?

Ursula brought me broth and tried to make me eat. I averted my face.

"Now, now, dear lady, if you do not wish to eat, do you at least wish for news?"

Her tone held a cheery note. I turned my head and looked at her. "There is to be a council meeting in Coventry on the first day of December," she said with smiling eyes.

I struggled up to my side, my heart beating wildly. *John would be there!*

"There's more. . . . The queen has sent Somerset away to Wales on royal business. He is not expected to return until the council convenes in Coventry, when the Duke of York arrives. We leave London tomorrow. You have only a few weeks until you see your love again, and who knows what news he brings—or what the future brings? Now, sweet lady, eat your soup."

With wagons loaded, carts creaking, and horses neighing, the court departed for Coventry early the next morning. I was barely able to contain my excitement, but while the music of minstrels incited me to dream of love, there was no mistaking the mood of the people. They hated Marguerite. All along the way, they gathered along the roadside, staring at us silently with sullen faces. No daisies had been fashioned to adorn the women's hair or the rude tunics of the peasants in honor of the queen, and their solemn expressions grew dark when she came into view, flanked by Egremont and the thick-necked, hard-faced Lord Clifford, another of Marguerite's young favorites who had lost his father at St. Albans. The people blamed their foreign queen for the loss of their French lands, especially Maine, the richest and most important dominion of all, which she had personally promised to her uncle, King Charles of France, and delivered to him soon after her arrival in England. In addition, she had prevailed on her malleable husband, Henry, to cede Anjou to France. Yet she had brought nothing in return except a brief truce. Even her gown had to be provided by Henry before she could be presented to the people, so poor had she been. Now she arrayed herself splendidly—perhaps too splendidly—and her favorites enriched themselves at the expense of the treasury.

She was blamed, too, for the death of King Henry's uncle Humphrey, Duke of Gloucester, who had accused the late dukes Somerset and Suffolk of mismanagement of the war. The people had loved him as they now loved the Duke of York, but he had been arrested by his great foe Suffolk and lay dead within the week. *Murdered,* the whispers said, *by the queen and her favorites.* They never blamed the king. They loved him. He was a saint, deeply religious; he hated bloodshed and pardoned every crime. But he was soft as churned butter in the hands of his Frenchwoman.

As soon as we arrived at Coventry, the queen dismissed me and all her ladies and, taking little Prince Edward, she went to join King Henry in his private apartments. The castle had been built in the eleventh century and rebuilt in the twelfth, and had fallen into disrepair. It was a gloomy place, surrounded by a great moat that ran red from the color of the soil. Its rooms had once been splendid, with embossed ceilings, inlaid stone floors in patterns of flowers and fleur-de-lis, gilded hammer-beam roofs, and much colored glass—but time had dimmed their beauty. Now the wind whistled loudly through the halls, moisture clung to the stone walls, and buckets stood in many rooms to catch the rain that leaked through the ceilings.

"Why does the queen choose to stay here?" Ursula inquired as we unpacked our coffer and hung the dresses to air on a peg in the corner of the dismal chamber.

From force of habit, I glanced around before I replied. "Coventry is Lancastrian, and London is Yorkist. She feels safe here."

Ursula placed her bright red head close to mine. "Yet she raised the taxes in Leicester fivefold in two years," she whispered. "How can they approve?"

I shrugged. Who understood anything anymore? It was all too complicated. "People see what they want to see," I said.

I spent my time in the queen's company, but never when she was with the king. In the mornings I helped her dress, arrange her hair, and make her beauty preparations, rubbing sheep fat into her face, tinting her cheeks with rouge, and darkening her pale eyebrows with charcoal from the pit of a burnt peach stone. During the day I ran errands for her, carrying her instructions to the far reaches of the castle, and sorted through some of the more personal petitions that came from the female servants, settling what problems I could and laying the rest before her. The evenings she did not spend with King Henry were spent in the company of her ladies. There we sang and I played my lyre, and read to her from her collection of illuminated manuscripts, and worked on a tapestry King Henry had designed that he wished to be ready for Yuletide.

I wondered about the queen. She had to know how matters stood between Somerset and me; yet she continued to show me favor. Not one to hide her feelings, she clearly enjoyed my company nearly as much as that of Elizabeth Woodville. Perhaps it was because marriage offers poured in for us both, and that pleased the queen's romantic nature. Yet Elizabeth had never expressed interest in any of her suitors, whether they were young or old. One had even come from a well-born retainer of the Earl of Warwick, and Warwick himself had written Elizabeth to press the knight's suit. It was a good match for a damsel of such low stock on the paternal side, the only side that counted.

"Do you not wish to wed?" I asked Elizabeth one day as we worked on the king's tapestry, unable to restrain my curiosity.

"Of course I do," she said with a throw of her haughty head and silver-gold hair. "What makes you think otherwise?"

"You are eighteen, well past marriageable age, and no one is fairer than you."

She laughed, but with a softer note than usual. It occurred to me that she liked being flattered. "Well, you can be sure I won't be going into a nunnery just to leave the field open to you."

When I recovered from my astonishment, I said, " 'Tis not why I ask. I only marvel that you have evaded marriage so long. Surely many have bid high for your hand."

"Not high enough for my mother, the Duchess of Bedford."

There was some tittering from the girls in the corner. When Elizabeth pointedly glanced their way, they wiped the grins from their faces and bowed their heads over the tapestry.

"Have you never been in love, then?" I asked.

"Love? What has that to do with marriage?" she demanded. "Only a fool seeks love when it is power and money that matter."

I was astounded, and my expression told her so, for she gave a laugh. "I see you are one of those silly fools who disagrees. Let me advise you that if you wed for love, you will surely regret it."

"But why, Elizabeth?"

"If Sir Lancelot lives long enough, he becomes Sir Fart-A-Lot, my dear. I thought even fools knew that."

MY ROOM AT COVENTRY CASTLE WAS SMALL AS a dungeon cell, and there was nothing to be seen from my side of the building except rooftops and walls. Yet I enjoyed Coventry more than I expected. The knowledge that I would see John again colored my thoughts and dreams, and Somerset's absence cheered me immensely. He was gone through November, and it felt as if the sun had broken through the clouds. In my lightened mood, I found myself clapping loudly for the mummers after our suppers and humming merrily as I helped decorate the queen's apartments with Yuletide greenery. The ugly bishop named Dr. Morton, who had startled me in the hallway at Westminster, frequented the queen's court at Coventry, and though a strangely unpleasant sensation always came over me at the sight of him, even this could not dull my pleasure.

"Only two more days, and John will arrive with the Duke of York!" I whispered to Ursula. The pealing of church bells through the day and the chant of monks at the holy hours kept tally of the passing time to remind me how joyfully near we drew to the first of December and the council meeting.

On the eve of John's arrival, as I took my customary leave of the queen in the royal chamber after Vespers, she said, "Seek out Simon the Toy Maker in town tomorrow morning and tell him we wish him to carve us an army of toy soldiers for our prince, Edward, as a Yuletide gift."

"Aye, my queen," I replied, grateful that my meeting with John was not forestalled. He had sent me a message to meet him in the king's sunken pleasure garden, near the dovecote, shortly after Prime, when no one else was likely to be there.

I did not sleep that night, so anxious was I to see my love—so filled with hope and happiness that all would somehow be well, and we'd find a way to wed! Morning finally dawned, heralded by the loud chirping of birds. I dressed with great excitement. Even dreary Coventry Castle, bedecked with lush greenery and holly and resounding with singing and laughter, had brightened to reflect my merry mood as I hurried to the sunken garden, laughing as Ursula ran to keep up with me in the light snow that had begun to fall.

"You have fleet feet!" she called out, and I giggled at her jest, for it was as we had shopped along Fleet Street before we left for

Coventry that a flower seller had flourished a bow and handed me a sprig of holly. Hidden in the greenery was a note from John, with instructions about where to meet him on the morning of the council meeting.

Church bells chimed the hour of eight as I lifted my skirts and tripped down the worn stone steps into the garden, stepping carefully in the snow, my mantle flowing behind me. John was already waiting by the dovecote, his hound at his heels. Leaving Ursula to guard our privacy at the top of the steps, I ran along the path deep into the garden and flew into his arms.

"My love, my dearest love," he murmured into my hair, swinging me into his embrace as Rufus barked a greeting.

I gazed up at him and fingered the noble lines of his handsome face, trying to imprint them on my memory. "I live for these moments," I whispered, grateful for the knowledge that he was safe at my side, however short the time would prove.

"One day we shall be together, my angel, never to be parted." He took my hands into his own and looked at me with a tender smile.

"Never to be parted," I repeated. "How good that sounds, my lord." I wondered whether John truly believed such a dream could come true. I wasn't certain I did.

A commotion by the garden wall startled me from my blissful reverie as Ursula cried out in loud warning, "My lords—"

"Get thee gone, woman, if you know what's good for you!" came the angry retort. Rufus leapt to his feet, barking fiercely, and I gave a gasp. It was Somerset's voice. He clattered down the garden steps and and a moment later came into view between the hedgerows lining the path. His color deepened to crimson when he saw us, and a vein throbbed in his forehead. He stepped forward, a hand on the hilt of his sword. Rufus let out a low growl.

"What have we here?" Somerset mocked, taking no notice of Rufus and exchanging a glance with a surly fellow at his side who had the look of a lawless ruffian. "I do believe we've caught lovebirds attempting to nest. What say you to divesting this cock of his feathers, Cockayne?"

The man called Cockayne gave a lopsided grin and drew his sword. John pushed me behind him. In the same instant, though I didn't see him withdraw his weapon from its sheath, the blade glittered in his hand.

"Two against one, how ungallant of you," John said, directing himself to Somerset. "Nevertheless, I thank you for the pleasure of divesting you both of your ugly hides." The shock of steel against steel clanged around me, and the thin wintry greenery shivered in the blast of the currents they stirred as John exchanged blows with the two men.

I pulled out the small knife I had carried in my sleeve since the night Somerset had accosted me. Awaiting opportunity, I edged back to the wall and made a wide arc around him and the ruffian until I stood at their backs. Rufus kept barking, but, like me, he dared not attack, for the men were moving too swiftly. While Somerset and the other man hacked at him, John parried their strokes expertly, but after a while the exertion of fighting two men at once began to tell on him. His movements slowed, and I heard his heavy breathing. I was preparing to lunge forward and thrust my dagger into the ruffian's arm to buy John time when a shout rang out. "Halt!"

I swung around; John and Somerset froze. The Duke of Buckingham and his armed retainers surrounded us, their sword points ringing the fighting trio. "Drop your weapons!" the duke commanded. "Disturbing the king's peace in his own garden—have you no shame?"

Warily, John lay down his sword. The other two followed suit.

The duke turned his gaze on me, and I saw that he understood clearly what had happened. He returned his glance to John and Somerset. "And you both, take heed. . . . The queen will not suffer either of you toying with her property. Now leave. You have a council meeting to attend. . . . As for you, Cockayne, you'll go before the magistrate."

At Duke Humphrey's nod, his retainers stepped back, opening a path for John and Somerset, who had been separated by Buckingham's men. Cockayne was rustled away with scant courtesy. John hesitated, ran a hand through his hair, and looked as if he would say something. Then he picked up his sword and, after a glance in my direction, strode off. Somerset straightened his jacket and retrieved his sword. He, too, threw me a look before he left, but one that spoke of loathing and anger. As John and Somerset disappeared from view, the Duke of Buckingham touched his velvet cap in farewell and, taking a different path out of the garden, departed at a rapid pace with his entourage.

I rushed after John. As I wound along the path, I spied Somerset a distance ahead, through an opening in the yews. He drew to an abrupt halt at the foot of the stone steps that led out of the sunken garden.

"We're not finished, Neville!" he shouted. "Tonight, in the village square, let's settle it once and for all!"

John, who was halfway up the snowy steps, turned and looked down at him. "Fear not, knave. I'll be there," he said, and disappeared from view without catching sight of me.

AS URSULA RELATED TO ME THAT MORNING WHEN I returned from running the queen's errand, she had run into the castle courtyard in a panic, calling for help. Her cries had been answered by good Duke Humphrey, who was just then arriving for the council meeting. By the time I returned from my errand to the toy maker in town, the entire castle was buzzing about the fracas in the garden between John and Somerset. As I feared, the queen knew about it as well, and a royal summons awaited me.

I hurried to her chamber, praying all the way and hoping she would not detain me long, for the matter stood unfinished and I had to warn Duke Humphrey of Somerset's plans for a fight that evening.

Seething with rage, Marguerite d'Anjou stomped to and fro before me. "*Alors*, this is how you repay me? 'Tis high time indeed that you were wed and we are rid of you!" I hung my head. She drew up sharply before me to glare before resuming her pacing. "Have you nothing to say for yourself?"

"The duke's attentions are unwelcome to me, my lady queen. I made that clear to His Grace."

She swung on me. "So he is not good enough for you?"

Bracing myself, I raised my head and looked directly at her. "My queen, I am not good enough for him, and well he knows that, or he would not choose to dishonor me. Even were it not so, I would never repay your great kindness with such malice, and I informed him so."

"Indeed?" Her hard look softened, and she drew closer. "What was his reaction?"

"He threatened me with rape."

The queen's lovely features twisted in fiendish rage. "*Sang dieu!* He shall soon know the full measure of our displeasure!" She dropped into a chair and placed a hand to her temple. Tears sparkled in her eyes, and her lips trembled with emotion.

So the rumors were true. *She loved him.* Had she also loved his father, killed at St. Albans? If so, then heartache and loss had proved themselves her steady companions for a great part of her life in England. I knelt before her.

"My dear lady queen, men are weak creatures for all their strength. But we are strong. . . . Look what we must bear."

Dropping her hand, she gazed down at me. We were but two females united in womanhood and the sorrows of love. Then a bright light struck in her eyes. "He shall pay!" she said.

I lowered my head so she would not see my smile of satisfaction. Following my interview with the queen, I fled in search of Duke Humphrey to inform him of Somerset's plans to fight John in town that night. To my shock, his suite of apartments lay empty. "Where's the duke?" I demanded of a servant sweeping the ashes in the hearth.

The man turned and looked at me, his face covered in soot. "He left after the council meeting this morning."

"Where is he gone?" I cried.

"I dunna know. But fear not, lady, he'll be back this evening."

"That'll be too late!" My mind raced in a thousand directions. "Is there someone who can tell me where he's gone?"

"Maybe . . . but I dunno who. They left with him, all m'lord o' Buckingham's men. . . . Maybe one of the grooms—"

But those in the stables who might have known had dispersed to attend other chores around the castle. I returned to Ursula in a panic.

"What can I do, Ursula? Somerset will kill him! There was murder in his eyes—"

Ursula made me sit down on the bed. "We'll get word to the mayor. He'll stop it."

I grabbed my cloak. Ursula laid a restraining hand on my arm. "Not you, dear lady. You've been through too much today. I shall go in your stead."

"But the mayor will never see you—"

"The mayor is a friend of my father's. He'll see me," she said firmly. "Now you must pray for Sir John. He is a valiant knight, and he's not lost a fight yet, but he can use your prayers and God's help. I'll bring you news soon as I can."

As weary as I was, I made no protest. I took Ursula's hand like a child and followed her obediently to the small castle chapel. Having deposited me there safely, Ursula left. I lit a candle for John. Falling to my knees before the wooden altar, decorated with ribbons and greenery for Yuletide, I fixed my eyes on the jeweled statue of the Virgin and Child standing in a niche flanked by holly and candles, and beseeched Heaven for his safekeeping. When my prayer was ended, I began my recitation over again, giving scant notice to the fading day or to the people who slipped in and out of the chapel, in search of God's help for their troubles.

Hours later, after darkness had fallen, Ursula returned. Fear and hope churning through me, I rose to my feet. She cast a quick glance around, then smiled. A cry of relief nearly broke from my lips as she whispered, "God in His almightly wisdom has answered your prayers, Isobel!"

As giddy as if I'd drunk too much fine wine, I grabbed the hand she offered, and hurried out to a secluded, shadowy corner of the court, now quieted from the day's bustle of noise and out of range of the light thrown by a flaring torch in a wall bracket. Ursula gave me a full report of the day's doings as the men at the watchtower exchanged ribald jests with each other, their laughter drowning out her words to all ears but mine.

"By God's will, when the mayor and the city fathers learned of Somerset's challenge, they were ready for him, and hundreds of armed citizens were in the village to drive him off when he arrived with his men," she said breathlessly in a hushed tone. "But Somerset was so angry at being thwarted that he killed three of their sentries. The irate citizenry wanted blood, and had the Duke of Buckingham not arrived in time to save Somerset from their fury, the mob would have killed him—"

"The Duke of Buckingham?" I repeated, stunned.

"Aye, he was returning from Leicester when he came upon the fracas."

"How do you know this is true?"

"It's true—I got it from a groom in the mayor's stable, who came back from town where he was visiting a maid in the household of a Coventry goldsmith. The goldsmith happens to be a good friend of the mayor's and was present at the melee."

I closed my eyes in relief. *John was safe.* In my mind, I saw the eyes of the rabble, armed with pikes, yelling curses, and ordering Somerset out of their city. I had seen the same fury and heard the same oaths in London.

That night I slept better than I had in weeks. The next day brought a missive from my uncle; I gave the boy messenger a coin and, with my mind spinning, broke the seal, unfurled the letter, and read:

My beloved niece Isobel,

Your letter has arrived safely, and I have given much thought to your request to intercede with the queen on your behalf. Sir John Neville, to whom you have given your affections, is by all accounts a man of impeccable character. As you know, I myself met him on many occasions years ago, when he was but a youth. I find no fault in him. However, I would be deficient in my duty to you and to your dead mother if I failed to point out the reasons why such a match is not in your interest. As it happens, I am due to come to court before my departure for Rome. We shall meet then and discuss this all-important matter in person.

God have you in his keeping.

Given this day, the first of December, 1456, at Dublin Castle.

Your loving uncle,
John Tiptoft, Earl of Worcester; Lord Lieutenant of Ireland; Royal Ambassador of His Grace King Henry VI of England to the Papal Court of His Highness Pope Callistus III in Rome

My hands trembled as I folded the missive and slipped it into my bosom. Seized with an urgency for prayer, I made my way into the chapel, seeking God's help in forming the words that would move my uncle.

He arrived a week later and lost no time sending for me. Soon after I had broken my fast, a page arrived with his summons. I followed the boy as he wove along the passageways, past retainers, messengers, servants, clerics, and all manner of folk both noble and plain, down several flights of worn stone steps, and across the inner bailey and up to my uncle's quarters in the east tower. My uncle's servants were carrying in his coffers and setting up his belongings around the spacious chamber. Not one to waste time, he stood dictating letters to two scribes at once, while interrupting himself to instruct the servants where to place various valuables. He looked up when I was announced by the yeoman at the door. His stern features softened, a wide smile lit his face, and he opened his arms. I flew into them.

"Uncle, dear Uncle, what joy to see you!" I grabbed him tightly around the chest, my eyes moist with happy tears as I gazed up at him.

My mother's brother was my only immediate family still alive, and he had owned a piece of my heart since childhood. He'd read to me on his knee, and played blindman's bluff with me, and had shown even greater patience with me than my nurse had. I loved my uncle Tiptoft with an all-abiding affection that neither time nor distance could erase. But I felt a pang of sadness to find him changed, for he had reached the seasoned age of thirty. *The years must leave their mark,* I thought, gazing up at his temples, brushed with silver now; at his cheeks, slack around the jaw; and at the frown lines between the eyebrows, which accented his only unattractive feature: his eyes, which, though a pleasant shade of blue, protruded sharply. Despite this, he was still a handsome man by any measure. Age had not bent him, and he held himself stiffly erect.

He dismissed the servants with a wave of his hand, and the door closed with a dull thud. "Dear child, here, take a seat—" He indicated one of the chairs a scribe had just vacated, and sat down at the desk, across from me. "You're looking very well," he said, scrutinizing me. "Very well indeed. Your mother would be proud that you have blossomed into such a beautiful young woman."

I dropped my gaze. I had been just six years old when the sickness had taken my beautiful mother, Joan Tiptoft, and I would carry her loss with me to the end of my days.

"Aye, she would be proud—as I am, dear child—" He contemplated me for another moment, and then he slapped his knees. "Now, what's this about Salisbury's son?"

My mouth twitched with the need to smile. My uncle was not a man to waste time in getting to the heart of the matter. I explained our situation, sparing no details. He listened intently. "I love him, Uncle," I concluded.

"That is reckless of you, my dear . . . most unwise. The Nevilles have sided with the Duke of York, and York's situation is precarious, in view of the queen's enmity. There is talk that he may be dispatched to the Tower now that King Henry has recovered. The queen hungers for his head."

"Living at court these past three months has made that very clear to me, but it changes nothing. I love Sir John Neville. We wish to wed. I cannot bear the thought of life without him." I reached for my uncle's hand. "When you lost your second wife, Elizabeth Greyndour, you were inconsolable. You swore never to wed again. You have kept your vow. You know what love is, dear Uncle. Save me from a lifetime without love."

He remained thoughtfully silent for a long while. Then he gave a sigh. "Very well, I shall do my best." Joy bubbled in my breast, but was dispersed by his next words. "But do not hope too much."

As I waited in the great hall later that afternoon, reading Horace, my eyes kept stealing to the windows of the state chamber where my uncle had been received by the queen to discuss matters in Ireland—and my destiny. By supper I still did not know what had passed between them, for my uncle had gone from that meeting directly to another with the archbishop of Canterbury. Although the queen invited me to sup at the royal dais with the distinguished company, my uncle's expression told me nothing, and her thoughtful gaze, which rested on me several times during the meal, added to my onerous burden of anxiety. After dinner, she issued a general invitation to the nobles and her ladies to join her for amusement in her solar. Church bells had pealed for Compline by the time I had a chance to learn from my uncle what had transpired between them.

In his apartment, he bade me to sit, while he stood, arms crossed, rubbing his chin as he gazed at me. "It appears you have had some impact on royal matters in the short time you've been here, Isobel. Thanks to you, the Duke of Somerset has offended the queen—so deeply that she has ordered him to Wales and has written James II of Scotland suggesting a match between Somerset and the king's sister Joan—"

An audible gasp escaped my lips.

"In response to my plea on your behalf—delivered so eloquently, I might add, that I nearly brought myself to tears!—she has agreed to give her consent to marriage between you and Sir John Neville."

I could barely breathe. I half rose to my feet in shock and sank back into my seat when my legs proved too feeble to sustain me.

"However, before you rejoice, let me advise you that she holds you in exceedingly high esteem. Since you are the sole heir to all my estates and titles, the price she demands for a match between you and Salisbury's son is exorbitant and out of all proportion to the income generated by your lands."

I clutched the armrest of my chair. "How much?"

"Two thousand pounds. You must agree, 'tis a queen's ransom. There's no way Salisbury can pay it."

I felt the room spin around me. I placed a hand to my temple to steady my dizzy head.

"In her own words," my uncle said, "she is determined to make some money from this."

I SAW SOMERSET ONE MORE TIME BEFORE HE LEFT Westminster. It was the night after my uncle's departure for Rome. I was returning from the privy when he waylaid me in the main passageway.

"So you would spurn me, would you—" He grabbed my arm. His breath stank of stale wine, and even in the gloom, I saw that his pupils were dilated with desire. "No one spurns me—"

I screamed for help and tried to shake myself loose. From deep in the darkness, a guard appeared. "Halt!" the man cried, drawing his sword.

Without relaxing his hold of my arm, Somerset turned and looked the man full in the face. The guard lowered the point of his sword and backed away, apologies dripping from his lips. I realized no help would come from this quarter, and I would have to save myself. Withdrawing my dagger from my sleeve, I slashed Somerset's hand while his attention was focused on the guard. He released my arm with an oath. As he staunched the flow of blood, I tore along the passageway back to my room, nearly tripping in my panic. Slamming the bolt into place, I fell quivering in Ursula's arms. The next day I kept to my chamber until Ursula came to tell me he was gone.

With Somerset's departure, calm descended over the castle. I spent much time in the chapel, beseeching the Virgin for help, even whispering the prayer of intercession silently during the hours I spent on my needlework as those around me gossiped and made merry. The great tapestry designed by the king for Westminster Palace was almost completed; soon it would hang in the great hall, where it would bring suitable reminder of the meaning of Yuletide to those who cared to ponder. *Thou Shalt Love Thy Enemies* was stitched below a scene of Jesus carrying the Cross to Calvary. Aye, forgiveness was a noble sentiment, and one sorely needed at court. Each time I gazed on the tapestry, the angry faces of Somerset, Clifford, Egremont, and others who had lost fathers and brothers at the Battle of St. Albans took form in my mind and replaced those in the mob of enemies that surrounded Christ.

I understood the king's intent. Gentle Henry had chosen aptly, wisely, and purposefully. But would they heed?

Though I had reason to celebrate the queen's assent to my match, I was thus seized with wanhope and yearning for John. The laughter and joyfulness of Yuletide assumed a strange hollowness around me, and I felt more alone and empty than ever in the midst of the merriment of the season.

Eight

JANUARY 1457

JANUARY BLEW IN ON A LIGHT DRIFT OF SNOW, and the throng of guests that had descended on Coventry Castle for Yuletide returned to their far-flung estates. I resumed my tasks of schooling the children, running royal errands for the queen, and attending the labors of the loom while awaiting missives from John. But no happy developments came to bring me joy. The queen, believing that the Earl of Salisbury could not—or would not—pay the mighty sum for my hand, actively entertained offers from other prospective suitors, thrusting me into a permanent state of terror that she would choose a match and pressure me to accept. So restless was the unease that dogged me in these early days of 1457 that I suffered from frequent headaches and slept with difficulty, even with the aid of warm possets.

On a bitter-cold morning, I returned to my room to find Ursula weeping, a letter in her hand. "What's the matter, dearest?" I asked, taking a seat beside her on the gray comforter and stroking her red hair.

Ursula turned swollen eyes on me. "My father's been taken to prison!"

My indrawn breath expressed the dismay I felt. "On what charge?"

"A false charge—the rape of a nun!"

I stared at her, stunned, shaken, at a loss for words.

"He didn't do it! He couldn't," Ursula cried. "It's all because of Elizabeth Woodville, I know it!" She broke into a fit of sobbing.

I gathered her close to me as my thoughts filtered back to her confrontation with Elizabeth in the tapestry room the previous week. The Woodville had been taunting a young, overplump servant for days until the girl finally dissolved into tears before us. Ursula had dared comfort her in Elizabeth Woodville's watchful presence, and at some point the word *"Witch!"* although given in a whisper, had sounded in the room. It was true that Elizabeth's mother, Jacquetta, Duchess of Bedford, was thought to indulge in witchcraft as a means of securing the remarkable good fortune that seemed to pursue her family, but none ever gave voice to the accusation, except behind the Woodville's back. To my relief, Elizabeth contented herself with a scowl in Ursula's direction and let the remark pass.

"Surely Elizabeth isn't that vindictive," I reflected. "Does your father have an enemy?"

"No—it's her doing, I tell you, Isobel! She's a bad one, rotten to the core! She has the ear of the queen, thanks to the French blood they share, and has shown her power many times with others who stood up to her—have you forgotten?"

Evil did seem to befall those who challenged Elizabeth Woodville. One girl's father lost his position as sheriff; another had her family home ransacked when her father left for London; and the lawyer father of another lost every case he argued in the London courts thereafter and was driven into poverty. Ursula attributed these misfortunes to Elizabeth Woodville, but I considered them merely unfortunate coincidences.

"What am I to do?" Ursula sobbed. "My poor father!"

"Ursula, I'll write John and ask for his help," I said, drying her tears with a handkerchief. "We'll get him out. Your father is a Warwickshire knight, and the Earl of Warwick will surely take an interest in his cause. The Nevilles are not without influence, even against the queen."

Despite my brave assurances, doubts assailed me as I composed my letter to John. The ignorant cruelties and violent prejudices of life weighed heavily on my spirits, and after many loving words to John, I paused my quill and gave vent to a few tears before continuing. Forcing a lighter note into my tone, I told him of my uncle of Worcester's visit and all that had transpired with the queen. Then I informed him of Sir Thomas Malory's predicament and begged his assistance in helping to free Ursula's father from confinement.

Only days later, a messenger bearing John's emblem of the griffin delivered John's reply.

Beloved Isobel,

Your gracious uncle of Worcester sent my father a full report of his treating with the queen on our behalf before he left for Italy, and therefore we are well aware of the sum she has set for our marriage. That does not mean our situation is without hope, Isobel. What is important is that she has agreed to the match. Agreed, *Isobel—*agreed! *My father shall come to Westminster and speak with the queen as soon as we have done with troubles here in Yorkshire unleashed by Egremont and his ruffians, who have broken into the homes of our tenants, smashing windows, stealing property, and killing livestock. On the Scots border, King James II has raided and burned many English farms and homesteads, and we must quieten the region as best we can ere we depart Northumberland. I will send you word as soon as I know more. In the meanwhile, tell Mistress Malory that I have informed my brother Warwick of her father's predicament and have received his assurance that he will do all he can to obtain Sir Thomas Malory's release as soon as possible.*

Be hopeful of a good outcome, my love, and send us your prayers

on all counts. With God's help, we shall right these wrongs, reach an
agreement with the queen, and see ourselves wed, Isobel, my angel.
  God have you in His keeping.
  Written in haste on Twelfth Night at Raby Castle by candlelight.

Yours always,
John Neville

I brought the letter to my lips and imparted a kiss to his signature, which was given in a clear hand as devoid of flourish and
ceremony as he himself. Nothing seemed impossible to John, I
thought, folding his missive and slipping it into my bodice. His
letter lightened my mood until the next morning, when Elizabeth
Woodville appeared at my side on the way to break fast in the
great hall. Ursula stiffened. I gave her hand a squeeze. Whatever
Elizabeth wanted, Ursula had to hide her true feelings about "this
venomous girl," as she called her. For myself, I still doubted that
Elizabeth was responsible for Malory's imprisonment. Every stone
has its flaw, but spiteful though Elizabeth was, I refused to believe
she could stoop to such malice for no great reason.

"I have news," Elizabeth announced, her nose in the air

"Good news, I pray, Elizabeth?" I said pleasantly.

"Splendid . . . I am to wed Sir John Grey, the heir of Lord
Ferrers of Groby."

I was stunned speechless for a moment. She had aimed high, and
she had scored. Such things rarely happened in a world where birth
determined how high one rose, and for the most part, one born a
yeoman died a yeoman. Yet Elizabeth's father, a mere knight with
no lands or standing, had wed royalty, and now she herself would
wed a lord. It was against all odds.

Elizabeth's father, Sir Richard Woodville, had met Elizabeth's
mother, the newly wed—and newly widowed—fifteen-year-old
Jacquetta, Duchess of Bedford, in France. He'd escorted her to England after her husband's death, and the two young people had
fallen in love on the journey. But Jacquetta, being of royal lineage
and the daughter of Pierre I of Luxemburg, Count of St. Pol, re-

quired a royal license to marry. Aware this would be denied them, the young lovers had wed in secret and birthed three children before they were ever discovered. While Jacquetta's royal relatives were disgusted at her marriage, Henry's new French queen, Marguerite d'Anjou, enchanted by the love match, prevailed on her husband to grant them a royal pardon and then took Elizabeth into her favor.

I found my voice at last. "I am happy for you, Elizabeth," I said truthfully. Her marriage meant she would leave soon, depriving court of her contentious presence. My mind touched on Somerset, who had been absent for over a month now. His absence had greatly enhanced court life as well. Nevertheless, I ached with a strange inner pain at Elizabeth's disclosure. Heaven had seen fit to grant her prayers for power and wealth, while mine, for love, remained denied. " 'Tis always a great blessing to receive our heart's desire and God's favor," I continued in a sinking tone.

She smiled her catlike smile, and I realized she had caught the strain in my voice. Holding her head high, she swept past me to find a seat as close to the dais as she could wile an usher to give her.

FROM COVENTRY, COURT RETURNED TO LONdon. Though I lit many candles for Ursula's father, nothing was achieved with regard to Sir Thomas Malory's release, and he remained in confinement.

"These things take time," I sighed, reading to Ursula from John's letter.

She nodded miserably. "But the waiting, 'tis so hard."

I took her hand into my own. "I know, Ursula."

Then came a letter to delight my heart, even if it still reported no movement on the case of Sir Thomas Malory. John was coming to London!

With Ursula at my side, I left Westminster Palace early on the eleventh day of January, the day before the Feast of St. Benedict, and with light steps walked to the Fleet, where I would meet John.

With our last encounter in the castle garden at Coventry still fresh in our minds, John had decided we should meet in a saddler's shop, where we might enjoy a measure of privacy.

The Strand lay quiet, even along Savoy Palace and St. Clement's Danes, and we did not encounter many passersby, despite the fair weather, but once we left behind its elegant cobbled streets and turned into the Fleet, London grew noisy with the bustle of commerce. Everywhere, blacksmiths clanged their metal, street vendors hawked their wares, and donkeys brayed complaints as they plodded along, nodding beneath their weighty burdens.

The wintry day was bright with sunshine, but cold. We walked briskly in the wind, clasping our woolen cloaks tightly around us, taking care to avoid the potholes, mud puddles, and refuse piles that lined the roads. Peddlers called their wares to us. I passed up "hot sheep's feet!" and stopped to buy a trinket from a thin, pale old woman who looked as if she would drop from illness. With her blessings following us, we turned into Shoe Lane, where the saddler's shop was located. The narrow street, gloomy beneath the wooden upper stories projecting far over the lower ones of mud and plaster, was filled with litters bearing rich prelates and highborn ladies, and with horsemen in gorgeous apparel. Consulting John's directions as we walked along, we finally spotted the gilded black-horse sign of Ye Olde Saddler swinging in the wind between a boot maker and an inn. With a flutter of the heart I stepped through the open door. The heavy smell of new leather struck me forcibly as my eyes adjusted to the gloom.

John stood in profile, in a corner by a row of leather goods, admiring a saddle finely stitched with gold thread and studded with a ruby. As he turned, such a smile lit his face that it seemed bright sunlight had burst into the gloomy shop. The old saddler, hammering at the table, left his stool to close the oak door behind us and drop the bolt, and with another bow disappeared into a narrow passageway at the back of the shop. Ursula followed him, her receding footsteps ending in the loud thud of a shut door. In a lightning-fast motion, I was in John's arms. He kissed me fiercely, sending flaming heat rushing through my blood. Weak-kneed, my head reeling, I leaned back in his arms and glanced to where the old man had disappeared. "Are we safe here?" I breathed.

John laughed. "As safe as we'll ever be. Somerset's in Wales, Egremont and Clifford are fomenting trouble in Yorkshire, and the shop owner's a Yorkist, like most here in London. My family's done business with him for years, and I've bribed him generously. He'll not return lest we give the word, my angel." He dragged me back hard against him and recaptured my mouth with savage intensity. I felt the shocking, surging contact between us and returned his kiss with reckless abandon. At last, my heart hammering beneath my ribs, I parted for breath.

"That's the second time you've called me your angel," I said, locked in his embrace and giving a small laugh as I recovered my composure. "Haven't you noticed my hair is as dark as chestnuts? Angels have golden hair, my love."

"You pose two very important points, Isobel," he said gravely, gazing down at me with his twilight blue eyes. "First, in my own defense, let me say there is nothing I haven't noticed about you, including your chestnut hair. . . . Second, *my* angels have chestnut hair."

"Oh, John, my love," I whispered, laying my head against his shoulder, " 'tis heaven in your arms." *Heaven, and Earth; sun, and stars; summer, and spring; all things beautiful are mine in this place where joy dwells.*

He held me close for a long moment, his cheek against my hair; then he relaxed his hold, took my hands, and looked gravely into my eyes. "Isobel, my father is meeting with the queen as we speak to discuss the negotiations for your hand. I shall send you word as soon as we have news."

Despite the doubts and fears that were never far away, a hot, wild joy swept me. "I shall pray for us, my beloved," I said.

THE NEXT DAY, AS THE BELLS OF WESTMINSTER'S clock tower chimed the hour of noon, a page delivered a missive to my room, where I paced nervously to and fro. I took it with a trembling hand. It came not from John but from his father, Richard Neville, Earl of Salisbury, inviting me to the Erber, his residence in Dowgate. The earl's barge would be waiting to take me there at the hour of three. Had the negotiations reached a final resolution so soon? If so, was I being summoned to be informed of exceedingly good news? Or exceedingly bad? And why had John not written himself?

I glanced down at my gown, crumpled from the morning's wear, and picked up the small mirror from the bedside table to examine my face. I heaved a long indrawn breath and laid the mirror down again. Anxiety and sleeplessness had staked their claim; I looked dreadful. It seemed to me that I had waited all my life for this day, and now that it had come, I was unprepared to meet it.

I left in search of Ursula. She was not gossiping with the laundresses or the groomsmen to pick up news, but as I returned from the stables and emerged from the tower stairs into the arched passageway to the great hall, I spotted her bright red head leaving a near chamber where a gold merchant displayed his wares to a group of ladies. I caught up to her side and assumed a casual tone for the benefit of those within earshot. "Ursula, I have lost my silver brooch."

One look at my face told her that something had happened, and she played along. "Welladay, my lady Isobel, fret not, for I do believe I last saw it pinned to your green gown."

As soon as we were back in our chamber, I turned frantic and seized her hands. "Ursula, I've been summoned by the Earl of Salisbury to his London residence! What should I wear? Oh, my hair is terrible! I should have washed it on Saturday last, when we had sun for part of the day. Help me with my face, and hurry, I pray you—"

Ursula poured me a cup of wine from a flask standing in a corner of the room. "Here, to calm your nerves and bring the color back. White as bleached linen, you are. As to your attire, such an important occasion demands your lavish lavender sarcenet with the silver tissue that you wore when you first met Sir John—" She went over to the corner, and, drawing the gown out from behind the others, set it in front on the peg. Bustling about the chamber, she checked coffers and corners for necessary toiletries, speaking her thoughts aloud as she went. "Where is the pearl and crystal necklace? I was certain I set it in the jewel casket, but maybe I laid it with the hair ornaments—" Gathering a box here, a potion there, a brooch, a clasp, ribbons, and towels, she dumped her load on the bed and resumed her search for misplaced items until she had everything safe in a heap. "That vial of paste is so small, I can't see it even when it's clear in front of my eyes—ah, here it is—" She rummaged through the items and gave me a smile. "Fear not, dear Isobel. When I'm finished with you, no one will ever forget how you looked this day."

The wine had a soporific effect on me, and my hands no longer trembled. Ursula left to fetch a pitcher of water, which she set on the bed table upon her return. Stripping me naked while I stood shivering, she went to work scouring my face, neck, and arms with a hot sponge steeped in herbs. She toweled me dry, rubbed rose oil into my skin, and threw a blanket over my shoulders. As I perched on a stool, she turned her attention to my face. She darkened my eyebrows and highlighted my eyes with charcoal, opened a small vial of pomegranate paste, and stained my cheeks and lips with the pink color. She unbraided my hair and brushed it vigorously with a boar brush till it fell in a gleaming stream to my waist, smooth as silk.

Now I was ready to dress. I donned my shift and stepped into my gown with great care. She hooked up the crystal buttons of the tightly fitted bodice and sleeves, adjusted the fur-trimmed plunging neckline to flatter the curve of my shoulders, and fastened my necklaces around my neck. "And your mother's lovely diamond brooch shall go here—" She pinned it high on my shoulder, on one side of the miniver collar. After fussing with the folds and voluminous train of my gown, she placed a gilt circlet with a dropped pearl over my brow and wove crystals into my flowing hair before attaching a gauzy veil.

She stepped back to assess her handiwork. "You sparkle like a faerie queen, but 'tis a black swan you are, with your long neck and shining dark eyes and hair. Here, see for yourself—" She drew back and held up the mirror for me.

A broad smile lit my face as I gazed at my reflection. Tenderly, I regarded the one who had wrought my magical transformation. "Thank you, dear Ursula." I hugged her tight.

Ursula disengaged herself when I didn't let go. "What's this?" she demanded as I hung my head. "Do I see a tear? You'll ruin my work!" she scolded. "What's the matter, dearie?"

"I'm so afraid, Ursula," I whispered. "What if—" I broke off, swallowing hard. *What if this day proves not my beginning, but my undoing?* In the silence that fell, I glimpsed a world of mist and grayness, where endless days followed one another in futile succession in a marriage devoid of love. Then I would drone on as thousands of others have done since the world began; I would be as they are and have been before me—a shadow living without light, color, or sound, until death stopped the heart with dust.

Ursula's voice brought me back to the present abruptly. *"Then—"* she said, seizing my shoulders and giving the word emphasis as if she read my thoughts, "you shall do as your father urged you. . . . What did you tell me he used to say?"

"The Wheel of Fortune turns, and if it brings us sorrow rather than joy, we must meet our fate with dignity and grace. For the Hand of God is in all things," I recited, seeing him smile at me in my mind's eye. I blinked to banish the image and took up a brighter thought. "But . . . but first I shall do as someone very wise once advised me. . . ." I closed my eyes and inhaled deeply before releasing my breath and meeting her gaze. " 'Chin up, bosom up—and all will be well,' " I said, forcing a smile on my face.

AT THE BARGE HOUSE, THE EARL OF SALISBURY'S elegant golden craft, festooned in ribbons and hung with tapestries, sat aglitter in the shining waters, but my breath stopped in my chest and I froze in my steps. John was not there. He had neither written nor come.

Fighting for composure, I let Ursula's hand slip and fingered my mother's ruby crucifix, which hung among the pearls at my throat. Then, lifting my chin, I forced myself forward with stiff dignity. A stout figure with a grizzled ginger moustache, wearing a tunic embroidered with the Neville saltire, headed toward me respectfully as I passed through the archway and emerged on the wharf.

"Sir John Conyers, at your command, m'lady," he said with a bow.

I had heard the name before. Sir Conyers was not only a seasoned warrior of the French wars who served in the earl's retinue, but a good friend of the Nevilles and related to them by marriage.

Ursula gave me a farewell hug. "Courage," she whispered in my ear. I gave her a squeeze in response. Gathering up my skirts, I accepted Sir Conyers's hand and stepped onto the barge.

"The Earl of Salisbury bids me inform you that Sir John Neville is at this moment returning from Bisham, or he would have come to escort you to the Erber personally."

I was momentarily speechless in my surprise. *God's Blood, but such a simple explanation for John's absence had never occurred to me!* "Thank you, Sir Conyers," I said, a new warmth surging through me as I took a seat on a scarlet cushion beneath the tapestried canopy.

The bargemen set their oars to water, and Ursula's figure receded into the distance as we streamed away. My mind filled again with a confusion of hope and fear, and my heart took up an erratic beat of anticipation. *Surely this is how many a knight feels as battle is joined and he knows not if he will see the morrow,* I thought.

Plain wood boats, gilded barges, and brightly painted craft crowded the blue Thames in the fine weather. Sir Conyers waved to one that passed us going in the opposite direction. "Sir Marmaduke Constable, another Neville retainer, and a good friend of mine," he explained.

I nodded and turned my face to the sun. Clouds flew by overhead, and the wind beat softly around me. We passed stately residences, bathhouses, taverns, and so many churches that their spires seemed to pierce the skies over London like a hail of arrows. The river bustled as densely with commerce as did the streets, but instead of the rumbling of carts and the smell of dung, there came the fresh, almost fragrant smell of water, the mewing of river birds, and the hurried flutter of swans' wings as they fled our path. Snatches of song reached my ears from seamen on passing ships bound for Calais with cargoes of wool, their sails billowing in the wind. From one of these, a captain standing on his deck removed his cap and threw me a courtly bow, lightening my heart.

A flash of silver caught my eye as Sir Conyers cast a coin to a passing boatman. The startled man dropped his oars and grabbed it. "Get repairs to your craft!" Sir Conyers yelled as we rowed past. The man stood up and waved wildly. "Thank ye, me good lord! Thank ye! May God reward—" His voice faded away into the distance as he cried out blessings.

Sir Conyers threw me an apologetic smile. "His small wood vessel is sorely distressed. I fear he won't reach shore the next time he takes it out."

I hoped my smile would convey my approval, for I was deeply touched by his noble gesture. I had seen many such craft and never given thought to the gap-toothed watermen who manned the oars. Turning my attention back to our journey, I saw that we were approaching London Bridge at a rapid pace. Crowded with shabby dwellings, vendor stalls, customers, tradesmen, and passersby going to and fro across, it teemed with bustle. As we drew into the shadow of its arches, I was assailed by the vile stench of traitor heads standing in a row along the bridge, impaled on iron pikes. I shrank back and covered my nose with a handkerchief. However, Sir John Conyers, undeterred, gazed up at the appalling sight of grotesque rotting faces, where ravens perched and pecked, as if scanning for someone he knew. A cold shiver ran down my back. There were always heads on the bridge, but until this moment I had given them scant heed. Now the thought froze in my brain that these were real persons—men who had left behind people who loved them. Drawing my mantle close around me, I lifted my eyes to their grisly remains and, making the sign of the cross, whispered a silent prayer for their souls as we passed beneath the bridge.

Sir John Conyers looked at me then. "You're cold. Here, m'lady, allow me to give you my cloak—'tis finest English wool and, though it is not furred, I vouch it will keep you warm. We are almost there—aye, there it is . . . the Erber. . . . You can see it now," Sir Conyers said. "The London abode of the Earls of Salisbury since the time of Edward III."

I peered into the distance. A fair and stately residence of white stone stood on a wide and welcoming breadth of the Thames in Dowgate. Bedecked with banners of the silver and crimson Neville saltire fluttering from its rooftops, the residence gave out a welcoming air. I lifted my chin and took a deep breath as we drew up.

Sir John Conyers helped me from the barge. With a cheery word of greeting here and there, he escorted me past the liveried porters, sentries, groomsmen, and men-at-arms, and through a broad and noble arch that opened into a gated court. We took the stairs over the buttery to the Earl of Salisbury's private chamber, and there Sir Conyers issued a gallant bow of farewell.

My heart missed a beat. John stood beside his father's chair, deep in conversation. One glance told me the room had been cleared of servants and retinue, and we would be alone. The usher announced my name. John looked up. I stood rooted to the ground, searching his face for the tidings he bore, and realization gradually dawned on my clouded, dizzy senses that his face glowed with joy. A quiver surged through my veins. *Heavenly Father, good tidings—can it truly be?*

John moved toward me, but with such strangely slowed steps that he seemed to float in the air. With my gaze still riveted on him, I heard a chair scrape the floor and a man's voice say, "Come in, dear Lady Isobel. We have been expecting you."

Flooded with rapture, my heart pounding in my ears, I regained motion in my frozen body and stumbled forward. John took my hand and placed an arm about my shoulders as I looked up into his face with wonder. He led me toward his father, who had risen from his chair and now stood before a glittering traceried window, the river sparkling with stunning brightness behind him.

The earl was regarding me with a kindly expression. "My child, I know you are anxious to receive the news, so let me dispense with all else and get to the heart of the matter without further delay. The queen has agreed to your betrothal to my son John, and has brought her price down to one thousand pounds, half the sum she had originally demanded. I have agreed to pay in ten installments over six years. Such a severe sum requires sacrifice, and so I regret the two of you will have hard days ahead. However, as John assures me he'd rather take you than all the gold in Heaven, I know you will find a way to manage. Naturally, I will help you as best I can. . . . Welcome to our family, dear child."

Welcome to our family.

Heaven had conspired with all the angels of God's realm to hand us a miracle! Floating in euphoria, I turned my gaze on John. Our eyes locked. Breathing in unison, we stood together as flowers of fire rained down on us in dazzling embers.

Nine

MERRYMAKERS SKATED AND SLEDDED ON THE frozen Thames, and children hurled snowballs at one another on the palace grounds despite the bone-chilling cold. But my heart did not notice, wrapped as it was in a cocoon of celebration. Laughter and sweet dreams, were my warm companions in these days as I waited for John to return from the North. I remained at court, but Somerset was still away in Wales and Elizabeth Woodville had retired to her family estate of Grafton Regis to prepare for her wedding to Sir John Grey, lightening the atmosphere so that even the tidings that came on the third of February, the day after Candlemas, did not dull my happy mood.

Though the queen had given her assent to my marriage, King Henry had attached his own conditions, and before we could be betrothed, the three Richards—the Earl of Salisbury, the Duke of York, and the Earl of Warwick—would have to fulfill them. Negotiations were to begin at once. These conditions included a demonstration of peace and goodwill between the chief Yorkist and

Lancastrian foes. The Yorkists were to found a perpetual chantry to pray for those slain at St. Albans, and the Duke of York was to pay reparations to Somerset and his mother for the loss of Somerset's father. John's brother Warwick was to do the same for the family of Lord Clifford.

Messengers came and went with their missives, and on occasion the Earl of Salisbury and the Duke of York made brief appearances at court to engage in discussion, but John, detained in Yorkshire by troubles on the border, did not come with them. Eventually agreement was reached. To seal the pact and celebrate the end of enmities, there was to be, by order of King Henry, a "love day" festival on the twenty-fifth of March, the Feast of the Annunciation. Our betrothal would be solemnized at St. Paul's immediately following the ceremony.

As February drew to a close, the Yorkist and Lancastrian leaders began to descend on the city with their retinues. The Nevilles were among the first arrivals, and my reunion with John was ecstatic. From the moment I flew into his arms, we were inseparable.

The Duke of York and his duchess, Cecily, were the next to arrive. They piqued my curiosity, for theirs had been a rare love match, and they were inseparable, so it was said. Cecily had always followed her lord wherever he went, even to France and the fringes of the battlefield, deterred neither by pregnancy nor by hardship.

The damp smell of the river floated through the open windows of their residence of Baynard's Castle, and gulls mewed noisily when we arrived to pay our respects. We found each member of the family in the solar, engaged in attending their interests: The duke stood by a massive carved desk, going over legal matters with his steward, while the duchess, clad like a queen in an opulent gown of azure velvet trimmed in royal ermine, supervised her servants as they unpacked her valuables. As John's father introduced me, I curtseyed low and kissed their hands. Despite the silver at his temples, York's sun-bronzed complexion and nut brown hair gave him a darker aspect than his fair wife, but he was not as austere as his lady and his smile held warmth. My eye lingered on the Earl of Salisbury's youngest sister, Cecily, whose namesake had been John's sister and my uncle's first wife. Called the "Rose of Raby" for her beauty and "Proud Cis" for her pride, Cecily, Duchess of York, was lovely and, though nearly forty years of age, had kept all her teeth so that her years sat lightly on her shoulders. More surprising, she was as tall as her husband and slender as a willow, even after innumerable childbirths. Ten of the children born to her had survived, of whom the youngest, a four-year-old boy named Richard, had remained behind at their castle of Fotheringhay with his brother George. The two oldest sons had accompanied them to London.

Fourteen-year-old Edward, Earl of March, York's heir, had been reclining on a window seat, stealing glances at a group of noble ladies on the quayside as he examined his sword for rust. Now he rose and gave me a courtly bow.

"My lady Isobel, I did not know Cambridgeshire grew such exquisite roses!" he said. Golden-haired and handsome, he'd already gained the full stature of a man. "I shall have to visit. Mayhap I can find one of such rare loveliness to grace my life, eh, Cousin John?" He gave John a merry slap on the back and chuckled good-naturedly.

"Roses it has aplenty," John replied, "but none as fair as my lady Isobel." His gaze on me felt as soft as a caress.

From Edward's side, his brother, thirteen-year-old flaxen-haired Edmund, Earl of Rutland, gave me a shy smile and a bow.

"We wish you well, my dear," the Duke of York said, "and we look forward to your wedding feast, which we plan to attend."

"Indeed," the duchess added, her generous, well-shaped mouth curving into a smile as she gazed at John. "You have chosen well, nephew." Turning to me, she said, "How fares your uncle, the Earl of Worcester?"

"Thank you for your concern, Your Grace. My uncle is leaving Rome on pilgrimage to Jerusalem as we speak. Instead of returning to England at the end of his service, he may linger to study Greek in Padua."

York and Salisbury exchanged a glance, but what it meant, I could not tell. Nor did I allow myself to ponder it. All I knew was that I would soon be wed to John, and that was all that mattered.

Nobles continued to pour into London over the next few days, and each brought so many retainers with them that the mayor feared fights would break out between the rival factions. But all went well, and peace prevailed. The last to arrive was Warwick. True to form, England's new Captain of Calais made a lavish, blazing entrance. With clarions blaring, he came by river in a large vessel, sails billowing, preceded by the music of twenty minstrels in two colorful barges painted in his colors of scarlet and gold. Thirty other barges followed, bearing his retinue of six hundred troops in scarlet jackets flaunting his emblem of the bear and ragged staff woven front and back in silver and gold.

Cheering crowds thronged the bridge and lined the river, some even standing in the water, their jubilant cries ebbing and flowing like waves as he sailed past. Warwick stood on the gilded prow of his sailing vessel, clad in crimson velvet and cloth of gold, his profile in relief against the rippling waters and blue sky as he glided toward us. He cut a fine figure; yet I found myself disturbed by his extravagant display, fearing it would draw more ire and envy to all the Nevilles.

While most of Warwick's retinue followed him by water, a stream of others came clattering through the massive gates of the residence, carting coffers of gifts, adding to the excitement. River birds shrieked and water lapped at the water gate as Warwick disembarked from his ship and climbed to the green where I stood with John, his father the Earl of Salisbury, his mother Countess Alice Montagu, and John's brother George, bishop of Exeter. The only absent family members were John's brother Thomas, who had remained behind in the North to maintain order in his father's absence, and Thomas's wife, Lady Maude Stanhope, who had elected to stay with him.

"Lady Isobel, allow me to congratulate you," Warwick said in his nasal tone, giving me a kiss on the mouth, as was the custom. He presented his lady, Nan Beauchamp, Countess of Warwick. Wearing the newly popular cone-shaped headdress with a trailing veil, and most elegantly attired in sable and a jeweled gown of damascene that befitted the wife of the richest baron in England, she was pleasant and petite, with blue-gray eyes, and hair that I guessed to be light brown from the tendrils that escaped her stiff head covering. Countess Nan greeted me warmly, and her two daughters, five-year-old Bella and three-year-old Anne, curtseyed sweetly. Both were fair-haired, pretty children, but it was little Anne who stole my heart. Fixing her large violet eyes on me, she reached up to take my hand and said, "Good to see you. Thank you for coming. I 'preciate it." Astounded, I looked at Countess Nan. "Did she just say what I think she said?"

Nan Beauchamp smiled widely. "She probably heard us greet our guests with those words. You'll find she's quite a mimic, our little Anne."

I glanced back at the child. She stood smiling up at me proudly, as if she understood quite clearly all that had transpired. I decided little Anne and I would be good friends.

Warwick greeted his family, then turned to me. "Ah, my lady Isobel, it seems your wedding gift has arrived—" His rings glittered as he made an expansive gesture toward a groom who was leading a stunning white palfrey across the green turf down to us at the river's edge. The horse's coat glistened so brightly in the sunshine that she seemed to sparkle as she paraded toward us. Coming to a stop in front of me, she flicked her silver mane and gave a snort and a stomp, as if to say, *Here I am!* I stared at Warwick in wonder. Could this glittering palfrey actually be meant for me? His lavish generosity was the stuff of legends, and he gave away to the common people as much meat and drink as they could carry home with them, enough that they jested the local taverns served his ale and sold his meat. But this was scarcely to be believed! This was a gift a king might give his queen.

"Aye, Lady Isobel," Warwick said, reading my expression as he took the jeweled reins from the groom and handed them to me. "She is yours. May you ride together in good fortune."

I accepted the palfrey from Warwick in stunned amazement, not trusting myself to speak. She wore an ornate and heavily gilded saddle studded with a large ruby. It was the one John had been admiring when I met him at the shop in the Fleet. My eyes misted with tears of happiness. Tears, whether of joy or sadness, had been my steady companions since the day I met him. Dipping into a curtsey, I bowed my head, recovered my composure, and, taking John's hand tightly as I regarded his brother Warwick, said, "But I am not worthy of such munificence, my lord."

"Indeed you are, Lady Isobel," Warwick replied. "Even this magnificent creature cannot dislodge our debt to you. But for your courageous warning to us at Barnet, the House of York might well have come to grief. It was your intervention alone that saved us. Now to more pleasant matters . . ." At a nod from one of his knights who was just drawing up in one of the barges, he said, "Where is Mistress Malory?"

"Why, she awaits there—" I replied, indicating the crowd by the wide-arched entrance to the gated court.

Ursula's bright red–haired figure appeared from their midst, intense astonishment on her face that she should be thus singled out by the great Earl of Warwick.

"Come, dear mistress," Warwick boomed. "For you, I have a more splendid gift—"

I heard Ursula gasp, and I turned behind me to look in the direction into which she gazed. A sad-eyed older knight, dressed in a gray doublet and hose, with long shaggy white hair, disembarked from a barge that had just moored, and began to limp across the dock. Ursula ran to him, skirts flying. "Father, Father!"

I swallowed back the emotion that gathered in my throat as I watched her joy.

THE DAY OF THE PROCESSION ON THE FEAST OF the Assumption, the twenty-fifth of March, dawned bright and sunny. Larks sang, narcissus and lilies announced the advent of spring, and London, wreathed in smiles, throbbed with anticipation. On each side of the street by St. Paul's, stands had been erected for the use of the nobles, and hung with gold-fringed banners and tapestries—Yorkist households on one side, Lancastrian on the other.

Heavy crowds had already gathered when I arrived at the Neville loge to observe the grand event. Waving white and red roses fashioned from cloth, wood, and paper, and jostling one another for space in the streets, on rooftops, on walls, and on balconies, the common people craned their necks in an effort to gain the best view of sworn enemies walking to St. Paul's to vow undying friendship. The Countesses of Salisbury and Warwick and the children Anne and Bella mounted the steps of the ribbon-festooned stand that was set aside for their use, and I followed behind them with Ursula, murmuring greetings to John's many sisters and their families. The top bench, however, had been left vacant for the use of the countesses. Amid shrieks of excitement, little Anne and Bella scrambled up to claim the seats between their mother, Countess Nan, and grandmother Countess Alice. I took my place beside John's mother, delighted to find I had a fine view of the street below.

Wild cheers erupted as the procession appeared in the distance, minstrels leading the way. "My lord the Earl of Salisbury comes first," John's mother announced.

We craned our necks to see his tall figure clad in wine and sapphire velvet. "He's walking hand in hand with Somerset," I noted.

Ursula leaned close. "Ah, I see Somerset now," she sniffed. "He doesn't look so good in crimson."

"He doesn't look so good in any color," I whispered back. We gave a giggle and parted to look further as John's mother fought to suppress a smile.

"There's my noble Earl of Warwick—he comes next, walking with the Duke of Exeter—" Ursula exclaimed with such rapture that I turned to look at her in surprise. "How magnificent a figure is my Earl of Warwick, our Captain of Calais!" she drooled. "The bravest, most chivalrous knight in Christendom!"

I glanced quickly at Countess Nan, seated farther along the row. She might not approve of Ursula's adulation of her husband, innocent though it be. But little Anne and Bella had raised such a chorus of delighted shrieks at the sight of their father that they drowned out Ursula's comments. Indeed, the jubilant cheers of the crowd and their cries of, "A Warwick! A Warwick!" made her words audible only to me.

I leaned close and whispered, "He always attires himself most sumptuously, and this costume of black cloth of gold suits him exceedingly well."

"Who can ever compare with him?" Ursula said, straining for another glimpse. "He overpowers the Duke of Exeter as the sun outshines the moon, does he not?"

"It would be hard not to, with such a load of gold and jewels," I whispered in her ear, growing bolder as I teased. "Warwick sparkles like the sun itself." Ever since Warwick had taken up the cause of Ursula's father, she had sung his praises. I had attributed this to gratitude, but now I suspected something more. *Welladay,* I thought, *admiration is kin to love.*

"And my lord of Warwick is so broad of chest, and Exeter is so thin," Ursula raptured amidst the cheering.

"Thin, and clad in drab gray. Without the Captain of Calais's huge sapphire and diamond cross to dazzle the eyes," I threw in. But Ursula, blinded by Warwick, failed to note the humor in my tone. He passed us now, smiling broadly in acknowledgment of the crowd's welcome, a hand raised in greeting. Beside him, Exeter's gaze burned as he regarded the new Captain of Calais, for it had been his command before it was taken away and given to Warwick.

A mighty roar went up and drew my attention back to those following behind them.

"Ah, 'tis the king who comes now!" I said, rising to my feet, as did everyone around us on all the stands. King Henry walked alone, clad in a white velvet gown unadorned by gems, wearing a plain golden circlet. I thought it fitting that he should process unpartnered. Everyone loved the mild and gentle king; he had no enemy in the world.

Another great cheer went up when the Duke of York appeared, clad in violet, hand in hand with Queen Marguerite, richly appareled in scarlet cloth of gold trimmed with sable, its thick folds garnished with diamonds. Here the crowds chanted, "York! York!" and while many a white rose was flung into the air, the people had not troubled to fashion any daisies. The queen wore an angry expression that gave me pause. Still, determined to enjoy every moment of this day of my betrothal, I banished doubt from my mind and let my glance search for John among the throng of Nevilles and Percies that followed the queen.

"There's John!" I exclaimed joyously when I distinguished him in green and silver striding hand in hand with puny Egremont. But the sight of Egremont's scowling face as he came into close view struck a jarring chord. A disturbing thought filtered into my consciousness: The king, taking his queen's approval of my marriage to the son of a Yorkist lord as evidence of a softening of her enmity, had seized the opportunity to push the lull into a peace, but there was nothing genuine about this lovefest, born of King Henry's simple mind. All was but hollow mummery. I drew my cloak tighter around me, suddenly chilled, and returned anxious eyes to King Henry's soft figure.

He was the only one still smiling as he disappeared into St. Paul's. Our meek and kindly king would rather pardon than punish, and chose mercy over justice, thinking to bring peace to his land. He did not comprehend that such a course might well reap a different harvest by driving good men from reliance on law to reliance on force in order to protect themselves against evildoers. King Henry truly believed in this day; he believed that hand-holding could heal the rift between enemies.

His queen followed him into St. Paul's, her expression hard as flint, her carriage unyielding. I stirred on the bench and looked at those around me on the stands. No one wore a smile; they all sat silently, staring after her. *They know,* I thought. King Henry's lovefest had resolved nothing; all remained as it had always been.

I came out of my thoughts abruptly. John had reached the top step of St. Paul's and stood looking up at the benches where he knew me to be. My distress vanished, and I leapt to my feet and waved wildly to him. He caught sight of me and, after throwing me a smile that warmed even across the distance, retired into St. Paul's.

What does anything matter when we have one another? I thought, resuming my seat. We were to be betrothed; then nothing could come between us, for betrothal was as sacred as marriage itself. The Countess of Salisbury clutched my arm, and I saw that the throng of Percies and Nevilles had vanished from the street. The time had come to leave for St. Paul's, and for my betrothal.

AS CANDLES FLICKERED AND INCENSE DRIFTED over us, John and I plighted our troth in St. Paul's, before the archbishop of Canterbury and all the peers of the realm. Immediately following the service, my head spinning with joy, we departed for Westminster Palace. King Henry had decreed that his feast of the "love day" be held in the great hall of Westminster Palace, the largest in Europe, normally reserved for such weighty matters as the meetings of the royal council.

With a gasp of awe, I drew up sharply on John's arm at the noble entrance of the splendid chamber. Strewn with rose petals, herbs, and fragrant ambergris, the gigantic hall dazzled with beauty. Every inch of stone wall between the long rows of traceried windows on either side of the room was covered with tapestries blazing with jeweled color in the light of flaring torches and thousands of candles set on the banquet tables. Silver goblets, platters, and saltcellars glittered, and urns overflowed with exotic oranges, lemons, and flowers brought in from faraway Spain. The famed hammer-beam roof crowning the room, now fully illuminated in the glorious light, appeared to soar on the backs of the long rows of hovering angels that were carved into the base of each arch, and which looked down now as if to bless all who entered. My eyes were drawn to King Henry's massive tapestry, hanging behind the royal table, which I had worked on since my arrival at court. Its admonition to "Love Thy Enemies" cried out across the long hall. From the wall niches, statues of Henry's kingly predecessors gazed out in stern reminder to Yorkists, on one side of the room, and Lancastrians, on the other, that they were all but one family.

Mounting the steps of the dais to be seated beside the queen, I caught the smoldering glance of Somerset, who was walking up at the opposite end to sit next to King Henry. No further word had been forthcoming on his proposed marriage to King James's sister, but this matter was of no import to me any longer. *Let the past be past,* I thought. Filled with magnanimity, I threw him a smile and a curtsey, whereupon he paused and gave me a gracious bow. I felt John stiffen beside me. I pressed his hand, and we resumed our steps up the dais and stood at our places. Clarions blared, and the king and queen entered. Nodding to right and left, they processed up to their thrones, Henry beaming and Marguerite barely smiling.

A sudden, dire thought came to me: *the king's peace and the queen's war.*

But this was the night of my betrothal. There was room in my heart only for celebration, and I dismissed the dark clouds that threatened my joy. I ate as ravenously as ever and drank to my heart's content. Soon enough John and I would be gone from court to begin our new life together. Only the legal formalities remained, and those would be tended to immediately the following morning.

MY HAND TREMBLED AS I SIGNED THE CONTRACT in the queen's presence at Westminster, the last to affix a signature before we left for Raby Castle, the seat of the Neville Earls of Salisbury. Our departure was set for the next day, for urgent business awaited the Nevilles in the North, and John had no wish to leave me behind at court at the mercy of the likes of Somerset. Since neither Ursula nor I in our blissful confusion were of any great use to anyone, I gave the packing of our meager belongings over to the Salisbury household servants.

Before we left Westminster, however, I had matters to attend. The first was to thank the queen, the power that had made my joy possible.

"My sovereign lady, a corner of my heart shall always be yours, and my prayers also, for as long as I have life," I said on my knees before her, tears of gratitude standing in my eyes. "You have been as an angel guarding me from harm and bestowing on me the greatest gift this earth can offer, that of love. . . . I shall never forget."

Marguerite sighed and clasped her slender hands together. I glanced up to find her staring far away into the distance with a strange expression of pain, as if some permanent sorrow weighed her down. A morbid thought came to me: Here stood one of those poor shadows I had feared to be myself, one who moved through the murk of endless days in a world without color or sound. Surely Marguerite had loved someone once—whether Somerset the father or Somerset the son, or perhaps a noble Frenchman? But it was a love that could not be, for she was royalty and must wed a king, though he be mad and chaste. So all her love and her hopes and her fire had come to reside in the child she had borne. And in memory of her lost love, she gave as a gift to others what she could never have herself. Therein her delight in arranging marriages and seeing love rewarded. My heart bowed with sadness for her.

The queen's hand took mine and raised me to my feet.

"Sweet Isabelle, your joy gives us more satisfaction than you can know. . . . Now, for a wedding gift—"

A lady-in-waiting brought over the gilt casket where Marguerite kept her jewels; they clinked softly as the queen rummaged through them and withdrew a gold ring in the shape of a swan, set with a sapphire for the eye. It was the emblem of her son, Edward of Lancaster, that she held out to me. "Take this as a token of our affection. You have been a loving and gracious presence here in our court, and we shall miss you. Go thee with God."

I kissed the hand she offered.

But soon the sadness of the lonely queen was forgotten. Riding in front of John on his palomino, Saladin, I nestled against him, half covered by the folds of his cloak, as we left Westminster for the Priory of the Holy Trinity within Aldgate. Sœur Madeleine had returned to London from Marrick Priory, where she had gone when court had left for Coventry in October, but she had returned for the lovefest. I wished to bid her farewell.

We went by the guildhalls of the silversmiths, harpers, and tapestry makers along the river, and through the crowded streets of the burgher sector, with its grand brick and half-timbered houses. In my drowsy delight, the bustling London streets seemed quite charming, and I bid them farewell with nostalgia. My eye passed over the scene and settled on Rufus, trotting beside us proudly, looking around as if he owned the city. I nudged John. "Checking for Percies, is he?"

"You laugh? I tell you, he can smell one a mile away," John replied.

"Does he never tire of walking?" I inquired.

"Sometimes."

"What do you do with Rufus, then?"

"Didn't I tell you? He has his own horse now."

I couldn't control my burst of laughter. When I finally caught my breath, I said, "Surely you jest."

"I do not."

"Can Rufus ride?"

"Better than you, m'lady."

I punched him hard in the stomach with my elbow. And thus we laughed our way to the Priory of the Holy Trinity, and Sœur Madeleine.

We waited in the parlor while a novice went to fetch her. The room was dim and musty, lit by a few sputtering candles and starkly furnished with a table that held an open Bible and two rough-hewn chairs. The rustle of garments drew our attention to the door. An old nun entered, a smile on her face.

"Sœur Madeleine," I whispered, curtseying, flooded both with joy and sorrow—joy to see her, and sorrow that this might well be the last time we would meet, for she was ailing.

"You have your heart's desire now, dear one," she said kindly. Then she turned her smile on John. "And you, my young sir, what do you have to say for yourself?"

John knelt before her and kissed her hand. "Thank you, Sœur Madeleine. You have filled my heart with gratitude to you for all time." I looked at him, puzzled. "Sœur Madeleine sent an entreaty of her own to the queen," he explained, "after my father presented his request that we be wed. To have gained the gracious sister's blessing is no small matter, for Queen Marguerite puts great store in Sœur Madeleine's counsel. She was her nurse."

I stared at her mutely. Sœur Madeleine had played a greater role in my happiness than even I had known. I fell into another deep curtsey at her feet.

"*Alors—*" She broke off, seized by a coughing spell. She turned aside until she had caught her breath, then she said in a weak voice, " 'Tis not so grand a thing. In truth, I merely reminded the queen that her devoted servant for whom she holds great affection, Lord Tiptoft, Earl of Worcester, is your uncle. Since he espoused your cause in this instance, it must have merit." Taking our hands in hers, she whispered a prayer over our heads as we knelt and blessed us with the sign of the cross. "May Love, the great reconciler, unite Lancaster and York in your union, *mon enfant.* . . . *In nomine Patris, et Filii, et Spiritus Sancti.*" She wore a smile on her face, but her eyes brimmed with tears as she reached out and touched my hair, and I knew she was seeing someone else. *A child lost—a child with dark hair.* My heart twisted for her. Women went into nunneries for many reasons. When life took too much, and left too little, there was always the house of God, where those whose lives had ceased could await their own end. She raised us both to our feet. On impulse, I flung my arms around her, wimple, coif, voluminous cloth and all, and held her close a long moment. I knew that I'd never see her again.

"I will write you, *ma chère-aimée* Sœur Madeleine," I said, my voice breaking.

"I will pray for you always, Isabelle," she replied, her lips working with emotion. I watched her turn and walk away. The door closed behind her. I stood for a moment, gazing after her. Then I took John's hand, and together we stepped out into the bright sunshine.

THE MIGHTY RETINUES OF THE EARL OF SALIS-bury and the Earl of Warwick covered the hillside as far as the eye could see, but I felt alone in the world with John as we trailed after them, exchanging loving glances as we pranced along on our mounts, north to Raby Castle in County Durham, Northumbria.

At Middleham, Warwick parted company from us, taking with him Sir Thomas Malory, who had joined his retinue. Little Anne, standing with her parents, gave me a close embrace and waved farewell, crying out to me, "Forget not—you come back!" I felt my heart melt within me. On the third day, we reached Raby. Standing on a rolling hillside of white narcissus, veiled in soft mist, the castle drifted dreamlike in and out among the trees, its towers and turrets beckoning to me, filled with eternal promise. The sheer beauty of the place made me draw breath sharply.

"Raby Castle," John said, "where I was born."

"And where we shall wed," I murmured softly. "Its gifts to me are boundless, my love."

He took my hand to his lips and implanted a kiss of such tenderness, my breath caught in my throat. With my white palfrey by his golden stallion's side, we clambered together over the meadows into the mist toward beckoning Raby, and our destiny.

Ten

AS WE DREW NEAR, RABY CASTLE CHANGED ITS
demeanor and showed its true face: a stronghold of soaring towers and impregnable walls daring foes to attack at their peril.
Nearly a hundred years old and built by the powerful Nevilles
on the site of a fortified manor of King Canute, from whom
they were descended, it stood tall and defiant, its history rolling
back nearly six centuries. Even the intricately carved figures on
the battlements seemed to cast a fierce eye on us as we cantered
through the stone gatehouse that guarded the drawbridge over
the castle moat.

The castle servants and household, gathered in the court, welcomed us with loud cheers. Many fell to their knees. Clasping their
hands, they called out prayers of thanks to the Almighty for our
safe arrival. Even the dogs barked greeting, running up to Rufus's
mare with great excitement. He jumped down from his horse's
back with an aplomb that brought surprise and laughter to many a
face around us, for he had newly learned this trick. Though I had

witnessed his acrobatics several times by now, I couldn't suppress my own amusement.

Taking my hand, the earl introduced me to the household and announced our betrothal. Cheers and dancing erupted at the news. His son Thomas embraced me warmly and called me "sister," while Thomas's blue-eyed wife, Maude, locked arms with me and took me from John, saying, "She will be yours soon enough. Till then you shall have to share her with us."

That evening at dinner I noted, with a softening of my heart, that John had acquired his love of hounds from his father, for the earl showed great tenderness for them.

"Come, Joselyn," he said to one of the dogs, "here's a fine bit of rabbit for you. . . . Now, now, Bridget, no need to get jealous, there's chicken for you. . . ."

As the days passed, I learned even more that pleased me. Every day John's father distributed five gold nobles in small coins as alms at his gate.

"I much admire your kindness, my lord," I said to him one evening.

"The poor are our neighbors," he replied. "When the mouths are many, and the money scarce, a farthing's worth of mussels is a feast for such folk. It gladdens my heart that we can help with their burdens."

Aye, Raby Castle was a merry place, filled with music, song, and many guests, for the earl's generosity extended to everyone. The hall was always full with knights and squires, and no one who asked for lodgings was ever turned away. The earl also much enjoyed new and fanciful dishes, but not for himself. Whenever these were served up to him, he immediately sent them to the tables of his knights and squires, and his guests.

I once read that you can tell more about a man by the way he treats those below him than those above him. By this measure, John's father was a man of impeccable character, and I felt supremely fortunate to be marrying into such a splendid family. During the three weeks I spent at Raby before my marriage, I never witnessed him using harsh words or mistreating a servant, and no guest ever left him without a gift. In all these ways the earl lived up to his family motto, *Ne Vile Velis*—"Wish Nothing Base"—and Raby was, I thought, a house of honor.

If the Earl of Salisbury had a fault, it was in the care he took with his accounts, to ensure that every pence due him was paid and none stolen by his receivers. I did not blame him for the stern eye he placed on his finances. The king owed him tens of thousands of pounds for the wages of the troops whom he had paid in the French wars, and the Crown had never made good this debt, placing an onerous burden on his finances.

In this house of merriment, laughter, and charity, the earl's second son, merry-eyed Thomas, John's favorite and closest brother in age, reigned the star, for he had a playful and jesting nature despite his mature twenty-seven years, and his perpetual merriment lit up the castle. I learned that first night that it was his wont to never let a song pass at dinner without his banging his tankard on the table and crying out that the song needed drink, which never failed to elicit laughter. Nor did he miss an opportunity to charm us with his wit. One evening, an aging knight-errant passing through described a feast, given by Duke Albert in Rottenburg-on-the-Neckar, that he had attended with Somerset.

"Duke Albert was most gracious," the old knight said. "He presented the Duke of Somerset with the princely Order of the Salamander."

Thomas leaned over to me and whispered, "The princely Order of the Flea would have been more fitting, for the man is a pest!" He pretended to scratch himself, and I bowed my head to stifle the giggles that choked my throat.

He also had a way with children, though he had none of his own. Each time he arrived home after being away for a few days, they rushed to greet him from all ends of the castle, and it mattered not whether they were of noble or peasant birth, for Thomas always twirled them around the same. Once I caught him bent double in the midst of giggling children, a hand protruding from his head, braying noisily, pretending to be an ass. At other times he'd amuse them with a sleight-of-hand trick, taking coins from their ears or finding roses in their sleeves. Often, with one voice, they'd beg, "A story—a story!" and after setting a little one on his knee, he would regale them with tall tales of knights and feats of arms. On one such occasion, I found myself listening behind the chamber door as he charmed them with a rhyme about a sea of milk:

> *In a slumber visional,*
> *Swam a sweet milk sea.*
> *With high hearts heroical,*
> *We stepped in it, stoical,*
> *And rode the billows so dashingly,*
> *Smote the sea so splashingly,*
> *That the surge sent, washingly,*
> *Honey up for ground.*

"More, more!" they called, giggling with delight, and off he went about a castle with ramparts of custard, where butter formed the bridge, and bread the floor, and dry beef the door. This castle had cheese for columns, a roof of curd, and cream for beams. "More!" they insisted, and he complied without hesitation:

> *Wine in well rose sparkingly,*
> *Beer was rolling darkeningly,*
> *And merry malt moved wavily,*
> *Through the floor beyond.*

"Well done, Thomas!" I announced, applauding as I revealed myself. Startled to learn he had a secret audience, he blushed like the root of a beet.

"And the rhyme maker smiled sheepishly," I said, inventing a line of my own. Tom blew me a kiss.

I never laughed so much in my life as I did in those early days at Raby.

Thomas and his youngest brother, George Neville, differed like wool from silk, for George was bookish and found more enjoyment in scholarly pursuits than in people. At the tender age of twenty-three, he had already been made bishop, and he came to call the banns on the three Sabbaths preceding our wedding. One night, while the earl and his family were away taking care of matters at their castle of Sheriff Hutton, and Warwick was in Calais, I sat embroidering in a lower chamber, listening as John and two of his brothers discoursed on the vices and virtues. Empty flasks of wine lolled about at their feet, and the heads of St. Margaret and the Four Evangelists looked on from the painted murals on the walls. At length, Thomas, growing weary, lifted a flask and toasted the wall. "Hail to the virtues and St. Margaret, good brothers!" he cried, draining the last remaining drops.

"Sobriety is one of the virtues, brother," Bishop George reminded him gravely. "Look how many dead soldiers lie here, thanks in main to you."

"And not one of them died without a priest, did they, brother?" John replied merrily, slurring his words.

Thomas gave John a slap on the back in approval, and Bishop George shrugged in surrender.

Of John's mother I knew little, save that she came from the noble line of the Montagu Earls of Salisbury, and as her father's only child, had inherited his title, which had passed to her husband. Though unfailing in her courtesy, she did not exchange more than pleasantries with me, and indeed, had not much time for idle chatter and tapestry work. The affairs of running the castle kept her occupied during the day, and at dinner she devoted her full attention to her lord. Since we each sat facing the hall on opposite sides of the earl, lengthy discourse was difficult between us, and if the truth be known, with John beside me, I had little mind for it myself. After Vespers, it was the custom of the household to retire to the chapel to attend nocturnals from the psalter, and prayers from the ritual to the Virgin and the Holy Ghost before Compline sent us to bed.

So was life arranged during those blessed early days of my betrothal.

★   ★   ★

ON THE TWENTY-SECOND OF APRIL, THE EVE OF the great Feast of St. George, Warwick himself arrived with his family in tow, bringing Ursula's father, Sir Thomas Malory, with him. Ursula fled into her father's arms, beside herself with joy, and Malory himself did not stop beaming all that day.

"What a knight my lord of Warwick is, m'lady!" Ursula cried when she prepared me for bed later that night, her eyes alight. "So handsome, such a princely bearing! They say he alone has turned Calais into a force to be reckoned with, by his courage, hard work, and the power of his personality alone—" My silence must have given her pause, for she interrupted her praise to frown at me. "Do you not agree that he is the most amazing knight alive?"

The question she posed was an easy one. "No, I don't, Ursula," I replied. "John is." Then we both broke out in laughter anew.

Two days after the Feast of St. George, happiness kept me from sleep as church bells chimed the strokes of midnight that ushered in my wedding day, the twenty-fifth of April.

I sat at my window facing the lake, hugging my knees. The spring night was tender, laden with the sweet fragrance of roses, lilies, narcissus, dianthus, and cherry blossoms, and my head grew light with their perfume. As night vanished with the cock's crow, dawn burst over the earth in an explosion of ruby and gold.

A knock sounded at the oaken door, and Ursula beamed at me. "Oh, dear Isobel! Oh, I can't believe this day is finally here! Oh, what joy, what fortune, how wondrous it is!" Since our arrival at Raby, we had not shared the same room, for she had the antechamber to mine. But tonight this would change again. I would move into a spacious apartment with John, and Ursula would reside in her very own chamber. I left the window seat and clasped her to me in a close embrace. "What's this?" she said. "Do you weep on such a day?"

"I shall miss you."

"Dearie, 'tis no cause for tears. I'm just down the hall. And you shall be with your husband from this day forth."

I burst into fresh tears.

"What's the trouble now?" Ursula clucked.

"I'm . . . so happy . . . Ursula," I managed, and hugged her again. "Why should Heaven grant me such joy?"

"You are hopeless!" she laughed, pulling away. "Only Heaven knows why it's chosen to grant you your heart's desire. Maybe your descendants will save the world one day, who knows? Now, enough of this foolishness. You have much to do to prepare for your wedding! Come, let us begin with the bath." She collected towels from one coffer, a fresh linen shift from another, and a comb from among my casket of rouges and unguents, and carted me downstairs to a low-vaulted, steamy bath chamber adjoining the passageway to the kitchen.

I stepped into the wood tub she had lined with linen towels and filled with warm water, and took my seat on the stool. As I soaked, she soaped me down with a sponge steeped in herbs, and then rinsed me off. When the bath was done, she dried my long hair vigorously with a host of linens and bundled me up in a camlet cloak. With my face upturned to the sun, I lay drowsy in the walled garden of the bath chamber, and sleep nearly found me there, but Ursula had every moment assigned, and soon she reappeared to pronounce my hair dry enough to proceed to the next task.

As we made our way back to my room, it became evident that the pace of activity at the castle had reached frenzied proportions. The shrill voice of the chaplet maker could be heard down the hall, screaming at her boy helpers as they fashioned the flower garlands of cherry blossom and white roses. "God's Knuckles, little fool, you'll break the blooms that way—Oliver, you do it right, but we don't have all day—make haste, haste!" In the kitchen, cook maids carried steaming pots hither and thither, and scullions chopped vegetables at a frenetic pace. Their knives pounded the long wood tables as streams of buckets of beans and onions were delivered to the chief cook, who bustled about, shouting urgent orders to his minions. "More salt—no, less! Set it here—no, there! Smaller slices—so, not so—what, did they collect all the village idiots and send them here to me?"

Climbing the three flights of tower stairs back up to our floor, we passed breathless chambermaids carrying linens stacked high in their arms, and panting servants carting firewood and supplies. We wove our way around pages sweeping rushes, and varlets polishing windows and dusting corners and crevices. Outside, there was also much noise and commotion as carpenters erected benches and tables for the procession. Their hammering mingled with a jarring scraping sound as gardeners dragged stone flowerpots along the pebbly ground. "Careful!" someone cried, and this was followed in swift succession by the shattering sound of breakage, and an oath.

In the distance, clarions announced approaching wedding guests, while in the courtyard the neighing of horses and a medley of voices proclaimed the arrival of others. Groomsmen hurried to and fro, leading away the steeds amid joyous greetings exchanged between the guests as they welcomed one another.

I recognized some faces, for I had met many of John's relatives and close friends during my three weeks at Raby, and my own excitement reached feverish pitch. "Look, Ursula, there's the Duke of York and his duchess, and there's their son Edward, whom I met at Westminster, and that fair lanky boy who is their second-eldest, Edmund . . . and, oh, those small children with them are so precious. . . . Look how that littlest one hangs back behind his sister's skirts—he must be Dickon. . . . And there's Lord Bolton, and his lady . . . and there are the Conyers. . . . I so like the Conyers, Ursula!"

"Be still, Isobel. How can I paint your face when you turn this way and that?"

I tried to cooperate, but my eyes, if not my head, kept stealing to the outer court. I wondered if the queen might come. She had said she might, but I doubted it. She would not wish to venture so deep into Yorkist territory, even after the love day.

"Isobel—" Ursula's voice broke into my thoughts. "You are ready for your chemise now."

The fine linen shift felt tender as silk against my bare skin as I slipped into it, and my shoes of soft leather, worked in gold, hugged my ankles as lightly as swan feathers. Then Ursula went to work on my hair. Untying the ribbons that held the locks she had wound into curls, she arranged ringlets of glossy hair around my face and wove crystals and tiny white rosebuds through the strands. I threw a loving gaze at my wedding gown, which lay spread out on the bed, shining white silk trimmed in miniver and embroidered in gold thread. Beside it my veil was held by a circlet of cherry blossoms and white roses, and edged with gold lace, crystals, and the glistening pearl that would be draped over my brow in a final touch.

"You're ready for the gown, m'lady dear," Ursula said, just as voices at the door announced the arrival of John's mother, the earl's countess, Alice Montagu, who had come with her daughters to help me dress and supervise my final preparations. But the countess entered alone; John's sisters and her ladies remained behind in the antechamber. Ursula quickly threw the camlet cloak around my shoulders so that I did not stand in my shift.

"Madam," I said, dropping into a curtsey. We had always been formal with one another. I did not yet know her well, and was unsure of her feelings about me. Was she displeased that her lord had paid such a heavy sum for my hand? Did she resent that I came from the Lancastrian camp? Did she see me as too lowborn for her illustrious family, who traced their lineage from kings of Europe descended from Charlemagne? I feared the answers, for I desperately missed having a mother of my own and hoped to have found one in her. But, though I might wish for a mother, with half a dozen girls she had no need of another daughter.

"Perfect," she pronounced to Ursula after examining my face by the open window. With a gesture of her hand, she indicated that I should turn. "You have also dressed the hair well. I find no fault with it."

"Thank you, my lady," Ursula said, stepping back with a curtsey.

"Now leave us."

I felt myself tense.

"Sit, my dear," the countess said, indicating the bench. "You have been on your feet for a long while—surely you need to rest before donning your wedding gown." She regarded me with an expression I could not read. "And it will give us a chance to talk." She settled into a high-backed chair and smoothed her skirts. "We have not spoken at any length, and I wish to begin by telling you something about myself. . . . As you may know, mine was an arranged marriage. I was the only daughter of my father, Thomas Montagu. My husband, Richard, was a younger son. Of course, he was well endowed by his mother, Joan, the granddaughter of Edward III and daughter of the great Duke of Lancaster and his beloved Katherine Swynford. But I daresay it appealed to my lord's father, Ralph Neville, the Earl of Westmoreland, that I was a great heiress, with an earldom for the man I married."

It was as I had suspected. She did not approve of me, for I brought John little and had cost him much.

"I cannot say I loved my husband when I wed him," she said.

I looked up sharply. Most marriages were arranged for reasons of commerce, not love; yet I had never heard anyone confess to it before.

"I was eighteen," she went on in a softer tone filled with reflection. "I prided myself on understanding—and accepting—how the world was designed. I had made a good match, and that was all there was to it, as far as I was concerned."

I stiffened. *Though I do not bring my husband an earldom, she has no right to shame me so openly.* I lifted my chin and said coldly, "My lady, I know what you imply—"

She reached out, took my hand. "No, you don't. Let me finish. I married without love, but God was kind. He sent it to me anyway. I was blessed with a good husband, but more than that, an honorable and wonderful man whom I soon came to love with all my soul and heart. . . . I have discovered a great truth in these years of my marriage. Love is more important than property, possessions, or power."

Taken aback, I was mute for a moment. "Aye, madam, and I do love John," I said at last.

"I doubt it not, Isobel. I am glad you have love from the start and shall waste no years finding it. I treasure all my sons, but John has a rare quality about him. He is a romantic. Such men do not love easily, and when they give their hearts, it is for all time. And though he appears strong, he is vulnerable at heart, and will have greatest need of you in times of deepest sorrow—may God forfend. But we live in an uncertain world, and who knows what life brings? 'Tis a great burden for you, Isobel, but also a great blessing to be so loved."

"I shall be at his side always, and I pray to prove worthy of him."

She pressed my hand. "I admit I was troubled when John came to us about you. But doubt not, you are indeed worthy of his devotion."

Again, emotion threatened to overwhelm me. The countess took a silk handkerchief from beneath her sleeve. "Child, you will ruin your makeup," she said kindly, dabbing at my eyes. "Now 'tis time you have my gift—" She turned toward the door and called in a raised voice, "Jane!" A young woman entered with a small casket, which she set down on the table before the countess. When she was gone, the countess spoke again.

"My son Richard was eight years old when he married Nan Beauchamp, so I did not give it to her. My son Thomas wed a widow, so I did not give it to her. My youngest boy, George, is a son of the holy Mother Church and has no need of it." She opened the lid and turned the casket around to face me. "Now I know the reason I did not part with it. . . . It was meant for you."

There, glittering in the brilliant sunlight, lay a necklace wrought like fine lace in the shape of many roses, with rubies for petals and diamonds for hearts. I gasped, and looked at her in wonder.

She smiled at the question in my eyes. "Aye, for you. Who better? It was given me by my mother-in-law, Joan Beaufort, hence the Red Roses of Lancaster. 'Tis very apt that you come to us from Lancaster. Now I pass it to you."

I fell into a deep curtsey at her feet. She raised me up. "Daughter, be happy. Love him, and all will be well, even through darkness. . . . We who have love, have everything."

We rose, and she clasped the necklace around me.

I fingered it reverently. "Your gift shall always remind me of the ruby dawn of my wedding day," I whispered. "And of you."

The Countess of Salisbury enfolded me in her arms and held me close. "On this beautiful day you wed in joy. May peace follow you always." She threw open the door to the chamber, and I was besieged by a flurry of ladies, including John's pretty sisters Alice, Eleanor, Katherine, Joan, and Margaret. Dressed in pinks, purples, and scarlet, they fluttered around the room, murmuring approval of all that met their eyes. Two helped me into my gown, two more arranged my veil around me, and another assisted Ursula in sewing fresh roses and cherry blossoms to the hem of my gown. Then they walked me to the looking glass that stood in the corner of the room.

I gazed at my reflection in the mirror, and gasped. *Can this magnificent creature truly be me?* Tulle and shining silk, cherry blossoms and miniver, crystals and glittering rubies had wrought a dazzling transformation, and I shimmered in the mirror like a vision from a land of enchantment. I looked mutely at the countess and Ursula, who each nodded and, stepping forward, held me in close embraces for a long moment.

" 'Tis time," the countess said, releasing me. John's sisters gathered up my skirt and voluminous long train, and we followed as she led the way down to the courtyard.

MOUNTED ON MY BEAUTIFUL WHITE PALFREY, Rose, my veil caressing my cheek in the breeze, I waited in the sunshine, as if in a dream.

Minstrels stood in a group in front of me. From the castle tower, Warwick's giggling little daughters, Bella and Anne, ran out to my side, shrieking with excitement. Garlanded and carrying nosegays, they made a delightful sight with their shining eyes as the countess positioned them behind the minstrels. Warwick appeared from the same entrance, dressed in sumptuous scarlet-and-purple damascene spangled with gems that flashed in the sun. With him came merry Thomas, who glittered in black cloth of gold. Thomas removed his plumed and jeweled cap to throw me a courtly bow, which I acknowledged with a broad smile. Then my eye caught on the noble archway directly ahead, which led to the chapel where John waited. The sight sent my heart soaring.

The countess arranged the folds of my gown over the rubied saddle that had been my wedding present from John. Rose, her braided mane adorned with cherry blossoms and golden tassels, endured the fuss patiently and then snorted, anxious to be off.

"You look like a princess, my dear," the countess said, smiling with approval.

"A most splendid princess," the earl corrected, stepping forward. At his nod, the minstrels struck the first chords of the joyful tune that announced the entrance of the bridal party. He gathered Rose's reins into his hands and led me through the stone-arched gateway of the chapel tower.

Wickets and gates had stood open since Prime to receive everyone who wished to attend, whether rich or poor, old or young, and from far and wide they'd come to wish me joy on this, my wedding day. Their smiling faces greeted me from all directions, and their sighs and cheers followed me. The white rose petals they threw showered me like blessed rain from Heaven, and like the murmur of the sea at ebb tide, their whispered praises and gasps of awe echoed around me as I passed, and wrapped my grateful heart in song.

Arrayed in emerald green velvet trimmed in sable, John stood on the chapel steps, which had been decorated with narcissus, heliotropes, and lilies. His tawny hair lifted in the breeze, a smile played on his generous mouth, and his blue eyes shone with happiness as he looked at me.

Thomas and Warwick helped me dismount, and the earl took me by the hand and led me to John. "Go forth in peace and joy, my son, and may long life together be yours," the earl said, removing his arm from mine and handing me decorously to John. The look John gave his father in return spoke all he felt and could not find words to say: affection, gratitude, and undying devotion to the beloved man to whom we both owed so much.

The iron-hinged doors of the chapel creaked open, and Bishop George emerged from the dim confines of the nave to stand before us in the open portico. The heady scent of narcissus, lilies, and peonies assailed me as I looked up into John's face, and I knew that were eternity to pass, I would never forget this moment. Hand in hand, we waited in the afternoon sunshine as George questioned us: *Have the banns been published? Are you within the forbidden degree of consanguinity? Do you have the consent of your guardians?* His voice droned on, and though I replied to every question, I barely heard the words until the very last. "Do you yourselves both freely consent to this marriage?"

We tore our eyes from one another and answered in one cry, "We consent!" *Oh, how we consent!* I thought.

George took the ring from Warwick's flower-bedecked little daughter Bella, and blessed it. He gave it to John, who slipped it in turn on three fingers of my left hand with the words, "In the name of the Father, and of the Son, and of the Holy Ghost," before fitting it on my third finger. Looking deep into my eyes, he paused, then said gravely, in a loud voice, "With this ring I thee wed."

Cheers exploded around me, and there came the flapping of a thousand wings as doves were released into the air. A bowl of gold coins was presented to us to scatter as alms to the poor. Laughing, we threw the coins into the air. They caught the sun's rays and fell glittering over the crowds like golden rain, reminding me of the fiery flowers I had imagined on my beautiful, never-to-be-forgotten night of the dance at Tattershall Castle. Enfolded in blinding happiness, followed by the wedding party, I entered the chapel for my nuptial mass.

THE EARL HAD SPARED NO EXPENSE ON OUR WEDding feast. Decorated with boughs of greenery, garlands of flowers, and countless flickering candles, the great hall had been made resplendent with beauty and light. No longer did I feel my feet carry me, as John led me to the head table, where two carved chairs had been set for us in the center before a golden taffeta curtain sprinkled with silver stars; I floated there on a perfumed cloud.

When the wedding guests had been seated and the wine poured, John pushed to his feet. Raising a golden goblet to me in salute, he gave me a gaze of heartrending tenderness. "Lady wife, God grant you health, honor, and joy."

"And a thousand sons!" yelled Thomas. The hall roared with laughter.

I stood and lifted my goblet to John. "And God grant you pleasure, peace, and health, my lord husband." It was the first time I had addressed him as "husband," and the word left an unbearably sweet, honeyed taste in my mouth.

A murmur of *amen*, accompanied by the rustle of fabric and the clink of silver cups, went around the room as guests joined their voices to ours. The earl gave the signal, and servers, carvers, and stewards sprang into action to present the wedding feast of beef, smoked mullet, veal, and all manner of venison, ducklings, capons, rabbits, boar pie with fennels, olives, and rich sauces. With great fanfare and torches blazing, they carried in whole succulent boars on their shoulders, and swans in their plumage. Beer, fragrant mead, and wine of many varieties, sweet, dark, and spiced, were poured from gargantuan barrels in endless streams. Between courses, tumblers performed handsprings, and mummers walked around on sticks like giants. Troubadours recounted the tales of Samson and Delilah, Priam, Helen, and Ulysses, and of Arthur and Guinevere, and accompanied themselves on pear-shaped lutes and stringed viols as they sang love songs. Before the course of sweets, John presented a troubadour to serenade me with words he had chosen:

> *My lady looks so gentle and so pure,*
> *That the tongue trembles and has naught to say.*
> *She walks with humbleness in her array,*
> *Seeming a creature sent from Heaven.*

Hands clasped, we exchanged a long look of love with one another as the song drew to a close. Amid grand applause, John threw the troubadour a gold noble, and guests rose to perform their own feats for us, vying with one another for the loudest praise. Then everyone joined hands and danced, accompanied by lute, viol, and tabors as servants presented sweets of marchpane, rice pudding, gingerbread, apples, and candied rose petals. Never was a hall so merry, filled with so much laughter.

As bells tolled for Vespers, John and I rose from the table to leave for our bridal abode, which had been set up in a cottage near a high waterfall on the castle grounds. Laughter resounded everywhere as our drink-laden guests struggled to their feet to accompany us. The drunkest of these was Thomas; the tallest, York's son Edward; and the most sober, Bishop George. Swaying, Thomas threw a hand around his cousin Edward's neck. "Where are you now, brave Percies?" he yelled, peering around the hall. "Here is a bridal party to ambush—'tis time to attack! Come, give us good sport—Edward and I stand ready to slay you like the hogs you are—" Grabbing a flask he had stuck in his girdle, he brandished it like a sword while he oinked merrily.

Edward grabbed the flask away from him. "Too good for Percies," he said, slurring his words, downing a sip. "Let us slay them with more sour stuff!" Roaring with laughter, the two cousins staggered out.

More sweets, more wine, more music followed us into the courtyard, where we were joined by a throng of feasting peasants. Purple sunset was falling over the world, and birds rejoiced loudly. While some merrymakers grabbed torches, others made John and me sit in chairs with long wooden poles extending out front and back. Hoisting us high on their drunken shoulders, they formed a wedding cortege a league long and carried us through the glowing gardens, along the narrow, winding path over the dimming meadows humming with crickets, past the darkening woods of larch and pine to our bridal cottage, singing, dancing, and nearly tipping us out many a time. But we were so happy and plied with wine, we merely held on to the wooden arms of our chairs, screamed merrily, and laughed the harder.

On our arrival at our bridal abode, Bishop George blessed the cottage from the thatched roof down to the wood floor, then the hearth and the nuptial bed, which had been prepared for us with silken sheets and down pillows and covers. With a last blessing, he

left us standing at the open shutters of the bedroom, waving farewell
to the departing revelers. Staking their torches into the ground as
they retreated, the merrymakers receded into the darkness and their
laughter died away into the distance, leaving only the roar of water
and the glitter of the waterfall as it reflected the lights of the flames.

We were alone.

John reached out, gently lifted the slender golden band of my
veil, and set it aside. My hair tumbled loose around my shoulders,
shedding white rose petals around me. He wound a lock around his
fingers, pressed it to his lips. I moved into the circle of his arms and
lifted my mouth for his kiss, but all at once he crushed me to him
and covered my lips hungrily with his own, sending a rush of desire through my body as fiery as the flames crackling in the hearth.
Without releasing me, he fumbled with the gilt circlet that held my
dress, found the clasp, and opened it. He tugged at my sleeves until
the gown slipped from my body. Then he released me, removed his
jacket and shirt, and threw them aside. I watched as he pulled off
his boots and hose and cast them away.

I dropped my linen shift to my feet. We stood at the foot of the
bed, gazing at one another without shame, lit by fire and moonlight. His eyes were darker than I had ever seen them. His kisses
swept my cheek, my neck, my shoulders, and I returned each with
savage harmony, my heart hammering in my breast. I threw my
arms around his neck, and he carried me weightless to the bed. I
felt his uneven breath against my cheek and the sweet bliss of his
hardness against me. It seemed to me then that there was naught in
the world but fire and thunder as our bodies entwined, united in
love, unto eternity.

"My wife . . ." he murmured when passion had been spent.

"Beloved husband . . . beloved, beloved . . ."

"Nothing shall part us ever again, my angel Isobel," he whispered thickly.

"Nothing," I echoed, engulfed in a fog of bliss. "Nothing . . .
ever, John."

Eleven

JULY 1457

OBLIVIOUS TO EVENTS IN THE OUTSIDE WORLD, John and I passed three intoxicating months together before July shattered the blissful cocoon we had woven for ourselves.

He had been gone more than a week with his father and brother Thomas to the seaside town of Whitby to meet Warwick, who had sailed in from Calais. I had expected him back before now, so when the Salisbury herald sounded his horn in the distance, I left the spinners I had been supervising and hurried up to the turrets to watch his arrival. Maude and the countess joined me there, along with many members of the household staff. We stood together, craning our necks as we scanned the green meadows rising to meet the rim of the sky, and waited with happy hearts for our first sight of the returning retinue. But our smiles faded when the column drew closer.

Maude spoke first. "Why is there so much dust? I can't see—"

I turned to the countess, and a cold knot formed in my stomach at the expression on her face. A sudden realization struck me with terrible force. *She knows only too well the signs of trouble.* "They're galloping up too fast. . . . The column is long with wagons." Her voice trembled. "They have wounded men with them—hurry! Get sheets and water, fetch the physicians and the priests—"

The first riders thundered in through the castle gates and slid from their saddles in the courtyard, their faces streaked with dirt, their clothes torn and stained. From their midst came the bark of a hound. A cry of relief burst from my lips. "John!" I flung myself into his arms and clutched him tight, closing my lids to hide my tears of relief. The earl and Thomas galloped up next and drew rein. I heard the sharp intake of air from the countess as she let out a breath.

"We gave battle at Castleton, we have wounded—" the earl began, dismounting from his horse as Maude ran to greet Thomas.

The countess swept to her husband's side. "We know, dear lord, and are ready for them. . . ." She paused, then added hesitantly, "Any dead?"

"Thanks be to God, no dead," replied the earl, limping forward.

The countess gasped. "You're wounded!"

" 'Tis nothing."

She gave him her shoulder tenderly. "Here, lean on me. Does it hurt?"

Behind her, Thomas laughed before the earl could reply. "Nay, lady mother! 'Tis a pain Father bears lightly, for look what gifts we brought you—" He turned to grin at two prisoners being hustled into the courtyard.

The countess's eyes widened with astonishment, and she froze in her steps. These were the Percy troublemakers, Thomas, Lord Egremont, and his brother Richard Percy. Egremont's face held no leer this time, only anger and loathing. With his muddy hair and disheveled appearance, he cut an even uglier figure than I remembered.

"Do we have suitable accommodations for these charming knights?" Thomas inquired, a smile tipping the corner of his mouth. "Perhaps a hog pen where they can help perfume the air, or mayhap someplace with goats?" He slapped Egremont heartily on the back "I know—how about a nice dungeon, eh, Tom? There you may sleep comfortably and not have far to go to plop your stool."

As he was led away, Egremont spat at Thomas, who wiped off the spittle, laughing.

The castle buzzed with delight as details of the battle emerged and we learned how the Percies had been completely routed. "Fortunate for us they're so stupid," Thomas laughed. Many hours of the days that followed were spent offering prayers of thanks in the chapel, nursing the wounded, and celebrating yet another victory of Nevilles over Percies. Within the week, the Duke of York himself arrived to take counsel with the earl on what was to be done with the prisoners. Until then, Egremont and his brother were sent to the earl's fortress of Middleham for safekeeping. After much deliberation, a decision was finally reached.

"We're going to let the courts decide their fate," John told me one night as we lay in bed.

"But wouldn't it be better to just keep them imprisoned at Middleham? Then they couldn't cause you so much trouble. The courts might free them."

"York stands for law and order, and our detainment of the Percy brothers has no legal sanction. We must deliver them up for judgment. All across the land, men are taking the law into their own hands. Maybe by our example, we can change that."

I nestled against him, my body in line with his, my cheek resting in the hollow of his back, my arm comfortably around him. "I hope so," I murmured as I fell asleep, the ills of the world banished by his closeness.

Little more than a month later, in early September, as I was giving Bella and Anne a counting lesson in the schoolroom, Ursula appeared at the chamber door. She had returned the previous week from her family manor at Newbold Revel in Warwickshire. She curtseyed breathlessly, an anxious look on her face. Leaving a nurse in charge of the children, I hurried out to her in the passageway.

"Something bad has happened!" she whispered urgently.

"John?" I demanded. He had left days earlier for his father's castle of Sheriff Hutton to attend matters there, and was not yet returned.

"No, no—it concerns the queen. York's own messenger brought the tidings!"

I shivered in apprehension. News carried by itinerant friars and peddlers could be dismissed if ill in nature, for it might well be mere rumor and have no basis in fact. This was different. A messenger had come from no less a personage than the Duke of York himself. The only remaining hope was that Ursula had mistaken its nature. I rushed to the countess's apartments and found the earl standing with her by the oriel window, a missive in his hand. Whatever hope I had that the news had been good evaporated when I saw their expressions. I halted in my steps.

The earl did not wait for me to question him but went directly to the point. "On August twenty-eighth Pierre de Brézé assaulted the port of Sandwich by land and sea, and ravaged, plundered, and burned the city, leaving a trail of dead in his wake."

I remembered Marguerite's ardent admirer, the gallant French general who had kissed my hand and showered me with compliments at my audience with the queen. "I don't understand—" I breathed in bewilderment. Could such a charming man do such a terrible thing?

"The queen urged him to it. Kent is a hotbed of support for York. Exeter, our noble Keeper of the Seas, left Sandwich open—no doubt on the queen's orders—and Brézé retired well-nigh untouched."

"Surely there's some mistake? England is her country now. She couldn't do such a thing to her own people. . . ." My voice drifted off.

"Her people are French, not English."

"But the king would never permit such a thing!" I cried in disbelief.

"The king has no knowledge of it, I warrant, nor was he consulted in the matter." The earl crumpled the missive in his fist. Turning his back, he gripped the stone windowsill and bowed his head.

Feeling suddenly weak, I sank into a chair.

Week after week, itinerants and guests brought us news, and for once, the reports did not deviate: All England bristled with fury and indignation over Brézé's attack and Exeter's shocking failure to act. At the end of September, the Duke of York journeyed to court with John's father to confront Exeter. On the earl's return to Raby in October we learned firsthand the results of that meeting.

"Reminded that he was Lord Admiral, Henry Holland, Duke of Exeter, finally put to sea in search of Brézé last week!" the earl said in disgust, hands clasped behind his back as he paced to and fro before us in the solar. "He sailed as far as La Rochelle, but achieved nothing. . . . Still, there is also good news to report." The earl paused, then turned to us. His tense features relaxed. "You are aware that we sued the Percies for damages at the York Summer Assizes? Well then, the verdict has just been delivered. . . . We have been awarded the sum of sixteen thousand and eight hundred marks!"

I stared at him, jaw agape. The figure was staggering—a king's ransom.

"There is no way the Earl of Northumberland can ever pay such huge reparations, my lord," the countess said.

"And the Percy brothers shall be kept in prison until they do," John grinned.

So John wouldn't have to face any more perils at the hands of that abominable Percy, Lord Egremont. Maude clapped her hands in joy and hugged Thomas.

"Are such my paltry thanks, lady, after all I've done?" Thomas demanded. To her puzzled look, he laughed. "It was I who captured Egremont and his brother—single-handedly, I might add! Father and John here had naught to do with it, did you?"

"Take all the credit you want, brother." John grinned. "All I wish is peace, which I have from the knowledge that those two scoundrels shall be locked up till they gray, God willing."

"Nay, if the truth be known, 'tis John to whom Father and I and our men are indebted," Thomas said, his tone turning grave. "Not just this once, but time and again. He's the most brilliant commander alive. Don't you agree, Father?"

"He'll do," replied the earl, his eyes sparkling with pride.

Thomas turned to his brother, his voice husky with emotion. "As long as you're with me, I know I'm safe, John. Thank you, fair brother." He clasped John's shoulder tightly for a long moment.

I had never doubted the love of the Neville family for one another, but this brought home to me the strength of the bonds between them.

MORE JOY FOLLOWED, FOR AS THE LEAVES TURNED gold and crimson and September faded away, I discovered I was with child.

Our babe was due to be born in April 1458. Many times during the night, and during those rare moments of the day when I found myself alone, I caressed the small bulge in my stomach and whispered sweet nothings to my forming child. For John's sake, I hoped for a son, for men had need of sons, but for myself, I wished a little girl: a sweet darling like Warwick's little Anne with the beautiful violet eyes, who had won our hearts with her charm and tenderness.

In the long golden dusk of an early October evening at Middleham, an alarm was raised that Anne was nowhere to be found. No one had seen her for the past hour. Leaving the castle staff to hunt for her inside the walls, John and I were among those who went out to the mound in search of her. Rufus bounded ahead of us, first in one direction, then the other, until at last he stood by a pile of leaves beneath a spruce tree in the woods behind the castle, barking loudly. We found Anne curled up in them, hugging her pet rabbit and weeping copious tears. I took the rabbit from her, and John lifted the child up into his strong arms.

"Why, little lassie, are you so sorrowful? Has it not been a beautiful day? Is it not a lovely twilight? Will the moon not be full tonight?"

The little one nodded, rubbing her eyes, but she still sniffled with sobs she could not suppress. "Pray, tell what ails thee, my sweet," said John gently, stepping carefully down the hill with the precious bundle in his arms. He loved children, and Anne most of all among his nieces, and I knew that he was as impatient for our own little one as I myself was.

Still sniffling, little Anne hid her head in John's shoulder. After much coaxing, she confided to us the reason for her sadness. "I am four years old, and I still can't touch the moon!" she said, pointing up to the glowing silver circle in the sky. John exchanged a look of sweet sorrow with me. Stroking Anne's hair, he pressed the child to him. "Aye, little Anne, 'tis a common problem, but one I daresay will be remedied when you are older."

FOR YULE OF 1457, THE SALISBURY HOUSEHOLD moved to the earl's castle of Middleham, surely the most splendid built in testimony to power and privilege. An outer staircase of wide, cream-colored marble led inside to the great hall that dominated the keep, and colored windows abounded everywhere, sprinkling fragmented rainbows through all the passageways and rooms. Stepping between two tall angel figures on either side of the arched doorway, I followed the family into the grandest hall I had ever seen, and looked around in awe. The chamber stretched before me with a mighty cluster of gilded columns of stone carved with roses, crosses, griffins, and crowns. Its walls were adorned by rich tapestries, colorful murals, and screens of ebony wood carved fine as lace. The floor was patterned with a mosaic of rose, azure, and honey-colored marbles inlaid with semiprecious stones, and most wondrous of all, it had a ceiling painted in such a way that it fooled the eye into seeing a soaring dome overhead.

Warwick himself arrived a day later. His brothers and his father met him in the castle courtyard. Shoulder to shoulder, the four strode to the earl's council chamber. *They make a splendid family,* I thought, watching them through a traceried window. *Each tall, handsome, and well made, even the earl, who, despite his silver head and fifty-seven years, carries himself as erect as any of his sons.* To my great comfort, I saw that their faces were creased with smiles. That night at dinner Warwick himself made the announcement.

"It has been shown to the satisfaction of all that our French queen was indeed behind the shameful rape and burning of the city of Sandwich. The violent public outcry has forced her to take the office of the Admiralty from her inept favorite, Exeter, and hand it to me. I stand here before you as your Captain of Calais, aye—but also as your new Keeper of the Seas!"

The hall, crowded to capacity with the household staff, exploded with cheers and the stomping of feet.

"As you know, I was appointed Captain of Calais after St. Albans, but did not assume my command until a year later because the dead Duke of Somerset's lieutenant, Sir Richard Woodville, at the behest of the queen, would not turn Calais over to me."

At the name "Woodville," I jerked up my head. "Is he a relation to Elizabeth Woodville, Countess Alice?" I asked my mother-by-marriage.

"Her father," she whispered back. "The landless knight who married the Duke of Bedford's widow, Jacquetta, Princess of Luxemburg."

Dismissing the vague unease that suddenly gripped me, I nodded and returned my attention to Warwick delivering his speech.

"—Payment had not been made to the troops in months, and Calais's fortifications stood in dire need of repair," Warwick was saying. "At that time I pledged to use my own resources to remedy this. And I did! I pledged to restore discipline among the troops of Calais—and I did! Calais is again England's most important and impregnable garrison." He waited for the cheers to die down. "As your Keeper of the Seas, I make you this pledge—with God's help, I shall avenge our national shame and restore England's honor! Now I invite everyone—be he varlet or knight—to partake of wine, drink, and merriment—for which expense, my gracious lord father, you shall be recompensed!" He turned to the earl as everyone laughed. "Tonight we celebrate this great victory for York, for Kent, and for England—and all the victories to come!"

★   ★   ★

WARWICK SOON FULFILLED HIS PROMISE. OUR swashbuckling soldier-pirate brought honor to the Neville name and captured the hearts of Englishmen with his exploits on the high seas. Though outnumbered twenty-eight ships to twelve, he soundly defeated the Spaniards off the coast of Calais and captured six enemy vessels laden with goods and treasure. London, that city of traders, nearly rioted with joy, for against the angry protests of the Merchants of the Staples, the queen's favorites had been issuing licenses to their supporters, allowing them to evade the Staplers' monopoly on wool. By his action, Warwick showed a clear sympathy for the Staplers and other London traders whom the queen's favorites had been robbing for years.

All across England, in the taverns, the manor houses, the abbeys, and the counting houses, his victory was compared with that of King Edward III at the naval battle of Sluys a hundred years earlier, and everywhere the talk was of Warwick, whom people were now calling "England's champion." Even those who had not taken a stance either for or against Lancaster began to speak in favor of the cause of York. But, as support for York rose through the land, so did jealousy of the Nevilles and of the House of York surge at court.

"They call his feats 'acts of piracy,'" Ursula said in disgust.

"Only at court, not elsewhere," I replied, setting my spindle in motion and feeding it a handful of wool fiber. "London has turned so hostile to the court party that the queen has moved permanently to Coventry and Kenilworth, which are Lancastrian in sympathy."

"How is it piracy when Spain is an ally of France, and we're still at war with France? What about the piracy of the queen's favorites, who have been looting the merchants for years?"

"The Lancastrians will call it what they will . . . and do what they will."

" 'Tis a reckless lot they are," murmured Ursula irritably.

I paused the spinning wheel. "I fear the queen won't take Warwick's successes lightly."

Indeed, she didn't. Soon we learned that Egremont and his brother Richard Percy escaped from Newgate Prison, and the queen gave them refuge at court. On the heels of this news came disturbing reports of the measures Marguerite was implementing against the House of York. Across the land, from high office to low, from the Lord Chamberlain to sheriffs and judges, men whose loyalty to Lancaster was suspect were replaced by appointments from the queen's own household staff. At every turn—on the castle grounds, in the taverns of the nearby village of Staindrop, in the shops and on the streets of the city of York, where I journeyed with the countess to purchase dressmaking and other sundry supplies—people passed on the latest reports sweeping the country.

"The queen's sacked Shrewsbury and replaced him with the Earl of Wiltshire as Lord High Treasurer," a woman told a butcher as she bought a pound of sausage.

"The coward who fled the Battle of St. Albans for fear of ruining 'is pretty face?" the butcher asked.

"The same. The queen likes pretty faces."

"An' Wiltshire finds nothing prettier than a piece of gold, I reckon!" another customer interjected. "The fox guards the hen-house now, don't he?"

"And once they empties that, the queen and 'im, they'll find other ways to steal from us," the butcher replied. "There's no end to their greed, that lot."

As we feared, the Lancastrian appointments were soon followed by persecution and impoverishment of those loyal to the House of York. The lands of Yorkist retainers, yeomen, tenants, and farmers were confiscated, their manors and property ransacked. Money became a serious problem for us, and we found ourselves cutting back our expenses as best we could. We gave up the luxuries of spices, reduced the purchase of furs and woolens for the household, and made do with more fish from the pond and less meat. Countess Alice sent orders to the household that no clothes be replaced until further notice. What cash there was went to the armorers, for on armaments we dared not stint. One chilly day in mid-October, Ursula's mother, Lady Marjorie Malory, arrived at Middleham seeking refuge, having been driven from the Malory manor in Warwickshire.

"The marauders sacked the house and carried off the oriental fabrics the household wore," she wailed. "They had been passed on by Sir Malory's dead uncle! And they took the precious Rhodian wine we had conserved in the cellar for nearly twenty years! And the Saracen carpets my dear lord Sir Thomas inherited!" She burst into fresh tears. Ursula did her best to console her, to no avail. "We have nothing, Ursula! We are paupers now. Who will take care of us? Where can we go?"

"You are welcome with us for as long as it takes to restore your property to you, Lady Malory," Countess Alice reassured her.

I cast a look at the desperate, homeless faces crowding the great hall, wondering how long this could continue, for even as we cut back, more mouths arrived to swell the castle indigents, as others who had been expropriated by Marguerite sought succor from their lord, the Earl of Salisbury. But it was at Middleham, when Warwick's countess, Nan, visited from Warwick Castle, accompanied by the earl's sister Cecily, Duchess of York, that I came to appreciate the true extent of the breakdown of law and order across the land.

"Poor Radford," Nan mourned almost as soon as she greeted us. "Poor dear Radford . . . What they did to him, 'tis an outrage . . . an outrage. . . ."

I did not know who Radford was, but I soon learned. The Duchess of York gave us the tale over wine and sweetmeats in the silk-draped Lady's Bower.

"We knew Nicholas Radford well. He was man of aged years, and a lawyer of great distinction who represented our friend Lord Bonville against the queen's supporter the Earl of Devon. My lord offered him a high appointment during his protectorate, and Radford could have reaped riches in London, but he refused. 'If I leave, who will represent those that suffer at the hands of the Earl of Devon?' he asked. My lord husband was moved by his words."

She paused a moment, remembering. "Radford lived in Upcott, near Exeter. Late one night, he received a visit from Sir Thomas Courtenay, one of Devon's sons, who had been terrorizing the area.

He came with a hundred of his father's men. They surrounded Radford's residence and set fire to the gates. . . ."

Duchess Cecily hesitated. The laughter of children floated to us through the open window. I waited intently, half dreading what I was to hear. And terrible it was. As the duchess continued, the events of that night unfolded before my eyes.

The old man had gone to the window to find a rabble of men standing at the gates, their faces lit by flames.

"Who's there?" he'd called.

"Radford!" Courtenay yelled. "Come down from your chamber and speak with me. I swear on the faith and fealty that binds me to God, and on my word as a knight and gentleman, no harm shall come to you, or your property."

Assured by the solemn promise, Radford had opened the main door, and Courtney had entered with all his henchmen.

"So many, my lord?" Radford had asked, alarmed at their number.

"Have no fear," Courtney had reassured him. "Take me to your private room, where we can talk."

There, Devon's son partook of Radford's wine and held him in conversation, while his ruffians ransacked the entire house, removing whole beds, napery, books, cash, ornaments from the chapel, and other household goods to a value of one thousand pounds.

"The ruffians even toppled Radford's invalid wife out of her bed so they could take the sheets," the duchess added after a brief pause. "Then Courtenay said, 'Hurry, Radford, for you must come with me to my lord, my father.' Radford sent a servant for a horse, and the servant returned, trembling, to report that all the horses had been taken away, laden with the stolen goods. Radford turned to Courtenay and said bitterly, 'Oh, Sir Thomas Courtenay, you have broken your promise. I am old and feeble, and can hardly travel on foot, so I must beg of you to be allowed to ride.' To this Courtenay replied, 'Have no fear, Radford. You will soon ride well enough. Come with me.' They left the house, and when they were a stone's throw away, Courtenay had a few words with several of his men and galloped off, calling, 'Farewell, Radford!'

Then the men fell on Radford with swords and daggers, and slew him cruelly."

No one spoke or moved after Duchess Cecily delivered the tale. "I fear worse to follow," Duchess Cecily concluded quietly, making the sign of the cross.

We had not long to wait to learn the truth of her prophecy.

Twelve

1458

THE NEW YEAR OF 1458 ROARED IN ON A HAIL-storm. Warm and comfortable, with John at my side through Twelfth Night and my stomach large with child, I worked my broidery loom, played my lyre, and read in the earl's library. All was serene in our corner of the realm, far from court and trouble, and for this I sent many a thankful prayer heavenward. Thus passed January of 1458.

My babe was due to be born in March, but the pains came a month early, and on Candlemas, the second day of February, I gave birth to twin girls. We named the firstborn Anne and the second child Isabelle, in honor of John's little nieces. The night of my labor had been chill, and a light flurry of snow had fallen, leaving the windows edged with frost. But morning brought the sun, and in my hazy sight, clouded and dazed by the travail of childbirth, the light that lit the frosty panes seemed unduly sharp. I did not know whether to take that as a good omen, but I hoped that it was so. I gazed on the wailing newborns the midwife placed in my arms.

"Anne has your dimples, my love," I whispered to John.

"And Izzie has your chestnut hair, my angel," he replied, his face soft, aglow with love and pride. He stroked her down with a gentle touch.

"Angels have golden hair, not chestnut, John," I laughed. "Even I am not so far lost in my senses to know that."

He kissed my sweat-drenched brow. "My angels have chestnut hair," he replied, as he always did.

We passed our first wedding anniversary in glorious celebration, surrounded by our wailing babes, laughing and making merry. In June more good news came of Warwick's great success on the seas. After a running battle that lasted two days, he had defeated several Genoese and Spanish ships. Three of the enemy vessels were brought in triumph to Calais. Once again England blazed with pride in Warwick's victories.

The sweet summer months gave way to the ruby leaves of autumn. As October sunshine dissolved into dreary rain, I discovered I was expecting another child. On the second of November, All Souls' Day, when I was four months pregnant, John made an announcement.

"I'm going to Sheriff Hutton," he informed me. "And from there to Westminster."

I gave Izzie over to the nurse and looked at John blankly. "To court?" I said, a sick feeling in the pit of my stomach, a vision of Somerset's wrathful face swimming in my mind. "But why? What is so pressing that you must go to court?"

"The queen has summoned Warwick to report on Calais and explain his attack on the Easterling salt fleet, which she's calling an act of piracy. She's appointed Lord Rivers head of a commission of an inquiry. We know their intent is to take the captaincy of Calais from Warwick and give it to Somerset. I must be there for my brother in case of trouble."

"Who is this Lord Rivers?"

"You know him as Sir Richard Woodville, the queen's favorite. He's that landless knight who married the Duchess of Bedford. Marguerite's elevated him to baron now."

Elizabeth Woodville rises higher still, I thought, not without a pang of bitterness.

Sleep during these days proved fitful. I was plagued with bad dreams, fueled no doubt by the worries over John's forthcoming visit to Westminster. On the night after his departure, I sat restless at the window, looking out at the dark night and listening to the chapel monks sing their matins prayers. Abruptly an idea came to me. I would to go to London! But secretly, so no one could prevent me, and that they would surely do, since I was with child.

At first light, I went in search of the new man John had hired to attend my personal needs, and found him in the armory, giving a hand to the smith shoeing Rose.

"Geoffrey," I called. Though nearly fifty, he was strong and wiry, and still had his hair and a good set of teeth. He left the smith and wiped his hands on a leather apron, giving me a warm smile as he did so, for smiles came easily to him and he had an especially good nature. A soldier for most of his life, he walked with a limp from an old battle injury, so John had persuaded him to accept an easier livelihood, and he had newly joined my tiny personal household from the village of Sawston, where we held a manor house.

"M'lady?" he asked.

"I'm going to London. You and Ursula are to come with me. Saddle a brown mare for me. I'm not taking Rose." About to leave, I turned back. "She attracts too much attention, and 'tis a secret matter. You are not to mention it to anyone. We depart within the hour."

His eyebrows shot up in surprise, but he gave no other evidence of his amazement. "M'lady, I'll have everything ready."

THE GREAT BELL OF THE CLOCK ON THE STONE tower at Westminster was tolling the hour of five when I arrived in London with Ursula and Geoffrey. We heard it as far away as Bishopsgate, since many citizens had retired to their homes for the evening meal and it was quiet in the city.

November clouds hung heavy over Westminster as we approached, mirroring tensions everywhere. Guards searched our
faces longer than usual before giving us permission to enter the
palace grounds; groomsmen took our horses silently; and a varlet
helped Geoffrey remove my heavy coffer from our small cart with
averted eyes and barely a grunt. The large courtyard, with its great
fountain, teemed with the usual assortment of merchants on business, friars and clergy, knights, ladies, and hopeful petitioners. But
laughter and chatter were nowhere to be heard, not even among
the servants. I was troubled by the absence of the customary ribald
talk they used with one another to make light of their burdens as
they carried sacks bulging with flour to the kitchens, or bent over
to receive a load of firewood on their backs.

I approached a royal officer whom I knew to be in the service
of the chamberlain. After showing him my ring bearing Prince
Edward's insignia of the swan, I gave him a silver coin and requested the small room I had been assigned the previous year.

"I woudna do this for just anyone, you understand, Mistress
Haute?" he said, using the false name I had given him and pocketing the money quickly. "Not with times being what they are. But
yours is a familiar face, and sure I am it doesna harm."

We waited a long time before he returned to lead us to our
chamber. "The closet has been used for storage for the past month,
an' we had to move a bed back in," he explained.

Following him across the cobbled courtyard and up the tower
stairs, I made certain to keep my head lowered and my hood raised
to avoid being recognized, praying not to cross paths with Somerset. Many of the lords we passed stood together in small groups,
speaking in hushed tones, their expressions guarded, eyes darting
around and hands on the hilts of their daggers. Outside, by the
fountains and along the hedge walks, ladies strolled with anxious
glances and spoke to one another with heads close together, their
lips barely moving. Even the dogs that lay around the castle steps
and in the halls set cautious eyes on us as we passed.

Following the man through the main corridor, we passed the
great hall, and soon thereafter took the familiar left turn into the

narrow corridor where Somerset had accosted me the night he was drunk. At the end of this, we turned right into the even narrower and gloomier dead-end passageway that led to my former chamber. The man threw me a glance as he jangled his keys before the door.

"This chamber's close to the rowdy great hall, and isolated from the other ladies, but if you're sure 'tis what you want—"

"I am certain of it." I smiled.

He creaked open the oaken door into the low-vaulted, dark room with the high window, and departed with a bow. I sank down on the bed with a sigh.

"Welladay, Ursula, John is here to help his brother, should Warwick need it, and I come to help John, should John need it," I said. "Let us hope neither of us is needed."

Ursula said nothing. She'd already spoken her mind vociferously many times along the journey. She considered me reckless to undertake such a journey when I was with child.

A knock at the door announced Geoffrey. He entered with another man, struggling with the coffer. Though not very large, it was deep and heavy, for along with the clothes, I had taken the precaution of including some weapons. They set it down against the wall and withdrew. Suddenly weary, I looked up at the window high above. Darkness had fallen, and the sky had turned black. The clanking of dishes reached my ears; the supper horn would soon sound. I had no wish to eat in the great hall, where Somerset might see me, and besides, I wasn't hungry. "You may sup in the hall, Ursula. I doubt anyone will trouble you if you sit below the salt with the servants, but keep your ears open for news."

She helped me out of my travel gown and into a woolen shift, and draped a blanket around my shoulders. Worn down by worry and the long journey, I laid my head on the pillow and soon fell asleep to troubled dreams. Dull morning light filled the chamber when I opened my eyes. The washbasin on the table stood filled with water, a towel beside it. Instantly awake, I raised myself on my elbow to find Ursula watching me anxiously.

"What news? Did you find out where they're going to meet, and when?"

Leaning close, she lowered her voice to a whisper. "I fear some evil, dear Isobel. Last night I overheard a remark from one of the queen's servants, something about finishing the 'business' this day. I felt it was my lord of Warwick they meant."

After she had laced and buttoned me into my dress, I sent her on her way to break fast, with an admonition to find out where the council meeting was to be held. Turning over all kinds of dangers and plans in my mind, I paced nervously as I awaited her return. She came back within the hour, bearing bread and cheese. I listened to her report, nibbling thoughtfully. As it turned out, my concern was well founded.

"They have lost no time. From breaking fast, they went directly to their meeting. They're in a council chamber next to Westminster Hall—"

Good, we were close, as I'd planned.

"But matters are not going well. I heard the Earl of Warwick shouting at Somerset as I left, and men came to wait in the hall as soon as the servants began gathering up the trestle tables. They're lounging in two groups along the walls, Lancastrians on one side, Yorkists on the other. The Earl of Warwick seems to have a goodly retinue with him, but I fear the queen's men outnumber his by far." Ursula paused. "The way the royal attendants were looking at our lord of Warwick's men made me most uneasy, Isobel dear . . . like they were awaiting a signal—"

As if on cue, we heard shouts. I threw down the crust of bread in my hand and grabbed the dagger from under my pillow. The noise came from the great hall. With Ursula following close behind me, I opened the chamber door, then turned left a few paces and left again into the narrow passageway that led to the main corridor and the great hall. By the time I reached the opening, the din was a raucous clamor, punctuated by desperate cries of, *"A Warwick! A Warwick!"* The clanging of metal burst over my ears as men exchanged blows with swords. My heart hammering in my chest, I flattened myself against the wall and peered around the corner.

A chilling sight met my eyes. I gasped, drew back, and turned to Ursula. "Warwick's surrounded! He's fighting for his life!"

At the entrance to the great hall, in the midst of his retinue and heavily outnumbered, Warwick was beset by the queen's men. My eyes swept the thicket of pikes and swords as a wave of panic surged within me.

"There's John!" I cried. He was about ten paces away, his back to me. "Oh my God, he's been separated from Warwick and has only a few men at his side!"

I watched in horror as others streamed to join the melee from all directions, wearing King Henry's badge of the panther. Emerging from the stairwells that led down to the kitchens and pantries, they poured toward the fray like dogs to a cornered quarry, brandishing knives and cleavers, pestles and clubs. John, parrying blows with three ruffians at once, disappeared into a small chamber on my side of the passageway, only yards away. The clash of steel and metal now resounded with ear-shattering force. Suddenly a great group of men rushed out of the great hall. Slashing at the queen's men, they moved forward, toward Warwick.

In stunned joy, I turned to Ursula. "They're the lords from the council meeting! Led by Duke Humphrey! He's fighting his way to Warwick's side! Oh, Ursula, I think he means to save him!"

Duke Humphrey and the other lords cut a path open for Warwick down the hall toward the far stairwell that led to the river, where his barge was moored outside the water gate. As the queen's men saw their prey about to escape their grasp, I flattened myself against the wall and stole another look around the corner. Warwick had moved even farther down the hall; now it seemed he would make good his escape. *God bless good Duke Humphrey!* I thought, my heart swelling with gratitude. This was the man who had tried time and again to play peacemaker between the warring factions of York and Lancaster.

"But, Blessed Mother, where is John?" I peered around the corner again. Everyone had their backs to me as they parried with Warwick, trying to slay him. My heart was in my mouth when my husband suddenly reappeared. He looked pale and was unsteady

on his feet, his left arm dangling limp at his side as he fought a
lone ruffian. I covered my mouth to stifle the gasp that escaped,
but John heard me. A look of bewilderment flashed across his face.
Then I indicated the dagger in my hand. He gave me an almost
imperceptible nod, and I slid back into the hallway and waited.
Hacking wildly at his opponent, John forced him toward me. The
opportune moment came suddenly as a lightning strike. With both
hands and all my strength, I thrust my dagger into the man's back
and watched as he collapsed. Grabbing John's good hand, I drew
him out of sight and ran with him down the long passageway until
we reached my chamber. Behind us, Ursula mopped up the drops
of telltale blood from the floor with a strip of linen she had torn
from her shift.

John was about to sink onto the bed, but I cried out, "No! You'll
stain the sheets!" From the passageway came faint voices, then footsteps. John eyed the space under the bed. "No! Not under there," I
cried in a frantic whisper. "In here . . ." Wildly I emptied the coffer
of my gowns.

"I can't fit in that, Isobel!" John protested.

"You must. Get in! Hurry!" Grabbing the gowns, I dumped
them in a pile over his head in an unruly heap. "Quickly, Ursula,
get me out of this!"

Swiftly, she stripped me naked. I shook my hair loose and, to my
horror, I noticed a bloodstain on the floor near the coffer. I stepped
forward and covered it with my foot, and no sooner had I done so
than the door burst open. I let out a scream and hid my breasts and
swollen stomach with my hands.

Ursula stepped in front of me to shield my nakedness from their
gaze. "How dare you? Have you no shame?" she cried, feigning
anger.

The man averted his eyes. "We thought there might be a Yorkist
hiding somewhere down these halls."

"You can see for yourself there's no one here but us. Where
would he hide? The bed? The coffer? If he's that small, you've nothing to fear from him, now, have you? Get out and give my lady some
respect, or by Satan's horns, you'll answer to my queen for it."

The man took a moment to make his decision, and in that moment, I believe my heart stopped its beating.

"Very well," he said at last, turning to leave. But Ursula was enjoying this too much.

"And where's your apology, may I ask?" she demanded.

Eyes averted, he turned back as he closed the door. "You have it, mistress," he said.

GEOFFREY, WHO HAD SLEPT AT A COUSIN'S HOUSE, returned for us the next day with a small cart. Ursula and I rode away with him, my coffer rumbling along on the wheels attached to the horse's saddle. We were followed at a short distance by a tall Franciscan friar in a gray habit with a wooden cross, and with a knotted scourge dangling from a rope at his waist. The monk's face was protected from the cold by a thick wool cowl, and to his nose he held a handkerchief, which he removed from time to time to bless the humble folk he passed. No one in the courtyard paid him any heed, except the few who murmured their thanks, and he passed beneath the arched stone gateway and out into the streets of London, unnoticed.

THE WEEKS THAT FOLLOWED WERE DRENCHED in happiness and celebration. Not only was John safe and his arm healing, but Warwick, too, had reached the Tower and from thence had made his way to Calais. It was the season of Yule, and our babe was growing at a quickened pace. John took as much pleasure as I did in the baby's kicks, and on occasion he would place his ear to my stomach, hoping to hear a gurgle. As December approached, the castle filled with song and merriment. Servants dashed about, laying down fresh rushes, beating tapestries, washing windows, scrubbing murals, and preparing sumptuous feasts for the guests who arrived to partake with us. Though we still had concerns with expenses, since our impoverished tenants had trouble paying their rents, it was decided that we would not scrimp on the Yule festivities.

I found my heart light as I helped Countess Alice and Countess Nan deck the halls with ribbons, holly, and boughs of evergreens. Many guests came to visit, bearing gifts of spices, dried meats, and marchpane: the Scropes of Masham and Bolton; the Conyerses, Sir John and his son William, and their ladies; and many more of the knights in the earl's retinue, with their ladies and children.

Thus, with hope in our hearts, we rang in the New Year of 1459.

My babe was born on the first day of April, another beautiful little girl whom we named Elizabeth. But our joy was short-lived, for the tender spring that followed our babe's birth brought ominous tidings. It was clear to us that the queen had made a deliberate attempt to murder Warwick at Westminster; yet hope for reconciliation still held sway in our hearts. However, just before St. George's Day and our second anniversary, we learned that the queen, who had moved to Cheshire with her son, was assembling an army and distributing her son's badge of the swan.

In the solar at Middleham, attended by John, Thomas, and Warwick, who had come from Calais, and by York's golden-haired, magnificent son Edward, Earl of March, who had arrived from Sandal Castle to represent his father, the earl strode back and forth like the black bull of his emblem. From beside the hearth where I sat with Countess Alice, Nan, and Maude, pretending to bury my head in my needlework, I watched them from the corner of my eye and listened intently.

"She has ordered three thousand bows for the royal armory and commands the king's loyal men to assemble at Leicester," he exclaimed. "The warrant opens thus: 'Considering the enemies on every side approaching upon us by land and by sea—' " The earl slapped the missive. "Our names are significant by their absence! By excluding us, Marguerite makes it quite clear whom she considers the 'king's enemies.' " He threw the missive on his desk. "Is it not enough for her to rob the treasury, to impoverish us by every means possible, to rule the land without parliament for three years? Is this not enough for the venomous she-wolf who rules our mad king? Now she means to force us to make war on one another!"

"She would have us all dead to secure the throne for her son," John said quietly. "She knows, as does the land, that the Duke of York is England's true king by right of blood. Only in his death, and the deaths of his supporters, can she find rest."

"Aye, she fails to see my father as anything but a claimant to the throne—a threat to her husband, to her son, to herself, and to the ruling dynasty of Lancaster," said Edward, Earl of March. "While my father sees our mad and impotent king, Holy Harry, as the Lord's anointed! Had he seized power after St. Albans, all would have been resolved. Yet, even knowing that now, he continues to show self-restraint. Despite every provocation, he makes no attempt to displace Holy Harry, and proves time and again by both words and action that all he wishes is a change of ministers. Yet she thirsts for war!"

"Bitch!" snarled Warwick, slamming a fist down on the desk. "If the bitch of Anjou wants war, let us give her one, Father! We'll crush her as surely as we did at St. Albans, and be done with her once and for all."

"Do you know what civil war means?" said the earl, shocked, his wrath spent. He was not a man who harbored anger for long. "It means to tear the land in two. To divide families against themselves. To set brother against brother, and kin against kin. 'Tis the worst horror a land can inflict upon itself. We must not be hasty. We must do all that we can to avert civil war. War is the last resort. Only a fool chooses war when reason can still get him heard."

"But how? By all agreement, Marguerite believes only in the sword," Thomas said.

"We'll gather a force of our own and go to the king and plead with him, as we did in fifty-two and fifty-five."

"It did no good either time, Father! Even our victory at St. Albans proved for naught," said Warwick impatiently.

"This time is different. We are much stronger, and I daresay Marguerite understands strength. You'll bring us forces from Calais—the pick of the garrison—and we'll go with a large army. If we fail to get redress from Henry, only then will we take up the challenge and fight. Thus, we'll have given them every chance to settle matters reasonably." The earl gave an audible sigh and turned to Edward. " 'Tis a sad and sorry state of affairs. In Ireland your father stands for justice, and in England, for good government. To Marguerite d'Anjou—"

The earl broke off, unable to finish the thought. To the queen he was the enemy, the great devil that had to be destroyed before she could gather a good night's rest.

My hand trembled as I pushed a needle through the cloth, drawing a load of red wool in its wake.

"I have come to believe," said Edward of March quietly, "that, from the beginning, Marguerite d'Anjou never doubted matters between us would be settled by the sword. She has been lusting for war ever since Holy Harry's first bout of madness."

The air in the room seemed suddenly hot; I felt faint. Laying down my section of tapestry, I excused myself and quit the room.

WARWICK RETURNED TO CALAIS. JOHN LEFT FOR the Scots border to deal with the marauders burning English villages and stealing sheep and livestock, and Thomas rode back to Sandal Castle with Edward of March to inform the Duke of York of the deliberations at Middleham and to urge on him the need to call a council of war, and plan strategy.

And so the spring passed. I played with my babes as often as I could, and helped Countess Alice with the management of the household—arbitrating quarrels, receiving petitioners, and overseeing the work of the chambermaids, the kitchen help, the spinners, weavers, and embroiderers, and the education of the children. I tried to find ways to curtail expenses, by going over the money spent on supplying livery, buying stock, even the cost of the clergy we employed to sing masses and say prayers. When John was home and at my side, I clung to him, my feelings heightened by the uncertainty that pervaded our days and by the black specter of loss that always hovered in the background.

"My father is the most famous knight in the whole world!" Warwick's Anne announced one evening at Raby as she sat on my lap, playing with her wooden doll. "Nurse told me. She says England loves Papa as much as I do."

"Indeed she is right. He has made us all proud, sweet Anne."

"See, Jane has her head back," Anne said, holding her doll to my full view.

"Had she lost it?" I inquired.

Anne nodded. "Cousin Edward of March broke it when he kissed her."

York's seventeen-year-old son had earned himself quite a reputation with the ladies, but clearly he had fallen dramatically short in impressing Anne. She had such a disagreeable expression on her face that I had to laugh. "So how did Jane get her head fixed?" I asked.

"Uncle John did it when he got back from London at Yuletide."

This came as a surprise to me. The shoulder wound John had sustained as a result of the castle brawl had proved very painful and had taken weeks to heal. During that time, even slight movement had brought him excruciating pain.

"Did he use one hand or two?" I questioned.

"One. He had a bandage on his shoulder. He couldn't use two hands. He said he was sorry for taking so long to fix it. I didn't mind. Is Cousin Edward coming to visit again?"

"Not soon."

"Good," said Anne, giving the word sharp emphasis.

Again I found myself laughing. Here, at least, sat one young lady in no danger of losing her heart or her virtue to handsome, dashing Edward, Earl of March. Saddened to see her leave the next day, I blew her a fervent kiss as she departed for Middleham with Nan.

"Fear not—I be back!" she called in her sweet voice, leaning out of her litter as it passed through the gates, eliciting laughter from everyone around.

OVER THE SUMMER MONTHS, THE EARL AND THE Duke of York held many parleys, either at Middleham or at the earl's castle of Sheriff Hutton. Men answered their summonses, signed the contracts, collected their pay, and reported to Middleham to pick up their weapons and don the murrey and blue colors of York. Warwick, in Calais, was notified that he would join forces with his father at York's fortress of Ludlow in Wales. From there they would proceed to Kenilworth to remonstrate with the king. They intended to plead their case, present their grievances, and reassure him of their loyalty. For safety's sake, however, they had to go armed, and in strength.

On the twenty-first of September, 1459, just before St. Michael's Day, the earl left his castle of Middleham for the South. I bid John farewell with a heavy heart and watched the procession file down the hill and vanish into the dense fog. But before many hours had passed, while Maude, Countess Alice, and I were murmuring prayers for our husbands in the chapel, a messenger galloped up to Middleham, out of breath and in much distress.

"The earl's left? Blood of Christ, I came to warn him! The queen knows his plans to join forces with York at Ludlow! She's determined to prevent it and has advanced north to cut him off. She has with her a strong royalist army. The earl will be heavily outnumbered!"

The countess nearly swooned with the dire tidings. With panic rioting in my heart, I found a trusty young lad, helped him saddle a fresh horse, and with a sharp slap on the horse's rump dispatched him to find the earl and deliver the messenger's warning. My stomach clenched tight, I retired to the nursery. Rocking my babes to and fro in my arms, I whispered prayers and lit candles all that night until at last morning broke and the nurse took the sleeping babes from my weary arms, and left me to fall into drowsy slumber.

Thirteen

BLORE HEATH, 1459

AT MIDDLEHAM, THE HOURS SETTLED ON OUR shoulders like a black cloud as we awaited news. We didn't know whether our warning had reached the earl in time. Every few minutes we paused in our duties to strain our sight into the distant fields. One day passed, then finally another, and the next; the chapel filled with the murmur of prayers. A tense, fearful silence pervaded the castle.

One afternoon a huge cock was seen in the waters near Weymouth. He emerged from the sea with a great crest upon his head, a great red beard, and legs half a yard long. He stood in the water, so it was said, and crowed three times, and each time he crowed, he turned himself around and beckoned with his head toward the north, the south, and the west. And then he vanished.

Perhaps because I was with child again, I took this omen to heart. I didn't realize how it had affected me until Sir John Conyers galloped up one wet afternoon, nearly a full week after the earl had departed for the South. We had heard nothing from the messenger we had sent, and we labored with our tasks around the castle, oppressed by dark thoughts. I was patching a tear in one of John's cloaks when I heard the loud creak of the drawbridge and the noise of a commotion in the courtyard. Conyers rode up with a few Yorkist knights. From all directions we rushed to meet the small party as they dismounted. But the old knight seemed weary and made no announcement to the household that gathered around him. His silence chilled my heart.

He greeted us courteously but gravely. I knew the fear on the faces of the household staff was mirrored in my own as I fell in behind the countess to lead the way to her private apartments. We settled in the solar, and servants brought sweetmeats and ale.

Sir John Conyers spoke at last. "My ladies, I have news of both a good and bad nature."

We all stopped breathing at once. I gripped the carved wood arm of my chair.

"As I know not where to begin, I shall begin at the beginning," Conyers said in a somber tone. "The earl, with no knowledge that the queen was advancing to intercept him as he marched south to Ludlow through Market Drayton, set up camp for the night on Salisbury Hill, south of the River Trent. There your young scout found him and brought him your warning—"

The room filled with cries of relief and a rustle of fabric as we all shifted in our seats and breathed again.

"The Lancastrian force was far superior in numbers. Their intention was to attack his rear as he went south, but the earl immediately changed direction to evade them."

Countess Alice gave my hand a squeeze.

"Skillful he was in marching us across country, through woods and valleys, and hiding us from prying eyes," Sir Conyers said, fingering the tip of his ginger moustache. " 'Tis a marvel how he did it, an' I still wonder at it. . . . A skilled general he is, my Earl of Salisbury, with many a trick up his sleeve. He got us all safely away and took up a strong defensive position on Blore Heath."

I sat still as a statue, holding my breath; my chest felt as if it would burst. *They gave battle. There will be deaths.*

"There is no doubt the queen had sent the lords Audley and Dudley to slay him." A soft gasp escaped the countess's lips, but she made no further sound as she sat stiffly erect. "My lord of Salisbury was outnumbered five to one, for the Lancastrians came prepared for battle, and he only to parley. But he chose his position well an' was protected by a broad stream. He's a wily old fox when it comes to giving battle, m'lady, but more than that, he had the protection of God Almighty Himself, as you'll see—" Conyers said, addressing the Countess of Salisbury. He fell silent a moment, shaking his head in admiration. "He tricked Audley and Dudley into thinking he was about to retreat. The Lancastrians took the bait and attacked. What's more—and here the good Lord Himself saw fit to intercede on the earl's behalf—they charged up the hill mounted on their horses!"

As there was no reaction from us, he cleared his throat and added, "You see, 'tis a fool thing to do, to charge uphill on horseback, m'ladies. Audley should have known better. He, like the earl, had experience in the French wars, but it seems he understands nothing of warfare. My lord of Salisbury released a hail of arrows into their midst. Men and horses fell, and those that didn't bolted to the rear." After a pause, he added wryly, "The Lancastrians have a monopoly on stupidity, m'ladies, and here's proof they learn nothing from their mistakes. Audley ordered a second cavalry charge!" He gave us a wan smile, but my heart, rioting with uncertainty, could not let me return his smile. Neither did anyone else. We were all waiting for the bad news.

"The battle lasted four hours," Conyers resumed. "The Lancastrians were routed. Audley was killed and Dudley taken prisoner. The earl pressed his pursuit relentlessly all night until Lauds. When it was over, two thousand lay dead. They're calling Blore Heath 'Dead Men's Den.' Here we come to the bad news. . . ."

Though fear glittered in their eyes, no one said a word, and none asked questions. My stomach clenched itself into a tight, painful knot. Maude reached for my hand. At her touch, a chill raced through me. I wondered if my fingers felt as icy to her as hers did to me.

"Sir Thomas and Sir John—"

I leapt from my chair, a hand to my frozen heart, unable to breathe, to see, to feel. Across a wilderness I heard the countess cry out and Maude's soft voice begin to recite the Ave Maria.

"Nay, my ladies—courage, they *live!*" Conyers exclaimed, stressing the vital word. "They live, but are taken prisoner. They pursued the Percies too far into Lancastrian territory, and on the morning after the battle they were captured and imprisoned in Chester Castle. They are well treated, so we understand. We have taken prisoners too, and well the Lancastrians know that should harm come to ours, theirs will suffer."

I closed my eyes, a grateful prayer on my lips, and sank back down.

"Lady Isobel—" Sir Conyers said gently.

I opened my eyes. My heart pounding, I moved to the edge of my seat. "There is something you haven't told me," I whispered. "Is John wounded?"

"Aye, m'lady. He was, but in the thigh. . . . 'Tis not mortal. . . ." His voice trailed off, for he knew the comfort he offered rang hollow. Many a man had died of an infection that began in a minor flesh wound.

Countess Alice's arms encircled my shoulders as I bit my lips and averted my face, but a sudden restless scampering at the door gave me a moment's respite. Rufus ran in, barking with great excitement to see me, and pressed himself against my skirts. I gave him a warm reception, for he was dear to me now in a way he had not been before.

Sir Conyers gave a nod of dismissal to the youth who had brought him. "I held the hound back," he said, "fearful you might misconstrue events if you saw the dog before I had a chance to explain his presence. I thought Sir John might wish you to keep him."

"You did right, Sir Conyers," I said in a choked and teary voice, struggling with the knowledge of John's capture.

The countess spoke. "My lord the Earl of Salisbury, where is he?"

"He went on to Ludlow, m'lady, to join the Duke of York as planned."

"And what happens now?" asked Maude.

"Now we await the arrival of my lord of Warwick's seasoned force from the garrison of Calais." Sir Conyers sighed on an audible breath, "Pray God, the final outcome shall soon follow and be favorable to York."

Images rose in my mind, flashing like sheets of lightning before me: Egremont's face, hideous with hatred; Clifford's small, truculent eyes glaring from his thick-necked, square-jawed face. I saw Somerset grab my arm in the gloomy passageway, his breath stinking of stale wine, his pupils dilated with passion. *So you spurn me, do you? No one spurns me*— In my heart, unsaid, thundered the words I could not bear to hear: *If York loses, who will protect John from their wrath? And me, from a fate worse than death itself?*

After we were dismissed and we dispersed to our duties, I took Ursula aside grimly. "I'm going to the queen."

" 'Tis too dangerous, dear Isobel! You are with child again! And what of Somerset? He might be there, and there's you without protection!"

"I can't just sit here and wait, Ursula. I must at least try to use my influence with the queen—if I have any left—to persuade her to release John!"

"It will be pointless to seek mercy from her, my lady. From the sound of it, the queen has changed. She is not as you remember her. I beseech you, Isobel, do not go to her! There is nothing to be gained, and harm may come to you."

"What of the harm to John? Nay, I must go! We'll leave Coventry the minute I've seen her."

I did not tell the countess or Maude, but excused myself with an explanation that I needed to check on repairs to my manor of Eversleigh—something that John had intended to do. The journey south made no imprint on me. My mind, heart, and soul were centered on our arrival and the words I would use with the queen. We crossed the great red moat into the courtyard. The sun sent shards of light glittering off the jewel-colored windows, and the wind stirred the golden leaves of autumn as we followed the old, familiar winding path through the pleasure garden to the royal apartments in Caesar's Tower. But nature's beauty brought me no solace, for the castle was filled with people and commotion, and the faces that passed me seemed more somber than ever. Ursula departed for the kitchens to see what she could glean that might prove useful, and I left in search of the queen.

I found Marguerite in the low-vaulted antechamber that she had always favored at Coventry. With an ornate ceiling, stained-glass windows, and a colorful inlaid stone floor, the room that adjoined her solar glittered darkly as I approached. She was pacing violently as she dictated a letter. Her six-year-old son, Prince Edward, kept her company, slouching on an immense treasure chest set in the corner of the room as he cleaned his fingernails with a miniature dagger. A little dog lay nearby, watching him, and in a silver cage hanging in a corner a trio of yellow finches twittered.

The man-at-arms announced me. The queen broke off, and the gaze she turned on me was so hostile that I froze in my steps. I fell into a deep curtsey.

"Ah, Isabelle! Rise, dear," she said in the affectionate voice I remembered. "For a moment I mistook you for someone else. Sometimes I think we are surrounded by enemies, but no matter—you are welcome. Edward, my prince, do you remember Lady Isabelle Ingoldesthorpe?"

Prince Edward set his gaze on me and lowered his dagger as I made obeisance. "You are fair," he announced.

I smiled and looked at Marguerite, who laughed and tousled his hair. "*Mais oui*, my dear *Edouard*, she has a French look, has she not?"

He nodded. "I shall not cut off her head, Maman."

His words shocked me, but I kept my composure. The queen laughed again. "Indeed, *non*," she said, gazing at her boy tenderly. "Lady Isabelle is our friend, and we do not cut off the heads of our friends, only of our enemies." For the second time in as many minutes, a chill ran through me.

"Come," she said, leading the way across a gaudy Saracen carpet patterned with large bloodred flowers. She took a seat by the fireplace and arranged her skirts carefully. As I took the low chair across from her, I could see that she had aged greatly in the two and a half years since the love-day fest. A servant brought us spiced wine and sweetmeats, but I was too nervous to eat. I accepted the wine and held my goblet firmly with both my hands, for they shook.

"Isabelle, dear, so much has happened since you left!" the queen said, taking a sip of wine and setting her golden goblet on the damascene-covered table between us. "I have had such troubles! And I have tried so hard, as you well know. . . . Remember the love-day fest? Everything looked so promising then—" Into my mind flashed the memory of the queen walking hand in hand with the Duke of York, her stance rigid, her face stony. I remembered thinking then that perhaps, for the first time in his marriage, King Henry had managed to coerce his queen into doing something against her will. Yet she appeared to remember the day quite differently, and with nostalgia.

Welladay, people see what they want to see. I came out of my thoughts abruptly.

"When I agreed to have you married into the House of Neville," she was saying, "my expectations had been of a new beginning between the Yorkists and our government. But in spite of all my efforts and sacrifices, all my attempts to gain their friendship, all my patience, they have betrayed their oaths repeatedly and taken up arms against us! Only a week ago they came to attack the king at Kenilworth, and I had to intercept them with the royal army!" She buried her face in her goblet, visibly distressed.

I was taken aback by her words and the tears in her voice. Could she truly see herself as a peacemaker? If so, how did she explain— even to herself—the constant ambushes, the numerous attempts to murder the Duke of York and his sons, and Salisbury, Warwick, John, and Thomas?

But these were not questions I could ask. I remained silent, though my thoughts rambled on in this vein, answering each assignation of blame with my own silent defense: Had the Yorkists not been heavily outnumbered and taken by surprise each time, proving they never planned to use force against the king? Had they not survived thanks merely to simple good fortune, great bravery, or ingenious military strategy? Had they not won the battle they had been forced to fight against Lancaster, yet kneeled before Henry VI immediately afterward to beseech pardon, when they could have just as easily seized power and set the king aside? Had they not shown by both actions and words that all they wanted was what they had asked for time and again—good government and a redress of ills?

And did all this not constitute remarkable self-restraint in the face of extreme provocation?

"*Mort de ma vie*, I regret that I allowed your marriage to John Neville, my poor child!" she said, her words slicing through my thoughts like a dagger through silk.

"Oh, no, my queen, I thank you for this gift with all my heart! The day you gave us your blessing was the beginning of all my joy in life. Would that you knew my lord as I know him!"

"He has not beaten you, then?" she asked to my great surprise.

I hesitated, stunned, at a loss for words. "My beloved queen, Sir John Neville is one of your finest knights. Never could he mistreat anyone."

"Then why does he fight so recklessly against our loyal lords?"

I had to choose my words with utmost care. She saw no wrong in Somerset, Egremont, or her other favorites, for she was a good friend—and a bad enemy. I lowered my eyes and said softly, "My queen, men have quarrels that we women cannot understand."

I reddened beneath her piercing gaze.

"I see," she said, and her tone told me she understood perfectly the meaning I had given my words. She leapt from her chair and began to pace angrily again. "Unlike my own Henry, most men are like cocks, always strutting to and fro, spreading their feathers, trying to impress us. 'Tis how nature made them, I suppose, but 'tis tiring!"

" 'Tis why they stand in sore need of your patience and guidance, for you are mother to them all, my queen."

"*Pardieu*, you speak truth!" she exclaimed, wringing her hands. "I have undertaken the management of the realm for my Henry's sake, and my lords try me with their quarrels as sons try a mother! But more than any of them, 'tis York who tests me. Nothing is enough for him! He puts out lies about the paternity of my child! He impugns my honor! He wishes to be king—to steal my son's throne, and that I will not permit, never, on my soul, by the flesh of Christ—"

"Who is trying to steal my throne, Maman?" Edward interrupted the shrieking birds he was teasing to ask his question.

"The hateful Duke of York, but fear not, your *maman* will not let him have it, *bijou*, not on my soul, never! *Sang dieu*, I shall have his head first—"

Watching her ghastly look as she hissed these words, I erased from my face all trace of the emotion I felt, and kept my features deceptively composed. Fear thundered in my chest; I did not know how much longer I could keep myself contained. "My queen, is there no other way?" I implored.

The queen halted in her steps and her features reassembled themselves into a more normal aspect. " 'Tis my hope that we shall find a peaceful resolution, though I doubt York will be interested. We in our patience and in our mercy are anxious to avoid further hostilities. We have sent a messenger to Ludlow with an offer of amnesty if the Yorkists disarm immediately."

I breathed again and found the courage to broach the subject that remained foremost in my heart. "My liege, I have not the worries of a kingdom as you do. All I have is the love I feel for my husband, and concern for his safety. Without him the world would turn to frost for me—" I looked at the little prince now cooing to his birds, holding out bread to them to console them for his vigorously shaking their cage moments before. "We love whether we should or should not, and our world turns on that head we love."

The queen shifted her gaze to Edward with eyes as soft as the sweet grapes of her native land. I gained courage, then went on, "I have come to ask your mercy for the man I love, Sir John Neville, who is imprisoned in Chester Castle."

Her face hardened. "He fought against us. I cannot release him."

"My queen, we have children now, and well I know you understand a mother's love—"

"Not even for your children."

Panic rioted inside me. I fell to my knees before her and seized her bejeweled hand. I laid my wet cheek against the cold stones, more conscious of the bony fingers I held than of the soft flesh. "Madame, I carry another in my womb! I pray you, do not wrench from me all hope, do not condemn me to be companioned by salt tears for the rest of my life—" I broke off, slipping her ring from my finger. "You said to return this to you if I ever needed you. I need your mercy now, my queen."

She stared at the golden swan emblem of her son for a long moment. "I cannot release him," she said finally. "But he shall not be harmed."

Relief overwhelmed me. "He is wounded, my queen. Can you command a doctor be sent to treat him?"

"Aye."

Lifting my tearstained face to her, I said, "And his brother Thomas?"

She hesitated, then gave a nod.

"Thank you, my liege, thank you!" I cried.

"But do not come again," she said angrily, slipping the ring on her finger. "This is the last favor you shall ever receive from me. I am done with York."

THE MOMENT I SAW URSULA'S FACE, I KNEW SHE was bursting with urgent news. I waited impatiently in the court for Geoffrey to bring out Rose and to saddle the other horses, and then we bustled out of Coventry while keeping our silence, for the highway thronged with traffic and we were within earshot of too many. A distance from the castle, the road split. I was about to take the north fork, when Ursula leaned over and restrained me with a touch on the arm. "We go south," she said, "to the Erber." I understood her immediately. She had learned something that had to be passed on to Warwick, who was due to arrive in London on his way to Ludlow to join forces with the Duke of York and the Earl of Salisbury. My heart took up a quickened beat and my mind filled with worry. But I did not question Ursula further. I merely nodded and turned Rose south.

When we were safe in the quiet countryside, with only sheep around us, Ursula broke the news. "Somerset is planning to intercept my lord of Warwick at Coleshill as he journeys to Ludlow to meet with the duke!"

"Coleshill . . . that's only a few miles from Warwick Castle. Warwick has to pass through there on his way to Ludlow. But how do you know it's true?"

"I told my friend Mavis the cook that you were hoping to see his lord of Somerset. She informed me that he wasn't here and wouldn't be back for a while. I didn't learn any more until I overheard Mavis talking with the chief cook. They were laughing together about there soon being a vacancy in the captaincy of Calais, thanks to the pleasant surprise Somerset was planning for my lord of Warwick at Coleshill. They were betting on whether it would be Somerset, Exeter, or Wiltshire who would get the post."

I closed my eyes.

At the Erber, I sat listlessly on the riverbank, waiting for Warwick and watching the traffic on the Thames. I felt a great relief but also enormous concern. John was safe, but hope of a peaceful solution seemed to be vanishing. Edward of March was right. Queen Marguerite, despite all her protestations to the contrary, believed it was by the sword that the problems of the realm would be settled. She came from a line of stubborn women, who had ruled their weak-willed men with an iron fist and viewed absolute power as their queenly right. While Marguerite's father, Good Duke René, had made rhymes, her mother had made war—and signed treaties only when no other alternative remained.

Nay, Marguerite would never share power with a man who was not her equal. Not for any reason—be it good government, justice, or peace. Such things meant little to her. Peace for her was a last resort, something that belonged to the vanquished. Only when they were driven to it by defeat did the women in her family make peace.

Such were the dark thoughts that crowded my mind.

I sent a letter back to Maude and the countess at Middleham explaining my visit to the queen and the promise I had wrung from her about John and Thomas's safety, and then took to my bed. I was with child again, after all.

For the first time in weeks, I slept hard and long, knowing John would not be harmed. As bells pealed for Prime, Ursula awoke me with great excitement. I opened a bleary eye, still so tired that my bones felt like a leaden weight. "My lord of Warwick has landed in Kent and is on his way to London! The city is afire with the news! Maybe we can see his arrival!"

I dressed quickly and swallowed some wine and hot bread. Soon we were elbowing our way through the cheering crowds that thronged the streets. They were a merry bunch, as joyous as on any feast day, jostling one another, cheering, and waving their caps.

"There he is, my lady! There—"

Ursula pointed. We heard the sound of clarions, and a great cheer went up, moving through the packed crowd like a giant wave. Standing on tiptoe to peer over the heads of the crowd, I saw the mayor and aldermen walking up to greet Warwick. The welcome was called out, a few words exchanged, and then Warwick continued toward the Erber with his procession.

"Behold the great Earl of Warwick!" a mother told her babe in arms, lifting him high for a better view. "Hurrah for England's champion!" a man roared. "Long live the Captain of Calais!" another yelled. Finally I was able to get a clear view of Warwick. He was enjoying his reception and rode with a hand on his hip, smiling and nodding to the crowds as if he had not a care in the world. Behind him marched two hundred men-at-arms and four hundred archers, all clad in scarlet tunics bearing his emblem of the bear and ragged staff.

"Which one's Trollope?" asked a youth who stood in front of me. I took him for a fishmonger, for he reeked of the sea and his leather apron was stained with blood.

"You mean the hero of the French wars?" replied a baker, dusted with flour even to his lashes. "He's the one with a patch on his eye and the kerchief tied around his head, just behind Warwick. You can't miss him."

I followed the direction of his gaze to a burly, scar-faced man swaggering behind Warwick. He was ferocious-looking; I was relieved he'd chosen to side with York and not Lancaster.

Warwick was surprised to see me at the Erber. As Ursula went to greet her father, who had returned with him from Calais, Warwick threw himself into a chair, knees wide, and listened to my report. I warned him of Somerset's plans to intercept him at Coleshill and quickly brought him up to date on Blore Heath, the capture of his brothers, and the promise I had extracted from the queen.

"So she sees herself as the one who wishes peace, and believes we are determined to destroy her and her dynasty?" Warwick demanded incredulously. He slapped his thighs and rose. "Then I must spare no effort to set her straight in language even she can understand." Summoning his scrivener, he dictated a manifesto.

"The laws of the land have been subverted, and the king's income is so reduced that people are being robbed in order to meet the expenses of the royal household. Neither is there justice in the land, for crime is encouraged instead of punished—" He fell silent a moment as he paced back and forth by the great window that looked out over the Thames, his head bowed in thought. "However, the blame for this rests not with the king, but with certain persons who hide the truth from him. Therefore we and our friends propose to go to King Henry, acquaint him with the facts, and beg him to remedy these ills and punish those responsible."

"And add this. . . . We are not interested in taking power from the king, or in enriching ourselves, or in exacting revenge on anyone. We have come with an army at our back only for our own safety, because so many attempts have been made on our lives."

He paused to look at me. "That should be clear enough even for the bitch of Anjou."

Warwick lost no time departing London, staying only long enough to rest his men and the horses, and to issue his procla-

mation. We rode north with him, and all along the way to Warwick Castle, we saw crowds swarm to behold him, men cheering,
women holding up their babies for his blessing. But no one joined
his ranks. Perhaps it was because they loved the king more than
they hated the queen; perhaps it was because they' didn't yet realize
that it had come to the sword.

And perhaps I am wrong, and all may be resolved amicably, I thought,
watching his colorful procession weave along past the crowds that
lined the roads. Surely melancholy born of John's absence evoked
these feelings of despair. . . . I was nineteen, a mother now, expecting another child, parted from the husband I loved. Hiding my own
fears, I smiled at others, listened to their talk, and prayed on my
knees until they were worn out. And I waited for news. A life of
such uncertainty, devoid of a calm, steady routine, had to exact a toll.
Then I chided myself. What of the good fortune I had known? I
had married the man I loved, against great odds. I had beautiful children, and my husband, though captive, was safe. What more should
I ask of Heaven? Banishing the gloomy thoughts that plagued me, I
resolved to dwell only on my blessings.

"They are receiving my Earl of Warwick like a king," Ursula
said proudly.

"And you are indeed in love with him. Try not to swoon,
Ursula." I smiled.

She reddened like a beet, then said sullenly, "You have to agree
he looks royal. Far more so than Holy Harry."

"True," I conceded reluctantly. I didn't know why, but something about Warwick had come to irk me with nagging persistency.
His princely bearing, generosity, and charm could not be denied,
yet I cared not for his arrogance and his need for acclaim and
power. There seemed a certain hollowness at his core. *While my
John is as solid as granite and needs no worship,* I thought. *He wishes only
to do his best for his king and country, and to live up to his motto: Honor,
Loyalty, Love.* John had always walked in his brother's shadow, and
the higher Warwick's sun rose, the darker and broader the shadow
Warwick threw over him. John had to feel he was the forgotten
one, but if he did, he kept his thoughts to himself.

There are still things I do not know about my husband, I thought
with a sigh.

After a long day's ride, we glimpsed the tips of the towering,
mighty walls of Warwick Castle on the distant horizon, a welcome
sight after our weary travels. But our smiles vanished as we drew
near. The castle and Warwick's estates had been plundered and lay
in waste, and all across the fields, tendrils of smoke floated up into
the sky. A stony-faced Warwick addressed the desperate villagers,
assuring them that those responsible would suffer punishment and
pay restitution. Then we parted company, he to hurry to Ludlow
and I to Bisham to join Nan and her little daughters, and to de-
posit the contingent of armed men Warwick had sent to guard his
family.

The hillsides I passed through lay so pastoral with sheep, nut
trees, and the occasional stone cottage that if I hadn't witnessed
for myself the turbulence of life, I could be fooled into believing
all the world was at peace. But, God be praised, when we arrived
at Bisham, we found good news awaiting us. Warwick had passed
through Coleshill safely, for Somerset had arrived too late to ambush him. We laughed at Somerset's fury at yet another of his fail-
ures, but our celebration proved brief. For it was here, to Bisham,
that the news came about Ludlow.

Fourteen

LUDLOW, 1459

WHEN THE LONE MESSENGER RODE UP ON ST.
Ursula's Day, the twenty-first day of October, I was seated in
Bisham's elegant wood-paneled council chamber with Nan, celebrating Ursula's name day. The minstrel played merry tunes while
we sipped wine and ate sweets and spiced fruits, including marchpane, which was Ursula's favorite, and dried figs, which was mine.
Nan's girls lay at our feet, munching cookies, chattering, and playing with their dolls. Across the way, the black-garbed monks of
Bisham passed serenely across the grounds of their beautiful priory
on the River Thames, which was drenched in autumn colors, pro-
viding for us a sense of deceptive tranquility as we made merry on
Ursula's birthday.

Even from the window we knew something was terribly wrong.
I laid down John's cloak, which I had been embroidering with his
emblem of the griffin, and rose to my feet. We hurried into the
quadrangular cloister that enclosed the manor's graceful courtyard.
The messenger, dusty and weary, dropped out of his saddle and

knelt before us, lifting anxious eyes to our faces. Warwick's two daughters, who had run out with us, pressed themselves against their mother's skirts.

"My ladies," he said, "I fear the tidings I bring are not good."

Nan turned ashen and drew her children close. I laid a hand on my stomach, as if that would shield my own unborn child. Around us had gathered all the household staff, from kitchen scullion to bailiff.

"The king replied to my lord of Warwick's manifesto by issuing a general pardon to everyone except the Yorkist leaders, my ladies. Again the Yorkist leaders asserted their loyalty and their desire to avoid force, but the king refused to meet with my lord of Warwick, and the royal army moved on Ludlow. As night fell, the two armed camps faced one another across the bridge on the River Teme. The Yorkists waited behind the fortified trench they had built—" The messenger hesitated. "But no trench could protect the Duke of York and his men from the real danger that threatened them . . . treason."

I heard myself gasp.

"As day broke, it was seen that Andrew Trollope, the leader of the Calais regiment who had been guarding the bridge, had absconded to the queen's side, taking with him the Duke of York's battle plans."

I remembered the fearsome one-eyed soldier with the kerchief knotted around his head, who had swaggered, grinning, at the head of Warwick's procession.

"The Yorkist leaders were forced to flee for their lives, my ladies. My lord of Warwick went to Calais with his father and York's eldest son, Edward of March."

Beside me, I heard Nan's labored breathing. I encircled her shoulders with my arms.

"By God's grace, the Duke of York and his son Edmund, Earl of Rutland, were able to get away. They have fled to Ireland with Lord Clinton. However, York's duchess, Cecily, and her two small boys, George and Richard, age ten and seven, were captured and made to watch the queen's revenge on Ludlow. . . . After plundering the town, Yorkist soldiers who had surrendered were hung, drawn, and quartered, and the queen gave the wild horde she calls an army— filled with Scotsmen and ruffians—permission to sack the village as cruelly as if it belonged to a foreign land. Her men, in their drunken orgy, raped women and set the church afire, burning those who had taken refuge inside, children and livestock among them."

The shock of this report must have proved too much for me in my condition, for the next thing I remember was a sharp pain in my abdomen, and nothing afterward. I awoke to find Ursula mopping my brow in my bedchamber.

"My baby—" I cried in alarm, my hand going to my stomach as I rose on an elbow to check.

" 'Tis well, Isobel, dear," Ursula said, pushing me back down gently and drawing the coverlet up to my chin. "You had a nasty fright, is all."

I lay back down, but the nagging doubts at the back of my mind would not be stilled, and many times during the nights that followed, I rose from fitful slumber to pray at my prie-dieu for my unborn child.

Soon another messenger arrived with orders from Warwick that, for safety's sake, his countess and their two daughters be taken to Calais to join him. In heavy rain, I took bitter leave of them, crushing little Anne in my arms as I knelt down on the wet, sharp pebbles of the courtyard. "Fear not—I be back!" Anne said, as was her wont. But instead of evoking laughter, this time it brought me tears. I watched the small party gallop off into the twilight, and misery engulfed me like a steel weight. Marguerite was tearing the country in two as every village, every household, every manor house, and every convent became divided against itself, and here I was alone, my husband and his brother imprisoned, his other brothers and kin driven from the land. Never had I felt so destitute, so bereft. *Where should I go? What to do? And what does anything matter anymore?*

I banished my moment of self-pity. I had to be strong. I was a mother now, and even if the whole world were lost, I had to survive for my girls and for the new life I carried.

The next morning, Ursula packed our few belongings, Geoffrey saddled the horses, and we set out north to Middleham. Many of the Bisham household staff came with us, fearful of staying behind in the unfortified manor house now that their lord could no longer protect them. Along the way, we passed traders, wool merchants, and farmers driving livestock to market. Everywhere doubts were expressed, more loudly than ever, that Henry was Prince Edward's father, and I heard more people refer to the queen by the nickname Warwick had given her: *bitch of Anjou.* Much of the talk centered on the ballad that had appeared nailed to the gates of Canterbury Cathedral, placing Prince Edward at the root of the trouble for being a false heir born of false wedlock. The Duke of York was the true King of England, it said. For his blood—he was descended from an elder son of Edward III and Henry from a younger son— was the more royal.

The sun was setting when we arrived at Middleham two days later after a hard journey. Maude and Countess Alice greeted me with the joyous news that Warwick had arrived safely in Calais, and the duke safely in Ireland, dispelling some of my tension. After supper, with my Annie asleep in my arms, and Ursula carrying Izzie, we gathered around the hearth with Nurse and baby Lizzie, and several highly placed servants of the Salisbury household, as the countess read us Warwick's letter, for the October night was cold and damp.

My gracious lady mother,

You surely know by now the events of Ludlow brought you by York's own messenger. For the first few days after Trollope's treachery, we were not certain we would be able to flee with our lives, for we had no money. However, with the help of a Devonshire gentleman who bought us a ship, and his widowed mother, who risked life and limb in protecting us and obtaining for us the provisions we needed, we put out to sea.

Fearing the sentiment of the Calais garrison after our heinous betrayal by one whom I had trusted and treated as friend, I was unsure whether to attempt to go there. However, our beloved cousin Lord Thomas Fauconberg wrote us from Calais that all was well and we should come. The garrison received us with every sign of joy, and I am now safe in my stronghold with my lord father, my countess, and our two girls, so concern yourself not about us. As you know, Edward of March is also with us.

Likewise the Duke of York was received in Ireland as if he were the Messiah, crowds of people running to him and declaring that they would stand by him unto death. By all accounts, the Earls of Desmond and Kildare vie with one another to see which can do the most for him, and the Irish parliament is said to be willing—nay, eager!—to do his bidding. I shall go soon to meet with him and finalize battle plans, for it is too dangerous to entrust them to messengers who may be captured and put to torture. One such sad report which may have not reached you yet, and which shall cause you much grief now, is the death of our kinsman Roger Neville. His head is impaled on London Bridge and his torso is sent to Warwick town, so I am given to understand. His was a fine legal mind, and he never did harm to another, but only attempted to secure for them a measure of justice in the courts. When you pray for his soul, also pray for us that we may avenge his death in a manner most fitting.

For revenge we shall have, by the grace of God Almighty.

Given the twenty-fifth of October, 1459, on St. Crispin's Day, at Calais.

Your devoted son,
Warwick

The apple-bobbing celebrations of All Hallows' Eve, which followed the earl's letter, were brief, joyless, and held only for the children, and the feasting on All Souls' Day and All Saints' Day also was meager and brief, for no one had heart for much else besides prayer. In mid-November we learned that in Coventry, the queen called a parliament stacked with her adherents, and attainted the Yorkist leaders.

Countess Alice herself poured ale for the messenger who

brought us this news. The man, a Benedictine friar, recited the details without faltering over a single word, for he had evidently repeated it many times along his journey north from Coventry.

"Attainted: Sir John Conyers, Lord Clinton, Sir Thomas Neville, Sir John Neville—"

My stomach churned violently, and a stabbing pain came and went.

"Attainted: the Earl of Salisbury, the Earl of Warwick—who is also replaced as Captain of Calais by the Duke of Somerset. Attainted: the Duke of York; his sons Edward, Earl of March, and Edmund, Earl of Rutland; his duchess, Cecily—"

"His duchess?" the countess exclaimed, staring blankly at the friar.

The friar heaved a sigh. "Aye, 'tis unusual to attaint the wife. But these days—" He shrugged and resumed. "The bitch of Anjou wanted the duchess attainted, claiming the duchess incited her husband to revolt. But that's not the worst of it, m'lady—nay, 'tis not. . . . The bitch also attainted the duchess's two little sons, George and Richard—"

I closed my eyes on a breath. *Dear God, has Marguerite lost her mind?*

"George and Dickon?" demanded Countess Alice, her voice trembling. "But they are mere children—what hand could they have had in their father's treason?"

"None, m'lady, and all the world knows it. It seems she wants to depose all male children of the York line. That's why they're calling it the Devil's Parliament."

I bit my lip until it throbbed like my heart.

"But—b-but . . ." the countess stammered in bewildered confusion, pushing herself into a standing position. "But if she does this, w-what will she n-not do?"

The friar gave her a look of surprise. "Why, she is French—who can say? But for myself, I fear there is nothing she will not do, m'lady." He gave a sigh. "Nothing."

★   ★   ★

ANOTHER MISSIVE ARRIVED SHORTLY AFTER THE
friar's visit, brought by a messenger disguised as a pilgrim who
begged harborage for the night. It was for the countess, from the
earl:

My well-loved lady wife,

> *As you are sure to know by now, we have been attainted by
> parliament, even York's duchess and two small boys. Clearly, 'tis the
> work of Holy Harry's foreign woman, who knows not honor and
> hesitates at nothing. The duchess Cecily and her children have been
> given into the custody of the Duke of Buckingham and his duchess,
> our sister, and by all accounts they are well treated at present. But
> their situation is perilous, as this can change at any moment, given
> the queen's passion and temperament. For this reason, I beg you to
> consider flight. You are not safe in England any longer. While I
> should like to have you in Calais with our Warwick, 'tis better that
> you head west for Ireland, so as not to arouse suspicion. The bearer
> of this missive shall guide you as to the timing and preparations.*

> *York is also concerned for his duchess and children and searches
> for a way to free them from Duke Humphrey's custody and bring
> them out of England, so that they not remain at the mercy of
> Harry's queen. However, Isobel's safety is not in question, due to her
> previous long association with Marguerite. Therefore, at this time
> and given her delicate condition, we consider it advisable for her to
> remain at Middleham.*

> *These are perilous times for us, dear wife. May the Lord have
> you in His keeping until He sees fit to reunite us.*

> *Written this day the twenty-fifth of November, St. Catherine's
> Day, at Calais.*

Your loving lord and husband,
Richard of Salisbury

With a trembling hand, the countess showed this letter to
Maude and me before burning it. As I read, a shiver of black fright

ran through my spine, and fearful images built in my mind. I turned respectful eyes on the pilgrim, whose identity was kept even from us. That men dared the terrors of the torture chamber in order to honor their convictions was not something I had been accustomed to dwell on, until now.

We soon learned that the bishop Dr. Morton had a special hand in drafting the bill of the Devil's Parliament. I remembered the bishop's fish-eyes. Whenever he had turned his gaze on me, my flesh had crawled. Yet I suspected that women were not his interest, for I had seen his expression when he looked at the choirboys. His eyes had lit, and it was not their angelic singing he admired. The thought, singularly distasteful, sent disgust into the pit of my stomach. I felt the babe lurch. *My poor little one,* I thought, stroking my womb gently. *I shall not think of it again.*

More tidings arrived. The queen had commissioned Lord Rivers to seize all Warwick's ships that remained on the English coast, and Somerset to assemble a large force that included Andrew Trollope and others of the Calais regiment, along with angry young men whose fathers had been killed at Blore Heath. Somerset then sailed to take Calais from Warwick, but matters had not gone well for him.

"What are you smiling about?" Maude demanded as we sat before our broidery looms in the Lady's Bower.

"Imagine Somerset's surprise when he approached Calais and they fired on him with their guns."

She grinned. "He must have been furious."

"Surely so . . . he had to settle for Guisnes instead." I laid down my needle. "How bitter is that? He thinks the world is his, and now he sees it isn't." I smiled and, resting my chin on my elbow, gazed out the window. "Imagine his jealousy, his dismay, each time he gazes over the marshes at Calais . . . being able to see Calais but not take it . . . the prize he's coveted so eagerly, for so long, the prize he can't have, that belongs to another." I turned to her happily. "I find it sweet, Maude."

Maude jabbed me with her elbow, laughing. "You could be Calais, Isobel—don't you see? You, too, are the prize he's coveted for so long and can't have."

I fell silent for a moment. Then I burst out laughing. "Oh, Maude, *imagine* being destined to failure in both love and war! How woefully sad. I am almost sorry for the wretch." We heaved in merriment.

Our glee proved brief, for tidings of great sorrow soon reached us. While Warwick, the Earl of Salisbury, and the Duke of York were out of reach of their enemies, their friends and retainers were not. The queen renewed her efforts to exterminate Yorkist support, and terrible reports came to us of the doings in the town of Newbury. There the Earl of Wiltshire—the coward who had fled the field of St. Albans—conducted an inquest with great harshness. Not content with confiscating all the lands and property of the people, he ordered a large number of the men to be hung, drawn, and quartered.

The duke's enemies were reaping a rich harvest from the downfall of York. Income from offices vacated by their removal, annuities from their forfeited estates, and fines exacted from those who had been pardoned were divided liberally among the queen's favorites. More heads appeared on London Bridge and more quartered bodies at the city gates. Exeter, who had hated Warwick since the day the Keeper of the Seas title had been taken from him, received a commission to put out to sea and destroy him.

If the queen thought to deter York's support in this brutal manner, she soon found herself mistaken. Her cruelty engendered even more sympathy for the cause of York, and yet another ballad made its appearance on the gates of Canterbury. Praising Salisbury as the essence of prudence and Warwick as the flower of manhood, it proclaimed the desire of the people that the Yorkist earls return with an armed force and assume the guidance of the kingdom.

In those days, as I helped Countess Alice supervise the household staff, keep a stern watch on purchases, receive petitioners, arbitrate quarrels, organize meals, arrange for repairs to the castle walls and defenses, pay the servants, plan their festivities, supervise the care and education of the children, and nurse the sick, my eye was never drawn long away from the castle gates, where those who entered might bring tidings. Journeymen reported what they had learned in towns where they had passed through seeking work, while merchants brought information they had garnered in abbeys and inns along the way where they had sought shelter for the night. Emboldened by her success at Ludlow, the queen had appointed more commissions of inquest in Kent and in other counties that had given warm reception to the Yorkists. The hated executioner of Newbury, the Earl of Wiltshire, had been named to these commissions in order to strike fear into the hearts of those who embraced York.

"But it is Wiltshire's own heart that is struck with fear," the countess commented one cold winter's day just after Christmas Day, after the subdued festivities of Yule were behind us. "Under guise of fighting Warwick, he went down to Southampton and commandeered some Genoese ships. Then he fled to Dutchland. It seems he is well aware of Warwick's regard for the common people, and is terrified of revenge for his cruel doings at Newbury."

"How brave he is," I said with disgust, remembering the pretty duke whom I'd first seen quitting the queen's audience chamber at Westminster.

"Indeed, it appears that the French queen surrounds herself with the most valiant and worthy hearts our land can offer," Countess Alice replied with biting sarcasm.

That evening, the last of the old year of 1459, we went together to chapel to light candles and pray. Countess Alice said, "No matter what comes, we must never lose sight of what matters most: Our lords live. As long as they are safe, we have hope that all will be righted in the end."

I nodded, and into my mute assent I poured all my heart. Wrapped in our thoughts, we went to the solar to sip a cup of wine and bid silent welcome to the New Year of 1460. The countess worked on her tapestry; I played the lyre; and Maude sat in the window seat, listening to my song while gazing out at the stormy blackness. It was a fearsome night. The wind moaned around the castle walls as I sang of love and death, and it seemed to me that the Four Horsemen of the Apocalypse rode in the night, bringing death, plague, wars, and famine, wreaking havoc, and promising worse to come. I lifted my eyes to the window, and in a trick of my imagination, I thought I saw their ghostly shadows galloping across the darkness, and that one of the figures was a woman and bore the form of Marguerite d'Anjou.

Ending the lament, I broke into a lilting melody, hoping the merry sound would banish my terror.

A few weeks later, on a foggy January night, the countess confided that she was leaving for Ireland. All had been readied, and there was no time to be lost. Maude and I packed her coffer in secret. After a tearful and anxious farewell taken in the dead of night, we watched her depart quietly with the pilgrim. When she wrote to us about her safe arrival there, she also informed us that Warwick was expected to arrive in Ireland shortly thereafter to confer with the Duke of York on their plans to return to England. "I regret I am not there with you, dear Isobel," she wrote, "to assist you with the birth of your babe who is soon due. I shall pray for you and the little soul that all goes well and that God grants you and my grandchild a safe delivery."

But all did not go well. In March, as winter gathered up its drab attire and the fields made ready for spring, I was in the stables, feeding Rose a handful of sugar, when the first pains came. I staggered outside. It was too early yet; my child was not ready to be born for a month. Several youths came running to carry me to my bedchamber. The midwife was sent for and attended me, along with Ursula and Maude, during my long and arduous labor. I heard them but dimly through the spasms of cramps that kept me moaning in pain through the night, conscious only of the hands that wiped my brow with cool water.

When morning broke, there was only silence except for the song of the birds. No running of feet or children's laughter; no commands or chiding of the servants by their superiors. No clanking of breakfast dishes. Only silence. I realized my pains had ceased. "Is it a boy or a girl?" I asked.

Neither Ursula nor Maude answered me.

I struggled to rise and see for myself, but my body felt like a leaden weight. I fell back against the sheets, drained, panting. "Boy or girl?" I demanded again.

After a hesitation, the midwife said, "A boy."

"Where is he? Is he all right? I want to see him."

"Later, Isobel. You are weak. You need your rest." Ursula's voice.

I sighed with relief and let my heavy lids slip down over my eyes. Ursula was right; I was exhausted.

"John will be so pleased," I whispered. "I shall name him John. *John*. Then I shall have two Johns to love."

I must have drifted off into sleep, for when I awoke, the light was fading fast and the sky had grown bleak. Stronger now, I easily pushed myself up on an elbow. Ursula was dozing at my bedside, but the movement startled her and her eyes flew open. The room was quiet. *Where was my babe?*

"I want to see my little John. . . ." I reached out my hand to Ursula, who gripped it tightly. She didn't reply. What was wrong? Where was everyone? Why wasn't my baby crying?

Ursula gazed at me. Her mouth trembled at the corners, and tears shone in her eyes.

"I am sorry, dear Isobel, so sorry, my dear lady. . . . Your babe . . ." she said in a thick voice, and broke off.

I stared at her in confusion. As the monks chanted the even-song, their voices drifted in through the open window. The music's sweet harmony conveyed to me the pain of loss wordlessly, urgently, as with the sharp blow of a sudden dagger thrust. Tears rolled down my cheeks. I turned my head and looked at Ursula.

"He took . . . no breath," she managed, squeezing my cold hand in both of her own.

My little one was gone from my arms before I had ever held him. My tiny, beautiful child was born dead.

I closed my eyes.

FOR THE NEXT WEEKS I DROWNED MY SORROW in the joyful babble of my children and buried myself in the management of the estate as I mourned my newly born babe and pined for John. Faithful Rufus must have missed him, too, for his eyes had taken on a sad look, and he followed me everywhere I went, as if I could lead him to John. The girls also marked his absence. "My friend John coming home?" asked my two-year-old Annie. I felt an instant's squeezing hurt. John had not been home enough for Annie and Izzie to grasp the concept of father, though Annie understood that of friendship. "Soon," I replied, flooded with sadness for my girls. "Your friend John shall be home very soon, God willing." And I pressed them both to my heart.

Many a sleepless night I kept to my knees in the chapel, praying for my living John and for my little one who had gone to be with God. April came, bringing with it springtime's beautiful flowers and blossoming trees, just as it had done on my wedding day three years earlier. Feeling a need to be close to John, I gathered up his cloak and journeyed to Raby with Ursula, taking a party of horsemen with me for protection. I spent the afternoon of our anniversary alone, hugging his cloak by the edge of the waterfall where I had passed my wedding night, and then I plunged into the pool for a swim, as I had done with John before breaking fast on our first morning as husband and wife. The falls thundered with the same mighty roar, but oh how much had changed in three short years.

I planned to spend the night in the cottage, embroidering more griffin emblems on John's cloak, for I had found this pastime brought me solace in times of distress. But the emptiness of the place mirrored my desolation and evoked none of the joy of my wedding night. The dying day took my strength with it as it departed. Slowly, wearily, leaving the splashing waterfalls behind, I wound my way back to the castle before darkness fell. The next day, drawn by an overpowering need for my sweet little girls, Annie, Izzie, and Lizzie, I returned to the safety of the fortress of Middleham.

In May, Countess Alice wrote from Calais with news that lifted our spirits. On their voyage from Ireland to Calais, she and Warwick had sailed past the queen's new "Keeper of the Seas," the Duke of Exeter, without the loss of one ship. For lack of money, or for fear, Exeter had not tried to attack, but had watched Warwick sail past him without a shot.

"He holds the grand promise of another Somerset," I said to Maude with a small laugh.

Then, in early July, Warwick's own messenger arrived. We received him in the open courtyard, where all the household could hear his tidings.

"My lord of Warwick bids me inform you that he landed in Kent on the first day of July. Men have flocked to his banner, and he is marching to London at the head of a large army!"

Cheers went up. The messenger presented the letter he had brought and, placing our heads together, Maude and I pored over it in silence, for it contained nothing of interest to the household, only cordial greetings to us, advice regarding the repair to a castle wall, and assurances that the countess was well in Calais. But then we came to his last paragraph. Maude and I exchanged a fearful look, and my heart jumped in my breast. Breathing in shallow gasps, I read it aloud to the household:

" 'Wishing to avoid bloodshed, again I begged an audience with King Henry, stating that I would speak with him or die, and again I was refused.' " I braced myself so that my voice would not shake as I read Warwick's last sentence. " 'Battle is imminent.' "

IN A STATE OF TERRIBLE ANXIETY, I PRAYED WHILE I awaited further news, and embroidered more griffins on John's cloak. But the dire thoughts that drummed in my head were never far away: What if York lost? What if Warwick was killed? What then for John and Thomas—would the queen keep her word and let them live? Would she release them, or keep them in confinement forever? One thing was certain: If the queen won the battle, she would send the Percies to take Middleham and Raby, and turn us out into the streets. Attainted of treason, we would likely receive no pardon, and if pardoned, we would be homeless, as would be all our friends and kin.

Two weeks passed. No other messengers came. Evil dreams

plagued my nights when I slept. Then, one day, clarions sounded in the village. I dropped the chain of daisies I was making with little Annie and Izzie on a patch of turf near the fishpond, and rose to my feet, my heart in my throat. All around me servants froze in the midst of their tasks; then they sprang to life and ran screaming into the castle, into the kitchens, into the stables, wherever they thought to find refuge, while retainers and men-at-arms grabbed their weapons and clambered to man the ramparts. Suppressing the sheer black fright that swept through me, I gathered up my girls and hurried into the chapel. I fell on my knees before the altar and with my eyes closed recited the Ave Maria.

"*Ave Maria, gratia plena, Dominus tecum—*"

A clamor arose outside. I closed my eyes tighter, murmured the Ave louder. Then, strangely, Rufus bounded into the chapel, barking wildly.

I opened my eyes. John stood smiling down on me, shining like an archangel in the flickering light of the burning candles. I blinked to focus my vision, unable to believe the evidence of my eyes. *John?* Slowly I rose. My hand shook as I raised it to his face to make certain he wasn't a dream, that this was truly him. His cheek was rough with the growth of a beard, but around his smile I glimpsed the dimpled creases I so loved. I traced the line of chin and nose and found it solid; I touched the hair, and it was as thick as I ever remembered. The impact of his penetrating blue eyes engulfed me so completely that my knees trembled.

John was safe.

He caught my hand and placed a kiss on my open palm. The touch of his lips was almost unbearable in its tenderness. He lifted his shining head and looked at me as he had done at Barnet, when I had risked all to warn him of Somerset's ambush.

"My angel," he said in the rich voice I remembered. "My love . . ."

I flung myself into his arms with a wild cry, burying my face in his throat. His hands locked against my back. We clung to one another as I wept tears of joy. How many times had I dreamed of being crushed in his embrace? Now his strong arms enfolded me once more. My pulse pounded in my ears as I laughed; I had forgotten what true happiness there was in laughter. The chapel resounded with my laughter, and the candles wavered in my joyful breath. "John, John . . ." My voice trembled like my hand; the light of his eyes blurred my sight. "My love, my love . . . Dear God be thanked, oh, my love!" In euphoria, between sobs and laughter, I stole kisses from him, kissed the creases in his cheek, the point of his nose. I could not get enough kisses.

"Who dat, Mama?" asked a small voice. A gremlin with dark blue eyes framed by chestnut hair emerged from behind my skirts and was joined by another.

I forced myself to part from John and look down at our children. " 'Dat' "—I laughed tenderly—"is your papa," I said, sweet tears running down my cheeks.

Fifteen

INCESSANT RAIN SPOILED FRUIT ON THE TREES and grain in the meadows, and swept away dwellings, bridges, and mills. Yet, to me, the sun seemed to shine brighter than ever on us during these blessed summer days of 1460, filling Middleham with happiness. We toasted to freedom, to one another, and to York's win over Lancaster at the Battle of Northampton, and celebrated merrily. For days on end I could not take my eyes from John's face, so handsome did he seem to me, so good was it to have him home. Sometimes I reached out and touched him simply to make sure he was real, for I had already lost one John. When I had broken the news to him of the death of our babe, he'd held me close for a long moment and released me in silence, and I'd known that his sorrow ran too deep for words. Later, he'd gone riding alone. That night I'd not slept, but had lain awake beside him, pressing kisses to him lightly with the tip of my finger, in the hope that somehow my love could heal his ache of loss. In my heart I said many a silent prayer of thanks to the Almighty for his safekeeping, for truly I felt it a miracle to have him beside me as I learned of what had happened at Northhampton.

Near London, on the tenth day of July, Warwick defeated the Lancastrians and captured King Henry. John was released from Chester Castle soon afterward. He had galloped home to bring me the news himself.

"On hearing of Warwick's advance from London, the king's supporters lost all heart and resigned en masse," John grinned. "King Henry came down from Leicester to meet Warwick, and entrenched his army in a meadow near Northampton. Wishing to avoid bloodshed, Warwick begged an audience with him, but the lords around Henry refused."

"Did good Duke Humphrey not try to persuade Henry to negotiate?" I asked.

"Duke Humphrey was as determined as the others to keep Warwick from Henry's presence." John's tone held a note of bitterness.

"But why? He was never rash. He always used his influence to mediate for peace."

"That changed when Marguerite arranged the marriage of his son to Margaret Beaufort, the richest heiress in the land, and of his daughter to the Earl of Shrewsbury's son. Even good Duke Humphrey had his price," John said.

"Had?" I asked.

"He died at Northampton, along with our mortal enemies Shrewsbury and Egremont. Warwick found their bodies strewn around the king's tent."

"How—?" There was so much here to grasp. That Egremont was gone gave me not a moment's care. He had been an evil man, and his petty hatred and jealousy of John and Thomas had contributed greatly in fanning the troubles and dividing York from Lancaster. As for Shrewsbury, his name had come up occasionally as one of the implacable lords around Marguerite, but I didn't know the man, though I'd seen him at court. What baffled me was that so many lords should have died at one time. Lords were never killed in battle, unless the fighting was heavy. They were usually taken for ransom. "Was it such a fierce battle?" I asked.

"No, only three hundred men lost their lives."

"Why, then?"

"Reversing custom, Warwick ordered his troops to slay the lords and spare the commons. He has no quarrel with the people, only with Marguerite's lords."

"I see." My heart warmed to Warwick. I thought it a great kindness on his part, for the commons had no choice but to fight and die in the wars that were of their lords' making. "Yet I do mourn Duke Humphrey's death. He saved your life and York's many times. He wasn't like the others. He had integrity, and he abhorred bloodshed as much as you do. Loyalty to Henry was his abiding principle, though he cared little for Marguerite."

"Aye, his personal devotion to Henry was admirable. He stood by him to the last. . . . Maybe he saw no way to avoid bloodshed, or maybe he was outvoted by Marguerite's zealots. We shall never know. In any event, Northampton proved an easy victory. The battle was over in a half hour."

"So quickly?"

"Aye, for two reasons. Weather played in Warwick's favor. Henry's guns were rendered useless by torrents of rain, and his men hampered by the flooding of the meadow in which he was entrenched."

"And the second reason?"

"Treason," replied John.

I gasped.

"Lord Grey of Ruthin extended the right hand of friendship to Warwick and came over to our side."

I didn't know what to say, how to react. I was delighted that York had won the battle, naturally—but treason . . . Treason was abhorrent to honorable men.

"As Trollope did at Ludlow," I said coldly.

"Aye, treason is a hideous thing," John replied, and fell silent. "Incidentally," he resumed at length, "Edward of March, York's son, fought with splendid courage. He's quite an impressive young man."

"That surprises me. Warwick has never said anything positive about him."

"Warwick considers Edward dissolute and good for nothing more than the pursuit of pleasure." After a moment's pause, he added, "My brother is sometimes guilty of hasty judgment, which nothing then can change."

His comment gave me a rare glimpse into his inner thoughts, and again I wondered how hard it must be for John, living in his brother's shadow when he had to know he was the finer man. And once again the realization struck me there was much about my husband I had yet to learn.

WE ARRIVED IN LONDON IN TIME TO WITNESS King Henry's return to his capital. Though the king was a prisoner, Warwick accorded him all the imposing pomp and ceremony of a monarch entering into his kingdom, and he himself, bareheaded, carried Henry's sword of state before him. The bishop of London loaned his palace as a royal residence, and the crowds that received Henry did so with honor and solemnity.

At the Erber we enjoyed a joyous reunion with John's father and mother, and with Warwick's countess and his daughters, Bella and Anne, who had come over from Calais now that it was safe to do so. Their exile had had a pronounced effect on them all: Nan seemed more nervous and jumpy than ever; her daughter Bella, now eight years of age, had grown more playful and merry, as if laughter could banish her fears; and six-year-old Anne had become more sensitive and thoughtful. She refused to eat flesh of any kind, which made for many an argument between her and her parents. Yet little Anne, so gentle and sweet, did not relent in the face of their disapproval. She merely buttoned up her lips and quietly refused the food they tried to force into her. I couldn't help but admire her courage for proving so strong in the face of such determined opposition. I knew I couldn't have held out against Warwick's bushy-browed frowns and Nan's daily chidings, especially not at the age of six.

One day I asked Anne why she had an aversion to animal flesh. Turning her bright Neville blue eyes on me, she'd replied with a question of her own: "Would you eat your friends, Auntie Isobel?"

From then on, though I did not dare gainsay her parents, I showed Anne in all other ways that I approved of her mutiny—and we exchanged many a secret look of triumph after each of her little victories.

In all, these were happy days, and we had much joy. John was appointed as King's Chamberlain and was elevated by parliament to the peerage as Lord Montagu. Still, much work remained to get the government moving again, and I saw little of him during this time. All our men had their hands full attending meetings, receiving petitioners, appointing good men to offices vacated by those Lancastrians who had either died or fled, and dealing with others who caused unrest in various parts of the country. King James II of Scotland, unable to resist the opportunity offered by the upheaval in England, attacked Roxburgh Castle, and John's father was immediately called away to raise an army and deal with the Scottish threat, leaving John in charge of Henry's person. But in a divine moment of justice, King James was killed by a misfire of one of his own guns, and peace was promptly restored.

At the same time in August, Warwick, after hearing that Somerset was willing to negotiate the surrender of Guisnes, left for Calais. Meanwhile John's closeness to Henry's person gave me an opportunity to see another side of them both. I was impressed and deeply touched by the tenderness of the care John gave his king. I myself spent much time with Henry, who seemed delighted by the company of our two Annes and Isabelles. He played games with them, threw balls to them, and chatted patiently with them as though they were grown ladies, which pleased them all immensely.

Henry also sympathized with Warwick's Anne when he learned about her aversion to flesh. "Ah, my dear little lady, you are far wiser and kinder than I, for I do enjoy a good piece of mutton, though I love the lamb. 'Tis a failing in me, but one I am too weak to correct. Will you pray for me?"

Little Anne nodded readily, and added, "I shall pray for you forever, King Henry," whereupon Henry laughed and gave the top of her golden head a tender kiss.

That he missed his seven-year-old son, Prince Edward, was evident to me. Once, he placed his arm around little Anne and said wistfully, "My Edward would like you."

"Is Anne not too gentle for the prince?" I asked, my curiosity piqued.

"Gentle as the tiny red finch that flees not the fierceness of winter." Henry smiled.

Anne, the little red finch, had defied the power of her fierce father in refusing to eat flesh.

Only once in all these months did Henry dare mention Marguerite.

"Have you had any news of my queen?" he asked John timidly. "I cannot help but wonder how she fares. . . ." His voice trailed off meekly, as if he feared to offend.

John informed him as gently as he could of Marguerite's adventures. "The queen and Prince Edward are safe in Wales, my liege. She left Coventry as soon as she learned the outcome of Northampton. She was robbed of her jewels along the way, but came to no harm." John didn't give the details of Marguerite's harrowing ordeal with the robbers, or add that she was stirring Heaven and Hell to raise an army against the Yorkists and rescue her husband.

"I have prayed for my dear queen," Henry said sadly.

But Henry's favorite topic remained God, and his favorite friends were monks. With them, for long hours at a time he pondered the mysteries of the spirit and the universe. I had believed Henry to be a dull man, incapable of true feeling or thought. Now I realized how I had wronged him, what injustice I had done him! I came to revere him for his goodness. Even if Henry failed as a ruler, he did not fail as a person; he was pure in thought and deed, a true man of God in all ways. *Henry,* I thought, *has the sheen of a saint about him.* Even Warwick, who could be harsh and arrogant with those he despised, showed Henry deference, honor, and respect, for no one could be harsh with gentle Henry except one who had no heart.

As for intellect, in matters that interested him Henry was exceedingly clever. He asked questions of the monks that confounded them in their intricacy and drove them back to consult their ancient books.

And so passed the last tranquil, beautiful days of the summer of 1460.

AS UNREST WAS QUELLED AND GOOD GOVERN-ment restored, word came that the Duke of York had sailed for England from Ireland. On the tenth day of October, as the leaves turned scarlet, he arrived in London to the jubilation of the multitudes, who welcomed him with a veritable sea of white roses. The emblem of York waved from the hands of children, adorned the hair of maidens, and was pinned to the caps and collars of men. Everyone jostled for space; nimble youths climbed rooftops and high walls to gain a better view, and fathers set their children high on their shoulders.

From the balcony of the earl's house on the Thames, we watched the Duke of York's arrival as he crossed London Bridge. His procession advanced midway along the bridge, then halted abruptly. "What's happening?" Maude asked, straining for a better view. "Why have they stopped?"

No one replied. Then we saw that men were taking down the pikes on which were speared the rotting heads of traitors.

"Oh my God!" the countess said, swallowing hard. "Roger . . ."

"Blessed Virgin," I murmured, my stomach tightening with revulsion. They must have seen Roger Neville. They were taking down all the rotting heads for Christian burial. Still the procession did not resume.

The sun grew hot on the balcony, aggravating my confused and uneasy state of mind. Finally the crowd on the bridge began to stir, and a cheer went up. The procession resumed its forward motion, but now with clarions blowing and tabors beating. The duke emerged clearly into our view, and a sudden hush came over us all. He was resplendent in the murrey and azure colors of the House of York. But he came with his sword borne upright before him like a king. The duke had brought with him at least five hundred retainers clad in his colors, and around him were gathered his son Edmund, Earl of Rutland, his good friend Lord Clinton, and several other lords in livery of azure and white embroidered with fetterlocks, the personal badge of the Duke of York. Above him floated a banner of the lilies and leopards, the arms of England.

The mayor and aldermen of London received him with much ceremony, and though we couldn't hear what was said, the crowd's hails of approval that punctuated the speeches reached us clearly.

The spectacle left me mute. After a moment, when I had recovered from my astonishment, I leaned close to Maude. "What can this mean?" I whispered.

Maude was ashen-faced. "He comes to us as king, no longer duke."

"Be silent, Maude!" Countess Alice said sharply. "Such words must not be uttered!"

"York has assured my lord husband that he remains Henry's loyal subject despite all," whispered Nan under her breath. "He would never attempt to seize the throne."

A page informed us that our barge was ready, and we left for Westminster, our mood far from festive, though our colorful streamers blowing in the wind gave out a different impression. We found the duchess Cecily already seated in the gilded gallery of the Painted Chamber, and after a crosscurrent of greeting, we took our seats beside her. Within a few moments, the duke himself strode in. He presented himself to the lords, then threw a glance up at his wife. I saw Duchess Cecily give him an almost imperceptible nod. As I wondered about the significance of this, the Duke of York crossed the floor to the dais and mounted the steps to the empty throne.

He laid his hand on the blue cushion.

I gasped. Without realizing it, I rose to my feet, as did everyone present. Below, in the hall, there was only a horrible silence. My eyes flew to John, Warwick, and the earl. They, like the rest of the lords, shrank back, repelled and dismayed, standing as still as the painted figures that looked down on them from around the walls. No one appeared more astounded than John's father, whose mouth hung agape. The Duke of York's motion to claim what he considered his rightful seat had met with appalled disbelief from every quarter, even his allies.

York withdrew his hand angrily, turned to face the lords, and stood awkwardly beneath the canopy of state as if still expecting welcome. After a tense silence, the archbishop of Canterbury ventured forward. "Does the Duke of York wish to see the king?" he asked gently.

" 'Tis not I who should go to Henry. 'Tis Henry who should come to me," replied York.

The archbishop stood looking around at the lords, wringing his hands. Then he turned and quit the room. After a moment, York, rebuffed, descended from the dais and stalked out.

From outside the gallery, in the passageway that led to the royal apartments, there sounded a commotion. We abandoned our seats and ran out to see the duke emerge from the stairwell. I saw him from the back as he made his way behind the archbishop to the king's chamber, followed by his retainers.

"Out of the way!" York called to the archbishop. The cleric halted and moved aside in fear. The duke stood before the king's door. "Open it!" he commanded.

His men turned the latch and pushed, but the strong oak door remained shut. "It's barred from within," someone said.

"Then break it down," the duke commanded.

No one moved.

"Break it down!" the duke said through clenched teeth, eyes flashing.

His men didn't need to be told again. A few hard kicks and shoulder thrusts, and it flew open. Henry rose from the chair where he had been seated, a book in his hands, a monk at his side. "You are to vacate these chambers!" the duke said. "They belong to the king, not to you."

"Where shall I go?" Henry asked meekly.

"To your wife's apartments. They will do for now."

By this time the earl, John, Warwick, and the duke's eldest son, Edward of March, had caught up with the duke.

"My God! What are you doing, Richard?" Salisbury said, looking from Henry to the duke.

"What I should have done five years ago! I'm claiming the throne that is rightfully mine! This man and his foreign woman have no right to rule us, and it's time to be rid of them. We've suffered enough misery at their hands."

From the distance I saw John turn pale. "Gracious Uncle," Warwick said, "this is unwise. The people love Henry. You will divide the realm, cause civil strife. Always you have stood against bloodshed!"

"Where have you been? Where have you all been?" the duke demanded, looking around in fury. "What do we have now but civil strife and bloodshed? Because of him—" The duke pointed a wrathful finger at Henry. "Because of this usurper!"

A loud gasp resounded all around.

John's father said, "You can't take the throne, Richard! The people won't stand for it."

"I tell you they've had enough rapine, murder, and injustice—as I have—and they will back us! You saw how they hailed me in the streets!"

"You misjudge the people! They will not accept you. They hailed you with joy—not to depose Henry, but to rid themselves of Marguerite and the Earl of Wiltshire, and her rapacious favorites," Salisbury said. "The people still love their mad, mild, pious king in spite of the humiliations they've suffered under him."

"Don't you understand?" the duke said, glaring at each man in turn. "We can't get rid of the bitch without getting rid of this idiot! Only the sword can settle matters now—Marguerite knew this from the very first, and for that she is smarter than all of us. How many times did she try to murder me? How many ambushes did she set for us—she and her favorites? It was always only about the sword—but we were too fool to see it!"

"Aye, the people loathe Marguerite and her unscrupulous favorites," the earl replied. "But they love their poor, frail king. 'Tis not Henry they hold responsible."

"Yet he is responsible! This pathetic man and the foreign woman who wears him like a crown have made us bleed. And the bleeding won't stop until he's deposed. *God's Blood, his is the head that enables the Hydra's snake-arms!* Only when he's gone shall we be done with the bitch of Anjou, who's plundered our nation to its bare walls, invited the French and the Scots to rape our women, murdered and looted with impunity all these years—thanks to this pathetic creature you call a king!"

Silence.

The duke spoke the truth. But the truth was treason, and treason was the most heinous crime a man could commit against God. Henry was an anointed king; he was God's chosen. We had all taken oaths to him. To go against our oaths was not only to dishonor ourselves, but to put our immortal souls at risk. I had been watching Henry through all this, wondering what he thought. He stood half-hidden at the threshold of his chamber, behind the throng of men, and his eyes had followed the conversation; yet he bore a calm expression, and on his lips hovered a kindly smile. Had he not understood what had just happened?

York's son broke the silence that held us in thrall. Elbowing his way out from behind Warwick, he said gently, "Father, better government is sorely needed, but 'tis the willful Marguerite and her favorites, not poor, dull-witted Henry here, whom the people hold responsible. We have all found Henry blameless. You saw what happened down there—they will not back us. But I believe they merely need time to get used to the idea. Let us present our claim to the Lords and have them debate it. In due course they will see its merits."

"Indeed," Warwick said, "let us present your claim to the throne and have Henry proven a usurper. Then we can set him aside without tearing the land asunder."

The Duke of York pondered this for a long moment. At last he gave a nod.

THE HOUSE OF LORDS DEBATED THE DYNASTIC question for a month. All agreed that the crown was York's by right of lineage, but since Henry occupied the throne as an anointed king, they reached a compromise to save the king's honor and appease the duke. Henry would rule for life, and after his death York and his heirs would succeed to the throne.

"But the Duke of York is ten years older than Henry. Does it not trouble him that he may never be king?" I asked John one night as we climbed into bed.

John heaved a sigh. "Despite what happened at Westminster, York is a reasonable man. When the House of Lords brought him the compromise, he said, 'I need not the title of king, only to know that my hand will guide the ship of state, for the good of all.' It was seeing Roger's head impaled on that pike that unsettled him and made him decide on the spur of the moment that there was no other way except to depose Henry. But he is prudent by nature, not rash, and so he accepted the offer."

The archbishop of Canterbury took the compromise to King Henry for his assent. "I have no wish to shed Christian blood," Henry told the bishop, "and shall agree to this accord." Henry then sent Marguerite a missive bidding her to return to London. Her furious, scathing reply arrived soon afterward. "Unlike you, dear king, I am not made of butter to be molded into shape by such knaves as those who seek to steal what rightfully belongs to us. Hell shall boil over with ice ere I consent to such abomination and sign my son's birthright over to York. These devils shall be made to swallow their words, seal and all, and with God's grace, I shall soon send them to the bowels of Hell, where they rightly belong."

Nonetheless, on the ninth day of November, 1460, York was proclaimed heir apparent to the throne. The substance of power was now York's, the shadow Henry's. We didn't know how or when Marguerite would return, but that she would move Heaven and Hell to raise an army and be back for another fight, we knew all too well.

Nor did it take Marguerite long to invade. She raised a large army of Frenchmen, Welshmen, and Scotsmen. By threatening loss of life or limb to every man between the age of sixteen and sixty, she recruited soldiers from the north region of England, where

York had few adherents, and placed them under the command of Andrew Trollope, the traitor of Ludlow. In return for the help of the Scots, she agreed to give them the great castle of Berwick, which for centuries had protected England from their invasions. Then, leaving Clifford, the Earl of Northumberland, and Somerset at Pontefract Castle to ravage the estates of the Yorkists and murder their tenants, she moved south on her invasion of England, a vindictive foreign queen at the head of a wild and savage horde.

"My lord Warwick has told me this leaves no doubt in anyone's mind that she is the enemy of England. No reasonable man can truly see her as our rightful queen now that she's given away England's chief bulwark against invasion from the north," Nan said with a sigh.

Indeed, as this motley and unruly force crossed the Trent, it swept away by its excesses King Henry's last hold on the nation. Reports came that unrestricted pillage of England south of the River Trent had been agreed to by Marguerite as part of her payment to the Scottish and Northern men. Nothing was spared from this plunder, not even the books or the vessels of the altars.

"Henry's government has long been recognized as a failure, but Marguerite's outrages have divided England into North and South for all time," Countess Alice said heavily. "Where was God on the day Suffolk and Somerset sold us out to the French in return for the hand of that penniless she-devil Marguerite d'Anjou . . . ?"

Her voice faded away so that I knew not whether she expected an answer of me or of God.

While Marguerite plundered the land south of the Trent, her favorites ruthlessly carried out her orders to burn the estates of the Yorkists in the North. Pleas for help came to the Duke of York at Baynard's Castle, each more desperate than the last. As a result, York, armed with legal authority to put down rebellion, dissolved parliament on the ninth day of December and set out for Wakefield and his northern castle of Sandal, taking with him his son Rutland, the Earl of Salisbury, and Thomas. Warwick and John stayed in town, and Edward of March was sent to raise men on the Welsh marches. In the meanwhile, an armistice was reached with the Lancastrians so the holy week could be observed. For the Yule of 1460 was almost upon us.

We took our leave of the earl and Thomas at the Erber, beneath a cloudless winter-blue sky. It was a beautiful day. Freshly fallen snow wreathed the world in bridal white, and icicles glittered from the branches like diamonds. Birds chirped loudly, celebrating the glory of the season. Maude took a long moment to embrace Thomas. As I stood watching their farewell, my heart filled with pity that they should be parted over Yuletide, and I gave a silent prayer of thanks to the Holy Mother that John remained at my side. I knew this scene was repeated across the way at another house, where Duchess Cecily took her leave of her husband, the duke, and her seventeen-year-old-son, Rutland. No doubt she and her family waved them farewell as calmly we did, unaware of what Fortune held in store for us—what appalling evil, what unspeakable horror awaited. . . .

Sixteen

WAKEFIELD, 1460

FOR ME, YULETIDE OF 1460 WAS A HAPPY ONE, AT the Erber. John was at his most attentive, his most loving. For three weeks, surrounded by those I loved, I knew poignant joy, and so I celebrated the Christmas festivities gaily, reveling in games of Hoodman Blind and hide-and-seek with the children, munching sweetmeats and the dried figs I loved, strumming my lyre and singing and dancing merrily, content in my belief that all was well with the world despite the reports of ill omens that kept coming to us. As in Norfolk, where a strange two-edged sword in the heavens, pointing toward Earth, was seen as a portent that God was about to wield the sword of vengeance for the actions taken against King Henry; or in Bedfordshire, where a bloody rain fell—a sign for some that blood would soon flow like water. But in my happiness, I chose to ignore the omens.

On the morning their truth was proven, the first day of the New Year of 1461, the wind howled outside, driving everyone indoors so that no song or joyful noise came from street revelers. Engaged

in a game of Hot Cockles with the children in a corner of the
chamber, I did not immediately see the wounded when they first
rode into the Erber. But I heard the screaming and shrieks of the
servants, the shouts and curses of the men in the courtyard; I heard
the medley of loud clangs and bangs as trestle tables dropped out
of the hands that carried them and buckets fell to the paving stones
from the shoulders that bore them, all this against the harsh, stri-
dent cawing of ravens perched on the rooftops and the wild barking of hounds. Glancing out the window, I saw a wounded man
drop from his saddle into the snow. Others ran to his assistance, and
from the shadow of the arched gate, more wounded trailed into the
court behind them. A few of these disappeared into the stairwell
that led up to the great hall, and others scattered into the direction
of the kitchens and the stables, leaving a trail of bright red blood
behind in the snow. Maude and the countess came running out
into the passageway from their chambers, their faces deathly white.
We all hurried to meet the messengers in the hall.

If I live a thousand years, I shall never forget a detail of what
happened next.

Surrounded by the entire Salisbury household and the wounded
still able to stand, a man with bloodstained white hair knelt before
the countess, an arm hanging limp at his side. She gestured him
to rise, which he did, and the expression in his eyes tore my heart.
Panic rioted within me as I waited, holding my breath.

"I am the bearer of the most grievous tidings a man can bring a
mother, a sister, a wife, a daughter, a son, a father, or a brother. My
lady—" His voice caught. He coughed, cleared his throat. "Our
much-loved and most gracious lord, your husband, Richard Neville, Earl of Salisbury, and your son Sir Thomas Neville . . . are dead.
Dead, too, are two thousand of our Yorkist army. . . . May God in
His mercy assoil their souls."

My breath froze in my throat as screams, wailing, and the most
raw and visceral sounds that human pain can summon rent the hall.
Arms reached out to the countess reeling where she stood, and
held Maude, white as ash, who was drooping into a faint. When
the screams quieted, the man resumed, slowly, haltingly. "The earl's

kinsman Richard Plantagenet, Duke of York, died with them, as did his second son, Edmund, Earl of Rutland, and many others whom we knew and hold dear, and whose loss we shall mourn evermore—" His voice broke. More screams pierced the air and gave way to a burst of moaning, terrible and unearthly. The man's voice came again. "The duke, the earls, and Sir Thomas Neville dedicated their lives . . . to justice and honor, and to the care of the common man . . . and they died with their men in the cause of that justice and honor. . . ."

With great effort, I raised my eyes to the faces that pressed around me, stained with tears, loss, and agony. The moaning ceased, and there fell a silence that howled like an empty wind as it blew through us, changing everything, binding us together in a massive chain without shape or substance. Forged of grief eternal, this chain was more powerful than any steel, for it secured us in its black claws for all time and was never to be broken.

The painful, terrible details emerged over the next days, some so horrible, they were kept from the countess and Maude.

Violating the Christmas truce they had agreed to observe, the Lancastrians on the thirtieth day of December attacked the duke's men as they foraged in the woods between Wakefield Bridge and Sandal Castle. York saw the fighting from the castle and immediately called for his armor. His advisors urged him not to go forth, but to wait until he was at full force, since his men had scattered to their homes in celebration of Yuletide. But York dismissed this counsel. "To sacrifice these men I cannot do," he said. "Death is preferable to such dishonor." Ordering the drawbridge lowered, he led his men over the moat and galloped into the woods. Outnumbered three to one, he fought valiantly and fell at the head of his troops. York's son seventeen-year-old Edmund, Earl of Rutland, escaped the melee and tried to reach sanctuary. He was almost there, only a few yards away on Wakefield Bridge, when Lord Clifford caught up with him. Rutland, unarmed, begged for his life, but Clifford cried, "By God's blood, thy father slew mine, and so I will do thee and all thy kin!" and thrust his sword into the boy's heart. The Earl of Salisbury died the next day, but how, no one was sure.

"My father escaped the slaughter but was captured during the night by one of Trollope's men. He was taken to Pontefract Castle. All we know is that he pleaded hard for his life, offering a huge ransom, but he died there. Whether he was beheaded or"—John swallowed hard—"or murdered, we cannot say."

I took a long, unsteady breath as I watched him sitting on the edge of the bed, his head in his hands. After a while, he lifted stricken eyes to me. "There is more."

I looked at him, stunned. How could there be more? Deceit, treachery, fighting during the sacred season, death by ambush, the murder of an unarmed boy . . .

"Dear God," I whispered, "what more can there be?"

John leapt to his feet in a sudden motion, turned eyes on me that blazed with fury. Startled, I took a step back. "Clifford cut off their heads and took them to Marguerite, who had them nailed to the gates of York. Marguerite demanded, laughing, that a paper crown be placed upon the duke's head, since he would be king."

I shrank back in horror, a hand to my mouth. To dishonor the fallen—men who had died valiantly in battle—I couldn't comprehend a thing so vile! By her actions, Marguerite had broken all the rules of engagement. Never, ever, even in my darkest nightmare, had I envisioned her capable of such sacrilege, such incredible cruelty. Now it was war *à outrance*—war to the knife, and the knife to the hilt. I felt suddenly weak. I reached out for the bedpost and let myself down to the bed. Raising bewildered eyes to John's haggard face, I opened my mouth to speak, but no words came. Overnight the world had changed. Nothing would ever be the same again.

Dimly I heard John turn on his heel and leave the room. He did not return for many hours that day, and I learned that he had been riding across the moors, which were as bleak and desolate as his spirit. To my torment, words Thomas had spoken echoed in my mind: *As long as you're with me, I know I'm safe, John.* I closed my eyes on a breath. John had not been with Thomas, and Thomas had died. I feared his brother's words would haunt John for as long as he lived.

Eventually I shook off my terrible lethargy and dragged myself to check on John's mother. As I moved along, wrapped in my thoughts, soft voices floated to me. I halted and, retracing my steps and approaching on tiptoe, I followed the drifting voices into a small chamber behind me. They were all gathered together in a tight group on the floor near a charcoal brazier, Warwick's little Anne and Bella, now six and eight, and our twins, Annie and Izzie, who were nearly three. Nurse was nowhere in sight, though I knew she had not left them for long. They talked so quietly, I had to strain to hear them.

"They've gone to Heaven," Bella said.

"What's 'Heaven'?" our little Annie demanded.

I flattened myself against the stone wall as I listened, tears forming in my eyes, a terrible heaviness weighing down my heart.

"It's a place in the sky," Warwick's Anne answered, her voice reflecting a measure of pride that she knew the answer.

"What they do?" our Izzie demanded, curious.

Clearly Bella had never considered this, and the question took her by surprise. After a long moment, she said, "They just sit there."

"On chairs?" our Annie asked.

Bella frowned in thought. "I guess so. Or maybe thrones."

"Will Uncle Tom come back and make me laugh?" asked Warwick's Anne. She had loved Thomas best, and into my mind came an image of him twirling her around in a room glittering with filtered sun as she screeched with delight.

The soft patter of footsteps drew my attention down the passageway. Nurse was hurrying toward me, mumbling in distress, and I heard the word "privy." I placed my finger on my lips to hush the flow of her apology, and touched her arm in reassurance when she drew alongside.

"We forgot about the children," I whispered, blinking away my tears. Then, swallowing my anguish, I forced a smile on my lips and entered the chamber with Nurse.

"Uncle Thomas is waiting for you in Heaven, little Anne," I said, gathering the child to me. "One day he'll make you laugh again. When you go to Heaven yourself, he'll make you laugh as much as you wish, and all will be joyful and merriment. . . . I promise."

★   ★   ★

THE QUEEN WAS MARCHING SOUTH FOR BATTLE,
her troops looting, ravishing, and murdering along the way. Reports
flooded us of Northerners breaking open the pixes and throwing
out the Holy Sacrament, carrying off books, chalices, vestments,
and church ornaments of every kind, and murdering priests who
dared object. For Marguerite had promised her soldiers that whatever they could seize south of the River Trent was theirs.

Desperate, terrified people in her path fled their homes and
flocked to London for refuge, making a pitiful sight as they overflowed the churches and huddled together in the wintry streets,
cradling their babes, begging alms and bemoaning their loss of
hearth and home to any Londoner who had heart to listen. Everywhere I went, I was surrounded by the sound of tears and wailing
from all directions, so that it seemed the very walls of the city wept
with grief. My heart broke for the poor, some of whom had lost
sons forced to fight for Lancaster against their will. Like us, they
mourned the loss of those they had loved, but even worse, they
were reduced to beggarhood, for their homes were gone as well as
their breadwinners. Their plight tortured me day and night until I
devised a way to help them.

Nan and I met with the priests of St. Mary's and arranged for
food to be served to the destitute sheltering in the streets of Dowgate. Our efforts proved so successful that we met with many more
priests from churches throughout the city over the next few days.
When we put out calls for straw pallets, Londoners brought them
to us by the cartload. We delivered these to the churches and then
asked for donations of coarse dark bread of barley and rye. Again
people rallied to our cry, delivering them to us at the Erber by foot,
horse, and cart. Since we had little ready gold, we placed orders for
weak ale at all the London inns and taverns, and hired cooks of the
London houses to prepare barrels of potage with the promise of
future payment. The establishments readily gave us credit.

I was deeply moved by the gratitude of the people we helped.
Men and women, young and old, in rags, missing teeth or limbs,

smothered our hands and the hems of our skirts with kisses and sent a litany of blessings after us: "God bless the Nevilles!" they cried, and, "May the Lord keep the Earl of Warwick, the savior of England, and all his kin!" and, "God bless the House of York, for without York, we are lost, lost!"

Except for the children and John, of whom I saw little in these days, the Erber was devoid of solace for me. Memories swirled through its halls and passageways, of the earl, whom I had loved as a father, and of Thomas, the brother I'd never had. The work I did for the poor gladdened me, for it occupied my mind and gave me release from the Erber, returning me exhausted at the end of the day, so that I did not dwell on the countess and Maude, who no longer slept but sat staring listlessly out the windows with unseeing eyes, as if expecting their husbands to return home from the grave. Of them both, it was Countess Alice whom I pitied most, for Maude had youth and a future, while the countess had only memories.

It pained me how sorrow had aged John's mother beyond recognition. Her once-rosy cheeks hung gaunt and pale, and weight poured off her limbs so that her clothes hung loose on her frame, and her hands resembled those of a skeleton.

Though I was weary, sleep did not often find me in these days. Each night I lay beside John, tracing the lines of his handsome face with my finger, lightly so as not to awaken him. Laying my palm lightly on his heart, I felt its rhythmic beat. That he was able to rest comforted me, for he would need his strength if it came to battle. When this black thought descended upon me, I'd take a candle and light my way to the chapel. Sometimes I found comfort there, but sometimes the tiny chapel seemed too confining for the breadth of my appeal to God, and as morning broke, I left the Erber and made my way to the more spacious church of St. Mary's to light more candles and offer more prayers.

On one of these sleepless nights that followed Wakefield, craving fresh night air, I arose from bed and stole down the tower steps to go to the river. Sometimes merely gazing at the brilliant starry vastness where God resided in His Heavens helped ease my soul.

But I was startled to find the countess hovering at the foot of the staircase that led out of the keep. "I came . . . for something . . . I lost," she said in a strange voice, with an odd, vacant smile. "But I . . . I can't remember what it is. . . . I only know I can't live without it. . . . 'Tis something precious . . . but . . . but I don't know what it is. . . ."

I realized that she walked in her sleep, and what she sought could never be found. A line from Aeschylus came to me: *Even in our sleep, pain, which cannot forget, falls drop by drop upon the heart.* Hot tears rolled down my cheeks and splashed my hands as I led her back to her bedchamber and gave her over into the care of her dozing servant.

As for Maude, she proved inconsolable. "Life is a war, so why can't I just die?" she said one day, pushing away the broth I brought her, her voice a barely audible whisper. I placed my arms around her shoulder tenderly, smoothed her fair hair, and laid a kiss on her pale brow. I understood her despair, for Thomas was the second husband she had buried, and she had no children to laugh around her in her darkness. The Erber, emptied of Thomas's merry jesting and laughter, seemed an unbearably silent place, even for me. But soon Maude would leave for Tattershall Castle to be with her jovial uncle. Once she was away from memories, I felt sure, healing would begin.

Meanwhile, since London's mayor was a Lancastrian, Warwick and John had much to do to keep the city under control, while also gathering up a new army to replace the one lost at Wakefield. Men galloped in and out all day long, bearing news. Led by John and Warwick, the council chambers at the Erber and Westminster Palace filled with the harsh harangue of male voices arguing policy and strategy. During these bleak days for York, one of Warwick's most vital tasks was to reassure his foreign allies that the Yorkist cause still lived. He dispatched letters to his friends Philip of Burgundy and the Duke of Milan, and also to the Pope, in care of my uncle in Rome, whom he designated his papal ambassador. That his friends did not desert him upon the death of the Duke of York and the rout of the Yorkist army attested to his reputation and prestige throughout Europe. Loss and danger were all around us, and no one could predict what the future would bring, but we had Warwick, and so we still had hope.

At this time of disaster, however, I gained a new insight into Warwick's heart, one that did not please me. I was passing his council chamber as he stood dictating a letter to the Pope. Distinctly, so that I could not doubt what came to my ears, I heard him refer to the deaths of his father and brother as "the murder of my kin." Shocked, I halted in my steps. The earl and Thomas—how could they be mere "kin"? *They were his father, his brother!*

Gathering my composure, I resumed my steps. But this I knew I would never forget.

NOTHING MARGUERITE HAD DONE IN THE PRE-vious decade alienated her from the people as did her actions at Wakefield. This was no rabble that had died there, but the noblest blood of England—the most honorable and patriotic. Common decency had demanded their dead bodies be treated with respect. York had lost to Marguerite, aye, but not because he was no match for her or because she was more clever. He had lost because he was not as ruthless as she. He had been a white knight fighting a black queen, a native son battling a foreign intruder. And the people came over to York as they had never done before.

Yet even now, even after the queen's ghastly doings at Wakefield, John urged Warwick to try to gain an honorable peace agreement with the Lancastrians and put an end to the fighting. "For the sake of the poor devils of this land who must fight and die for us, we owe them to set aside our own feelings and give them peace, if peace is attainable," John said to me one night, adding after a pause, "And for poor Henry's sake, too, and for the oaths we took to him before God."

But Marguerite's ears were deaf. She was already planning a triumphal march on London, where she meant to deal with Warwick as she'd dealt with the Duke of York. Henry was to be rescued, and then she and her favorites—Somerset, Clifford, and the Percies of

Northumberland—would divide the spoils and rule as they saw fit. The specter of another battle loomed so darkly over us that when John entered our chamber with a smile one day, I cried out, "My love, if there is good news, I beg you to tell me!"

"There's been a battle at Mortimer's Cross. Edward of March won! He checked the advance of the Lancastrians Jasper Tudor and the Earl of Wiltshire—and he did it without Warwick's arm! By this victory Edward has borne out the promise I foresaw in him."

Oh, how good it felt to see that smile I so loved! I threw myself into his arms and covered his face, neck, and hair with wild kisses and tears of joy. Over a celebration of spiced wine and the hot rye bread and coil of sausage that John loved, as we sat lounging on cushions by the fire, I learned what had transpired, and what a splendid tale it proved to be!

"On Sunday, Candlemas Day, the portent of three suns was seen in the sky."

Startled, I sat erect. "Three suns? I've never heard of such a thing. . . . Weren't they frightened?"

"Indeed they were. The sign created confusion and alarm in the Yorkist ranks. The men thought it an evil omen and took it to mean the terrible conflict of the king and the queen and the Duke of York, which had resulted in the captivity of the king, the flight of the queen, and the death of the duke. They saw it as their defeat. But March turned this around and claimed it auspicious. 'Have no fear,' he told them. 'The three suns betoken the Holy Trinity and our victory! Therefore be heartened and in the name of Almighty God let us go forward against our enemies.' "

"How old is he now?" I asked, pondering his wisdom.

"Nineteen," John replied. "He was outnumbered by Marguerite's army, yet he still won the battle. They say Edward is taking the sun as his emblem along with the rose."

"The three suns may have been a good omen for Edward of March," I said with a happy heart. "And Edward of March is a good omen for England."

"I do believe he'll make a worthy king, God willing," John replied.

"What about Wiltshire and King Henry's brother, Jasper Tudor? Do they live?"

"Tudor escaped. . . . Wiltshire fled the scene before battle." John was unable to resist a smile. I gave a giggle and shook my head, savoring this light moment offered us by England's great coward.

In a change of tone, John said gravely, "For the rest, Edward dealt with his father's murderers as they had dealt with his father—" He fell silent, and his mouth worked with emotion. I knew he was thinking of the earl and Thomas. I averted my eyes until he was able to speak again.

"Three thousand Lancastrians died at Mortimer's Cross. Jasper's father, Owen Tudor, was beheaded in the marketplace at Hereford. His head was placed on a pike, and then a madwoman combed his hair and washed away the blood on his face."

The thought struck me that this woman had loved Tudor, and grief had turned her mad. For now I knew the power of grief. Pity flooded me.

John's voice interrupted my dismal thoughts. "Tudor never believed he was actually going to die. Not even when he saw the headsman or when they stripped him to his doublet. Even then he expected pardon, for he'd played no true role in the conflict. Not until the collar of his red velvet doublet was ripped off did he realize he was going to die. Then he said, 'Now that head which used to lie on Queen Catherine's lap, shall lie on a pike.' And went to his death bravely."

"So ends the handsomest man in England, who rose from Groom of the Wardrobe to wed a queen . . . and many another who took no willing part in this conflict."

Our eyes met, and we clinked our goblets together. "To all the fallen, both Lancastrian and Yorkist . . . may they find eternal rest," John said quietly.

ON A STORMY DAY IN FEBRUARY, A WEEK BEFORE the Feast of St. Valentine, scouts galloped into London to inform Warwick that Marguerite was closing in on London. Leaving the city in John's hands, he immediately led his army north to meet her. One morning, I found John in the great council chamber at Westminster Palace, alone, pondering a missive in his hand. He was lost in thought.

"From Warwick?" I asked anxiously.

He laid down the letter with a sigh. "I fear I must go to him, Isobel. He needs me, whether he knows it or not." Rising from the table, he went to the window and gazed at the river. I watched him run a hand through his hair, a gesture I took for weariness and uncertainty. Again I wondered about my husband, how he really felt about his legendary brother, whom the world hailed as another Caesar. I went to him and laid a hand on his sleeve.

"And why do you feel Warwick has need of you, when he asks not for your help?"

"On the way to St. Albans, scouts reached him with differing reports of Marguerite's whereabouts, so that he knows not where she is." John heaved an audible breath. "I know not why, but I sense that something is wrong. . . . Warwick is out of his league. He may be admirable on the seas, but despite his own belief in himself, he is no great soldier on land."

"But what will happen to London in your absence? 'Tis too dangerous to have it unguarded."

"I'll leave Sir John Wenlock in charge. He's Warwick's protégé, completely devoted to him, a good man and trustworthy. . . . He can manage things till I get back."

"Go to Warwick, then, and doubt not that he will be grateful to have you at his side, for though he'll not admit it, he holds your counsel in high regard, my love. Nan has told me so."

He turned and looked at me, his eyes soft. He bent down and kissed my brow. "I shall leave at cock's crow," he said.

"John . . . can you send Sir Thomas Malory to report back to me as soon as—" I broke off, finding the words difficult to utter. "—If—after—you give battle?"

He looked at me sharply. Reading my great fear, he drew me to him and laid his cheek against my hair. "Aye, my angel."

In the courtyard by the mounting block, I took my leave of him the next morning in the light of a bleak gray dawn. It was the six-teenth of February, two days after the Feast of St. Valentine. Gazing up at the sullen sky, I offered a silent prayer for John's safe return and watched him depart with Rufus beside him, riding his own mare. But the sight that had brought me laughter so many times no longer had the power to do so.

As John had promised, he sent Sir Thomas Malory to report to me. He arrived on the eighteenth of February, and it was ill tidings he brought.

"The second battle of St. Albans, fought yesterday morning"—he hesitated—"ended in defeat for York, my lady. The Earl of War-wick has fled to Calais."

I bowed my head and gave pause for a silent prayer of thanks to the Lord for Warwick's escape. But Malory had said nothing of John.

"And—and my lord husband?"

Malory took a moment to reply. "M'lady, I have saved for last the news I had no wish to bring you. . . . My lord of Montagu is captured."

I bit my lip to stifle the cry that rose from my heart. He gave me his hand and guided me to a chair. As I stared at him, my mind in chaos, Malory broke the rest of the news.

"The Earl of Warwick stopped in London on his way to Sand-wich and Calais to apprise Duchess Cecily of his defeat at St. Al-bans. Fearful of Marguerite, she persuaded him to bear her small children, the lords Richard and George, to Calais with him this very night."

"What about Nan and the children?"

"Sir John Wenlock is to take them to Calais as soon as possible. Warwick believes you have nothing to fear from Marguerite and has made no arrangement for you to leave with the rest of the fam-ily." He regarded me gravely.

I nodded in assent. "Aye, I agree with my lord of Warwick."

"That is good, for he has left a task in your hands that concerns my lord of Montagu."

My mind was a mixture of hope and fear as I waited for the old knight to remove a missive from inside his tunic and hand it to me. "My lady, the Earl of Warwick gave me this ere he fled, and bade me bring it to you with instructions that you lose no time taking it to the queen, now that disaster has befallen York. In this lies Lord Montagu's only hope." I accepted it with stiff fingers. The missive, addressed to Marguerite, bore Warwick's seal, and before Malory took his leave of me, he explained its contents.

"Have Geoffrey saddle Rose!" I cried to the sentry at the door. "Find Ursula! Fetch the children! We leave immediately for St. Albans!" I tore out of the chamber.

Seventeen

TOWTON, 1461

TAKING THE TWINS AND LEAVING LIZZIE BEHIND
in her nurse's care, I galloped north toward St. Albans, accompanied by Ursula and a dozen men-at-arms. But the picture Malory
had given me of what had transpired seemed incomplete, and many
unanswered questions preyed on my mind. *How did York lose this
battle, when they have won every other battle so brilliantly, even against the
heaviest of odds? What went wrong?*

"I can make no sense of it!" I said to Ursula as we rode together.

She said nothing. I threw her a sharp look and realized there
was something she kept from me. "You know what happened,
don't you? Your father told you, didn't he?"

Silence.

"Ursula, I have to know!"

"I shouldn't . . . mustn't—I promised I wouldn't!"

But she did, for we were closer now than sisters, and there was
nothing we could keep from one another. Filling in the details her
father had omitted, she gave me a full account of the disaster that

had taken place. "You must never repeat what I'm about to tell you! My father owes his freedom to my lord of Warwick, and never would he wish to offend."

"It dies with me, dear Ursula. I vow it on my father's soul."

As Ursula related, Warwick and John had argued. Warwick had decided to await Marguerite at St. Albans and fixed his camp on a field called No Man's Land, fortifying it with many guns and a load of curious devices called caltrops, as well as nets and shields bristling with nails, which he hid in the ground. Mortified by his brother's choice of location, John had argued for a change in the positioning of the camp. "You've left your rear open to attack, brother!" he'd exclaimed, shocked.

Always sensitive to criticism, Warwick had replied heatedly, "No one attacks from the rear."

"You've gone to such length to protect your front, you're forcing Marguerite to attack your rear!" John had shot back.

"Who are you to question my judgment, I, the hero of England?" Warwick had bristled, squaring his shoulders.

"God's Blood, Dick, Father always put his trust in my advice— not because he cared less for you, but because there are a few things he knew I understood better than anyone else, and one of those is strategy."

Warwick relented. "Very well, then. If you insist, we'll adjust the position tomorrow."

"But you've no time to lose! It lies unprotected tonight."

"No one attacks at night," Warwick flung back in disgust. " 'Tis dishonorable!"

John had looked at him as if he'd taken leave of his senses. "Has she not proven to you with our father's head that she cares not a whit for honor? You can't afford to take the chance!"

Warwick had shrugged his broad shoulders dismissively. "In any case, there may not be time."

"How close is she?" John demanded.

"I don't know . . . exactly. The scouts are not back yet."

John had stared at his brother with disbelief for a long moment. "For God's sake, man, send out others! You've got to find out where she is. But you must begin adjusting your position—*now*. If Marguerite catches us here, she'll destroy us!"

Warwick refused. A compromise was reached. When the scouts returned, if time permitted, the camp's position would be readjusted. A scout came back later that night to report she was eleven miles away.

"If we begin right away, we can be done by daybreak," John said.

Warwick gave a nod of assent.

"I wish you had started earlier, brother!" John said as he left to supervise the change of position, still troubled by Warwick's unprotected flank.

But Marguerite had not been as far away as the scout had reported. On learning that Warwick was at St. Albans, and that his flank lay open to attack, she pushed on under cover of darkness and arrived in St. Albans at three the next morning. Warwick, caught in the midst of his preparations, was taken by surprise, completely unprepared. Utter confusion broke out in the Yorkist camp. In the darkness, Warwick's guns proved more dangerous to his own men than to the enemy, and many were killed by his own side. After Marguerite's victory, the town and abbey of St. Albans were thoroughly pillaged by her rampaging troops, who were giddy with victory. Not even the beggars were spared. Three thousand men died that night, mostly Yorkists, but only two Lancastrian nobles fell. One was Lord Ferrers of Groby, the lord Elizabeth Woodville had ensnared as husband.

This time Elizabeth Woodville's sad tidings brought me not a moment's glee. It was merely another sorrow to lay with the rest. *Pray God, I'll be spared her fate.* My hand strayed to Warwick's missive, which I'd tucked into my bosom in search of reassurance. "Thank you, Ursula. Now I understand everything. But I'll not dwell on misfortune while there is hope."

AT THE FAR REACHES OF MARGUERITE'S CAMP, I ordered Geoffrey and the others to return to London for their own safety. He argued with me as hard as he dared, but I stood firm. I cared too much for him and for each of these lives to place them in Marguerite's hands. Then, girding myself with resolve, I nudged Rose forward.

Night had fallen, and campfires burned before us as far as the eye could see, glittering like stars in a dark firmament. Men were clustered around them, some warming their hands, others roasting meat on the spit or drinking and making merry with their female company. The aroma of cooked meat filled the air. I went up to a group of sentries and asked to be taken to the queen's tent. One man, picking his teeth with a splinter of wood, merely pointed a thumb to someone else farther up, a barrel-chested man-at-arms, evidently his commander.

The man drew himself up to his awesome height and approached me. "Who are you?" he demanded fiercely in the thick twang of the Northern men.

"My name I will not give," I replied, summoning the haughty dignity of rank to garner his respect.

"Your business, then?"

"My business is urgent, and it is with the queen. 'Tis not for your ears."

He scrutinized me with beady eyes, his gaze moving between Ursula, the children, and me, and back again. After a long moment, I said, injecting a measure of disgust into my tone, "What? Are you afraid of women and small children?"

The man gave a nod. "All right, the royal tent's straight ahead. Ye canna miss it."

I made my way through the camp, followed by the tittering of ruffians and much frank and lecherous assessment of my form. Then, suddenly, in the distance, someone called my name.

"Lady Montagu—"

A man with curly brown hair came running up to me out of the shadowy light of the campfires. I drew up my palfrey, and waited, puzzled. *What friendly face could possibly know me in this place of enemies?* The man reached my side and looked up. With pleasant surprise, I found it was William Norris.

"My lady, 'tis good to see you again," he said, panting.

"And you, William. I've wondered how you've been in these years since we last met."

"I thank you for your concern, my lady. . . . Have you come to see the queen?"

"I have."

"Aye, I heard Lord Montagu was taken prisoner."

I swallowed thickly.

"I hope the queen grants your request for his pardon. . . . He is a valiant knight. You made a worthy choice . . . Isobel."

He said my name so softly that it was barely audible, but I caught the tenderness in his tone. Such, then, were the men who had died in these battles of York and Lancaster: men who loved, men of goodness, men who had fought because honor and their lords commanded it. Tears stung my eyes, and I bit my lip against the emotion that flooded me. "These are sorry times for us all, William. I regret the death of your lord Duke Humphrey."

"He was a fine man," he said.

A silence fell between us. Some ruffian called out drunkenly, "Hey, Norris, give 'er to me if ye dinna want her! I'll know what to do wi' 'er." I heard guffaws. William looked at me gravely. "May I escort you to the queen?"

"That would be a kindness," I replied.

He took my bridle and led my restless palfrey forward.

AT MARGUERITE'S TENT, MY WAY WAS BARRED again by another sentinel. As William reasoned with him for admittance, the flap was pulled back and a man emerged. I swallowed as I looked upon the face of the Butcher of England. Lord Clifford's truculent brown eyes glared up at me with hatred. "You have no business here!" he spat, and whirled on William. "You, too! Begone." William cast me a look of agonized helplessness as he made his obeisance and withdrew.

"You are mistaken," I replied. "I bear tidings of a most urgent nature for the queen."

"Urgent to yourself, no doubt. Be assured the queen has no de-sire to see you. You may leave." He pointed the way I had come.

Another voice came from inside the tent, and a man stepped out. It was Somerset. He froze in his steps when he saw me, and a rush of color flooded his cheeks. After a moment, he recovered. "Lady Montagu—"

I was surprised to hear him address me by John's new title, awarded by York's parliament, and I softened somewhat before him, for he seemed changed. Certainly he was nothing like Clifford. I searched for the word that eluded me, and it came at last: *humbled*. Time seemed to have humbled Somerset.

"I'll handle this, Clifford." He waited until Clifford disappeared back into the tent. "Here, allow me to assist you from your palfrey," he said, offering his hand as gallantly as any true knight.

I gripped it tightly and alighted. "I thank you, my lord Somer-set." I looked up into his face and met his eyes. But I looked away hastily at the disquiet I saw there. He led me into the tent and an-nounced me to Marguerite, who was pacing as she dictated a letter to a scrivener. The tent surprised me with its spacious opulence. It bore every comfort: a large silver coffer, many candles, a table covered in damascene with a pitcher of wine and a plate laden with apples, a large bed covered in blue satin embroidered with the prince's insignia of swans and feathers, several gilded camp stools, even a settee. Many lords stood about Marguerite, and in a carved chair beside the scrivener sat Henry.

She swung around when she heard my name, and Henry smiled. "Welcome, my dear—"

Marguerite didn't let him finish. "She is not welcome!" She turned to me in fury. "I told you last time never to come to me again for a favor! The nerve of you to seek me out, after all you have done to make me suffer, you and your kin—the damned and contemptible Nevilles, who made their alliance with the Devil himself, York!"

I stared at her in astonishment. A wild look lit her eyes, and she trembled from head to toe.

"Have you forgotten his deceptions—that falsely sworn traitor whom my lord King Henri pardoned time and again? That malicious traitor who—against all the oaths he swore—put forward a false claim to the throne and spread lies about us to provoke our subjects into fighting against us? And, *mort dieu*, all this while declaring he intended us no hurt, but merely sought the welfare of the realm. That liar and slanderer! But now his venomous purposes stand revealed for all the world to see! York was after the throne from the first—he lied and killed for it! As God has shown, we are the true monarchs, and God Himself has seen fit to punish York and those that rose up with him against their oaths!

"Now you come here expecting me to pardon your husband—a traitor who, with the connivance of his foul brother Warwick, slandered my name, impugned my honor, called me *bitch* and our royal prince *bastard*? Who drove me and my child into the forest at Northampton, and into the hands of robbers? Have you any idea what I suffered there? God alone knows! Aye, God"—she pointed a finger up to Heaven—"God helped me to escape them. Those ruffians fell into an argument over their booty, and He sent me a fourteen-year-old boy to help me ride away with him, all three of us on one horse!

"We fled through the forest. Do you know what it is to be friendless and alone in the forest, at the mercy of robbers and every hideous evildoer who hides there? One of these accosted me—*très hideux et horrible en l'aspect*—and the ruffian prepared to take advantage of us. But I knew what to do! With the help of God it came to me—I confided to that *hideux* man our rank and placed my child in his hands and said, 'Save the son of your king!' He proved loyal and we reached Wales—*oui*, God helped me to survive all this, and has given me victory over my mortal enemies this day! Never will I forget or forgive what these foul Nevilles and Yorkists made us suffer. So there is your answer. Your husband dies!"

And with that she fell silent, glaring at me with a triumphant look that bespoke her own madness. A gentle voice broke the silence. "Nay, dear queen, John Neville is a good man. He was my chamberlain. I pardon him—"

Marguerite whirled on Henry. "You pardon everyone! That is precisely the problem! You shall remain quiet, my lord, because they all die, all of them. Not only the Neville, but also the others to whom you promised pardon, your captors who held you while we fought—Lord Bonville, Lord Berners, and Sir Thomas Kyriell."

"They didn't hold me. They protected me."

Marguerite ignored Henry and turned back to me. "This time they have gone too far. We shall crush them all—all the voices against us shall die. Then we shall rule as before."

"Nay, Marguerite, dear wife," said Henry, rising from his chair. "That is not the way. I promised them pardon, and we had a good time together, singing and laughing under the apple tree—"

"Henri, sit down and be quiet before I dispatch you to a monastery."

"I like monasteries. 'Tis peaceful in—"

Breathless with rage, she glowered at him. He dropped back into his seat and sat quietly, mumbling to himself under his breath. Then she turned her wild eyes on me. "Go now—" She pointed angrily to the entry flap.

"My queen, I fear you have misjudged my intent in coming here today. I come not to seek a favor, but to parley one life of value against another."

Marguerite hesitated. "What do you mean?"

"The missive I bring informs more eloquently than I, my liege—" I held it out.

Marguerite nodded to Somerset. I placed the missive into his hand, and he bent his head to read. When he looked up, his eyes held an anxious expression. He came and knelt before Marguerite. She frowned in puzzlement as she gazed down on him.

"My queen, they hold my brother Edmund prisoner in Calais. If you execute Neville, Warwick threatens to slay Edmund. I beseech you for mercy and pray you to grant pardon of life to John Neville so that my brother may live."

The queen stood motionless as fury, tenderness, and fear battled for supremacy. After a long moment, she said, "Rise, loyal Henri of Somerset. If this capture of Edmund can be proven true, John Neville will not be executed with the others."

I curtseyed low and withdrew. Somerset escorted me outside. We stood looking at one another for a moment. "Where do you go now?" he inquired.

"I know not . . . maybe Eversleigh . . . maybe Bisham. . . ."

"You cannot ride alone. You will need protection." He motioned to the sentry and murmured some instructions, and the man hurried off. I heard him calling for Ursula and the horses.

"Isobel," Somerset said in an odd yet gentle voice, taking my hand, "there is something I wish to say to you ere you go."

I looked at him in surprise.

He drew a thick breath. "I was wrong about you. That wild quality which drew me to you, 'twas not recklessness, but courage. You are the most courageous woman I have ever known, Isobel. I owe you an apology for my discourteous—nay, my insolent— behavior of years past. I regret it."

I was unnerved by the change in him and stood there baffled. "I don't know what to say—"

"Say you forgive me."

I wavered, trying to comprehend what I was hearing. Then I realized that here before me stood a man facing the harsh realities of war. "I forgive you," I said softly.

Somerset kissed my hand and regarded me strangely. "God keep you, Isobel."

The sentry returned with Ursula and the horses. Little Annie and Izzie were babbling with delight, excited about something, but what it was I did not know. Then I heard barking, and Rufus bounded to me out of the darkness and circled my skirts, giddy with joy. I bent down and gave him welcome. He must have fled into the woods during the fighting and returned to camp in search of John. When I looked up again, William Norris had appeared with a party of men, and my horse.

Somerset took Rose's reins and helped me mount my palfrey. He passed me the reins and stood looking up at me for a long moment, his hand over mine. "Fear not," he said under his breath.

"John Neville is safe. You have my word." He threw Norris a glance. "Take good care of her!" He gave Rose a slap on her rump, and she leapt forward.

When I looked back, he was gone.

I MADE MY WAY TO BISHAM LISTLESSLY, MY BODY engulfed in tides of weariness and despair, my mind awash with tortured thinking. Was John cold or hungry? Was he in pain? Would he survive? William Norris was the perfect squire, courteous and attentive but unobtrusive, his demeanor offering no hint of his own feelings for me. Ursula and I spoke little, and chose our words carefully when we did. The only laughter came from the children, who chatted merrily with Norris and asked questions of the other men and even of Rufus trotting along beside us. We passed through many small towns on our way north, and I found the journey as arduous as when I had first come to court with Sœur Madeleine, perhaps because then, as now, I nursed an aching heart.

I was relieved that John was safe, but little else offered much solace. King Henry's gentle face came and went before me as we climbed hills and descended into meadows. . . . Poor Henry. The events of the past months had unhinged his mind. A mild, simple, endearing man ordained a king in some jest of Fortune, he was no ruler, but a pathetic shadow of a king who passed without resistance into the hands of enemies and rescuers alike. He preferred mercy to justice but, mild and simple, he could give his land neither, for his actions were dictated by his wife.

My hands tensed around my reins. The half-mad smile on Marguerite's face as she had ranted about the Duke of York had told me more than I ever wished to know. I thought of the beautiful and learned young woman I had first met. In Marguerite, cruel Fortune had played yet another jest on England. It had coupled a monk-king totally lacking in ambition with a proud, willful, and boundlessly ambitious consort, who wielded power ruthlessly and arrogantly. Her reach for absolute authority had torn England into two and turned her into a demented she-wolf whose bloody fangs could be appeased only by yet more blood. Her mind, like her husband's, had become unhinged by events, but her insanity, unlike Henry's, bore a dark and brooding quality.

I thought about Somerset, too. A strange sadness came and went. He was no longer the same man who had accosted me in the passageways of Westminster, but as to what had engendered the change, I did not ponder. As I had witnessed with Marguerite, life had a way of changing people.

If there was beauty in the landscape, I didn't see it. We passed a woman who had covered herself with a sheet to keep out the cold wind, and a peasant in coarse cloth whose toes stuck out through the rags that wrapped his feet. We passed others working in the fields whose rough mittens, with worn-out fingers, were covered in mud. We passed beggars pleading for alms: one-legged beggars; one-armed beggars; one-eyed beggars; beggars with terrible, oozing sores. The wars had created a plethora of beggars.

For luncheon we rested our horses in Little King's Hill, at a tavern in the market square, just past the churchyard, near a dyer's shop releasing noisome waters from its vats. A few people sat eating. With a wary eye on my Lancastrian guard bearing the insignia of King Henry's white swan, they conveyed without commentary the reports they had heard. Though they spoke in low tones, I heard their conversation and wished I had not. Marguerite's little prince, Edward, resplendent in purple velvet and gold, had presided over the trial of Bonville, Berners, and Kyriell, the lords who had offered to remain behind to act as Henry's bodyguards while the battle raged and to whom Henry had promised pardon. The king's pardon was set aside, and the seven-year-old prince passed judgment of death on them. Then he watched their beheadings.

Across the street, a butcher came out of his shop with a cage of chickens. He removed one from the group and very methodically axed its head from its body and flung the decapitated trunk into the air. The hapless corpse flew some distance before dropping lifeless to the ground. Behind him, a cloud of flies disturbed by the commotion settled down again to banquet on a slab of meat hung to dry. My stomach clenched with full force.

At Bisham, the reeve received us with great joy, but when he learned that our escort was Lancastrian, he fell quiet, though he made them welcome with ale and sausages and dark rye bread, as I instructed. But the next morning, when I came to bid William Norris farewell, I found the reeve and some of Bisham's younger female servants gathered around the party of Lancastrians, laughing and making merry. The reeve even offered to ride with them through town, to make sure they received safe passage out of Bisham, which was deeply loyal to Warwick. "Good that you came thro' after dark," he told them as he mounted his horse, "or that swan on your livery might have caused yer a spat o' trouble."

I went up to William Norris. I wanted to wish him a safe journey, peace, and a good and long life, but I did not. Our fates lay in the hands of capricious Fortune, and if he prospered, perhaps that meant that John would not. And so I merely thanked him and bid him Godspeed.

MOST OF BERKSHIRE HAD GONE OVER TO YORK now, and the danger of threat from Lancastrians was past, so I rested well in Bisham, especially since I was reunited with my babe, Lizzie. From there the following week I made my way north to Burrough Green in Cambridgeshire, where I was born. I needed the comfort of my old home. The fortified manor house I had inherited from my father dated from Saxon times, and while it was not designed to keep out an army, it was certainly strong enough to protect us from the bands of marauders that posed the greatest threat.

Soon after we arrived, I left the household behind and went to the empty east wing, where I used to spend so much of my time as a child, running through its long halls and hiding from my nurse in its many nooks and crannies. Taking the familiar narrow passageway with a ceiling of multiple arches covered in red brick, I passed many of the chambers it serviced before pausing in front of a nook where a coffer used to stand. Laying my hands over the redbrick wall, I pushed gently. The false wall gave way, and I stood in a small room lit only by a narrow pane of window and the light that seeped through the floorboards of the room above. Before me, a rope dangled from a large round metal hook in the ceiling. I shut the door. As a child, I used to leap for the end of the rope; now I took it into my hands. Dropping my gown, I caught the rope and began to swing as I'd done when I was small. Twirling, twisting, I gathered force, and it seemed to me that I flew through the air with the freedom of a bird, and I was a girl again, running through the long grass, shrieking with delight, chased by my nurse. The world turned around me, and time took shape and form, and became a thing of substance. I felt its sensuous touch on me like silk, melting the years away. Again I heard my nurse's complaint to my father: *She ran away and almost fell into a well. She's too reckless for her own good. Let me tame her with the rod!* And my father's reply: *Nay, there's a fine line between recklessness and courage, and she'll need all her courage to get through life.* Then a magical thing happened. I saw myself beside me, a laughing child of six, twirling and twisting and whirling on the rope in imitation of each movement I made, and from that child's face as she laughed and twirled, I saw that time was touching her too, for she changed as I gazed, and innocence melted away, and then she was no more.

During the next weeks, I pored over the household accounts and carried on with my daily chores of household management. Tallying the candles, doling out the rushes, and darning the woolens, I struggled to manage expenses carefully, for there was never enough money. At night I worked on John's cloak, embroidering more griffins so that it now had a wide border of them around the collar, and when I finally grew weary, I hugged it to me and fell asleep.

"Are we poor?" little Izzie asked me one day as Annie and Lizzie pressed close. I gathered my children to me and explained as best I could that we had to be careful until Papa came home again. "But don't worry, poppets," I said. "Mama will make sure you never go hungry."

In these days I listened avidly to all tidings brought my way by those who passed though Burrough Green. With Warwick's defeat and Sir John Wenlock's flight to Calais, and with him the departure of the Duchess of York and Warwick's family, there remained no one in London to urge the city to remain true to York.

"Yet despite this," a visiting Kentish merchant told me, "and despite the rumors—no doubt put out by the queen—of the Earl of Warwick's capture and of Yorkist outrages by Edward of March's army marching on London, the city stands firm for York, and has barred its gates to her. All this despite the pleadings of the mayor and city magistrates, who are Lancastrian." He shook his head in wonder, and I poured him more wine. After a long sip, he leaned close and added, "The land would rather part with Henry, whom they love, than put up with his queen, whom they hate!"

A friar from London came next. "On February twenty-seventh London flung its gates wide to Edward of March!" he announced. "On March first he was proclaimed king with the blessing of the archbishop of Canterbury!" With a glad heart I listened to the rest of his tidings.

"They sang and danced around him—" The old man rose from his chair and, lifting his skirts, performed a little jig. *"Let us walk in a new vineyard,"* he sang in a high voice, mimicking what he had heard, *"and make a gay garden in the month of March with this fair white rose, the Earl of March—la-de-he, la-de-he!"* I laughed and refilled his wine.

One day a carpenter from York on his way south to seek work at St. Albans stopped at our doors to beg a night's shelter. "The queen has set up in York while she awaits to give battle," he said. With an anxious heart, I asked him, as he awaited his supper, if he knew anything of my lord husband.

" 'Tis said she holds Lord Montagu captive in the dungeon at York."

I knew I should give thanks that John lived, but a dungeon— "You may pour yourself more wine," I said heavily, and departed.

Days later, a minstrel arrived offering music for a night's shelter. "My lord of Warwick has returned to London with men and reinforcements for Edward of March. They go north to fight the rest of the queen's forces!" I served him a plate of mutton and potherbs, and had the servants bring him wine. Though he played his flute well and my spirits lifted somewhat, I was unsure of John's fate and found it hard to rejoice. The last battle awaited. The sword would decide who wore the crown. And York could not afford to lose.

ABRUPTLY, ON THE SUNNY MORNING OF THE FIRST day of April, as narcissus spread a yellow mantle across the fields, clarions sounded in the village. My breath caught in my throat. I ran to the window and peered into the distance, but I couldn't see anything, for the trees were budding into leaf. Then Rufus stood up and barked wildly—and at that moment, a pennant came into view for just a bare instant. It was all I needed, for it bore the emerald green and silver of John's griffin emblem. Screaming, I fled the room, frightening the servants. Seizing a stunned Annie and Izzie from the nook where they sat playing, I ran wildly from the house with my little ones under my arms, out the door, down the stony path, my hair flying.

At the head of his men, John saw me. Breaking loose from the others, he galloped to my side. Oblivious to his men, he slid from the saddle and whirled us around joyously before giving me a long, lingering kiss on the mouth.

Over dinner that evening, I learned there was much to celebrate in addition to John's release from captivity.

Edward of March had lost no time marching on the queen. On Palm Sunday, the nineteenth day of March, Lancaster and York clashed at Towton. Again, Warwick, reversing tradition, ordered his men to slay the lords and spare the commons. Hour after hour, for fourteen hours, in a raging blizzard, the two sides fought one another, wreaking carnage the likes of which England had never seen—and, God willing, would never see again! Tens of thousands of men died fighting, and it looked as though the battle would go to the Lancastrians when—out of the driving snow—the Duke of Norfolk rode up with his army! York emerged triumphant. Somerset escaped, but nearly all the other Lancastrian lords were slain, and the frozen ground on which their butchered bodies were strewn became a field of ice and blood. The queen and her son fled England. King Henry went into hiding. The Yorkists stood triumphant, and Edward of March, the Duke of York's gloriously handsome son, was now King of England!

Immediately after his victory, leaving Warwick to bury the thousands slain in the battle, Edward lost no time marching to York with one purpose in mind: to take down the agonized heads of his father, brother, uncle, and cousin Thomas from the city gates, and to punish the people of York, who had done nothing to stop Queen Marguerite, just as Lancaster had punished the town of Ludlow for not rising up against the Duke of York. Finding John safe in the castle prison at York, Edward had freed him. Then he had turned to his men and issued the order to destroy the city as if it were a foreign land—to smash it utterly, and with such cruelty that the punishment of York would live forever in men's minds.

"Edward shook with such fury as he issued his command that no one dared ask mercy for the hapless citizens," John said quietly. "So I did." He fell silent for a long moment.

"What did he say?"

Silence again. Then John replied, "He granted my plea." ·

I knew there was more to it than John was willing to relate to me, but whatever it was, he couldn't bear to tell me now, and I didn't press him.

John lifted his cup. "To peace," he said softly.

I lifted my cup and met his eyes. "To peace," I echoed, giddy with happiness. Laying my hand over his, I whispered, "And to love."

Eighteen

CORONATION, 1461

BUT PEACE HAD YET TO COME. SOMERSET HAD survived Towton. Taking refuge in several Northumbrian castles still loyal to the House of Lancaster, while Marguerite went to Scotland to seek aid against the House of York, he plagued the land. It fell to John, my valiant knight and England's brilliant military commander, to drive the Lancastrians out for good. I took my leave of him by the mounting block at Burrough Green. On the twenty-sixth of April, the day after our anniversary, he kissed me and our babes farewell and set out for the Scottish border. John gave me a lingering smile of tenderness before he turned Saladin and left the gate, followed by Rufus on his mare. I watched until he disappeared over the horizon. Soon messages arrived to inform me that he had relieved the Lancastrian siege of Carlisle, and his forays into Scotland had met with such success that the country had made a truce with the House of York.

Although I continued to worry for John's safety, my spirits lightened greatly since he had sent much good news. Our property, confiscated by Marguerite d'Anjou, was now restored to us, and in addition, Edward confirmed the barony of Montagu that the Duke of York's parliament had bestowed on John. Edward also conferred on John a grant of the gold-producing mine in Devon at a rent of a hundred and ten pounds a year, easing our money woes. Further, the king had evidenced his faith in his Neville relatives by sending his eight-year-old brother, Richard, to be raised at Warwick's castle of Middleham.

I was touched—but also annoyed—by John's fondness for the fatherless boy and his many visits to Middleham to supervise the child's knightly training.

"You have made four trips this month alone, John," I said as I helped undress him for a bath. "Why do you push yourself so hard? Others can teach Dickon the skills he needs for war. You should rest when given a chance, not undertake the arduous journey from the border to Middleham as often as you do, my sweet lord."

John had thrown me a sharp look. "Surely you don't resent the visits I make to the boy?"

I could not deny it. He had struck at the truth. I decided the time had come to speak of what troubled me. "Why don't you come to see me instead? Is it because I haven't been able to give you a son?" I asked in a small voice.

John's expression softened; he took me into his arms. "Isobel, Isobel . . . 'Tis not the reason I go so often to see Dickon. . . . God gives us all some work to do—if not great deeds, then small ones. A cup of water to one of His children. Nay—even less than that! A word of advice, something lent to another. A vexation patiently borne, or the fault of thoughtlessness by another repaired without their knowledge . . . Dickon has suffered much. He was born as our troubles with Lancaster began, and has known more violence and grief in his brief life than others many times his age. He has no father to guide him, and no mother to comfort him—" John broke off at the disloyal thought he'd spoken aloud. Yet it was the truth. John's aunt Cecily had borne a brood of children, but mother she was not. Since her husband's death, she'd shut herself up at her castle of Berkhamsted, where she prayed and fasted like a nun, as if she bore no responsibility to anyone but herself.

"The boy is in sore need of reassurance," he continued. "He lacks confidence in himself and is much hampered by his left-handedness, which makes the knightly arts more difficult for him." He tipped my chin so that I met his eyes. "God will recompense all a thousandfold, my sweet. Surely you see that?"

Swept with shame for my jealousy and for my own perceived failings as a woman, I nodded, recognizing the truth of what he said. How could I begrudge the boy love when by the tender age of eight he'd suffered so much—witnessed the horrors of Ludlow and endured the hardships of captivity, exile, and death? John's words opened my eyes and my heart, and from that moment forward, I took Dickon to me, as John did—as if he were our own son, in place of the little one we had lost.

Young Dickon's experiences had left their mark on him, and each time I saw him, the sadness in his gray eyes made me remember Ludlow, and wish to crush him in my arms and kiss away his pain, while his adoration of his brother Edward stirred a nerve deep within me. *All his life long, no matter how hard he strives, or what he achieves, Dickon will walk in his brother's shadow, just as my John walks in Warwick's.* I knew it with a certainty I didn't question, and so I tried, whenever I had the chance, to show him a mother's tenderness.

One evening, when Ursula's father, Sir Thomas Malory, visited Burrough Green, we took wine together in the solar.

"How fares the Countess of Salisbury?" he asked.

"Not well," I replied, an image of Countess Alice as I'd last seen her at Middleham filling my mind. Afflicted in both body and spirit, she lay bedridden, no longer able to speak or to recognize us. "I fear the countess is lost to this world."

The old knight murmured kind words about John's mother and fell silent. I poured more wine into his cup and changed the painful subject. "You were present when my lord husband was released from imprisonment in York. How exactly did it come to pass that Edward chose to pardon the citizens of York?"

Sir Thomas gave me his answer in storyteller fashion, as I imagine he wrote his tales.

"A splendid knight he is, my lord of Montagu . . . the finest. . . . There we all were, you see, citizens and knights, pressing around King Edward, and he, seated on his black horse, his handsome face pale as the moon as he gazed on the rotting heads of his valiant father and of Edmund, the brother he loved, and of the kindly Earl of Salisbury and his merry son Sir Thomas Neville, all these nailed to the gates, buzzing with flies and covered with maggots. 'Take them down!' he commanded. 'And send them to Pontefract to be reunited with their bodies for decent Christian burial!' He didn't say another word for a long time, but sat there still as death itself, staring at Micklegate Bar, and we thought that the end of the matter.

"Then he looked around him with a glittering eye and said, 'Burn this city, rob it to its bare walls, rape its women, and hang its men so no eyes dare live that did naught to take down my father's head in these three months since Yuletide!' And his voice was like the hiss of a snake, and everyone that gathered close around him, friend and foe alike, turned white as the clouds above their heads, and trembled to hear his words. No one dared ask the king to spare the city, lest he turn his black fury on them—none, that is, except my lord of Montagu. . . . He stepped forward and fell to a knee. He looked up at King Edward and said, 'Noble king, fair cousin and valiant conqueror, I beseech you to forgive the unkindness of the citizens of York, for they had no power nor might to withstand the bitch of Anjou and her evil hordes, and took no part in this horror, which was committed by a woman without honor or mercy before God or man. These are good people, your people, and given a chance to serve you, they shall not fail you, but shall prove themselves your most devoted subjects.' "

"The king gazed down on Lord Montagu's bowed head for a long time, and we quivered for Lord Montagu, everyone there who watched, for we were certain he would be smitten down by the king in his rage. Then King Edward lifted his eyes, and the fury had fled from them, and he said, 'Lord Montagu, if you can ask this of me after seeing the heads of your own father and brother rotting on the gates of this accursed city, then you are a better man than I, my fair cousin. . . . Your request is granted.' And so the town of York was spared the horrors that befell Ludlow."

Silence throbbed in the room. Ursula and her mother wiped tears from their eyes. Neither could I speak, for my heart brimmed with pride that left me mute.

MUCH GOOD NEWS CONTINUED TO ARRIVE FROM John. He liberated castle after castle for York and subdued the wild hordes of thieves and cutthroat murderers on the border, keeping the Lancastrians on the run. But years of civil strife and lawlessness were reaping a bitter harvest of turmoil that fed the hopes of the Lancastrians, and so he rarely had a chance to return to me and taste life's sweets. I fretted greatly over his hard lot, so devoid of much else but fighting.

One warm summer day, as John's birthday approached, a trader on his way to Norwich stopped in Burrough Green to show me his wares. As I looked into his sack, the glitter of bronze, half-hidden by fabric bolts and a load of baubles, caught my eye. The trader fished it out.

"A veiled dancer," he said, his sharp dark eyes watching me carefully, "from Alexandria, cast in bronze by a Greek sculptor three hundred years before the birth of Christ . . ."

I traced the lines of her perfect features and the graceful flow of her veils with my finger. An undergarment fell in deep folds around her and trailed heavily; atop, the figure wore a sheer mantle drawn taut over her head and body and across her cheek so that only her eyes and hairline were visible. The sculptor had caught her in the midst of a twirl, and as I gazed on her, she seemed to come to life before my eyes.

I paid the exorbitant sum the trader asked, though it set me behind with my expenses for the entire month. If the merchant had not lied, hundreds of years had passed since an ancient sculptor of the Hellenistic age had lovingly cast her beautiful image into the golden metal. The past seemed alive to my touch.

"I wonder who she was," I mused to Ursula. "Did she love someone? Was she dancing for him?"

"She was beautiful, that is for certain," Ursula replied. "You can see it even beneath the folds of her veils. . . . And she was a fine dancer . . . like you, m'lady."

"I wish I had the chance to dance for the man I love . . . even veiled."

In one of those rare coincidences of life that can never be explained, a troupe of Gypsy dancers came to Burrough Green the very next day seeking to entertain us. My purse drained by the purchase of the statuette, we reached agreement on a payment I could afford, and they hauled their cart and donkey inside. I invited all the household to watch their entertainment, and our small hall filled with revelry as everyone clapped to the tunes of their gittern, cymbals, and tabors. And as I watched them twirl and beat their tambourines, a curious idea took shape in my mind.

When the entertainment was over, I summoned the dance troupe to the solar. "I wish to surprise my lord husband, who holds camp on the Scots border with his army," I told them. And I presented my scheme.

Over the next days the dance troupe helped plan my intricate dance steps, and I practiced them to the music of the blindfolded minstrels, for I had no wish that their men see me dance so suggestively until I performed for John. For another full day I experimented with a drape of veil over my form, and after this they pronounced me ready. For my attire I chose a red bodice and a rich skirt of multilayered red and purple veils sewn with tiny beads of colored glass, and a purple mantle embroidered with silver flowers. Now we were ready to leave.

The day dawned cool and bright. I was excited. Even the horses caught the scent of something special in the air; they snorted and neighed, stamping their feet as if to demand that we hurry. How we managed to load up the carts and not forget some vital necessity that would have ruined the entire plan, I shall never know. For I scattered my orders to the groomsmen with only half a mind, in a flutter of nervousness, amidst the incessant giggles and chatter of the dance troupe. At last I climbed into my litter and drew the curtains to protect my identity, and we set our course north for Doncaster.

Now that I was truly on my way, the sheer recklessness of my prank struck me with full force, and I was assailed with doubts. Lancastrians were everywhere. What if they abducted me to use as a pawn against John? I could end up being the means of his destruction. This was mad, complete folly! Even if I managed to surprise him, his reaction could be far from the joy I had anticipated; it could be anger that I had chanced such disaster. Mayhap I should turn back.... Then his face would rise up before me, his Neville blue eyes gazing at me, filled only with me, the way they were on the night of the dance when we had first met, and my body would flame with passion. What if I didn't go—and God forfend he was taken from me forever in the next battle? Would I ever forgive myself for my cowardice? Could I deny us the ecstasy of a last reunion?

Then courage braced me like a knight's armor, and my doubts fled for a time.

The trip went by uneventfully. I spent two uncomfortable nights in inns along the way, sleeping with Ursula on hay mattresses filled with bedbugs, but the ale helped us abide them. Late on the third evening, the spire of the town church announced our arrival in Doncaster. Nearby lay John's camp . . . and that of the Lancastrians. From this point on, we had to proceed with the greatest caution.

"HALT! WHAT IS YOUR BUSINESS?" DEMANDED THE man-at-arms fiercely. Around him was gathered a large group of soldiers, and behind him John's camp stretched out into the distance, a maze of tents beneath the setting sun.

Geoffrey drew out the missive I had written in my own hand and presented it to the guard. I drew my mantle tighter across my face as I watched them. In order not to attract undue attention, I had left my litter and donned a veil just before we arrived at the camp, and now I rode an old mare, which I shared with one of the eight Gypsy dancers. But we could not have more than one veiled woman, or suspicions would be aroused that we might be men in disguise, hoping to gain entry and sabotage the camp. Thus Ursula had been given a gray-haired wig to wear and told to walk with a stoop, so she would not be recognized.

The sergeant took my letter warily but didn't break the seal to read. I wondered if he was illiterate.

"This is a dance troupe," Geoffrey explained. "As you can see from the seal, Lady Montagu has dispatched us here to entertain her lord husband and his camp. I myself am well-known to those in His Lordship's retinue. Send for anyone close to Lord Montagu, and they will vouch for me, as I vouch for this Gypsy troupe."

The man moved down the line, stopping at the litter. He drew back the curtain and riffled through the costumes that lay strewn there. His gaze then moved over our group and settled firmly on me, though I sat in the midst of the riders. But he could see little, for I took care to bow my head and draw my Saracen veil tighter across my face.

"Why is that one covered up?" he demanded.

Geoffrey laughed. " 'Tis her custom—she dances veiled. 'Tis not from modesty, either, I assure you, as she is a ribald little thing— welladay, not so little, since she is as tall as I, though some will say I am little—however it be, you will see for yourself tonight. 'Tis enough to bring a blush to your own cheeks, I warrant!"

Geoffrey exchanged a look with me, and it took all my will to suppress the laughter that threatened to convulse me. He was quite the mummer, though I had never known it. Clearly he was enjoy- ing himself with a freedom he would never taste again, and my raised eyebrow told him so.

"We'll see about that," the man-at-arms said with a scowl. "Wait here."

Patiently we sat beneath the fierce gaze of the guards while the Gypsy captain stood holding the reins of the lead horse, fearful to stir lest they unsheath their swords. The man-at-arms finally re- turned with Conyers who held my missive, the seal now broken. I shrank into my saddle, but Conyers strode directly to Geoffrey and barely glanced my way. He broke into a broad grin.

"Geoffrey, you rogue," he said with a slap on Geoffrey's back that nearly felled him, "how did you gather this bevy of wild beauties? I half expected you to be dancing for us tonight when I heard you were here. Never would I have guessed women were one of your many talents."

"Sorry to disappoint you, my lord." Geoffrey grinned back good-naturedly.

I realized suddenly how fond I was of these two men, loyal friend and loyal servant. Conyers turned back to the sergeant-at-arms. "Let them pass, and offer them what comfort there is. We have few here, my ladies"—his smile passed gallantly over us all—"as you will soon see, but we are happy you came, and most likely some of us will be even happier tonight."

Geoffrey broke into a broad smile and shepherded us and our cart of supplies past the guards into the camp.

IN THE DINING TENT, MEN CROWDED THE LONG plank tables, filling the space with rowdy conversation and bursts of laughter as they drank their ale and awaited their commander's arrival, for one sweep of the scene told me John was not yet present. While my dance troupe dressed and made ready in a small area at the back of the enclosure, I hid behind the curtain that shielded us from men's eyes and watched for him, my gaze touching nervously on the table, set with tall-backed chairs, where he would sit with his highest officers.

At one side of the enormous tent, a wide flap stood open, admitting the fading light of day and a view of the fields lit by the rosy glow of the setting sun. As I looked in that direction, a general commotion took place, and there was the rustle of garments as men stood to receive their commander. John entered with Sir John Conyers and his knights. I pulled back behind the curtain to catch my breath. Then, fortified once more, I looked again. John was making the rounds, greeting a man here, a man there, laughing and pausing to rest a hand on many a shoulder as he passed along to the high table. It was a side of him I had never seen before. He

evinced a genial ease and camaraderie with these men that could
exist only between those who had fought together and shared danger, who had entrusted one another with their lives and proven
true time and again. Here was his own private world, a world of
which I could never be part. I drew back, overcome by an inexplicable sadness.

When everyone was seated and the first course had been served,
the Gypsy captain gave the signal to the minstrels, and the merry
notes of the first melody floated over the hubbub of conversation.
I nodded to four of the dancers and parted the curtain for them.
They twirled into the hall, bright and beautiful in their costumes,
midriffs exposed, hips swaying, their raven hair loose, bare legs visible through the slits. Men cheered and whistled. The girls smiled
and blew them kisses as they danced, eliciting hoots of admiration
from the soldiers, one of whom suddenly stood with a hand to his
heart and cried out, "For mercy's sake, either marry me or slay me
now!"

I peeked out from behind the curtain, seeking John. He sat engrossed in conversation with Conyers and paid the dancers no heed,
his mind clearly elsewhere. This distressed me. *What if he doesn't
notice me? What if he leaves the hall before I have a chance to dance?*

Rousing applause broke into my thoughts. The first number
had ended. The girls moved to the beat of the next melody, which
was faster and wilder than the one that had gone before. John ignored them, still absorbed by his thoughts. Although he glanced up
when the dance ended, his eyes held a faraway expression. A silence
fell. I waited for the clash of cymbals to announce my entrance,
and checked that my veil was secure against my hair. The music
changed to a slow and sultry beat. My heart in my throat, I glided
onto the floor, surrounded by a circle of dancers who shielded me
from sight with blue and green ostrich feathers. I struck my pose,
head turned shyly over my shoulder, eyes downcast, a hand holding
my veil away from my body, the jeweled toe of one bare foot pointing out from beneath my gown. The girls withdrew their plumes.
Men gasped at the strange sight I made, a dancer veiled from head
to toe. They had never seen such a thing.

With one hand gripping my veil tightly over my face and the other sweeping its folds back and forth across my hips, I took long, languid steps to one side, then to the other, careful to keep my face averted from John. The minstrels quickened the beat of the music, and I broke into a long, sensuous twirl. Across the dance floor I writhed, veils sweeping around me, hugging my body, revealing a glimpse of jeweled ankle here, a glimpse of thigh there. I saw many of the men put down their ale to watch more intently, not knowing what to expect but unwilling to miss whatever came next. I twirled across the floor, pausing to reach out here and there to brush a shoulder, caress a cheek, or meet a glance with a promise in my eyes, all the while keeping my veil secured firmly across my face. Finally, my breath in my throat, I dared to look in John's direction. Oblivious of me, he had tilted his chair back to talk to his friend Marmaduke Constable, behind Conyers, a gesture reminiscent of the banquet at Lord Cromwell's castle that squeezed my heart in memory.

But, dear Heaven, doesn't he recognize me yet? On either side of him, Lord Clinton and Conyers sat relaxed in their chairs, giving me their full attention, smiling in enjoyment but also without a hint of recognition. *Have I disguised myself too well?* My heart cried out to John—*John, it's me, my love, look at me, want me, I'm here. . . .*

The hoots and calls of the soldiers, and the gazes of Clinton and Conyers, who now leaned close to watch, finally penetrated John's concentration. He tilted his chair back to the table and gazed over at me, but still with only half a mind. This was my chance. I twirled forward to his table, stepped up on tiptoe and swung a thigh swiftly, boldly, across the table at him, and retreated again. The minstrels broke into the melody of our first dance at Lord Cromwell's castle and I cast my outer mantle to the floor. Dancers whisked it away. I was now covered only by a single sheer veil, as are Saracen women of the harem when they dance for their lords and masters. While some of the dancers fanned me with the ostrich feathers and others clapped to the beat of the wild melody, I writhed sensuously before him, letting my veil slip from across my cheeks for a mere instant. Then, as he lifted a goblet of wine to his lips, I displayed a leg, bare to the mole on my thigh.

John froze. He leaned forward in stunned disbelief. Tearing his gaze from the mole on my thigh, he ran his eye up my leg, up over my bosom, to my face. He met my gaze. He set his wine cup down and stared at me. Then slowly, very slowly, a grin began to spread across his handsome mouth, and the creases I so loved made themselves visible to me.

I widened my own smile and gave him a wink.

I RETURNED TO BURROUGH GREEN, WREATHED in joy. My mission had been accomplished successfully, and as John assured me when I left, he would not soon forget my Gypsy dance. "The memory shall keep me warm on many a cold winter's night," he promised as he kissed me farewell. As if our reunion had brought us good fortune, more news arrived from John on the heels of my visit. He had raised the siege of Carlisle and killed six thousand Scots. His victory meant that King Edward no longer had to hurry back to the North and delay his coronation. The date was set for June twenty-eighth, four days after John's birthday on St. John's Day. John came home to celebrate his name day, and the following morrow we left for London to attend Edward's coronation.

However, everywhere along the way to London, we heard the people murmuring about the choice of date. "Sunday?" they'd gasp. "But Sundays are unlucky this year!" Then they'd cross themselves to keep the Devil away. I'd had the same reaction when John had given me the news; even he had been troubled. For the day of the week on which fell the anniversary of the Massacre of the Holy Innocents, December twenty-eighth, was unlucky throughout the year. And this time it had fallen on the Sabbath. King Edward apparently cared naught for superstition. That date suited him, so preparations went forward for the crowning of England's Yorkist king.

When we arrived, we found London thronged by cheering masses displaying the White Rose of York, which was sold by the cartload on street corners and by hawkers from aprons brimming with the flower. "Fresh white roses for sale!" they cried. "Buy a fair white rose for our fair White Rose King!" The palace of Westminster, where we went to greet King Edward and John's brother Bishop George, now his chancellor, bustled with the coming and going of innumerable staff. Cooks and helpers milled in the kitchen, conjuring all manner of toothsome delights into creation; carpenters hammered and pounded, making necessary repairs around the palace and on the royal barge, building tables and making chairs; while cages of swans and pheasants, and sacks of fruits, vegetables, sugar, and spices poured into the royal kitchens on carts, horses, and the backs of mules. The halls teemed with courtiers and nobles, and their retinues and ladies, and we had to thread our way through crowds everywhere we went. On our way to the king's chamber, I gave a cry of joy, for my eyes alighted on a dear, familiar figure.

"Maude!"

She was with her uncle, Lord Cromwell. We embraced with delight.

"How are you, Maude?" I said. "You seem happier.... Are you?"

"Indeed I am. The defeat of the bitch of Anjou has done my heart much good."

Promising to seek one another out over the next few days, we left for the king's chamber. We found him chatting amiably with a goldsmith whose wares, spread out on a table, gleamed and flashed in the light.

"This is the goldsmith Master Shore, and he has made us a fine sword that shall be our offering as soon as the crown is placed upon our head," Edward laughed and, flinging an arm around the man's shoulder, he pointed to a golden sword set with rubies. Unaccustomed to familiarity with royals, the man colored and attempted an awkward bow. Edward removed his arm and moved to embrace us. "He's the best goldsmith in London," Edward said, slapping the man's back before he left. "Almost as good a goldsmith as you are a commander, Cousin John! I owe my coronation to you, you know. If you hadn't raised the siege of Carlisle, I would have had to come north—but now—"

He gave me a lingering glance filled with admiration. "Truly, you sacrifice yourself for your king, John. To think you could be at home with your beauteous wife instead. . . . Here, let us walk together. The garden is profuse with the most splendid adornments." He put a hand on John's shoulder, and we strolled out to the garden. But as Edward talked of finances, state troubles, and military strategy, his glance touched on each of the ladies we passed along the rose-lined paths. I realized that, for him, adornments meant not flowers but women.

In spite of the money woes that seemed to plague the young king—for he'd had to borrow ceaselessly these past three months to pay the troops and expenses of the government—King Edward threw himself a lavish coronation. He made his state entry into London the next day, and was met by the mayor and aldermen in scarlet and four hundred citizens clad in green. They conducted him from Lambeth Palace across the bridge to the Tower. At a rich banquet that evening he created thirty-two Knights of the Bath, two of whom were his young brothers, eight-year-old Dickon and eleven-year-old George, and he gave each knight a sumptuous gift. The following afternoon, the king rode in procession from the Tower to Westminster, preceded by his Knights of the Bath in their blue gowns with hoods of white silk.

His coronation took place on Sunday morning in Westminster Abbey. The archbishop of Canterbury anointed him and placed on his head the priceless crown of King Edward the Confessor, which he wore to Westminster Hall as he walked beneath a glittering canopy of cloth of gold. He took his seat at the dais, beside his brothers and other members of his family, while we arranged ourselves around an adjacent banquet table. To my surprise, the hall was dimly lit, with only a few torches on the walls, and no candles. At first I thought this was a money-saving concession. But as we took our seats in the low light, torches appeared in the shadowy dark depths of the cavernous hall and moved toward us out of the blackness, accompanied by soft chanting. As the torches drew closer, we saw that they were borne by hooded monks. They divided into two long rows and filed past the dais and down both sides of the hall, chanting their song until it faded away into the darkness that enfolded them.

Immediately varlets scurried to light the candles on the tables, and the hall filled with light. In the flicker of their flames, the beautiful colored glass in the soaring windows came to sparkling life, as did the banners and tapestries that decorated the walls, while the jewels that encrusted the hats and gowns of the nobles dazzled the eyes. All at once, from above, came the flapping of wings. We looked up to find hawks and falcons swooping and diving through the hall to our delight, pausing now and again to seize an apple or a plum from the silver bowls on the tables. The jangle of tambourines caught our ears, and a brightly colored Gypsy troupe made their entry to the beat of the lilting music of their strolling Gypsy minstrels. They were dressed Saracen-style in low-cut bodices with their midriffs exposed over their jeweled skirts, and I recognized the captain of my troupe when he passed close to our table. He gave us a low bow, and I threw him a white rose. John leaned over to me and whispered in my ear, "Warwick arranged it at my suggestion." Then he gave me a naughty wink, and I laughed knowingly.

And so it continued through the night—acrobats whirling in the air in the most stunning and unbelievable acts as we marveled; the finest troubadours in the land singing to us as we listened dreamily; and a set of twin dwarfs and their magnificent black bear performing daring and dangerous feats to bring us to the edge of our seats.

The ancient hall of William Rufus, filled to capacity with its illustrious guests, rang with cheers and brimmed with the boundless gaiety of those celebrating the end of war and a new beginning. We feasted on goose, swan, and pigeons in puff pastry with rich sauces, fried trout and partridge tails, and rice pies decorated with flowers; and we drank the finest, sweetest wines, spiced hippocras, malmsey, and fragrant beverages, toasting the health of our handsome new king at every opportunity. At the conclusion of the evening, in a spectacular display that drew gasps of awe from us all, an angel in white silk and silver dropped down from the hall's magnificent hammer-beam roof to bless King Edward IV and bid us a good night.

The festivities resumed the next morning, and later that day, King Edward created his brother George Duke of Clarence, and his little brother Dickon Duke of Gloucester. Before we departed for the North, I heard Edward promise Dickon the gift of a golden garter. "You shall have it, Dickon," he whispered, "as soon as I can pay for it."

Amid such merriment, we took our pleasure and, finally exhausted with joy, we made our way back north, drowsy with delight, the evil omen of the Massacre of the Innocents long since forgotten.

FOR THE REST OF THE YEAR THAT FOLLOWED Edward's coronation, I enjoyed a measure of calm and life took on a pleasant uniformity I'd not known during my marriage. The best news in these months was the death of Marguerite of Anjou's cousin King Charles VII. His loss robbed her of all French support, at least for the present. Charles's son, the new King Louis XI, had hated his father and always sided with his father's enemies. He not only imprisoned Marguerite's envoys, but sent her friend Brézé to languish in a gloomy prison. Nevertheless, King Louis cared deeply for his kingdom and could be swayed to change policy. For this reason, Warwick was determined to wed Edward to a French princess. But according to various reports that came our way, King Edward, whose support rested on the favor of England's merchants, preferred a trade alliance with Burgundy over a marriage treaty with France. I knew enough to be concerned by this. It would not bode well for John if his brother and the king fell out with one another over France.

In November, a messenger arrived from Nan, who had taken up residence at her castle of Middleham. She wrote that the ailing countess was sinking fast. I packed up the children and journeyed to see her. While my spirits were immediately lifted by Warwick's daughters, little Anne and Bella, who ran to embrace me with shrieks of delight and open arms, I was deeply saddened by the sight of the countess. Maude had married again and moved on to a new life with her third husband, Sir Gervase Clifton, but the countess remained trapped in that moment in time when the news of Wakefield had been brought to us.

"How long has she been like this?" I asked Nan.

"For months . . . I lose count," Nan replied.

Refusing to eat, the countess had wasted away, and her skin was stretched taut over her bones. Whereas she was once unable to sleep, now she lay in permanent slumber, not even opening her eyes. I went over to the bed, where she lay stiff and still as a corpse. Her matted gray hair was strewn across the pillow, and her face bore an expression of deepest pain. But whether it had roots in the body or in the mind, I could not tell. I touched her hand and found it ice-cold; I bent down and kissed the sad, furrowed brow. She did not stir. But it was then I heard the moan that came from her lips as if entwined in her breathing, without beginning or end, rising and falling in volume and dying away like a soft wind that passes gently through a field only to stir again.

"Nearly a year has passed since the earl and Thomas died," I said, stroking her cheek. "She never recovered, did she?"

Nan met my eyes, and in them I saw my own sorrow reflected. "No . . . she died at Wakefield, too." She turned her sad gaze on the lifeless figure who still lived.

I kissed John's mother one last time and heard the sighing of her breath. "Your many kindnesses to me live in my heart," I whispered.

THAT NIGHT WARWICK CAME STREAKING THROUGH Middleham as unexpectedly as a star streaks through the heavens, blinding all else in the light of his glory. Nan rushed around frantically to attend his every whim. Wine flowed, and we spent the evening feasting lavishly on boar, peacock, and swan. Even beggars at the door were given generously of the rich fare, for it was Warwick's custom that every man be allowed to take away as much meat as he could fit on a dagger, and those too poor to own one were permitted to fill their stomachs until they could swell no further. Thus fortified, they set out again into the cold world, carrying their praise of Warwick all over the land, so that even those in faraway Bohemia heard of him. He carried the name "Kingmaker," for having unmade Henry and put Edward on the throne.

The evening was splendid in all regards except for one: John was not at my side. He was detained in the North. Warwick relayed his greetings to me, and a welcome message.

"He has left to pick up a party of Scottish nobles from the border and escort them to York. They are to meet with Edward's commissioners to discuss a peace treaty. He says to tell you that he is determined to make a visit to you very soon."

"Papa, why do you have to leave again?" his little Anne demanded tearfully.

"I must go to London to talk to the French ambassador, my child," Warwick said, stroking her hair as she sat on his knee. "I am planning a marriage for our brave King Edward."

"Indeed?" I said. "Who does King Edward wish to wed?"

"Edward? He's too busy whoring to give that any thought, so I shall decide for him," Warwick replied. "I intend to secure a treaty with Louis XI and seal it with marraige to a French princess, so that France does not render aid to the bitch of Anjou."

I was shocked by the manner in which Warwick spoke of the king, and I couldn't help but wonder what King Edward would think of Warwick's wedding plans when he was told. A little shiver ran along my back. The Sun may have risen in splendor, but the future suddenly seemed vague and darkened by shadow.

YORKIST
ENGLAND

1462–1471

Nineteen

1463

I LOOKED AROUND OUR MANOR HOUSE AT SEATON Delaval, much contented. A gentle snow drifted past the windows and bright sunlight flowed through the slated shutters, casting a glow through the great hall, which had been decorated with ribbons, greenery, and berries for Yuletide and the New Year festivities of 1463. On the dais, the hearth crackled with burning logs, giving out warmth. In one corner, men played at dice; in another, ladies held hands and danced in a circle; and in the center of the room, children played Hoodman Blind, shrieking with delight as they tried to escape the clutches of the hooded one. The smell of spiced wine and gingerbread cake floated in the air as servants carried around great trays laden with sweets and fragrant drink. *How much there is to be grateful for!* I thought. So many good things had happened for us in the nearly two years since King Edward's great Yorkist victory at Towton.

There was only one thing I would change. Our family had grown by yet another daughter. Margaret gave us a brood of four girls, and though I loved them deeply, it also pained me that I had failed to provide John with the strong arms of sons. My hand had hesitated as I put quill to paper to inform him of the birth of our girl. I knew he had to be disappointed. A man needed sons to help him fight his battles, whether in the courts, on the field, or on the manor. Yet his reply bore no evidence of it. He talked about the joy the news had brought him, how he looked forward to seeing his beautiful little daughter, and how he hoped matters on the border would settle down long enough to permit him a visit to Burrough Green. I had brought his missive to my lips and kissed it tenderly, but with an inward sigh. After all these years, he still stood alone, no boys at his side to help him in the world.

There's plenty of time to have more children now that we're close and he comes home more often, I told myself, remembering.

I had made the decision to move to Northumbria the previous year, 1462, for we saw little of John in Cambridgeshire. He was always in the North, securing the Scots border and fighting against the Lancastrian remnants that still vexed the land. To excise that cankerous sore and rid the realm of their threat, John had placed the three Lancastrian-held castles of Alnwick, Dunstanburgh, and Bamburgh under siege. Faced with the prospect of not seeing him for months on end, I moved our household from Burrough Green to the fortified manor of Seaton Delaval, far north in Northumberland, which had been confiscated from the Delaval family and given us by King Edward.

We had set out on our journey north as soon as I regained my strength after Maggie's birth in September. Along the way, news reached me of Countess Alice's death. Though I was grateful that she had finally been granted rest, I was unable to shake the painful sense of loss that dogged me, and I wondered how John did and wished I could be there to comfort him.

Autumn colors still clung to the Midlands when we left, but winds already blustered in gloomy Northumberland, and freezing sleet covered the earth. No livestock grazed outdoors, and we encountered few travelers along the way, for animals were given shelter and wise men did not venture out in such weather. Trotting our horses and rolling our carts across the rugged and lonely terrain of Northumbria, we had traversed hills and valleys, passed endless barns and small dwellings, and sometimes a shivering traveler that necessity had forced outdoors. As we'd entered the final stretch of our journey, the road before us climbed so steeply that all we saw was the vast sky rising ahead, so that it seemed the stony path would lead us directly to Heaven. I took it as a good omen.

At last we'd turned our horses through the sleepy village of Seaton Delaval and out into the arable farmland that surrounded the manor, marked on the horizon by the bell tower of an old Saxon church. The porter had let down the rusty drawbridge amidst a terrible shuddering and ear-shattering screeching that scattered the swans and herons on the moat with a wild flapping of wings. As we clattered up to the gatehouse, I'd made a mental note to have the drawbridge oiled. The reeve had met us with anxious eyes and a troubled air, no doubt wondering his fate under a Yorkist lord, and, while two grooms came running to hold the horses for us as we dismounted, he showed me around my new home.

Near the kitchen, a stream flowed through the garden to a well, and a windmill turned its sheeted arms, billowing like sails on a ship. Pigeons flew around the dovecote and the air bubbled with their loud cooing, while geese, poultry, and partridges wandered around the yard, squawking and sounding their horns. I was shown the spacious kitchen wing, the washhouse, the brew house, and the bake house, from whence had floated the smell of baked bread. My stomach had growled with appetite, and my throat thirsted for the wine and ale to be served at luncheon. Inwardly, though, I'd given a sigh. The manor required much hard work and expense to make it comfortable, for it had an unkempt air, with its run-down dovecote and rampant weeds, the half-rotted wood of the byres, and the ripped sheets of the windmill. Much tending was needed; we'd have to engage the services of many itinerants to mend farm buildings and implements.

We had entered the main house then and taken the creaky wooden staircase up to the living quarters. I'd noted many buckets that stood ready to catch drips from the leaking tiled roof, but the great hall was paneled and had a lovely minstrels gallery, and the wonderful old Saxon chapel, with the tall tower that I'd seen from the road, radiated warmth. In preparation for our noon arrival there was much bustle in the hall. The tables were already laid with freshly laundered cloths and pewter goblets, and varlets were bringing in saltcellars and spoons and setting them in their appropriate places.

At the end of the tour, I was shown our bedchamber. To my delight, it commanded a view of the surrounding fields and gardens, and had a privy that was set with sconces on either side of the arrowhead window. I had changed out of my journey-stained attire and, thus refreshed, had made my way to the hall for luncheon. Most of the household staff had already gathered in the hall to await me. I invited them to sit, and with my nod to the ewer, they were offered water in which to wash their hands before grace was said.

For the next two months I had thrown all my energies into fixing up the house and controlling expenses so that we could squeeze in extra repairs. I went over the household accounts with the reeve, suggesting ways to cut back on the purchases of clothes, wax, wine, spices; on the cost of alms given; on the money spent on supplying livery and buying stock; on the cost of the clergy we employed to sing masses and say prayers; on the expenses of the varlets engaged to clean windows and floors, and to keep the fires, candles, and rushlights lit; even on the number and cost of the staff that took care of the children. The money saved paid not only for additional repairs, but for adornments such as tapestries. And by Yuletide, the manor had repaid my efforts by taking on a truly inviting air.

The decision to move to Seaton Delaval had been a good one. John had seized every opportunity to come home, and though his visits were usually brief, they filled the house—and my heart— with great joy.

As we prepared to usher in the New Year of 1463, the sieges of Alnwick and Dunstanburgh went so successfully that Somerset surrendered both to John on Christmas Day. Now only Bamburgh remained in Lancastrian hands. On Twelfth Night, John arrived at Seaton Delaval with a very special guest in tow. "Look who I brought you," he said, his dark blue eyes twinkling.

"Uncle!" I cried, throwing myself into his arms in a most unladylike display of affection. "Oh, Uncle, 'tis so good to see you!" Linking arms with him, I turned to lead him to the house, when a familiar voice sounded behind me. I looked back to see Somerset dismounting his stallion with the help of a man-at-arms, his hands bound before him. He stood for a moment gazing at me. I stared, not comprehending. Somehow I hadn't understood that when Somerset surrendered the castles, he had also surrendered himself.

"My lady of Montagu, I greet thee well," he said in a gentle tone.

"My lord of Somerset—" I broke off, finding no words. I inclined my head in a nod of acknowledgment, aware of the strange look John threw me. Then John gave a curt nod to the man-at-arms, and Somerset was hustled away. A stream of other captives followed.

"What will happen to them?" I asked, speaking my thought aloud.

"They are traitors," my uncle said. "What do you think will happen to them, dear child? Now let us dine." He rubbed his hands together enthusiastically. "I am good and ready to sup!"

Over dinner, my uncle recounted his wonderful adventures in Jerusalem, Padua, Florence, Rome, and Rhodes. We downed spiced wine and hippocras, and worked our way through a dozen courses. But all the while, I thought of Somerset.

"So York rules over Lancaster at last," my uncle marveled, toying with his goblet. " 'What glory can compare to this, to hold your hand victorious over the heads of those you hate?'—Euripides, you know . . . For a time there, I had not much hope of it. The manner of the Duke of York's death changed the minds of many, I daresay."

"Indeed, it did," John murmured thoughtfully, pondering his wine before downing it in a gulp. A sorrow came over me, for I knew he was thinking of his father and Thomas.

"Aye, ' 'tis a rough road that leads to the height of greatness,' " my uncle said, quoting the poet Seneca.

"A road forced on us by Marguerite," John replied pragmatically.

" 'She to Ilium brought her dowry, destruction.' 'Tis what Aeschylus said about Helen of Troy, and it is proven true again in our day. Ah, history has a way of repeating itself, does it not?"

John gave a polite assent and moved to another topic. "As to the prisoners, my lord of Worcester, may I suggest we request a general pardon for them from King Edward?"

"Nay, make an example of them!" my uncle retorted. "Put them to death—and a slow death, at that!" He changed his mind about stabbing a slice of venison and waved his dagger around instead. "Impalement, that is the way! I observed this manner of death employed in Transylvania. 'Tis slow and torturous, and has proved most effective with the Turks. 'Tis how Vlad Dracula solidified his hold over his unruly region of Transylvania. Victims are either impaled through the anus or, in the case of women, their female part. His people live in such fear that none dare break any laws in his land! He has a gold cup placed on display in the market square of Tirgoviste, unguarded from any thief, and the cup remains, even through the night. 'Tis said he has made mothers eat the flesh of their own babes for fear of being impaled if they refused."

A varlet offered him spitted boar, and he nodded with appetite. Another servant heaped a load of boiled cabbage on his plate and moved to me. I swallowed hard on the wave of nausea in my mouth and waved the food away. I couldn't believe what I had heard. Neither did John, for he had turned pale.

"These are not Saracens," said John thickly, "but our own people, some of whom were forced to fight for Lancaster against their will."

Despite the effort to inject civility into his tone, he sounded angry. His face had hardened as he listened, and a muscle twitched in his jaw.

"Nevertheless their suffering will serve as an example and discourage the Lancastrian cause," said my uncle. "Do you wish peace?

Do you wish the return of law and order? Fear is the most effective weapon there is! Vlad Dracula had his mistress disemboweled for having lied about being pregnant with his child. Now people dare not lie in Transylvania, or even cheat, for terror of coming to his attention."

I put down my wine cup, my mouth flooded with the taste of bile.

"England is not Transylvania. And you yourself were Lancastrian once," John reminded him.

"My situation was quite different. I never fought for Lancaster. I owed my earldom to Henry, but I was connected by birth with the Duke of York, and to your family by marriage and friendship. How could I choose sides? 'Tis why I left the country."

"These men were duty-bound to fight for their lord, whatever side he happened to choose, whether they agreed with him or not. They were too poor to leave England," John said.

"That is not your problem, nor mine, John," sighed the earl. "They fought for Lancaster! What matters now is our duty to King, and that duty is to support him with every means at our disposal, including fear. And spare no man for his rank! The only concession Dracula made to rank was to impale his noblemen on longer spikes, and as for the Turks, hear what he did to—"

I could take no more and rose to my feet abruptly. "Pray, my uncle, some other time, perhaps? I fear I am not up to such talk—" I forced a laugh, and to excuse my rudeness, I placed a hand on my stomach.

I saw John's startled look.

"By the rood, you are with child?" my uncle exclaimed, scraping back his chair and rising to take my hand gently into his own. "Must be love that keeps you in such fair shape and glowing with happiness, for no one can tell by looking at you that your condition is so delicate, my dear."

Much as I cared for my uncle, I was sickened by his talk of torture and had summoned up the only excuse that would not oblige me to feign sickness for his entire stay, be it short or long. Yet I had not exactly lied—my stomach was indeed churning. "And that happiness I owe to you, dear Uncle," I said lightly, to change the subject. "If it hadn't been for your intercession, and your golden way with words, the queen would not have agreed to my marriage to my lord husband."

He patted my hand. "It does my heart good to know you are wed to such a splendid knight. 'One word frees us of all the pain and weight of life: That word is love.' Is it not?"

"Indeed it is, and Sophocles was wise to know it," I replied, eager to bid him good night.

John stood, looking stunned by my disclosure. I smiled, gave him an almost imperceptible shake of the head, and when I brushed his cheek with my kiss, I whispered, *"No!"* in his ear. To my relief, his eyes changed, and I knew he understood. He bowed to me and sat down.

But instead of retiring to our bedchamber, I stole down to the cellar, where Somerset was held captive. His room was a mere storage cell between some barrels of wine, and the surprised guard gave me entry only upon my insistence, for he had been commanded not to let anyone in.

I stepped into the chamber, and the key turned behind me. At first I saw nothing; my eyes had to adjust to the darkness. Then I made out Somerset sitting with his head in his hands. He hadn't looked up when the door had been unlocked or when it was locked again behind me.

"My lord of Somerset," I said.

He jerked up his head. He didn't move for a moment; then he blinked and rose to his feet. He stood gazing at me.

"Isobel," he said, almost reverently, "do I see true? Surely you are not real but a vision sent me from above. . . ."

"Nay, I am real enough," I said, suddenly regretting I had come.

He put out his hand, and after a hesitation I gave him mine. He kissed it and held it tenderly in both his own. "My lord of Somerset, I have come to thank you for the promise you made me at St. Albans, which you have kept."

"I need no thanks, Isobel."

"It was a kindness that greatly eased my mind," I replied, ignoring his denial.

"I did it for you. . . . I would do anything for you."

I dropped my lids, blushing furiously, glad of the darkness as I withdrew my hand from his. "Your Grace, I only wish you to know that I shall always be grateful to you."

"Prove it."

My eyes flew back to him. "What?"

"Kiss me."

I took a step backward. "You're mad!"

"I'm a dead man. I don't want your prayers. If you wish to thank me, do it now . . . with your lips."

Before I knew it, he had closed the distance between us and swept me savagely into his arms. "Isobel—do you not wonder why I never married? 'Tis because of you!" he said roughly. "As long as the wars raged, I had hope. But now hope is gone!" His mouth swooped down to capture mine, and I felt his burning body against mine. I struggled against his kiss, which suffocated me so that I could not cry out, and fought him hard, beating against his chest with my fists. But he was too strong for me, and I flailed in his arms like a dove in the claws of an eagle.

The key turned in the lock with a loud click. Jolted by the sound, Somerset relaxed his grip, and I removed myself from his grasp with such haste that I ripped my sleeve. John stood in the entry, staring at me. I pulled my hair and the torn sleeve of my gown over my shoulder, but the look on his face, so wounded, full of pain and disbelief, cut me to the core. In the next instant, his hurt look vanished, replaced by rage. He raised a fist to strike Somerset, but I lunged for his arm, which I caught at the elbow. "Nay, my lord! Strike him not! 'Tis not worthy of you to strike a prisoner—one who did you kindness!"

"Kindness?" John looked at me with hatred. "Is this kindness—that you steal down here to be kissed by my mortal enemy—the one who murdered my father and my brother—"

"I had nothing to do with that," Somerset protested. "I tried to dissuade them from it."

"So you say now, when no one is left to gainsay you," John hissed. "I have a good mind to throw you to her uncle—you know what he'd like to do to you?"

"John, I beg you, say no more! Let it be! I came to thank him for your safekeeping! He promised me at St. Albans that no harm would come to you—and he kept his promise! Oh, John, forgive this trespass—I only wished to thank him, 'tis all."

With a jerk of his arm, John shook me off. After glaring at Somerset for a long moment, he spun on his heel and strode out of the room. I ran after him, to no avail. Stony-faced, he would not speak to me and was deaf to my entreaties.

For the first time in our marriage, John did not come to our bed.

THE NEXT MORNING, I WAVED FAREWELL TO MY uncle with a troubled heart. As soon as he had gone, John dispatched Somerset to the safety of the fortress of Middleham, to be kept there until the king arrived. For the next three days, he held a military hearing in the market square, where he pardoned most of the prisoners and hung the rest. I knew he had acted swiftly so that my uncle would have no opportunity to carry out his designs against the hapless captives. Yet I felt such speed unnecessary, for I had recalled something I'd been unable to share with him. My uncle's talk of impalement was mere bluster, and his hard demeanor hid a soft heart that could never inflict cruelty. I knew, because he had read me the tale of the doomed royal lovers Tristan and Iseult when I was a child, and before we reached the end, he broke down and wept at their suffering.

Even at the tender age of six, I understood my uncle to be a proud man who would not wish others to know his weakness. Thus, I never spoke of what I had witnessed, and put it out of my mind so completely that I almost forgot it had happened.

On the last day of the executions, I did not see John at all, and on the night before he left again, he stayed away from our bed for a third time. I paced in my chamber restlessly, as though movement could grant me peace from my agony of mind. The doleful tolling of church bells sounded the hour of matins, and the nocturnal chants of the monks came floating to me across the stillness of the night. I could bear it no longer. Donning my chamber robe, I went to John in the room he had taken down the hall.

His eyes were closed. "John," I murmured, "are you awake?"

In the moonlight, I saw him open his eyes, but he said nothing.

"About what happened . . . Surely you know I intended no harm by thanking Somerset?"

He didn't reply, but at least he didn't turn his back.

"John, I've never given you reason to question my fidelity. Somerset grabbed me. Couldn't you see I was struggling to get away when you walked in? What more could I do? You are my first love and my last. When we're apart, I yearn for you, and only when you are safe at my side do I feel I truly live. We are granted so little time together, my love—'tis a terrible thing to waste our moments. Tomorrow you depart again"—I cast a look of dread at the black window—"and I shall be alone; for how long this time, I know not. . . ." I broke off wretchedly.

His continued silence was extinguishing my hope of forgiveness, but I gave it another effort. "Life is uncertain, my dear lord, and well do we know loss, you and I. Though you've won every battle you've ever commanded, the fear is always with me that the next one shall claim you. Sometimes I feel that I walk with the shadow of death at my shoulder—" My voice broke, but I forced myself to go on. "If you leave me now, angry and bitter as you are, how shall I bear that? If we part this way and misfortune comes to us, what then? Somerset has cost us much. Do not let him take more."

John did not move. I swallowed the despair in my throat and turned to leave, and it was then that I heard his sigh and felt his hand take mine. He drew me down to his side. I gave a small sob of relief as I stretched out beside him on the bed.

"You are right, Isobel," he said softly. "We should not waste time on such nonsense, for in the end that is all it be." I kissed the pulse in his neck. " 'Tis just that your uncle upset me at dinner, and when I came to you for comfort and you were not there . . ." He heaved an audible breath. "To see you in another man's arms—'tis a sight I hope never to witness again. It well nigh drove me mad. I couldn't help myself, I wanted to kill Somerset."

"My love, let us put it aside, and forget. All that matters is that we are together."

Twenty

"THANK YOU, GEOFFREY," I SAID, ACCEPTING THE missive my uncle had sent from court, and giving him a warm smile as I opened the letter.

I had grown very fond of this man, who had become my right arm. In John's absence, he guided me in my dealings with our various bailiffs, rent collectors, reapers, grangers, carters, smiths, plowmen, shepherds, herdsmen, and other farmworkers on our scattered estates, and I found in him a veritable fountain of knowledge. With his genial good nature, he reminded me of King Edward, and not only was he pleasant, but he worked hard and accomplished much. As Heaven knew, we sorely needed his help. Our money woes never seemed to leave us, despite the income from the gold mine, and limited the help we could hire, but this older man accomplished more in a day than most youths did in a week.

I broke open the seal and bent my head to read.

My dear niece Isobel,

Much has transpired since I left you. I have been made most welcome in London by our gracious sovereign, King Edward IV— long may he reign over us!—and I must admit to you that I have been extremely impressed by him. He is the handsomest man and prince I have ever laid eyes upon, being taller than all other men I have known and broader of shoulder, and he is also extremely amiable. But, clearly our young king is nothing like our meek Henry. Exceedingly able and perceptive, as well as a great and courageous military leader, he is a great statesman. Recognizing my talents immediately, he found merit in my arguments against leniency. My dear niece, you may take pride in knowing that your uncle, already a high peer of the realm and famed as one of the world's great scholars, has been duly recognized by our King Edward IV. In appreciation of my wise counsel and staunch devotion to the cause of York, His Grace has appointed me Lord Constable of England, with the power to try cases without a jury and no right of appeal from my courts.

I lowered the missive in my hand, my mind reeling. Great power had been placed in my uncle's hands, a power that would test his true mettle. He had always been proud, and now I feared his pride blinded him to the truth about himself. Like Marguerite d'Anjou, who saw herself as a peacemaker even as she drove men to the sword, my uncle had thought himself a loyal Lancastrian even as he'd fled for Italy to avoid the wars.

But what troubled me more was his belief in his own righteousness. My uncle was noted for his piety; yet he'd watched with admiration the gruesome sight of Saracens being put to death by impalement, this man who'd wept at the tale of the fictitious lovers Tristan and Iseult.

Which was the real John Tiptoft, Earl of Worcester, my uncle?

I made the sign of the cross and bent my head back to his letter.

*However, our new king is too merciful, and despite my strenu-
ous objections and the greater wisdom conferred on me by my years,
King Edward has extended Somerset the olive branch. Embracing
him as his cousin and his friend, the king said, "Let us put the past
behind us where it belongs, Henry," and granted him forgiveness and
favor, and Somerset knelt to him in acceptance.*

I laid down the missive. My uncle was mistaken: It was not
learning and age that made for wisdom. It was a man's heart, and I
need not doubt that King Edward's remained in the right place. *For
shame, is this your thanks to the uncle to whom you owe your happiness?*
I thought, swept by guilt. However, only days after his appointment
as Lord Constable of England came tidings that fanned my misgivings again. John brought them to me himself.

"The Earl of Oxford and his eldest son have been arrested for
treason."

"Are they guilty?"

"Most people feel they are not. But your uncle will decide the
matter."

John said nothing more, and I dropped the subject. My uncle
had become a sensitive subject for us both. Not long afterward
came the news that my uncle had found the earl and his son guilty,
and the earl had been beheaded on a scaffold still wet with his son's
blood. The whole matter made my stomach tighten into such a
knot that I was unable to take food for two days.

John, who was at home when we received the news, took to his
horse, and I didn't see him again until dusk. He returned long after
dinner had been cleared away. I sat with him and watched as he ate
silently, a faraway look in his eyes. I knew he was remembering his
own father and brother, and Clifford's brutal treatment of them at
Wakefield. Whether my uncle's executions were warranted or not,
there was no need for the added cruelty of having the son executed
in front of the father, and of making Oxford lay his own head down
on a block lathered in his son's blood.

Edward, in a burst of generosity, had not attainted the Earl of

Oxford, so his remaining son, seventeen-year-old John de Vere, who'd taken no part in his father's treason, would inherit his father's earldom. But how could this kindness ever outweigh my uncle's ruthlessness? Soon afterward came news that this young heir had come to blows with another youth over some disagreement, and this had brought him before my uncle's court once again. He was sentenced to have his arm severed at the elbow. This time, however, King Edward commuted the sentence, which was considered unduly harsh by everyone. My uncle, this man I had seen weep at a manuscript, was carving himself a reputation for great cruelty.

The weeks passed. My concerns about my uncle faded in the glow of better tidings. Marguerite, despairing of Scotland's help, had left England to seek help in France, and only the fortress of Bamburgh, where King Henry resided, remained in Lancastrian hands. Sir Thomas Malory, traveling to the border on royal business, stopped at Seaton Delaval for a brief visit with Ursula and brought us interesting news.

"Shocked by the sight of their young king bareheaded and un-armed, riding beside Somerset, and believing King Edward to be in mortal danger, the people of Grantham tried to drag Somerset from his horse and slay him!" he said. "But golden-haired Edward laughed and told them that he and his erstwhile foe were now the best of friends! The townspeople scratched their heads at this turn of events. . . . On my soul, King Edward is the most amiable, good-natured, and courageous monarch that ever sat the throne of England!"

"King Edward is not only generous, he is right," I said thought-fully. "We must put the past behind us and move forward as best we can. But, Sir Thomas, isn't Somerset in a difficult position? Not everyone is as forgiving as Edward, and now he finds himself trying to gain acceptance among men who are kin to those he has slain." I was thinking of the many ambushes and attempted murders of the Nevilles. *How must John feel?* Somerset, even if he wasn't physically present at Wakefield, had taken a hand, however reluctantly, in the slaughter of the Earl of Salisbury and of Thomas, and he had cer-tainly been active in the many other ambushes and waylayings.

"Aye," Sir Thomas Malory sighed. " 'Tis an impossible situation in many ways. There are those who will never forgive. I have seen him taunted. Some even turn their backs on him when he walks past. They whisper openly and snicker behind their hands. So I know not the answer to your question, my lady. Only time will tell."

Indeed it did. Before the year was out, Somerset had defected back to the Lancastrians, joining King Henry at Bamburgh. From that fortress, he and his Lancastrian friends wore John out keeping the peace as they raided the surrounding countryside. John's visits home to me grew fewer in number, and shorter in duration.

Though he had promised to return to Seaton Delaval for our seventh anniversary, he didn't arrive until after dark on the twenty-sixth of April, and his homecoming wasn't what I expected. He rode up wearily, an expression on his face that I had come to see in the days when Marguerite ruled the land. At his side rode faithful Rufus and John's new squire, Thomas Gower, the one I had known as "the pilgrim" in the depth of the troubles with Lancaster.

"What happened?" I asked.

"We gave battle at Hedgeley Moor," John sighed, dismounting. I took his arm as we walked together. "One of our Neville relatives—you know that rabid Lancastrian Humphrey—"

I nodded. Humphrey Neville was descended from a first marriage made by John's grandfather, Ralph Neville, Earl of Westmoreland, to Margaret Stafford, while John's line was descended from Earl Ralph's second wife, Joan Beaufort, daughter of the Duke of Lancaster. Humphrey's quarrel with John's father concerned the inheritance of certain property he felt should have gone to his side.

"I discovered he had plotted with Egremont's brother to ambush me—"

A gasp escaped my lips. Egremont was long dead, yet his legacy lived on and the Percies still made trouble for John. I had come to loathe their name, which had been coupled so often with the word "ambush" that it never failed to remind me of the anguish of those days that had led to the horror at Wakefield.

"Nay, have no fear, 'tis over," John said. "The Percy is dead, but

Humphrey escaped to Bamburgh." He sighed heavily as he sank down into a chair in our bedchamber. "There can be no peace in the land until I find a way to wrestle that impregnable fortress on the sea away from the Lancastrians."

Rufus made himself comfortable by the hearth. He cast John a sad look and wagged his tail in commiseration. I sent Tom Gower away and undressed John myself, pulling off his high boots, removing his doublet and hose, and untying his shirt. After sitting him down by the fire and covering him with a blanket, I went to the door and sent a servant down for wine and sweetmeats.

"Let us worry about that later," I said, returning to his side. "Now we shall eat, drink, be merry . . . and make love." I kissed the back of his neck as he sat in the chair, and I slipped my hands beneath the blanket and down over the rippling muscles of his chest. He turned and reached for me.

AFTER JOHN LEFT, HE WROTE ME DAILY. ONE BY one, the castles in the North and the West surrendered to him, until only Harlech in Wales held out. Favorable reports also came from across the land about King Edward. His charm was so great that he had won the hearts of his people, and they adored him almost as much as they loved Warwick. Merchants' wives pressured their husbands to loan him money, and men, too, often gave generously to Edward's purse, though they could not be sure they'd ever see their gold again. But each time I met King Edward, I heard the same troubling refrain from him. "Money, money," he'd moan, "why is there never enough money?" Well did I understand his concern, for it was the same as ours. But then he'd turn his gaze thoughtfully on Warwick, who was richer than any king, and I felt that cold shiver run down my spine again.

At this time, Warwick decided to reunite his mother in burial with his father and brother at Bisham Priory, for in his will the earl had expressed his wish to be buried with his Neville ancestors. Accompanied by John and Warwick riding bareheaded, with banners fluttering before them in the cold wind, the bodies of the earl and

Thomas were conveyed from Pontefract to Middleham, to join Countess Alice, and from thence the three were taken to Bisham. All along the way, people gathered to pay their last respects, removing their caps to stand quietly and watch the chariots rumble past, covered in black silk and drawn by gleaming ebony stallions. At the priory we were met by John's brother George, the bishop of Exeter, now Edward's chancellor, and Edward's young brother, fourteen-year-old Clarence. But the king had not come. Again I felt that cold shiver of warning that told me something was amiss.

Attired in black, my face covered by a veil, my mind awash in memory, I rode behind the caskets of the three I had come to love as my own kin. I saw merry Thomas in the hall at Raby, surrounded by children. *Wine in well rose sparkingly,* he sang; *beer was rolling darkeningly, and merry malt moved wavily, through the floor beyond....*

I wiped away a tear.

At the door of the priory church, John performed his father's bequest and distributed forty pounds in gold coins to poor maidens about to be married. I watched the earl's last act of charity on this earth, a charity characteristic of him throughout his life. As clarions blared farewell, tabors drummed, and monks chanted their dirges, the coffins were lowered into their sarcophagus. One by one, I blew them a kiss in my heart.

Immediately after the funeral, John took to horse and did not return for many hours. I watched him ride away, wishing he could turn to me for solace. But, strong and silent as he was by nature, there was much he knew not how to share with me, and much that eluded me about him. *He is like the wind,* I thought, *and one cannot capture the wind.*

The next day, I went back to Seaton Delaval. Before any word arrived from John, a travel-dusty pilgrim appeared at our door one May evening, begging shelter. Ursula came to me in the kitchen, breathless. "The pilgrim has news, dear lady! Come—" Seizing my hand, she dragged me to the hall, where a man sat eating at a trestle table.

"See," he explained, repeating what he had told Ursula, "my lord o' Montagu delivered the Scottish nobles safely to York, and he was on his way to his headquarters in Newcastle to await my lord o'Warwick and King Edward when he learned that Lord Somerset and King Henry were encamped near the town of Hexham." The man spoke between long draughts of ale and mouthfuls of bread soaked in broth. "My lord o' Montagu needed no second invitation, m'lady! I was passing through m'self and saw the fight, and afterward I spoke to one of the soldiers—"

"Is Lord Montagu safe?" I demanded, my heart in my throat.

"Safe and snug as a bug in a soiled mattress in a dirty tavern, m'lady. Have no fear—"

With a wide smile, I ordered him a capon and wine. As we waited for the bird to be cooked, he told his tale of Hexham.

"As I was saying, this man-at-arms, he was one who took part in the battle, and I'm relating it to you as he himself told it to me, so upon my soul 'tis as God himself saw it—" The pilgrim took time to cast an eye heavenward and make the sign of the cross. " 'My lord o' Montagu,' he says to me—the sergeant says this, mind you—'My lord o' Montagu is the most valiant knight and the best commander a fighting man can have! Here's the traitor Somerset camped in this meadow near Hexham on the banks of Devil's Water, and without waiting for reinforcements, m'lord o' Montagu galloped to meet treacherous Somerset, whose life King Edward said was forfeit on capture—' " The pilgrim paused to down his ale. " 'Crushed 'em like that—' " He snapped his fingers. "This is me talking now. . . . God's own truth, m'lady, I saw it with m'own eyes—may the Lord Almighty smite me down if I lie! M'lord Montagu attacked with such suddenness and so fierce, that's why the entire battle took but minutes, though Somerset's army outnumbered his by more than two hundred men. . . . Aye, England never 'ad a finer general or a more manly knight than good Lord Montagu—may God bless him and reward him, so say I!"

The wine and capon were brought, and he settled down to dig into his meal. Even if this last compliment had been inspired by the hope of more wine, it deserved a full reward, and I took the pitcher to pour his cup myself.

"King Henry escaped," the man added, licking his lips as he

watched me pour. "But Somerset was caught, and he lost his miserable head in Hexham's market square—and good riddance to him, I say!"

My hand stilled, the wine half poured.

"M'lady!" the mercer said anxiously, putting down his knife and leaping to his feet. "M'lady, ye've gone so pale! Is there anything I can do for ye?"

I inhaled a deep breath. " 'Tis nothing but a passing faint," I replied, setting the pitcher down.

I retired to my prie-dieu, and there, before my prayer book and an urn of lilies, I said a prayer for Somerset's soul, and my eyes filled with tears I did not understand.

TWO DAYS AFTER THE BATTLE AT HEXHAM, I learned from my maidservant, Agnes, that one of John's soldiers, who had been wounded, had come to stay with her while he recuperated. The soldier was a cousin of Agnes's husband, a tanner by trade, and unmarried, with no family to care for him. I gathered together some compotes and jams, wine and dried beef, and what coins I could spare, and rushed to her house, accompanied by Geoffrey.

We had not far to go, since Agnes lived just past the village church, but the journey was not pleasant in the cold rain. Assailed by the rancid stench of the dyes and animal hides in the adjacent tannery, where Agnes's husband worked with his sons, we dismounted in front of the rude abode, of wattle and daub, that stood in a small field. Hens squawked and flitted out of our way, and a cow ambled over to sniff us as we crossed a path made uneven by muddy ruts. We reached the shelter of the low-hanging thatched roof, and Geoffrey banged on the door. A young girl welcomed us inside. Blinded by the darkness, I stood for a moment, waiting for my eyes to adjust. The two-room house had only one small, unglazed window to let in the light. The shutter was half-closed over it, and the room was sooty from the fire lit the previous night in the center of the hut, making it hard to see. A clay pot of burning rushes soaked in sap provided the only light in the house and stood on a trestle table in the corner of the room, where a man lay on a pallet, his chest bandaged. He had been staring at the ceiling, but now he turned his head to look at me.

"M'lady of Montagu!" he cried out in great excitement, struggling to kneel to me as I crossed the floor of rammed earth covered with straw. There came a thump and a groan as the old soldier tumbled heavily to the floor. Geoffrey rushed to his side and got him back into bed, but he tried to rise again. I rested a hand on his shoulder. "Nay, be still, my good man," I said.

With moist eyes, his voice trembling, he seized my hand in both his own and covered it with kisses. "M'lady, I am not worthy—"

"Indeed you are," I said. "You fought for my lord husband and were wounded in the service of our king. You are most worthy." Smoothing my skirts, I took a seat on the stool. Geoffrey brought the basket of gifts he had dropped at the door when he'd run to the man's assistance, and set it down beside me. "Here are a few items that I pray will help restore you to health—" I showed him the meat, wine, and compote. Then I presented him with the coins. "I hope that you can buy whatever else you need with these. . . ."

The man stared at the coins and looked up at me with moist eyes. "I canna take it," he said.

I stared at him. "Why?"

"M'lord of Montagu gave me money already. . . . He gave us all money. Even the dead."

I was momentarily speechless in my surprise. "What do you mean?"

The man explained. Soon after the battle of Hexham, John had caught a Lancastrian envoy loaded with gold and silver in the huge amount of three thousand marks. The money was meant to buy armor and supplies for King Henry's troops at Bamburgh, and—more important—to pay the wages of the Lancastrian soldiers. The men had not been paid for months, and had refused to fight unless they received what they were owed.

"The gold rightly belongs to me lord of Montagu as commander. But he didna keep it as he might have . . . as anyone else would have. . . . Nay . . . he didna keep it, but ordered it divided equally between his men, every last one of us, even the ones who had been slain, and this he had delivered to their widows. . . . For many, sore hurt and sick, the money was a godsend, m'lady. It rescued them and their families from dire straits." He fell silent for a long moment. When he spoke again, his voice shook with emotion. "There's nothing we woudna do for him, m'lady," said the tough old soldier. "We'd march to the ends of the earth for him, m'lady, every last one of us."

LESS THAN TWO WEEKS LATER, I RECEIVED A MIS-sive from John. He'd been summoned to York on Trinity Sunday, the twenty-seventh day of May, 1464, to meet King Edward, who was on his way north. I immediately made preparations to join him in the city with the girls, whom he hadn't seen for a month. With a cart laden with the children and a travel chest rumbling behind us, we sought lodging at St. Mary's Abbey in York. John arrived the next morning, but King Edward had reached York earlier than expected, and John had not long to spend with me.

"I hope to dine with you tonight," he said as he mounted Saladin. We were surrounded by nuns, whose gazes shadowed us as they moved through the grounds, so he embraced me only with his eyes.

After taking luncheon in the hall, I sat near the banks of the River Ouse while my girls frolicked on the lush grass, playing Catch Me If You Can and shrieking with delight as they evaded one another. It didn't seem possible that the twins had already celebrated their sixth birthday, Lizzie had turned five, and Maggie was nearly two. I watched a flock of magpies fly overhead, their cries mingling with the pealing of church bells and the children's laughter. A bottomless peace drenched my spirits. *What more be there to life, when I am here with my children, and the man I love is safe?* Life had been so busy of late that I'd had no time to reflect on my blessings, but now I shut my eyes and sent a prayer of gratitude up to Heaven.

The dinner hour came and went, but still John did not return. After hymns, Ursula put the children to sleep, the nuns retired to their cells, and the abbey grew silent. Back in my room, I reluctantly let Ursula prepare me for bed. I had just removed my gown, and stood in my shift, when the loud sound of heavy rapping and shouts came at the gate, followed quickly by the shout of a distressed nun. I flew to my barred window and threw open the shutters. With the help of several sisters who had rushed to her side, the nun was cranking the gate open. I stood on tiptoe, straining to see through the high, barred window. There followed the clippity-clop of horses' hooves as four riders galloped in, some bearing torches. Amid the neighing of horses, they dismounted. I did not recognize the men in the darkness, for their faces were covered against the cold wind, but even in the blackness I had no trouble making out Saladin. With a broad smile, I turned back to Ursula. "It's John!"

"Is Geoffrey with him?" she asked softly, rushing to my side. I threw her a glance. Even in the gloom I saw that she blushed. *So that's how it is.* . . . I gave her a smile. "Go to him, Ursula," I said softly. When I looked out again, John was striding to my room. I threw open the door, not knowing what to expect—whether good or bad. But that something had happened, I did not doubt.

John stood beaming at me with such a look of elation on his face that he lit up the passageway like a torch. I drew him inside. "Tell me!" I cried. He seized me so fiercely by my arms that I almost cried out with pain. "Isobel," he said, his voice deep, exultant. "I come to you no longer as Lord Montagu, but as the *Earl of Northumberland!*"

Twenty-one

1464

WE SLEPT LATE THE NEXT MORNING. JOHN CRA-
dled my head on his arm, and I snuggled close to him, for it was
cold outside, and the wind howled.

"And how is the Earl of Northumberland this fine morning?"
I inquired.

"Very fine, dear lady, for the Earl of Northumberland is a rich
man, and he will never have to borrow from his brother again,"
John replied, planting a kiss on my brow.

"How rich is he?" I asked, stealing a look at his face.

"Oh, about a thousand pounds a year."

I gave a little gasp.

He laughed. "You find that impressive, but what if I told you
he was powerful too?"

"Tell me about his power."

"This Earl of Northumberland, he has a brother, and between
them the two rule a great swathe of territory across the whole of
northern England—the Midlands, in the South, and into Wales.

They are the realm's greatest peers and the mightiest force in the land."

"And where does this great Earl of Northumberland live? Surely not in some leaky, drafty manor house?"

"Of course not. He owns castles . . . Alnwick, Warkworth—"

"Warkworth? Warkworth is exquisite and designed for every comfort!"

"So it is. I have heard tell that the Earl of Northumberland receives his food steaming hot, for the varlets can reach any room in the castle from the kitchen within minutes, it is so well designed."

"If that is so, I think I shall wed the Earl of Northumberland, for I should like very much to live at Warkworth and dine on steaming-hot plates of delicious food, and be powerful, and have nice dresses and jewels to wear. Besides, I have heard tell he is very handsome and of great prowess."

"That he is, for I have seen him myself," John laughed. "And when would my lady like to wed him?"

"The sooner, the better," I replied, climbing on top of him.

I COULD NOT BELIEVE THAT THE TWO JEWELS OF the earldom of Northumberland, the castles of Warkworth and Alnwick, were ours! While John chose Alnwick as his favorite, Warkworth soon became mine.

Alnwick Castle lay on a wide stretch of the River Aln, in the far northern reaches of England, so near to Scotland that John could come home for a night's stay when he was patrolling the border. With its stateliness and life-size stone sentinels guarding the battlements, it looked what it was: a powerful fortress designed to repel enemies. But Warkworth, a few miles farther south, on a loop of the River Coquet, was smaller, and felt to me like more of a home. Each stood high on a hill bordered by forests, and each commanded magnificent vistas of river and rolling terrain. We moved with ease between the two residences, sometimes as often as three times a year, for in our absence, repairs were made and cleaning done without disrupting our peace.

But while John had shed his poverty, he could not shed his responsibilities. As I was soon to learn, these would claim ever more of his time and energies. In the meanwhile, two months after John received his earldom, I learned the joyful news that I was expecting another child. This time I knew for certain that it was a boy. So, while John returned to his duties on the borders and to Bamburgh Castle, where Henry had taken refuge, I occupied myself with moving from Seaton Delaval into our sumptuous residence at Warkworth Castle and making preparations for the delivery of our son.

In celebration of John's elevation to the earldom, I threw a feast for him at Warkworth and invited everyone dear to us—the lords Clinton, Scrope of Bolton, Scrope of Masham, and Marmaduke Constable, and their wives and children. The king's brother Clarence came, for he was deep in love with Bella, and Dickon of Gloucester came with him, for Dickon was in love with her sweet sister, Anne. Both princes hoped to wed Warwick's daughters, and Warwick had urged the matches on Edward. But, so far, Edward had remained noncommittal.

Even Maude came from Tattershall Castle, where she lived with her new husband, Sir Gervase Clifton, whom she had married just before Lord Cromwell's death in '62. And what joy it was to see her! She had grown plumper since the coronation, but otherwise had not changed much.

"Your castle!" she said, stepping into the great hall with its semioctagonal walls. "Look at those grand soaring windows, and this passageway of arches, and that stone table built into the wall! Why, I've never seen such a thing."

"And that small stairway in the far corner behind that pillar—" I drew her toward the dais. "It connects with the wine cellar and the kitchen, so that wine and food can be brought to us at a moment's notice!"

"This is no fortress, but a true home." Maude gave me a long and loving look that mingled remembrance of things past with hope for the future. "And now, another child to bring laughter into these splendid halls," she said. "I'm so glad for you, Isobel!" As she embraced me, I felt a touch of sadness, for Maude still had no children.

Bishop George officiated at the thanksgiving mass we held at the church, where twenty choirboys sang for us in angelic voices, and afterward we moved outside for the banquet, set on the riverbank. It was a lovely summer evening. Rushing breezes swept the poplars and the weeping willows, bearing the sweet fragrance of flowers, and twilight bathed the castle walls with a rose glow. As we dined—on liver pie, roasted pheasant, turtledoves, pastries of capers, truffles with raisins, and hot capon fritters sprinkled with sugar—I glanced at John, and my heart warmed. He wore his silver circlet, and rich earl's robes of bright blue velvet furred with miniver and trimmed with gold, and never had he looked so handsome, or so happy.

JOHN CAME HOME OFTEN IN THESE DAYS, BUT Bamburgh Castle weighed on his mind, for it remained in Henry's hands, and the Lancastrians continued to make trouble by raiding the countryside around them. Their continued hold on the castle posed a significant threat to the Yorkist regime, for it stood on the sea and could be used by Marguerite as a point of invasion. But in August 1464, despite the urgency of Bamburgh, as the sun shone gloriously over radiant orchards rich in fruit, and fields bright with green and gold crops, parliament was cancelled, and John was abruptly summoned to a royal council meeting at Reading Abbey.

"How can it be more important than securing Bamburgh? What can it mean?" John said as he stopped for the night at Warkworth on his way south.

"Does Warwick have any idea?"

"Nay . . . none . . ."

I grew troubled and knew I'd have no rest until I heard back from John. But when his missive came a week later, I realized that my worries, far from being over, had only just begun. I read no further than the first paragraph before my hand began to tremble uncontrollably.

"Ursula!" I called, rushing into the nursery. She was not there. "Ursula!" I ran through the arched passageway. *Blessed Mother, how can this be true?* "Ursula—"

She was by the well, with Geoffrey. She turned, and grew pale as she looked at me. In one swift movement, she was at my side, a hand around my shoulder. I showed her the missive, for I could not form the words. She read, and cried out on a breath. Closing her eyes, she put out a hand to Geoffrey for support.

King Edward IV, England's twenty-two-year-old golden warrior king, had cancelled parliament and summoned his lords to Reading to inform them of a matter of far greater import to the realm than a threat of invasion by Marguerite. While this new matter also constituted a threat, it lay close to the king's bosom and he did not see it as such, for he was a man blinded by love. On May Day, the first of May, 1464, Edward had taken a wife and wed her secretly at the manor of Grafton Regis. Born the daughter of Jacquetta, former Duchess of Bedford, and a lowly knight, she was the mother of two small boys and the widow of Sir John Grey, son of a Lancastrian lord, who had died at Towton—

She was Elizabeth Woodville, Marguerite d'Anjou's former lady-in-waiting.

Shaken by the thought of the woman to whom I had bid farewell with such a happy heart seven years earlier—a great beauty, to be sure, but also coldhearted, vindictive, arrogant, envious, and avaricious—I pressed close to Ursula as I read the rest of John's missive. The royal houses of Europe were already buzzing with the news, which they found more scandalous than when John of Gaunt, Duke of Lancaster, uncle to the King of England, had wed lowborn Katherine Swynford seventy years earlier. For this was the king himself. And while John of Gaunt had obtained the king's consent, King Edward had wed his bride secretly. By this marriage, a deed committed behind Warwick's back and hidden for four months, Edward meant to proclaim that he was his own man and would not answer to anyone, not even to the one who had made him king. As John had written, Edward made the situation blazingly clear to Warwick at Reading. "Be forewarned, Cousin. I may be young," he had said, "but I am no stuffed wool sack to be pushed around like Henry, no crown to be worn by others—especially you."

But Elizabeth Woodville, Queen of England?

For some reason, Duke Humphrey's last words came to me. As he'd sat on his horse, awaiting the Battle of Northampton, where he died, it was claimed that he said, "Here we are, all that we tried to avoid has caught up with us now, God help us all."

My hand shook violently around John's letter. "Holy Mother Mary," I said to Ursula, unaware that I spoke aloud until I heard my own words. "May God save England. . . . May God save us all."

That night I had a bad dream, the same one I'd had at Westminster before my marriage. I was caught in the rain, and I was wet, shivering. I had hugged myself and realized it wasn't rain that had soaked me, but blood. When I'd looked up again, John smiled at me. He gave me a flower: It was a white rose, and happiness enfolded me. Then I dropped it. He bent down to retrieve it for me, and when he stood again, it was no longer him, but the stranger whose face I could not see. He handed me a red rose, and I saw, with horror, that it was merely a white rose soaked in blood.

I had awakened to find myself sitting bolt upright in bed.

A dream, 'tis all it is, I thought with relief. *Oh, thank God!* For it had felt so real, just like that other time. From now on, I would have to put thoughts of Elizabeth Woodville aside and focus on our blessings. I had not seen her in a long time. Perhaps she had changed. . . . Perhaps, she had softened as Somerset had. . . .

But it proved difficult to get away from the subject of Edward's marriage, for everywhere the talk was of her. The news had raced its way across the land like a wildfire that would not be put out until it was quenched by the seas. When John and I paid Warwick a visit at Middleham two months later, he seethed.

"Rivers?" Warwick spat. "Bah! He's a Lancastrian lordling, a nobody for whom no one has anything but contempt. All England has laughed at them. Now his daughter is queen!" He paused, his face a livid red, a pulse throbbing in his forehead. "All my great plans for the kingdom have been foiled by the arts of a woman and the infatuation of a boy."

"You do Edward wrong by dismissing him in such manner," John said quietly. "He is no boy but a fine military commander who has pulled off two great victories against impossible odds."

"And since Towton, he's contributed nothing—*nothing*," Warwick spat, "to his own success! And you're a fine one to take up his defense—don't you know what he said about you? He said, 'I shall stay where it's warm and comfortable. Let Montagu take care of sieges and Lancastrians. He's more suited to rough beds and inclement weather, for he's a soldier by nature.' Edward was busy whoring in Leicester—that's why you had to fight Somerset alone at Hexham!" Warwick slammed a fist on the table.

I listened with a heavy heart. Clearly the king had no idea what John sacrificed for him in performing his duty and winning him the many victories that kept his throne secure. And certainly Warwick had reason to be angry. King Edward had played him for a fool and humiliated him in the eyes of all Europe by sending him on an embassy to France to discuss a marriage with a French princess, when Edward had already been married.

OUR CONCERNS VANISHED WHEN, WITHIN TEN days of the Feast of St. Valentine, the twenty-fourth of February, 1465, nine months after John had received his earldom, I gave birth to a beautiful boy child we named George.

Our joy, though pure, was short-lived, for Elizabeth lost no time stirring up trouble, and shocking news soon arrived that affected us personally. Ambitious and vengeful, she and her brood of twelve siblings swarmed the echelons of power, stuffing themselves with the riches of others and destroying those who stood in their way. In a shocking display of raw greed directed at us, the richest noble lady in the land, John's sixty-five-year-old aunt the Dowager Duchess of Norfolk, whose husband, the late duke, had saved the day for Edward at Towton, was made to wed the queen's eighteen-year-old brother, John Woodville.

"I swear I shall have that Woodville's head one day for this diabolical marriage they have foisted on my blood!" Warwick fumed to us at Middleham. "Wherever there is money or a title to be had, they force themselves on the premier families of the realm, and in defiance of law and convention marry the heirs against their will, no matter how young! Even worse, the Woodvilles subvert the laws of inheritance so that wealth and titles, once in their hands, cannot pass to the next of kin if their spouses die before they are old enough to have children of their own! And Edward, the fool, blinded by love, scarcely notices."

And because he lets her have her way, his queen grows bolder, I thought.

"You'd best not wait to find an heiress for your babe," Warwick warned John, "or by the rood, there won't be one left for him by the time he reaches marriage age. These Woodvilles breed like maggots!"

After he left, I went directly to the nursery. Putting Elizabeth Woodville out of my mind, I cradled my child close to my heart and sang to him as he stared at me with Neville blue eyes as dark and clear as his father's.

> *Hush, sweet Georgie,*
> *Hark to the birds,*
> *They sing for you.*
> *See the blossoms that drape the May,*
> *They bloom for you.*
> *Breezes blow,*
> *Windmills turn,*
> *Peace reigns o'er the land,*
> *Peace reigns. . . .*
> *So hush, my sweet Georgie,*
> *God's in His Heaven,*
> *He smiles on you.*

John took his brother's advice and negotiated the betrothal of our little George to the king's nine-year-old niece Anne, the heiress of her father, the exiled Lancastrian Duke of Exeter.

"It cost a hefty sum, and there won't be enough money this year to repair the cracked tower at Warkworth, so it shall have to wait. But it's a grand marriage, and nothing is too good for our son," John said, gazing at our babe asleep in my arms. He bent down and gave him a kiss as I watched, and my heart burst with love for them both.

ELIZABETH WOODVILLE WAS CROWNED QUEEN OF England in May 1465, on the first anniversary of her secret May Day wedding to Edward. It was a lavish affair, on which King Edward spared no expense. In an effort to accent her royal lineage, he sent with great ceremony for her mother's relative James, Count of Luxemburg, who came over to England accompanied by a brilliant retinue, in a ship decorated with flowers, ribbons, and silk cloth. No Nevilles attended her coronation. Warwick was away in Boulogne to negotiate a treaty with Burgundy, and John had his hands full on the border keeping the peace, besieging Bamburgh, and negotiating with the Scots. Edward's chancellor, Archbishop George, assisted John.

No doubt many others would have liked to stay away but dared not, for no one was pleased about this marriage except the Woodvilles—and perhaps my uncle, the Earl of Worcester, who had apparently won the queen's favor. His letters to me from court were filled with praise of her beauty and charm, and I wondered that such an intelligent man could be taken in by her. Ah, but my uncle had always been an incurable romantic who admired female beauty with the ardor of the knights in his manuscripts. If a woman was fair, he believed, then she was good, and love was worth any price a man had to pay. No doubt he had flattered Elizabeth Woodville with his appreciation of her beauty and of a marriage made for love, and with adoring acceptance had carried out her wishes and commands. And Edward's vain queen had responded with her favor. Naturally, since I was well acquainted with her character, I did not believe for an instant that she loved Edward. But that he loved her was what mattered.

When King Henry was betrayed by a monk in Abingdon some two months later, he was turned over to Warwick, who paraded him through London with his feet bound to his stirrups and then committed him to the Tower. King Edward at least saw to it that he was given spacious quarters, and that his imprisonment was a comfortable one, even permitting him visitors from time to time. I went to see him there myself, bringing with me a basket of sweet-meats and candied rose petals.

"I remember with affection your many kindnesses to me and my lord husband over the years. I pray for you daily, Your Grace, that you remain content and receive comfort," I told him. More than that I dared not say.

"You have my deepest thanks, my lady Isobel," Henry replied gently.

But before I could present him with my basket, the door opened to reveal one of Elizabeth Woodville's three brothers, Bishop Lionel Woodville, attended by the queen's two sons, eight-year-old Thomas and six-year-old Richard Grey. I would have departed then, but Henry didn't allow it. "Stay, my dear," he said, waving me back into my seat. "You have only just arrived."

Bishop Lionel brought up a point of clerical law with Henry, while the two boys chased one another around the room in a game of pretend swordplay. Suddenly, to my horror, I heard the older one say to the younger, "Ah, I have won! And I, King Edward, shall slay you, Henry the usurper!" I turned to see him holding his wooden sword to his brother's chin. The younger boy, finding no answer, turned to King Henry and said, "What do I say to that?"

Henry rose gently and came to the boy's side. Resting a hand on his shoulder, he faced Thomas Grey. "Here is what you say, dear child. . . . 'My father had been King of England, possessing his crown in peace through his reign. And my grandfather had been king of the same realm. And I, when a boy in the cradle, had been without delay crowned and approved as king by the whole realm, and wore the crown for forty years. Every lord throughout the land paid me royal homage and swore fealty to me, as they had done to my fore-fathers. . . . My help cometh from God, who preserveth them that are true of heart.' That is what you say, my child." With a tender smile on his face, he resumed his seat.

The boys looked at one another in confusion, and Thomas lowered his sword from his brother's throat. "So who won?"

Henry smiled but made no answer, and returned to the point of clerical law Bishop Woodville had raised. And the boys began to chase one another around the room again, this time as Saladin and Richard the Lionhearted.

My heart went out to Henry. Had he wed a woman of a different quality from the one who had been chosen for him by the Dukes of Somerset and Suffolk, the destiny of this gentle-hearted king, and of England, would have been very different.

THE NEXT TIME I SAW WARWICK, IT WAS AT THE glorious celebration he threw for George, who had been raised to archbishop of York by King Edward. Never did I attend such a glorious feast. All the nobles of the land were present, including the king's bosom companion, Lord William Hastings—except, since Warwick had shunned Elizabeth Woodville's coronation, the king and queen were absent.

Three hundred tuns of wine and a pipe of hippocras flowed all night; and so many pigs, swans, and thousands of other birds and beasts were slaughtered for the occasion that it required the services of sixty-two cooks. Among the elaborate subtleties presented was a life-size Samson in marchpane, and many other courses of the most artfully prepared and toothsome delicacies of jellies, tarts, and custards. For entertainment, Warwick brought in a Nubian, who performed incredible feats with butterflies. They flew about the hall, sorting themselves by color into crimsons, yellows, and blues, and forming circles, spirals, and figures of eight. When they were done, they disappeared into a large painted urn. The event proved so extraordinary that the feast became legendary through the land. As I heard later, it also became the talk of the Continent, which no doubt pleased Warwick. Even his friend King Louis of France was said to have been impressed.

Remembering Elizabeth Woodville, however, and the evil things that happened to those who drew her ire, I gave a shudder.

"Such as she can never be happy," I said to John one evening. "Her happiness lies in making others as miserable as she is herself. And if she doesn't succeed in this, her sense of failure leads her to strike back until she does triumph. Look at poor Cooke. . . ."

Thomas Cooke was a rich merchant and a former mayor of London who had refused to sell a tapestry to Elizabeth's mother for the paltry sum she offered. It was said, in fact, that he had not wished to sell at any price. But when he refused it to Jacquetta, Duchess of Bedford, he was suddenly accused of treason and thrown into the Tower. At his trial, he was found innocent by an impartial and distinguished judge, but Elizabeth Woodville had flown into a rage and demanded of the king that Cooke be tried again. Aware that his queen had much to do with the charge of treason brought against the old mayor, the king appointed a panel of appeal judges that included his brother Clarence and Warwick—two of her many enemies. They released Cooke, but she had demanded a third trial, whose verdict had yet to be determined. Meanwhile the queen's father ransacked the old mercer's house, pretending to search for proof of his guilt, and carried off all his valuables, including the tapestry in question.

That evening, over a flask of wine in our solar at Alnwick, John broached the subject with Warwick, who was visiting for the night. "Wicked she is, the queen, but your blunt condemnation of her is dangerous, brother. Why not hide your feelings as everyone else does?"

"I, and the king's brother Clarence, have decided not to make pretense of how we feel about Edward's choice of wife, for one simple reason: We are the only ones who can. 'Tis our hope that by so doing, we shall make Edward aware of the true nature of the despicable woman he has so rashly wed, and of the damage she does to his reputation. She is another Marguerite—and, like Marguerite, she'll cost him and his heirs the throne in the end."

"Edward is blinded by love—you cannot make him see things as they are. Hide your disdain, brother. No good can come of it. I fear for your safety, and our own. You hold our destiny in your hands. I beg you to reverse course while we can still save ourselves."

"I know what is best for us, and for England!" Warwick had replied, red in the face, as he stormed out.

John plunged himself all the harder into pleasing the king by efforts to bring peace to the Scots border, but Bamburgh would not surrender. Yet we managed to find comfort, for after a year, there was still no sign of a royal child.

"Maybe we have nothing to fear," I said to Ursula hopefully.

"If she proves barren," Ursula whispered back, "we will be safe." And, taking a candle offering, she gave me a knowing look as she went into the chapel to pray.

AS THE YULETIDE OF 1465 APPROACHED, I LEARNED I was with child again. I hummed as I decorated the castle for the sacred season, dreaming of another son for John. Meanwhile John turned his energies into winning Bamburgh from the Lancastrians. Blasting a hole in the walls with one of Warwick's cannons, he stormed the fortress. The Lancastrians surrendered under a general pardon when they found their captain, Sir Ralph Grey, dead. However, Grey regained consciousness the following day; he had been merely knocked unconscious by the ceiling that fell on him. Though wounded so badly he was unable to stand, he was taken before my uncle, who presided at trial in Doncaster. My uncle had him propped up on pillows to hear his sentence, and Grey was shown no mercy. He was carried onto the scaffold to be beheaded. I was troubled by the ruthlessness my uncle had shown. But, determined to enjoy the Christmas season, I didn't permit myself to dwell on it.

John finally arrived at Warkworth on Christmas Eve, exhausted and nursing a violent cold and a raging fever. I put him to bed, my first concern, as always, to ensure he received the care he needed to bring him back into not only bodily health but also good spirits. To that end, I engaged the best minstrels and mummers I could find, and invited many friends to feastings at our gorgeous castle of Warkworth, where we had moved for Yuletide. There, we whiled away many evenings in the company of such as Lord Clinton, Lord

Scrope of Bolton, Sir John Conyers, and their ladies and retinues. Though Warwick could not attend, he sent his troubadour to one of these feasts.

At Warwick's request, John wore his circlet and earl's robes, and the man, following Warwick's orders, dedicated his song to John and launched into the tale of Guy of Warwick, who first slew a giant cow on Dunsmore Heath and then slew the dragon of Northumberland. "Your noble brother Warwick the Kingmaker," announced the troubadour, "bids me declare before all ye gathered here that you, my lord, have slain the dragon of Northumberland with the same zeal and ease as the legendary hero Guy of Warwick!" The man pumped his fists in the air and called out to the hall, "Woe to Percies! Long live Nevilles!" He was hailed by roaring cheers and the stomping of feet.

By the Twelfth Day of Christmas, when he had to leave again, John was back to himself. At this time came exceedingly happy news. The Lord Lieutenant of Ireland, the Earl of Desmond, the beloved, brave, and noble friend of the Duke of York's who had, at great risk to himself, taken up the cause of York and given the duke refuge in Ireland after the disaster at Ludlow, was coming to England in August to report on Irish affairs to his good friend King Edward. We were invited to attend the royal banquet planned in his honor at Westminster.

Twenty-two

The Banquet, 1466

THE FOLLOWING YEAR, ON THE ELEVENTH DAY of February, 1466, Elizabeth Woodville gave birth to a daughter she named Elizabeth. The babe was baptized by the archbishop of Canterbury and Archbishop George, with the two grandmothers, the duchess Cecily and the duchess Jacquetta, in attendance as god-mothers. Edward reached out to Warwick once again, inviting him to be godfather, an honor he accepted for the peace of the realm.

The ceremony of Elizabeth's churching that followed at West-minster Palace eclipsed even the elaborate fanfare over the birth of her first royal child. Warwick gave us the details when next he visited Alnwick. It seemed the parvenue queen, whose beauty had captured a royal heart as well as a royal hand, sat at a table in solitary splendor, on a golden chair in a magnificently bedecked hall, and before her had knelt the highest noble ladies in the land.

"Several Bohemian dignitaries happened to be visiting West-minster, and they could not believe what pomp and reverence the Woodville claimed for herself. For three hours she kept the king's sister Meg and her own mother, Jacquetta, on their knees before her, not deigning to utter a single word to them as she dined!"

"But this churching is known to have been done before," John replied.

"Aye, it has been done on occasion, but never for three hours—and those queens were of royal birth, not lowborn like her!" he roared. "Every so often, her mother would request permission to stretch her tired muscles, which was granted. But when the dancing began, the Woodville sat watching, and even the king's sister Meg had to keep coming back to curtsey to her. . . . The Bohemians had never seen anything like it!" Warwick's expression evidenced his utter disgust. As if to wash away the bitter taste in his mouth, he emptied his wine in a single draught.

On the heels of the birth of the princess Elizabeth came ill tidings. Little Anne Holland, the daughter and heiress of the Duke of Exeter, who had been promised in marriage to our Georgie, was snatched away by Elizabeth Woodville for her son Thomas Grey, with a payment of four thousand marks. Now I understood her puzzling attention to me at Desmond's banquet. She had been preparing the wound for the sting. When we saw the Duchess of Exeter at Middleham months later, she made us an apology as best she dared. "Matters of marriage are not necessarily ours to decide these days," she said.

More and more, Edward set Warwick aside for the Woodvilles. Not long after Elizabeth's churching, the issue of another marriage arose, straining the breech between Warwick and the king to its most threatening point.

The marriage of Edward's sister Meg, his only unwed sister, was a matter of vital national importance. Would she marry into Burgundy, as the queen wished, or into France, as Warwick advised? This alliance, already a bitter battleground between Elizabeth and Warwick, grew into a test of their wills.

I did not always side with Warwick in his opinions and his feuds, though he held our family fortunes in his hands, for he could be insufferably arrogant at times. But on this occasion I sympathized with him. No one had worked harder, paid a higher price, or risked more than Warwick to raise Edward to the throne and beat back his enemies. Now that Edward felt himself secure, he was moving Warwick aside, not for some other Yorkist supporter, but for the Woodville upstarts who had fought for and clung to the House of Lancaster until the very last moment.

We knew Elizabeth's jealousy of the Nevilles stood at the root of Edward's growing hostility to Warwick, including the question of Meg's alliance. To prove her star ascendant over Warwick's, Elizabeth was willing to go to any lengths, for there was a poison running in her veins that made her blind to the consequences of her actions. In this regard, and in many others, she resembled her friend Marguerite, who had held sway over poor Henry through the weakness of his mind. Elizabeth wielded the same power over King Edward, for an obvious but very different reason.

Warwick, on his part, might have improved his relationship with Edward had he struck a conciliatory note, but instead he quarreled with him at every turn. John, deeply concerned by his brother's attitude to the king, took the matter up with him when he visited Alnwick Castle again.

"You are richer than Edward, more popular with the people, and more admired throughout the land. Be content with that, Dick. Don't fan his jealousy. You cannot keep overshadowing the king, as you did with the Bohemians, by throwing a feast with sixty-four courses after he's given a banquet and served fifty! 'Tis dangerous. Edward will resent us even more."

"Edward needs to be reminded of our power! 'Tis all that keeps us Nevilles safe from harm."

"The king rules England, Dick, and he favors Burgundy over France for purposes of trade, not merely because his queen wishes it. 'Tis not for you to say what shall be done."

"I know best what's right for England. This wanton boy has no talent for anything but whoring! 'Tis his lust that gave us this vile queen. By pretending to be virtuous and refusing to bed him, the Woodville witch wiled that fool Edward into handing her a crown!"

John paled, placed a restraining hand on his brother's arm. "Guard your tongue, brother, or you'll bring us all down."

Warwick threw off his hand with an angry shrug and strode to the door.

John called out after him, "Beware, lest you force me to part ways with you! You are mistaken to believe that I will follow blindly wherever you lead."

Warwick turned around and glared at John for a long moment before he marched out. From this scene, I turned away with a heavy heart.

MY CHILD WAS ANOTHER GIRL, BORN ON THE fifteenth of June as summer bedecked the fields with wildflowers. We named her Lucy. Two months later, leaving all our children at Warkworth—for there was plague in London—we departed for the South, accompanied by a large escort of men-at-arms and baggage carts. Even Duchess Cecily, who had retired to a life of prayer at Berkhamsted and was seen little after her husband's death, came out of seclusion to honor the charming, revered, and much-loved Thomas Fitzgerald, Earl of Desmond, who had been such a staunch friend to the Yorkist cause.

I was a trifle nervous to see Elizabeth Woodville after so long, and wondered how she would receive us. But I should have expected it to be as it was. When I curtseyed before her, a spiteful smile descended to her lips and an icy wind seemed to enfold me from the dais. While the king bid us a warm welcome, she said nothing, but I felt her eyes bore into my back as we moved away. I wondered at her nature. Here was a woman who had not only achieved what she had set out to do, but had surpassed it to reach the very pinnacle of power; yet she had within her tight spirit not a groat of generosity.

The king had gone to great lengths to entertain his father's dear friend; we enjoyed three delightful days of feasting and merriment before the last banquet. On that unforgettable evening, the Painted Chamber glittered as never before, in the blaze of a thousand candles and torches and the flash of jewels adorning the nobles. The king himself shone like the sun of his emblem, in a yellow velvet gown richly embroidered in gold, while Elizabeth sparkled in black cloth of gold encrusted with diamonds, from the jeweled queenly circlet on her head to the tips of her royal toes.

Like all the lords and ladies in attendance, John and I wore new attire. I had chosen a magnificent crimson velvet sewn with garnets and edged in sable to match the stunning multitiered ruby necklace John's mother had given me, and John was clad in a rich velvet surcoat of azure cloth of gold bordered with brown sable and slashed with emerald silk, a furred mantle at his shoulder and a heavy gold chain set with sapphires around his collar. Though he had lost weight due to his exertions in the inclement conditions of the harsh Northumberland winter, he looked exceedingly handsome. As for myself, if I believed John's compliments, I did not pale in comparison to the other noble ladies.

"You look impossibly beautiful, my angel. Like a black swan gliding in shining waters. Your hair gleams a raven color against your ivory complexion, and no one can keep their eyes from you. You eclipse even the queen."

"Hush now!" I warned, half in jest. "Men have lost their heads for less." But I smiled. I did feel beautiful this night. I had never owned a more exquisite gown, and Ursula had coiled my hair in a new and most becoming style. Instead of flowing loose or being hidden away beneath a cone-shaped headdress and veil, it was caught at the nape of my neck in a silver net woven with diamonds and crystals.

No sooner had John left my side than Elizabeth Woodville deigned to pause and shed a few words over me as she swept past on her son's arm. "I understand you have a son now," she said, watching me carefully. I curtseyed and inclined my head respectfully. "An heir, whom you have betrothed to Anne Holland, the Duchess of Exeter's daughter."

Again I inclined my head. "Aye, Your Grace," I said as graciously as I could, hoping to avoid giving her cause for offense, for she was noted for perceiving slights where none were intended. Her young son Thomas Grey watched me with a haughty, remote look. She said no more and, dropping her lids, lifted her chin and moved on. I wondered at the purpose of her attention. Was she jealous because

I had a son and, as yet, she had been unable to give King Edward naught but a girl child?

John came and went as I chatted with the Countess of Desmond, whose company I had much enjoyed during our visit. Finally he left to seek out her husband, the illustrious Earl of Desmond. I had been charmed by both the earl and his countess over the past days, for the valiant, learned Desmond was a remarkably good-looking and congenial man, without arrogance but with a wonderful wit that reminded me of Thomas Neville. In his company I found much cause for merriment. Like my uncle, Desmond was a scholar who had studied the classics and enjoyed poetry and philosophy, but in Ireland he was known for not only his generous patronage of the arts, but also for his charity, humanity, and generosity to the poor. *Whereas my uncle enjoys a slightly different reputation.* I crushed my wicked thought and stole a glance at Desmond as he stood in conversation with John, Warwick, and Archbishop George. He was as tall as the Nevilles, and equally broad of shoulder and well made. Young Dickon of Gloucester came to join them, and Desmond, looking down with twinkling eyes, engaged the shy boy in conversation with easy grace.

"The Duke of York was very fond of your lord husband and spoke of him often in the most glowing terms," I said. "Now I see why. Your lord husband is charming, Countess."

"What happened to the Duke of York broke our hearts. He was a noble man, God assoil his soul. We loved him well." She fell silent, and her warm hazel eyes took on a sad, faraway look. "Young Richard of Gloucester reminds me of his father," she said abruptly.

"Aye, my lord husband is very fond of Dickon. He takes much time from his duties on the border to personally instruct the young duke in the art of warfare. He says he has never met a young man who is so determined and has such sense of purpose."

"To these qualities, I can add another, dear Countess Isobel. He is near as handsome as his brother King Edward."

"I shall tell him you said so. It will greatly please him, for the young duke does not have a grand opinion of himself."

"Humility is also a virtue. It seems Gloucester is laden with them . . . like his father before him, may he rest in peace." She sighed, made the sign of the cross, and added softly, "If York's sons fare well in this life, the father will not have died in vain, for we all wish for our children a life better than what we have known. Perhaps with this Sun of York on the throne of England, the people of England and Ireland can look forward to peace and contentment."

"Indeed . . ." I said, reflecting on such a life, one free from worries and war. "I wish we lived closer, you and I. We would be good friends."

"We surely would, Countess Isobel." She took my hand. "Perhaps Fate will be kind and afford us chance to meet again soon."

Without warning, the music that had been playing ceased, and a shocked murmur ran through the hall. Everyone turned in the direction of the entrance. A man with a long white beard and leather pants cut high above knobbly knees thumped his way through the room with the aid of a staff. I glanced at King Edward, whose hand had frozen with a wine cup halfway to his lips.

"Whoa!" he called. "What's this?"

The man ambled up to the king.

"Why, 'tis Clarence's fool," muttered Edward.

"Fool I may be," replied the Fool, "but tonight, sire, I am the King of Fools!"

"A dubious honor, I assure you, since fools have been known to lose their heads," said Edward with narrowed eyes. "Tell me, Your Foolish Grace, why are you dressed in this bizarre fashion?"

"Sire, my journey here was full perilous as any knight's. Many times I came near death."

"How so?" demanded Edward.

"I was near swept away by the currents, so high were *the Rivers*."

A deadly silence fell over the room. Everyone stared at the rigid queen. Then Edward let out a roar of laughter. The silence shattered, and relief swept me. Blessed Heaven, but Clarence had made his Fool take a dangerous chance!

I stole a troubled glance at Elizabeth Woodville. I feared she would not forget this.

*   *   *

EARLY IN THE NEW YEAR CAME A DISTURBING
letter from my uncle.

My dear niece,

   *I wanted you to be the first to know that I have been appointed
Lord Lieutenant of Ireland in Desmond's place. I shall be leaving
England shortly, mayhap even before you receive this letter. Our
beauteous Queen Elizabeth originated the idea, which was well received by our noble sovereign, King Edward, for Desmond has been
lax in some regards, and matters in Ireland stand sorely in need of
my attention. May the Lord watch over you and keep you safe until
we meet again.*
   *Given this tenth day of January, 1467, at the palace of
Westminster.*

*John Tiptoft, Earl of Worcester, Lord Constable of England, Lord
Lieutenant of Ireland*

"What does this mean?" I asked John. But my husband had no
answer for me before he left for Pontefract Castle, where he was
constable and had pressing business to attend.

Not long afterward, we all learned its meaning. Desmond, the
charming, beloved Irish lord who had risked everything to support
the Duke of York against Marguerite d'Anjou during the years
when few dared give overt support, was accused of treason by my
uncle, Worcester. When Desmond came in bravely to answer the
false charge, he was thrown into prison and his death warrant was
sent to the king for his signature. Sir John Conyers brought me the
news.

"At the banquet at Westminster, King Edward pressed Desmond
to tell him what he thought o' his queen, and Desmond told him
the truth—that his queen was beautiful, but it might have served
England better had King Edward secured the friendship of France

or even Burgundy by an alliance with a royal princess. And Edward related his comments to Elizabeth Woodville."

I turned away, my head reeling. *Is this sufficient grounds for which to execute a man? Dear God, what is happening?* With John away, I went to find comfort with Nan at Middleham.

"This is Elizabeth Woodville's doing, but the king will pardon his father's friend," Nan assured me. "How can he not? The Earl of Desmond stood by him through all the troubles with Lancaster, and he knows, as we all do, that the charge is false."

"You must be right," I replied. "It has been a month since Desmond's conviction. Edward could have signed the death warrant long before now, and he hasn't. It must mean he plans to pardon Desmond."

On the following Sunday in February, only days after the Feast of St. Valentine, Archbishop George was conducting mass in the chapel, when shouts and the clatter of horses sounded in the courtyard. We hurried outside. Two messengers dropped from their saddles and fell to their knees before Warwick, their travel-stained clothes and sorrowful expressions attesting to the ill nature of the news they carried.

"My lord, the Earl of Desmond is dead! He was beheaded by the Earl of Worcester on the fifteenth of February."

I stared, mouth agape, unable to believe the words they uttered.

"The king signed the death warrant?" Warwick demanded incredulously through ashen lips.

"Nay, nay! The king left the warrant unsigned in a drawer in his bedchamber, but the queen grew tired of waiting. She stole the king's signet ring and forged the king's signature. She sent the sealed death warrant to the Earl of Worcester, who executed the Earl of Desmond without the king's knowledge," the messenger said.

As we digested this horror, the second messenger informed us of another.

"His two boys, mere children of eight and ten, were sent to the block with him. One had a boil on his neck and asked the executioner to pray be careful, for it hurt."

Warwick groaned; Nan gasped. Archbishop George made the sign of the cross, his lips moving in prayer. I gave a shudder. The Countess of Desmond had lost not only a husband but two of her children. I remembered her praise of Edward: *Perhaps with this Sun of York on the throne of England, we can look forward to peace and contentment.* Instead the Sun had been shrouded by a vicious black cloud that rained down atrocities.

I hugged myself against the fit of shivering that seized my body. Once again Elizabeth Woodville had wreaked vengeance on an innocent man for a perceived slight. I had never believed, as others did, that she had committed sorcery to win Edward, and deep down I had always nursed the hope that she was not as wicked as she seemed, but now I faced the hideous truth: Her great beauty hid evil the way a gilded sepulcher hid the rot and stench of decaying human flesh. This creature that held the king in its fangs was a demon vomited up from the bowels of Hell.

"The king was furious when he learned what his queen had done," one of the messengers said.

Too late, too late! With dragging steps, I joined Nan and the others in the chapel to pray and weep for Desmond, and for his wretched countess, now left to mourn a husband and two sons butchered on Elizabeth Woodville's sacrificial altar.

AS ILL TIDINGS NEVER COME SINGLY, BUT IN threes, late one morning, after we had returned to Warkworth, I found Ursula missing. I searched for her myself until at last I spotted her red head in a far-off, little-used chamber, where she sat in a corner, weeping.

"What is the matter, dear Ursula?" I asked.

"My f-f-father—" she sobbed.

"What has happened to him?"

"He's been imprisoned . . . with T-Thomas C-Cooke—" She burst into fresh tears.

My breath caught in my throat. I sank down on the floor beside her. *Is there to be no end to the misery that Woodville causes?* The verdict on Thomas Cooke's third trial had come in. This time Cooke was convicted and assessed a fine so enormous, it cost him everything he owned. On top of that sum, Elizabeth Woodville, reviving an archaic law long since fallen into disuse, demanded a ruinous payment of "Queen's Gold." Cooke fled the country.

"But your father—what is his connection with Cooke?"

Ursula shook her head. "None . . . he was taken into imprisonment because of his connection to my lord of Warwick."

I stared at her, not comprehending.

"My lady Isobel," Urusla sniffled, " 'tis said the king suspects my lord of Warwick of treason, and since he is too powerful to be imprisoned, the queen has chosen others she wishes taken into custody in his place."

I could not speak for a long moment. Finally I said, with more conviction than I felt, "Dear Ursula, Warwick will find a way to get him out."

But it was an ill wind that blew through the land. Warwick was away in France on royal business during that summer of 1467, and we both knew the matter would have to wait until his return. Then came a fresh series of harsh tidings in swift succession. Taking advantage of Warwick's absence, Edward threw a lavish tournament for the bastard of Burgundy, and at the end of September, before Warwick's return, he announced Meg's betrothal to Charles the Rash.

King Edward had chosen Burgundy over France; Elizabeth Woodville had won over Warwick. Archbishop George, Edward's chancellor, who was to open parliament, absented himself with an excuse of illness. And Edward, in fury, rode to George's residence, demanded the return of the Great Seal, and appointed a new chancellor.

When Warwick returned and learned all that had transpired in his absence, he fell into a rage and went about the Erber smashing urns and furniture, pulling down wall hangings, hurling goblets, books, and anything not fixed to the wall. He knew Meg's future husband and despised him utterly.

"He's half-mad. You can see it in his eyes," he said on a visit to Warkworth. "His father, Philip the Good, loathed him and was sore troubled to leave Burgundy in his hands. Edward will rue the day he made his pact with Charles, for it frees Louis of France to back Marguerite against him—and back her he will!"

Warwick retired to nurse his rage at his fortress of Middleham, and King Edward, fearful of an uprising against his rule, surrounded himself with two hundred archers when he rode out from Windsor to spend Yuletide in Coventry.

"Not since that hated monarch Richard the Second has a king seen the need to protect himself with such a bodyguard!" Warwick huffed to us.

Nevertheless, for the sake of appearances and to reassure the land, Warwick made his peace with Edward as the New Year of 1468 blew in on a ferocious blizzard. Assuming a gracious demeanor in the spring, he escorted Meg from Blackfriars to Margate, where the *New Ellen* and thirteen other ships awaited to take the bride and her company to Burgundy. But as soon as he returned to Middleham, he summoned John to a meeting.

It was a sunny morning in the month of July when we left Warkworth for Middleham. But ominous storm clouds, hanging dark and low over the land, gathered in the distance as we approached Warwick's fortress. We wound our way through the pastoral countryside, our retinue at our side, trotting our horses through rolling meadows, past green pastures dotted with woolly sheep, along grassy riverbanks, and down steep wooded slopes. Wildflowers nodded in the breeze, and lambs bleated gently; the world seemed peaceful enough. But silence was all around us and we did not speak, for our hearts lay heavy in our breasts, and whatever it was that Warwick had to tell us, we knew it boded ill.

Northumberland's herald sounded the clarions in the Middleham market square, and villagers gathered to the castle with solemn expressions to watch us climb the hill. Warwick, Nan, and Archbishop George met us impatiently in the courtyard, their faces somber. As we mounted the stairs to the keep, I noted the strange hush that engulfed the castle. Chapel priests whispered their prayers, clerks buried their heads in their papers, and servants went about their tasks wordlessly. The knights, squires, and men-at-arms of Warwick's retinue sat around the halls and on the staircases, polishing their armor and sharpening their weapons, and while they stood to give us due obeisance as we passed, their expressions spoke their gloomy thoughts.

Nan and I hurried to a chamber adjoining Warwick's corner suite, which afforded us a clear view of his apartments and where we might eavesdrop on his conversation. Slipping the bolt into place stealthily, we tiptoed to the window and pressed ourselves flat against the wall on either side of the opening, straining to hear what was said.

Warwick blocked the window with his broad back so that I could not see John, who stood across from him. What passed between them I couldn't hear. Then Warwick shouted, "Elizabeth has made herself as hated as Marguerite ever was!"

Snatches of his words floated to us on the breeze drifting through the open window. "Malory still imprisoned . . . our brother deprived of the chancellorship . . . French ambassadors left with . . . leather bottles . . . empty promises . . . The Burgundian envoys . . . loaded like mules with gold . . . precious gifts . . ."

Nan and I exchanged an anxious look, not daring to stir. Warwick was mulling over the humiliation he'd suffered at Edward's hands on his return from France. He'd brought with him several French ambassadors and a generous offer from Louis for Meg's hand—but King Edward refused to meet with them and sent the embassy back to Louis with a few beggarly gifts.

Warwick spoke again, and though we both strained to listen, his voice was too low for us to hear. Then he boomed, "Woodville witch!" followed by, "John! Did you hear me, John?"

Warwick moved away from the window, and I caught my first glimpse of John. He stood at the large table with a stunned look on his face.

"What just happened?" Nan whispered.

I shook my head and raised a finger to my lips, for I did not know and feared to miss something. We both edged closer to the opening. "You've gone mad!" I heard John say.

Warwick crashed his fist on the table. " 'Tis Edward . . . mad with lust for his greedy witch. . . . I did not put him on the throne for this!"

What I heard next sent sheer black fright surging through me. "I put him up, and I can bring him down!" Warwick roared.

I watched John lean his full weight on his hands as he stood at the table, as if to steady himself. The pain I witnessed on his face made itself felt through my body, and tears sprang into my eyes. John spoke, but so quietly I heard not a word. My heart broke for him, and I ached to take him into my arms and soothe away his grief. I must have moved too dangerously close to the window, for Nan warned me back with a gentle kick.

Again John spoke, but I could not catch his words.

Warwick replied, "Not me . . . Edward's own brother Clarence, who . . ."

Nan nodded. She turned to me and held an imaginary crown to her head. *Warwick intends to make Clarence king!* For Clarence, Edward's ambitious brother, had long maintained he was the true king of England, and Edward but a bastard sired by an archer—a ridiculous tale concocted in the depths of Clarence's shallow and cloudy brain that made sense only to him. The men moved away from the window then, and all that came from the room was a mumble of voices. Archbishop George drew into view. "Aye," he said, "Dick is right. The Woodvilles are rats gnawing on the ship of state! They'll sink us unless we destroy them first. . . ."

He moved away and John came back into view. I heard him clearly now. "Easy for you to say! You've no convictions of your own, George, only ambition!" A silence. Then, "But I'll have none of it."

I began to tremble.

Warwick stared at John. "But you're a Neville," he said.

"And have always done what you wished, Dick . . ." John paused, and the corners of his mouth worked with emotion. "Except in this. I cannot—I will not. My duty is to the king."

"What about your duty to your kin?" Warwick stormed.

Archbishop George blocked the window with his back. "You

can't go against us, John," he said, and his voice sounded as clearly as if he stood in the same room with us. "You'd be fighting your own flesh and blood."

John mumbled a reply, which I neither heard nor cared to hear, for now I understood what had happened. Warwick was mounting a rebellion against Edward, a rebellion John refused to join. I could barely breathe. The room had grown so warm . . . so warm. . . .

I put a hand to my heart and felt it beating erratically, as it had done often of late. When John swept his gauntlets up from the table, a pain rose in my breast that squeezed my chest so tightly, the breath left my body and my legs folded beneath me. I slipped down along the wall until I sat on the floor, and I dropped my head into my lap.

Twenty-three

1469

ON THE DAY JOHN BROKE WITH HIS BROTHERS, there was a violent storm. As summer faded into winter, the Woodvilles became more detested, and tensions escalated between the king and Warwick. In this quarrel, the king's brother George of Clarence, driven by passion for his brother's crown and hatred of the queen's ilk, sided with Warwick. That hatred was making itself felt all across the realm. In Kent, Earl Rivers's estate was pillaged, and to the king came rumors of rebellion. As the situation deteriorated in England, so too did it worsen in Ireland. There my uncle proved a disaster for King Edward. Far from settling the land, his harsh measures had stirred it to the brink of rebellion. Only when my uncle, the hated "Saxon Earl," was recalled and the Earl of Desmond's good friend the Earl of Kildare appointed deputy governor was peace restored.

But the situation in England did not offer such easy remedy. The Woodvilles could not be made to vanish, and their spiteful acts continued to aggravate the realm. Soon rebellions broke out in the North.

The New Year of 1469 began with many sinister portents of disaster. A shower of blood stained grass in Bedfordshire; elsewhere, a horseman and men in arms were seen rushing through the air. In the county of Huntingdon, a woman who was with child and near the time of her delivery felt the unborn in her womb weep and utter a sobbing noise. And in the early spring, England heard about the first trouble, a rising in Yorkshire led by someone calling himself Robin of Redesdale, citing as grievances heavy taxes, injustice in the courts, and the rapacious Woodvilles, whose greed and impudence, they said, outraged honest men. No sooner did John put this down than a second arose in East Riding, led by a Robin of Holderness, who called for the restoration of Henry Percy as Earl of Northumberland. At the gates of York, John met the insurgents, crushed the rebellion promptly, and executed their leader.

"I've earned my earldom, Isobel, and been a good lord to them," John said. "Why should they call for Percy—what have the Percies ever done for them?"

From my window seat in our private solar at Warkworth Castle, I regarded my husband. In a fur-edged velvet tunic of my favorite emerald, his faithful hound curled up at his feet, he sat at an oak-carved table, writing a private missive to the king that he didn't wish to dictate to a clerk. My heart ached for him. I knew that the executions troubled him, that what he was really asking was whether he'd been justified.

Aye, he didn't deserve such ingratitude. Though he hadn't the means of his brother Warwick, his kitchens never turned away a hungry mouth and his door was never closed to those in need. He had in truth done many a noble deed. What Percy had ever sent firewood to the prisons or wine to the prisoners? What lord had thought to do it in summer so men wouldn't have to cart the heavy loads through the bitter chill of winter? Such kindness was a rare thing, but John cared so for everyone: his soldiers, his servants, his family. His king.

I stretched out my hand and he came to me. I lifted my eyes to his handsome face. Dear God, so much change! His decision to support the king against his brothers came to him at fearsome cost.

No longer did he sleep at night or have heart for amusement. How different was this careworn face from the glorious countenance I had fallen in love with on that precious night of the dance at Tattershall Castle! Gray dusted the tawny hair at his temples, and deep furrows marred his once-smooth brow. His generous mouth was now grim-set and drooping at the corners, and a fresh scar cut through his left eyebrow. I remembered the hopeful, dauntless youth he had once been, and my heart squeezed with anguish.

"Do not fault yourself, my dear lord. Robin of Holderness had no right to call for Percy's reinstatement. . . . And Robin of Redesdale, is he also against you?"

John turned. With a gesture, he dismissed the servants. The minstrel hushed his harp in the corner of the room and rose from his stool. My maidservant, Agnes, who had been moving quietly about her duties emptying chests and hanging clothes in the garderobe, set a hand basin of perfumed water down on a bedside table and withdrew.

John's eyes took on a pained expression as he met my questioning gaze. "I fear Robin of Redesdale is none other than our cousin John Conyers, Isobel."

I gave a gasp and rose from my place at the window. "Oh, John, my dear lord—" So the nightmare had already begun. So soon! I took his sun-bronzed hand into my own—such a strong, fine hand. I pressed tearful kisses to the long fingers.

John took me into his arms.

"Dearest Isobel, what comfort you are to me. . . . What comfort you have always been," he said softly. "I remember that day when you saved me from Percy's ambush on St. Albans Road. You came to me dressed as a nun then. . . . And later, before Edward conferred the earldom on me, and I was fighting the Scots and the Lancastrians on the border, and there was nothing all around but death and suffering, you came to me in my camp with your troop of women, disguised as a dancing girl. I didn't know you, and I didn't pay much heed at first, but seeing my men laugh for a change so soothed my sore spirits, Isobel. . . . And then I realized who you were, and I couldn't believe my eyes, and you winked at me. You cannot know how you have lightened my heart with your courage and joy in life. . . . Oh, Isobel, how I have loved you these twelve years!"

He pulled me close. With his cheek against mine, we watched swans glide on the blue River Aln and sheep graze on the lush green grass of placid hills.

"Sunshine is always brighter when I'm with you, and birdsong sweeter, Isobel. I forget all else . . . the gales, the fogs . . . the cold, weary men trudging over the frozen earth . . . the battlefields. . . ."

I snuggled into the warmth of his embrace. "For me, 'tis the same, John. . . . Our dance together at Tattershall Castle seems like yesterday to me. You were young and so handsome, my dearest, and I was so in love with you. . . . As for those frightful days when you were taken prisoner by the Percies at Blore Heath and I thought I might lose you, never would I relive them for all the earldoms in England." I pulled away and looked up at his face. "To think it was all so needless! You were taken prisoner, after a battle you'd won, only because you recklessly pursued the Cheshiremen into their own territory." An image of John flashed into my mind: a dashing Neville chasing a hated Percy with all the wild abandon of youth. I smiled. "What were you thinking, my love?"

John grinned suddenly. "I wasn't thinking. That was the problem."

How good it felt to see him smile again; how long it had been since I'd seen those dimples I loved! I watched his eyes go back to the window, the smile fixed on his lips. I turned in the circle of his arms and followed his gaze to the walled garden below, where our three-year-old George had suddenly appeared, romping and screeching with delight as his sisters made a game of chasing him around the hedges. George had been born nine months after John had won his earldom, and I felt myself blush a little, remembering that night in York.

"You've given me everything I cherish on this earth," I whispered.

John tightened his hold around my waist and brushed my forehead with a tender kiss. "One day George will inherit my earldom. I'm thankful I have that to leave him, Isobel."

Aye, the earldom, with its annual income of a thousand pounds, would greatly ease George's path. Had his proposed marriage to the daughter of the Duchess of Exeter not been snatched away by the Woodville queen for her son, little Georgie would one day have been one of the richest magnates in the land. I banished the sour thought. As John was fond of saying, "In last year's nest, there are no eggs." Looking back never did anyone any good; we had to set our face to the future. We still had many blessings to count; Georgie would not have to take out debts in order to last the year, as we'd been obliged to do. Or worse—far worse—carve his livelihood through bloody battlefields as his father had. John had sacrificed much for the earldom. He'd devoted his life to the king's business. Whether it was fighting battles or negotiating truces, the earldom of Northumberland had been hard earned. No one had a right to take it away.

"You are a good lord and the king's truest subject, John. He knows that—how can he not? As for me, I am the most fortunate of women to call you husband, my love."

"And I, my lady, am the most fortunate of men to have a nun as my lady wife—"

I looked at him sharply. "A nun?"

"Or a dancing girl. Which are you, Isobel?"

"A bit of both, I suppose." I smiled.

"No, neither . . . You are only what I always knew you were . . . an angel. I have watched you walk through the storms of our life with your head up and a smile on your lips, and never in all these years, with all that's happened, have I heard you utter a single complaint. I have an angel as my lady wife." He looked down at me, and my heart leapt to see those creases around his mouth. "Did I ever tell you, Isobel, that you have the most beautiful smile I've ever seen? I still remember when I first saw that smile. At Tattershall Castle, as I stood in the courtyard. In fact, right now, I can almost feel the breeze. . . ."

"That's because we have the window open, my lord."

He laughed. "What if I tell you I can almost see Lord Cromwell's castle?"

I shook my head. "Then you are the only one, since this is rugged Northumberland, not dainty Lincolnshire."

" 'Tis the truth, though. . . . I can almost see it . . . right there. . . . The glow of sunset reflects off the western battlements as I clatter over the drawbridge into the inner court with my small party. . . . I'm weary from the long, dusty journey from Raby, and I've thrown the reins of my horse to one of the groomsmen, wondering why my brother Thomas doesn't come out to greet me. . . . Surely we've made enough noise. And at that instant I hear a laugh light as silvery bells . . . a sound that seems to fall from the heavens like the beating of angel wings. I glance up—" He glanced up.

"What happens next?" I whispered, tilting his chin back down to me.

"I see a face. . . . Framed by the violet sky, the face gazes down at me from a high window. . . . It's the face of an angel, serene, beautiful, with a complexion white as lilies and hair dark as chestnuts . . . and a luminous smile, and eyes like jewels. . . ."

I stared at him, tears welling at his description—that he should remember so clearly after all these years the moment when he first saw me! His eyes had taken on a faraway look, and it seemed to me that he was truly standing in that courtyard, looking up at that window, seeing me again for the first time.

"I couldn't tear my gaze away," he said, returning to the present. "Your brilliant topaz eyes had me enthralled. I didn't even hear the jangle of steel, or the shouts of men, or the neighing of the horses as Thomas rode into the castle with Cromwell and a troop of men-at-arms. I heard only the lyre you played . . . and the sweet notes of the lament you sang."

I hummed a few bars for him now.

"Aye . . . and then you laughed . . . and it was an angel's laugh, sweet as chapel bells over the dales at morning time—"

I waited for him to continue, wanting to relive every moment of that exquisite evening . . . the night of the dance. But he said, "And Thomas called to me in his cheery voice, *'John!'* And he leapt off his horse and ran to me. His dark hair was disheveled and there were streaks of dirt on his cheeks, but his eyes were alight to see me. . . . I remember that he clasped me to his breast and said, 'My fair brother, what a relief you're safe! You were so late, we rode out to search for you. One never knows with those damned Percies—' "

His voice had sunk to a bare whisper, and I knew I had to interrupt the stream of memories, for horror lay in wait. So I forced a laugh.

"All these years you've called me your angel," I said, "and all these years I've been telling you angels don't have chestnut hair. They have golden hair, as any painter or colored-glass maker will tell you."

He grinned. "My angels have chestnut hair."

I took his hand and held it tight against my cheek. "I love you, John, and have loved you from the first moment I saw you."

John smiled into my hair as he rocked me in his arms. "That blessed twilight eve at Lord Cromwell's castle."

I threw him a glance. "Nay, 'twas not at Lord Cromwell's castle where I first saw you. I was fourteen and riding past the River Ure with my cousins. We surprised you as you came out of the water after a swim."

John flushed. "You mean you were with that party of giggling maidens on the cart that saw me—"

I laughed. "Aye, naked as Adam, standing on the riverbank! Thomas had the sense to cover himself, but you blushed red as a beet root and covered the wrong part."

"My face."

"That was why we were all laughing, my sweet lord."

John grinned. He bent his head tenderly to mine. "My love," he whispered softly, "you never told me."

Twenty-four

1469

OUR UNHAPPY TIMES CONTINUED, AND MEG'S MAR-
riage ushered in more troubles in its wake. Unsure whom to trust,
King Edward turned increasingly to his queen's relatives. My uncle,
who had done such a dismal job in Ireland and was hated in England
for his cruelty, was replaced as Constable of England by Elizabeth's
father, Earl Rivers. London became a scene of daily executions,
as men Rivers suspected of treason were arrested and executed.
The young Earl of Oxford, whose father and brother had been
put to death by my uncle, was thrown into the Tower but obtained
his release by turning witness against his friends. Others were not
so fortunate. Henry Courtenay, who was heir to the earldom of
Devon and generally regarded as innocent, but whose earldom was
coveted by a friend of King Edward's, went to the block.

We did not see Warwick in these days, for he had obtained a
naval command that gave him an excuse to reside at Calais. We
knew he was only biding his time until he could deal with Edward. That day arrived with news that shocked us all: In defiance

of King Edward, who had refused to sanction Bella's marriage to Clarence, Warwick had the two young lovers wed in Calais on Tuesday, the eleventh day of July, 1469. Archbishop George officiated, and the Earl of Oxford and five Knights of the Garter witnessed the ceremony.

"What possessed my lord of Warwick to defy the king on this marriage?" Ursula whispered, as stunned as the rest of England by Warwick's act of mutiny against the king.

"Warwick does so because King Edward defied him on Meg's marriage," I replied. "And he means to show he is the king's equal."

With a heavy sigh, I laid down my embroidery and gazed out the window at the peaceful Aln flowing past Alnwick's tall, mullioned windows. On the heels of Bella's marriage, Warwick issued a proclamation declaring his intention to arrive in London and tender a petition of grievances to the king, just as the Duke of York had done to Henry in the fifties. King Edward immediately left the city for a pilgrimage north to Walsingham.

" 'Tis a collision of wills between two giants, and where it will lead is anyone's guess," I added. "But one thing is certain. . . . There's no going back now."

I turned from the window to find John standing in the doorway. He entered the chamber with weary strides, setting his gauntlets on a table as he passed.

"Interesting observation," he said, dropping into a chair. No clarions had sounded, and I was so stunned to find him home unexpectedly that I rose to my feet and remained there, unable to move for a moment. *Something is terribly wrong.*

Recovering, I rushed to his side. "Oh, John, my dear lord, you look so tired. Is there anything I can get you?"

"You can get me a scribe," he said, putting a hand to his brow.

I knew that gesture. "What has happened?" I breathed through cold lips.

"The king has been taken prisoner by Warwick. The queen's father, Earl Rivers, and her brother John have been executed. So has their friend the new Earl of Devon."

I swallowed, struggled for composure. "How—?" I asked in confusion, sinking into a chair. *This is too much, too much!*

"There was a battle at Edgecote. In some strange coincidence, the king's forces under Devon and Pembroke going north to join the king at Nottingham collided with Warwick's troops moving south to London. Devon and Pembroke had broken with one another the previous night after a fight over a damsel, and they had separated their forces. Warwick caught them divided the next morning, and crushed them. Then he moved on the king and took him prisoner."

"Like Henry?" I murmured incredulously. "Two kings . . . two prisoners?"

John rose and went to the window.

My heart twisted to see the way he stood, leaning his weight on the stone embrasure, his shoulders slumped, a hand rubbing on the old thigh injury from Blore Heath that always ached in damp weather. "I'll send for the scribe," I said softly, not knowing if he heard.

I soon learned that none of this had shaken John's resolve to stand by his king. When a rebellion led by their rabid Lancastrian relative Sir Humphrey Neville broke out in the North, John received orders from Warwick to put it down, but he didn't answer his brother's summons. "Not while the king remains your prisoner," he'd told Warwick. Hoping that somehow all would be mended between his brother and his king, John turned his focus on the Scots and strove to keep peace on the border.

On a sunny autumn day in late October, as I was interviewing a new manservant, two messengers arrived, clad in Warwick's scarlet livery of the bear and ragged staff. My spirits lightened when I saw their smiles, and I ran to meet them. We gave them ale and nuts in the great hall and listened to the news they brought.

"My lord of Warwick has made peace with King Edward, and to celebrate the end of enemies, the king has ordered a love-day ceremony!"

It was as if a dark curtain dropped on my hopeful spirits. Oh, how I wished to exult with them at this news, seemingly the an-

swer to all our prayers! But half my heart bore the memory of
Henry's love-day celebration after the Battle of St. Albans.

Mounted on Rose, I journeyed to London with John, battling my thoughts all the way as I pretended gaiety. The sun shone
bright, and minstrels played their lilting tunes. But, engulfed by
the dull ache of foreboding, my misery was almost a physical pain.
I leaned over and patted Rose's silken neck as we passed through
Bishopsgate. It was near Henry's love day that Warwick had given
her to me. Gazing up at the birds wheeling in the sky, I remembered that other shining day, the other hopes. Now, as then, there
had been deaths. This time the queen's own father and brother had
died. Would Elizabeth Woodville forgive?

Time seemed propelled backward as I watched the procession
from my seat in the stands. Warwick and King Edward walked
hand in hand to St. Paul's. The queen followed the king, holding
Clarence's hand, enemies putting away enmity to swear loyalty and
friendship forever. As the Duke of York and the Earl of Salisbury
had done with Henry and Marguerite so long ago . . .

That day slid into this; memories shifted and I lost time, so
that I did not know for a moment where I was. Then I blinked:
The past fell away, and the present rose before me. Celebrated with
such hope, that other love day had proved as hollow as a dried egg.
Would this one follow in its footsteps?

We sat at the royal table, feasting and making merry with King
Edward at Westminster, and I caught a glint in Elizabeth Woodville's eyes when they rested on Warwick during the banquet. All
the doubts and misgivings of Henry's love day flooded me tenfold.
I stole a glance at John. He seemed preoccupied. This day must
dredge up even more painful memories for him—memories of a
time when his father and brother still lived and hoped, a time that
had offered promise of peace, a peace the years had proved elusive.
Sometimes I felt we were on a ship in an endless storm, waves ever
rising and crashing around us. We kept avoiding the rocks, but
could we do so forever?

Alas, within three months, Edward's love day proved as false
as Henry's. As at St. Albans, the deaths had been few, but as at St.

Albans, the bloodshed was neither forgotten nor forgiven. The Woodville queen, always vengeful, willing to behead a man for a minor slight, was scarcely willing to forgive the execution of her father and brother. Behind the scenes, Elizabeth worked to redress the books, fanning Edward's jealousy and Warwick's rage, until finally she forced Warwick's hand.

It was said she had tried to poison Warwick and Clarence at a Yuletide feast at Westminster, but they had been warned at the last moment. King Edward had defended his queen when the matter was laid before him, and angrily dismissed the plot as a figment of their imaginations. Following Elizabeth Woodville's attempt on their lives, they had withdrawn to their estates. John came to Warkworth to greet the New Year of 1470, but we had no heart for celebration, so we sat quietly together as church bells chimed the hour of twelve. I listened to the last stroke fade away. Though I knew cheer would likely not be our portion this year, when the last chime sounded I sent a silent plea to Heaven that glad tidings come to us. For the heart is stubborn and foolish, and hope always triumphs, even in the midst of disaster. On John's departure, I sought reassurance from a soothsayer, something I'd never done before. But the old woman, toothless and brown as a nut, with skin as wrinkled as a dried raisin, offered no comfort. "Beware the ides of March," she said, as another of her ilk had said to Caesar fifteen hundred years ago. Her words plunged me into a dark mood, and I could not shake the sense of gloom that descended on me.

Indeed, messengers were soon caught bearing papers that spoke of Warwick's intent to replace Edward with his brother Clarence. This was followed by reports that Warwick had lost a battle near Stamford in early March dubbed the "Battle of Lose-coat Field" since his fleeing army had shed their coats bearing his emblem as they ran. Taking his daughters and Nan, Warwick had fled to Calais with his son-in-law, Clarence—whose wife, Bella, was now eight months pregnant.

Reading John's letter, I cried out and clutched my chest. A frightful pain had seized my heart.

Ursula ran to me. "Isobel, dear lady . . . are you all right? Here, sit!" She helped me into a chair.

The cramp in my chest slowly receded; I inhaled deeply. "I am . . . fine. . . ." I lied, for my heart had been acting strangely for months. " 'Tis merely the letter. . . ."

Ursula took it from me, gasping and murmuring as she read. She laid it down with a heavy sigh. "One good thing," she said. "Matters cannot get any worse."

But they did. Even more dread tidings followed. Obeying King Edward's orders, Calais refused to admit their Captain. In the throes of labor, no doubt brought on by the harsh sea voyage, Bella gave premature birth to a son, born dead aboard the tossing ship, with only Calais's gift of wine as comfort.

I was at Warkworth, and John was occupied with his duties on the border, when the Northumberland herald arrived to inform me of even worse tidings from Westminster.

"King Edward has proclaimed Warwick and Clarence traitors, and placed a bounty on their heads. Your gracious uncle, the Earl of Worcester, has been reappointed Constable of England in place of the queen's father, Earl Rivers, who was executed at Edgecote."

Not trusting myself to speak, I inclined my head in dismissal. The man withdrew.

I yearned for the comfort of John's arms after this news, but he did not come home. I wrote to him and received no reply. This bothered me more than I cared to admit, for our thirteenth wedding anniversary neared and, except for the time John had been imprisoned after Blore Heath, this occasion had been filled with plans and celebration through all the troubles of the years. If I didn't know better, I might have thought he was avoiding me, but I did not permit myself such foolish thoughts. I knew many troubles preyed on his mind as he worked to maintain the peace of the realm against his own brother, and that the estrangement with his family weighed heavily on him. In my loneliness, how-ever, I could not find consolation even in my children's company, and I ached for him with a desperate longing. Every so often, like lightning from a summer sky, came the thought that thirteen was an unlucky number. Perhaps something had changed, and John was indeed avoiding me. But that made no sense; we had not had a serious argument since Somerset.

Meanwhile, fresh disturbances broke out in the North. Robin of Redesdale had been defeated once, but now he raised another rebellion. And, strangely, this news came to me not from John, who continued his silence, nor from itinerants, for they no longer came seeking shelter, but from Ursula, who learned it from the tavern keeper in the village before she left for York to buy almonds, sugar, and sundry supplies.

The notion that something was wrong grew harder to dismiss.

"AGNES, HOW IS THE FAMILY?"

She curtseyed, but did not look at me. "Fine, thank ye, me lady."

I watched her, troubled. Her demeanor toward me had changed sharply in the past fortnight, reflecting the same coldness of the shopkeepers in the village, in York, and everywhere else I went. "How is your husband's cousin, the one wounded at Hexham?"

She swallowed hard, and for a moment she did not reply. Then she said, "I know not where he be, me lady, but he has my prayers. With yer permission, me lady, I'll tend to the privy now."

I inclined my head, and she disappeared around the bend of the chamber. She had avoided my eyes both times. But it wasn't only Agnes; all the servants treated me differently, whispering together and falling strangely silent when I appeared. They did my bidding without smiles and disappeared quickly from my presence. I could not fathom the reason. I had always treated them well, and I was certain they knew how much I cared for them.

Making no further attempt to talk to Agnes, I quit the chamber, headed for the courtyard, and took the path to the stables. The chambermaids and servants I passed along the way stepped aside sharply and bowed their heads, with a murmur of "m'lady" that seemed sometimes fearful, sometimes sullen.

"Where is Geoffrey?" I asked one of the young boy grooms scrubbing the horses.

He retreated a step in my presence before recovering to give his obeisance. "M'lady countess of Northumberland, I know not, but if 'tis yer wish, I can go and find him for ye."

He seemed nervous. I shook my head. "No matter, thank you."

I found Geoffrey deep in conversation with the saddler, their heads together. "Geoffrey—"

Both men leapt to their feet. Geoffrey bowed formally to me from the waist, in a way I found disturbing. He had always been courteous, but never obsequious. I looked at the saddler, who seemed to shrink beneath my gaze. I nodded to him, and he hurried away as if wild boars were on his tail.

"Geoffrey, what is happening?"

"M'lady, I'm sure I don't know what you mean," he said, his color rising.

"I'm sure you do," I replied.

His color deepened to crimson. "M'lady . . ." He shifted his weight from foot to foot, weighing his words. "Perhaps you should speak to—" He broke off.

To whom? I thought. *To Nan, to Maude? To Lady Conyers, Lady Scrope, or Lady Clinton, whose husbands now fight for Warwick, in the enemy camp?*

"To the Earl of Northumberland," he said finally.

"As you are well aware, my lord husband is guarding the sea at Bamburgh from his brother Warwick." I hurled the words at him. "Who is there to speak to, Geoffrey?" I cried.

Geoffrey swallowed. "Ursula will be back soon from her trip to York."

"Why can't you tell me?"

He shook his head miserably.

"Send for her now," I agreed reluctantly. Ursula had a long list of shopping to do, which included buying materials for gowns for the children, and she might be a week unless I summoned her.

Ursula was back the next day, in low spirits. Just before my summons arrived, she had learned that her father's trial had been deferred yet again.

"The Woodville queen has managed on one ruse or another to keep my father in prison for three years without trial, just as Marguerite did in the fifties when he sided with the Duke of York," Ursula said despondently.

"What excuse did they give this time?"

"They said there were no jurors to try him."

I heaved a weary sigh. It could be true. Entire villages had been depleted of men as they all chose sides and left to prepare for battle.

"Ursula," I said, broaching the subject I had been waiting so desperately to bring up, "something has happened . . . something that is surely evil. No one will tell me what it is. Do you know?"

Ursula turned pale. "Nay, dear lady Isobel . . . I know not."

"Don't lie to me!" I screamed. "Everyone lies to me!" I broke into frenzied pacing. "They can't leave the room fast enough when I enter. If I bid them remain, they watch me like a mouse in the company of a snake. I am no longer welcome in the homes of the women I go to aid in childbirth! I have no friends. My lord husband has not come home for a month, nor has he written! Something has happened, and I must know what it is!" I seized her by the shoulders. "You have to tell me, Ursula, or I shall go mad! What have I done?"

Ursula averted her gaze. She grew pale, and I saw that she trembled. A cold knot formed in my stomach. "What is it? What's so horrible, Ursula?"

She gave me a look of utter misery. "May we go to the river?"

A choking fear caught at my throat as I turned to lead the way. Along the passageway of delicate arches, we went down the tower steps, out the gate, and over the cracked earth wet with patches of snow. We trod to the riverbank, where we had spent so many happy afternoons romping with the children. I took a seat on a stone bench and drew my skirts close to make room for Ursula. From across the way, edged by a long row of larch trees sighing in the wind, sheep watched us as church bells pealed in the village.

Ursula spoke at last: "You asked what you had done, dear lady. 'Tis not what you have done, for you are the kindest, most gracious mistress anyone can hope to have." She fell silent. I waited. " 'Tis what your uncle, the Earl of Worcester, has done."

I bit my lip until it throbbed like my pulse.

"I learned of it in York. I had hoped to keep it from you. I had hoped for you never to know. 'Tis naught you can change."

"Nevertheless, I must be told."

"I see that now...." She heaved an audible breath. "There was a sea battle. My lord of Warwick escaped to Calais, but Anthony Woodville captured twenty-three of his men. He turned them over to your uncle. The Earl of Worcester—" She broke off.

My hand shook as I pleated and unpleated a fold of my gown.

"They were of the better class, so it was thought they would be dealt with less harshly."

I closed my eyes.

"The Earl of Worcester executed them by driving stakes into their buttocks and out their mouths. They're calling him the Butcher of England, for he had them—"

My stomach wrenched violently, and the bitter gall of vomit flooded me. I covered my mouth with both my hands and dropped from the bench to the water's edge. Ducks scattered with a sharp quacking as I retched.

Ursula moved to my side. She knelt down and encircled my shoulder with a gentle touch. She helped me up and led me back to the bench. I fell onto it, my breath coming in audible gasps. "Agnes—her husband's cousin—was he—?"

"She thought he might be one of them . . . but, God be loved, he was not. He is safe with my earl of Northumberland. She received word this morning."

I closed my eyes. *Thank God for this small mercy!* Then the sick feeling came over me again. *But what about the others? What had they ever done to warrant such agony of death?* And the thought came to me, revolving in my head with the crash of cymbals—*I am the niece of the one they call the Butcher of England, the niece of the Butcher of England. . . .*

I winced and put my hands to my ears to shut out the horrible din, but it did no good. *I am the niece of the one they call the Impaler. . . .*

"You should not have made me tell you, for what good can come of knowing?" Ursula whispered. "I fear you will not soon sleep again."

She was right. I did not sleep again, except for one hour in twenty-four, nor could I eat. My heart behaved more strangely than ever, at times pounding wildly and knocking against my ribs, at other times lying still and missing beats. Fortunately the cramping did not come again, for it brought great pain. Yet nothing was as painful as my new knowledge that even John blamed me, and shunned me, and wanted nothing more to do with me. And how could anyone blame him? I was the niece of the Butcher of England, was I not? The niece of the man they called *ille trux carnifex et hominum decollator horridus.* That savage butcher and horrible decapitator of mankind.

I kept to my room all the next day, sitting on a chair, staring out at the river. By the time Ursula rapped at the door to check on me, I had reached a decision.

"Summon the household to the great hall, Ursula," I said, my voice weak. Never did I know speech could demand such effort. "Everyone must be there. I shall address them in one hour. In the meanwhile, I am not to be disturbed."

She nodded and withdrew. The door shut. I slumped in my chair and closed my weary eyes.

I LOOKED AT THE SERVANTS GATHERED BEFORE me. They were all present—Geoffrey, Agnes, the porters, the men-at-arms, the varlets, the grooms of the stable, the saddlers, the armorers and their boy helpers, the kitchen maids and cooks, the scullions, the butchers, the embroiderers and maids of the wardrobe, the nurses and the spinners, the weavers and the chaplet maker, even the reeve, the bailiff, the steward, the monks, and the friars. They stood watching me carefully, yet avoided my gaze by dropping their eyes when mine rested on them. All were wary and ready to dart away, like deer in a forest when the sound of human footsteps reaches their ears.

I braced myself and drew a deep breath.

"For the past month, there has been a change in your behavior that has not gone unnoticed. This change puzzled me, for I divined not its cause. Some of you have been with me for many years, and others are newly come, yet I believed you all knew how I cared for each of you. As your mistress, I have always striven to treat you well and fairly, arbitrating your quarrels in a just manner, and distributing your tasks between you equally so no one person would be taxed more than another. When you were sick, I did not permit you to work, and I tended you myself when you were in labor with child."

I paused.

"Now I have learned the reason why many of you have been troubled in my employ. I wish you to understand that I had no part in my uncle's decision to—to—to do as he did. Like you, I grieve with all my heart for those poor, unfortunate souls and for their families—may God in His infinite mercy take note of their suffering and forgive their sins! Men of the cloth tell us that in the eyes of God we are accountable only for our own actions, but in the eyes of man, I know we bear culpability for the actions of our blood kin. Anyone who wishes to leave my service may do so, and they shall receive an extra month's pay, and if ever they have need of me, they will always be admitted to my favor."

I waited, drained by my short speech, which had exerted me to the limits of my resolve. "That is all. You are dismissed."

Only one of my servants, a new hire, left my employ. The next morning, as Agnes made the bed, she comforted me. "He's too young to understand much o' life yet, but he'll soon learn. The rest o' us, we were fool to hold you responsible, me dear lady. You have no more to do with these happenings than us."

I touched her arm mutely in a gesture of gratitude. Then I left in search of Ursula. "I'm going to Bamburgh, Ursula," I said, hardly able to lift my voice above a whisper. "Have Geoffrey pack up the horses."

Ursula gave me a knowing, doleful look. She said nothing but merely nodded.

★   ★   ★

AT BAMBURGH CASTLE'S HIGH WALLS AND DRAWN
gate, Geoffrey announced me to the porter. The portcullis was
cranked open amid a great clattering of chains, and I entered. The
soldiers we passed gave me formal and cool reception, but I scarcely
noticed, my mind and will bent on what I would say to John. As
it was bitterly cold, and I was in a hurry, I did not wait for John's
captain, Sir Marmaduke Constable, to come to me, but asked a
man-at-arms to take me to him in the armory.

He gave me a curt obeisance. "My lord of Northumberland is
not here, my lady. We can make you comfortable in the antechamber, if it pleases you."

"Where has he gone?" I demanded. I had not come to sit and
wait.

"He rode out alone on the beach about an hour ago. He did not
say when he would be back."

"In that case, kindly seat my entourage by the fire, and give
them warm wine and food, for we have journeyed long and are
chilled. As for me, bring me a blanket and direct me which way my
lord has taken, and I shall find him myself."

It was past Vespers. The sun was beginning to set, and the wild
North Sea was a molten silver as the surf pounded the long, empty
stretch of shore. Stumbling down the hard slope, across the long
grasses and weeds that lined the edges of the sand, I wandered
along the desolate beach, searching for John. Then on the wind I
heard a dog's bark and a horse's whinny. Against the vast expanse
of darkening sky, beneath the thunderous clouds racing across the
earth, I saw Saladin and the outline of a tall, solitary figure standing
on a high bluff, staring over the deserted sea with somber intensity,
tawny hair whipping in the wind.

John.

I ran along the sand and climbed up to him in silence. Rufus,
old and arthritic, struggled to rise and wag his tail, but there was no
welcome from John. He didn't even turn to look at me. Inside my
breast, I felt a twist of pain. I wasted no words on useless greeting.

"John, surely, dear God, you don't blame me?" I cried.

He didn't reply; he didn't even look at me. He just stood staring out to sea, at the churning expanse of water, as if he did not know I was there.

"John, if you still have a heart, answer me!"

He spoke then, but without looking at me. "Those men your uncle skewered, they had families who loved them. They were human beings."

His voice was so cold, it chilled me more than the blustering wind whipping my blanket around me. "Don't you think I know that? Don't you think I care? I never, ever blamed you for what Warwick did! Why do you hold me responsible for my uncle's misdeeds?"

He turned his eyes on me then, and I shrank back at the anger I saw in them. "You always knew how I felt about Warwick's actions. 'Tis clear enough to the world how I stand. But never once have you said a word against your uncle, even now. For God's own sake, Isobel, those men were sons and husbands and fathers. What is your blood made of that you can ignore this? Or forgive?"

I could not believe my ears. I stared at him, mute in my bewilderment. Then words found me.

"I have always hated my uncle's cruelties! I thought you knew me, and so you knew how I felt! Loyalty kept me from voicing my condemnation, for we owe him our marriage. But if I could have dissuaded my uncle . . . if I could turn back the work of time and give my life so it never happened, I would do so in an instant! My heart breaks for them, for those men—those boys. What can I do to prove it to you? Oh, John, my love, how can you think I condone such brutality, such horror? I don't condone it—I don't forgive it, but he is my uncle, he is my blood. I cannot change what he did! I must find a way to abide it, but I'll never understand it, or forgive! Oh, John, why do we live in this hell? Why must it be so—"

I broke off, unable to continue, and through my tears and the sobs that wracked me, I flung out the thought that had been with me for years. "If only Wakefield hadn't happened, how different might all this be!"

"But Wakefield did happen," John replied coldly. "All else fol-lowed, and it is as it is."

"John, my beloved lord, you once said that I have been your comfort. Will you not be mine now?" I cried.

No response; his face hard, impassive, he did not look at me. To my horror, he turned to leave. *He cannot bear the sight of me!*

The ground rocked, beneath my feet, and the world I had known heaved itself over. Falling, I reached out for support and caught his hand as I sank to my knees on the thorny ground. For thirteen years, through all life's storms and blows, my belief in love had sustained me. Now love was gone, dissolving in my grasp even as I thought to hold it firm. I let go of his hand. Swept with desola-tion and grief, I covered my face and choked back my sobs. The wind howled around me, and I felt raindrops wet my face and mingle with the salt spray of the sea and my own tears. I knelt there, cloaked in my blanket, my mind numb, struggling to comprehend this terrible new world that had suddenly become mine.

But John had not gone. I felt him kneel beside me. "Isobel . . ."

He removed my hands from my face. Cupping my chin in his hand, he made me look at him. In the dimness, his eyes were moist, and his mouth worked with emotion. He wrapped his arms around me.

"Forgive me, Isobel. . . . Forgive me. . . . My dear love, the fault is not yours. 'Tis mine alone. . . ." His voice held a tone I'd never heard before. He turned his face to the sea, a faraway look in his eyes.

I held my breath, startled.

"I have lived with a secret I can no longer bear to keep, but you must hear it now, for it may help you to understand. . . ." He seemed to brace himself before he continued, and my mind reeled with dread. "I am a soldier, and killing is a soldier's work, yet I have loathed it to my core. All these years, I did it because I had to. To survive, to earn glory . . . I always told myself it would end one day. But it never did. When your uncle butchered those men, it made me realize how much I hated the killing. How much I hated myself for the killing . . ." He gave me a look of agony. "Forgive me, Isobel. I have been thoughtless and selfish. All my concern has been for myself."

I closed my eyes on an indrawn breath. *All these years, and I never knew. . . . This—this is what I had sensed . . . what he kept from me. All these years.*

"I thought I'd lost your love," I whispered.

"You have my love, Isobel. . . . You have it to my dying day. There is cruelty, and there is wickedness, but there is also love. We have been blessed, haven't we?"

"We have, my dearest lord."

A gust of wind tore at me, lifting my wool blanket and loosening the braiding from my hair. I shivered.

"Aye, 'tis bitter cold even for a March night, Isobel." He rearranged my blanket around me with a gentle touch. "Best we seek shelter. Let us hope tomorrow is a better day."

Together we rode back to the fortress on the sea, and though the mighty wind blinded us with eddies of sand and blew us backward for much of the way, I felt safe and protected, for love encircled me as I rode behind my husband, my arms wrapped around his strong chest, my head cradled in the hollow of his back.

Whatever the future brings, I thought, *I have had this.*

Twenty-five

1470

BEWARE THE IDES OF MARCH, THE SOOTHSAYER
had said.

The ides, on the fifteenth of March, had come and gone, but
they were not done with us yet, I thought as I read John's letter.
Robin of Redesdale has mounted another rebellion, he wrote, *and I must
decide what to do. Yet I fear I have no choice but to give battle.* John had
dealt swiftly and firmly with Robin of Holderness, but Holderness had not been kin. The rebellion led by our cousin Robin of
Redesdale was a different matter. John had struggled with his guilt
over the loss of relatives and friends who'd died fighting against
him, but hard as it had been for him with the first rebellion, this
time was worse. Robin of Redesdale's second uprising was far more
serious and widespread, and more lives stood at risk.

The letter shook in my hand, so tightly did I clutch it as I read.
Edward has no idea at what cost John delivers his victories! I sank into a
chair by the window and looked up at the dreary sky. How could
John kill his own kin? He had never been one to give voice to

what lay in his heart, but reading between the lines of his missive, I felt his hesitation, his depth of misery at the predicament he found himself in. I felt his agony. He hated killing. Now—once again—he faced having to kill those he held dear.

I rose and left my chamber, desperate for the laughter of my children, who played in the nursery. I had just passed the great hall, with its rows of marvelous pillars, and stepped through the arched door when Agnes came rushing up to me from the tower stairs. She was half out of breath but smiling broadly. There was news! *Good news!* I drew her into a small, empty anteroom.

"There are fresh doings at York, me lady! My husband's cousin rode in just before I left for the castle this morning. He was in York with my lord of Northumberland until last night. My lord persuaded Robin of Redesdale to turn himself in! He brought Lord Scrope of Bolton, Robin of Redesdale himself, and many others to King Edward at Pontefract to beg a royal pardon for them. And the king, generous as always, has granted it!"

Euphoria swept me! I broke out in a smile that didn't leave me all day, and in the nursery, I danced with my children and played silly games, laughing as ridiculously loudly as three-year-old Lucy. I dined well and went to bed much happier than I had been in many weeks, and this night my heart did not keep me awake with its restless, uneven beat. In the end John had done what he had to do—and did it so well that further bloodshed had been avoided.

It was late that night, well past matins on the twenty-fifth day of March, and the castle lay sleeping, when a great noise came from the courtyard. I rose from bed and went to the window. Rubbing my bleary eyes, I saw John by torchlight. He had only Tom Gower and Rufus at his side. I watched as he handed Saladin's reins over to Tom.

Grabbing a chamber robe and a candle, I slipped my feet into my slippers and ran down the tower steps, seized with foreboding. Why had he come home without warning? What could have possessed him to risk such a dangerous journey in the dead of night?

With his head bowed, he was mounting the steps toward the

keep when I reached him. A drizzle fell and the night was fearsome cold, but it wasn't the rain that chilled me: It was the way John carried himself, as if he had been mortally wounded in some terrible battle. I pulled up sharply before him and caught at the damp stone archway for support. He halted in his steps and looked at me. The candle I held in my hand sizzled in the rain and threw a flickering, uneven light around us, and what I saw in his eyes made me gasp: It was the same disoriented, disbelieving look I'd seen on that dread day when the news of Wakefield was brought to us. *Dear God, what has happened?* He opened his mouth to speak, but no words came. Silently I took his arm and, draping it around my shoulder, I helped him inside and up the tower stairs to our bedchamber. He fell into the chair by the window and dropped his head into both his hands. My heart broke to see him this way, but I did not speak. Instead I knelt at his feet and laid my cheek against his leg.

The candle burned out; the darkness thickened. Church bells tolled the hour, first twelve, then one, two . . . four. An owl hooted. On the mantelpiece, grains of sand hissed in the hourglass, marking the steady, inexorable passage of time. The moon crossed the dark sky and faded away; a cock crowed and was answered by another; bleak morning light strayed into the chamber. Still John sat. I wanted to cry out, but I did not. I waited. Waited as I'd waited all my life . . . waited, as if for death itself.

Finally I heard John inhale a deep breath and stir. I lifted my head. He dropped his hands and I saw his face again. I swallowed with difficulty and found my voice. "My beloved," I managed, "what ails thee?"

His mouth worked with emotion. He rose from his chair, turned his back to me, and stood looking out the window at the wintry scene. When he spoke, the words fell from his lips like one long sigh. "The River Aln is beautiful. . . ." he said. "I never rode past or crossed the three old bridges without thinking how beautiful it was, whether spring, summer, fall, or winter. How much it all meant to me . . . the meadows, the river, the castle . . . the earldom . . ."

I inhaled a sharp, burning breath. *"The earldom?"*

He turned to face me. He encircled my shoulders and drew me

close. "I fear we have looked our last on this place that has been our home for six years, Isobel."

"The earldom?" I whispered in disbelief, a faint thread of hysteria in my voice. I knew what his earldom meant to him. He had poured his blood into the winning and keeping of it, this earldom that had come with long and brutal service on the field of battle. He had fought on when few would have found the strength to keep going; he had stood erect through the wildest storms and against the cruelest winds Fortune can send a man in this life.

"The earldom is gone. Edward took it from me the day after I brought Conyers in for pardon. He gave it to Percy, whom he has released from the Tower."

I covered my mouth with both my hands to stifle my sobs, but to no avail. Through my choking sounds, my mind thundered on: *It isn't possible! It's not possible. . . .*

Then I buried my head on his shoulder and gave vent to a fit of weeping. I wept not for myself, but for John, for all the hopes that had been snatched from him and for the future that had been taken away. Every step on his harsh journey of life had been trodden stalwartly, with loyalty and courage, by an honorable knight who had not counted the cost to him, who had remained singularly faithful, who had striven with his every breath to prove his loyalty to his king when the temptation to treachery had never been greater for any man.

All his life he's endured for York, sacrificed for York, killed for York. Now, at the end of the long, hard, twisted road, this is what it comes to—Edward sacrifices him like a buck before a feast and flings him aside.

"John, oh, John!" I cried, weeping for him the tears he could not weep.

EDWARD HAD TOLD JOHN NOT ONCE BUT MANY times that he loved him entirely. *God help those that Edward "loves entirely,"* I thought with a loathing I had never known before. He'd stripped John of his earldom and elevated him in rank to Marquess of Montagu, but it was a hollow title, which came with the paltry sum of forty pounds a year from the county of Southampton. He had promised to wed our son, Georgie, to his firstborn daughter, Elizabeth, and had raised Georgie to the noble dukedom of Bedford, but again the title was barren, for it came with no estates. The settlement rang hollow; I don't think either of us ever believed that Edward intended to go through with the marriage—or that Elizabeth Woodville would permit it.

In our reduced circumstances, we could no longer afford more than a handful of servants, and so we chose carefully from among them. Ursula would come with us, of course, and so would Geoffrey. John's squire, Tom Gower, would also remain in attendance, as would Agnes. We bid the others a tearful farewell on a cold, foggy morning and moved out of Warkworth, taking the children and our few possessions back with us to Seaton Delaval in two carts. As we rumbled down the hill, I looked behind me. Mist swirled around the splendid castle, bestowing an unreal quality, as if it stood in a dream. And in the dream, aware of how well it had been loved, it magically waved its turrets, bidding me a sorrowful farewell of its own. A drift of fog floated across the main gate. It cleared the wall and the nearest tower, and I remembered how John, counting the cost of repair, had chosen to build the tower square instead of round like the others during that joyous first year of his earldom. Money had always been a problem, even with the earldom; the good years had not lasted long enough to make a difference in the end.

I glanced at him, riding beside me on Saladin. He didn't permit himself a backward glance but rode stiffly erect. *In last year's nest, there are no eggs.* Had he not always reminded me that looking back did no good? I turned my own face forward, so I would not look back to the place where I had left behind so many of my happiest memories.

Life at Seaton Delaval proved more difficult than ever before, burdened as we were by grief. We were enemies living among enemies, with no kin at our side, our friends blown away by evil winds. While the Percies rejoiced and feasted, we counted our meager income and drowned ourselves in work as best we could. It was hard on the servants, too, for they had to relearn their duties.

One day I caught Agnes replacing the rushes, and I had to tell her to never do that again unless I gave her the order. I kept careful tally of the candles, watching to make sure they didn't burn needlessly. And I helped the seamstress darn clothes and make new gowns for our girls, who, with the exception of little Lucy, too small to make much difference, outgrew their dresses every few months. But expenses were always high and income short, and John had to find ways to borrow. Every night I went to bed weary but never without a fervent prayer for his safety. For as hard as it was for me, it was worse for him: humiliated, derided, doing the work he hated, living the soldier's barren life with little warmth or comfort, his life and limb dependent on the outcome of the next skirmish.

As if to underscore our losses, a soggy spring damaged crops and reminded us that a poor harvest loomed ahead and many would die of starvation come the winter. We could help but little, for we no longer had the gold mines of Devon to draw from, and my own battles in these days lay with the household accounts. I went over them minutely with the bailiff, examining carefully the daily pur-chases of victuals and consumption, the number of meals served, the cost of the youths we kept for running errands and carrying messages. I questioned expenses and found ways to cut back on the number of scribes and clerks to deal with the correspondence and keep the records connected with the management of the estate. When the wages came due, I paid them myself, taking a moment to have a private word with each servant, to offer congratulations on a name day or the birth of a child or praise for good work done, or a suggestion as to where improvements could be made.

I saw little of John, who had been obliged to borrow money from his dear friend Lord Scrope of Masham, now that he could no longer go to Warwick. And Scrope had given it to him most generously, without requesting collateral. *Lord Scrope, who sided with Robin of Redesdale and Warwick in the feud against Edward.* This time, however, I understood John's need to be alone, for I myself felt the same.

There's so much to mourn, I thought, helping the chandler pour hot wax into the molds for the candles. Beads of perspiration formed on my forehead but, as my hands were not free, I wiped at them with my sleeve. We still received the poor and gave shelter to itinerants, but for one night at a time, for our means did not provide for greater generosity. The Four Horsemen of the Apocalypse, delivered to us at the New Year of 1470, were now rampaging through the land, and with an ever-growing sense of dread I listened to the tidings that were brought me. What I came to fear more than the pilgrims and mercers who stopped for a night were John's missives. More often than not, they imparted grievous tidings. Since I could not doubt their truth, it left me no room to hope the tidings might prove false.

In June, Edward followed up his brutal blow by taking from John the wardenship of the East Marches, which he gave to Percy, leaving John only the command of the West Marches, which bordered Scotland. John's visits grew few in number, since Seaton Delaval lay a great distance away. But now when he came home and felt an urge to ride the moors, I galloped at his side, and sometimes we made love in an old abandoned sheep shelter with the wind howling around us. Alone, surrounded by the vast landscape, we felt nature's healing touch, and the ancient Roman forts and burial sites that marked the scenery seemed to draw the thread of time around us and assign us a place in God's great plan. We always returned to Seaton Delaval tired but somehow fortified to meet the morrow.

That autumn John finally came home for a visit again. Rufus was no longer at his side, for he had died on my birthday, Lammas Day, the first of August, at the venerable age of fifteen, and John had acquired another pup, named Roland. My delight to see John vanished at the sight of his face, lined by inclement weather and ravaged by sleeplessness and mental anguish. I had to turn away for a moment and dig my nails into my palms to steady myself before giving him welcome. He had aged terribly this summer.

In our bedchamber, I bathed him in a wooden tub filled with warm water. The young pup watched us quietly from the hearth.

I fingered John's scars more gently than usual as I lathered him. He seemed fragile to me now, this strong man I had loved with all my heart, all my life, but never was he more precious. I sensed him slipping away from me, and so I fought harder to keep him close.

I offered him a loaf of the fresh, hot rye bread he loved, and a sampling of the finest aged cheese I could find in our meager pantry.

He shook his head and instead took the hand I rested on his shoulder and gave it a tender kiss. As I stood behind him, I bit my lip, my anguish almost overcoming my control. The pup wagged his tail when my glance touched on him, as if to give me courage. I forced a smile and, bending down, I laid my cheek against John's and slipped my arms around his bare chest. Inhaling deeply, I savored the warmth of his nearness. "I love you," I whispered.

"And I you, Isobel," he murmured. "To the end of my days . . ."

I rubbed him down with towels and an herb-scented sponge, and helped him into his chamber robe. Setting a flask of wine on the floor in front of the fire, I sat with him on the cushions and nestled in his arms. He remained silent for a long while, sipping thoughtfully. Then he said, "I bring news, Isobel."

I felt my throat closing up. "Not now, my sweet lord," I said hastily, smothering his words with my lips. "There's time enough for the tidings you bear. But now—now is our time . . . ours, for love. . . ."

His arms encircled me and his mouth came down hard on mine. My tired soul melted into his kiss, and in the frenzied tempo of our love, an exquisite harmony flowed between us as it had always done. The real world spun away, and we soared higher, ever higher, into the infinite heavens, where a million stars shattered around us, bringing us, at last, contentment and release.

THE NEWS JOHN CARRIED WAS SOMBER INDEED. Some of it I already knew from the itinerants, but it was worse to hear it from his lips. Warwick, incredulous that Calais had refused him entry, had sailed about for a month in disbelief before swallowing his pride and seeking refuge in France in May. During this time he came to accept the realization that England would rather keep

Edward on the throne than receive Edward's rash, foolish brother Clarence in his stead. Warwick and the French king had put their heads together and hatched their plans. What emerged from these meetings shocked the world.

'Tis too frightful to be true, I thought. But it was true indeed; we had to face it. The Spider King had lured into his tangled web both Warwick and Marguerite and turned them into allies against Edward. Together they would invade England and restore Henry VI to the throne. Their reconciliation was a tribute to Louis's powers of persuasion, for greater foes never lived: Marguerite hated no man more than Warwick, and Warwick loathed her more than he detested Elizabeth Woodville. For the Woodville had not done to him what Marguerite had done. Notwithstanding, Warwick had groveled at the feet of his father's and brother's murderer, singing his apologies and begging Marguerite's forgiveness.

Too horrible, I thought, walking in the woods being stripped bare by autumn's breath. John had left to attend his duties at Pontefract Castle, where he was still constable. Bitterly, I wondered why Edward had left him the post, for Edward had followed up his brutal blows of March and June with yet another cruel strike: He had deprived John of the wardenship of the West Marches on the Scots border, and given it to his seventeen-year-old brother Dickon.

Dried twigs crunched beneath my feet as I leaned against a tree to catch my breath. He might as well have plunged a knife into John's heart. "Why . . . what did I do?" John had asked me, mortified.

Nothing, I thought, *except sacrifice for your king, who's betrayed you and keeps betraying you.* Aloud, I said, "You have been true to your king, but your king has not been true to you, my love. Loyalty is a virtue that works both ways." I had come to loathe Edward, faithless and reprehensible as he was, but I stopped short of advising John to abandon him; it would be up to John to pass that judgment.

Finding it necessary to keep moving, I resumed my steps over crackling twigs and pushed back the thorny branches that barred my way. For some reason, I thought of Somerset. *'Tis an impossible situation in many ways,* Malory had said after Somerset accepted

Edward's pardon. *Only time will tell.* And in time, Somerset had returned to the fold of Lancaster and had died there.

Animals darted across my path; others froze to watch me cautiously. At a little brook, I sank down and, immersing my face in the water, drank thirstily. My tongue was parched and swollen, and my heart pounded in my chest so randomly, I feared my breaths were numbered. The brook murmured softly; I stared down at my rippling reflection and the sky behind me. It all looked so peaceful. . . . But peace was ever an illusion. I looked up at the sky, framed by the dying leaves. To seal their pact, Marguerite's sixteen-year-old son, Prince Edward, was betrothed to Warwick's daughter sweet Anne, who was in love with Dickon. Into my mind flashed an image of Prince Edward. At Coventry, when he was six years old, he had spoken with relish of beheadings.

The betrothal would take place in December at Amboise. Dickon had taken the news hard. Trapped at court among the Woodvilles, whom he hated as much as John did, he kept to himself. Loyalty to Edward was Dickon's fiercest trait; yet his lot was easier than John's, for Dickon still had one brother at his side. Both of John's brothers were traitors, and he was a hated Neville in enemy territory, discarded by his king and despised by everyone else, forced to endure many humiliations at Percy's hands. And Percy, being Percy, saw to it that the wound engendered by the loss of John's earldom and commands was constantly rubbed raw with insult.

John's predicament preyed on my soul night and day, depriving me of sleep and plunging me into an agony of heart I had not known before. John's brother George didn't present a large problem; he was an archbishop and safe from Edward's wrath, and he could make his peace with Edward one day. But Warwick was a different matter. He was a rebel who had risen twice against his king, and Edward had no choice but to hunt him down and kill him. How could John bear that? How could he help Edward slay his brother in battle, or deliver him up to Edward to be beheaded as a traitor? John had always hated treason. With his every breath he'd striven to live up to his motto: *Honor, Loyalty, Love.* For a long time he refused to see his brothers as traitors. Now he was one himself;

whether he supported his brother or his king, he was a traitor to one or to the other.

Dear God! I cried out. *Are You there? Can You hear me? Can You not help us?*

Whom would John choose—how could he choose? I threw my head back and screamed at the sky. *God curse you, Edward! God curse you, Elizabeth Woodville! May the devils of Hell feed on your rotten souls!*

FILLED WITH SECRET SHAME, I WENT ABOUT MY duties quietly after my rampage in the woods. I should not have cursed them; yet I had, and the curse, once released, could not be taken back. I would pay for it—there was no doubt in my mind about that—but it did not allay my guilt. I spent more hours at my prie-dieu praying for forgiveness, and even longer praying for John, that God grant him strength in the black depths of his despair, whatever choice he made. Then, one day, John came home again.

He was more gaunt than ever before. The loss of his earldom had taken all he had to give. He was like a hollow shell, merely going through the motions of living. I laid my head against his shoulder and we walked together to the house. In our bedchamber that night, we sat by the fire in one another's arms.

"Warwick has written me from France," John said. "He is returning to England with Marguerite to fight for Henry's crown. . . ." He looked at me with anguished eyes. "He begs me to return to his side and fight with him. He says 'tis where I belong."

I drew a deep breath and forbade myself to tremble. Half in anticipation, half in dread, I asked, "You've made your decision, haven't you?"

"I have no choice. I wasn't with Thomas, and Thomas died. . . . I must be there for Warwick." John's expression darkened with unreadable emotion.

So I was right. Thomas's words had haunted him since Wakefield, and he blamed himself for his brother's death.

"All my life I've fought for peace and tried to live an honorable life. But peace is a dream, Isobel, and honor an elusive quest. Whichever way I turn, I find no hope of peace, and no honorable way out. Right or wrong, I must stand with my brothers now. To go against kith and kin is to fight a gale alone, my love. I cannot do it anymore."

It was what I had wanted him to do; it was the only thing he could do. Now that the decision was made, I felt nothing. No despair, no joy, no doubts. Nothing.

I laid my hand on his. "You've always done the right thing, John. Not many can say that about their lives. So be it, my love."

On the night of John's departure, I felt weary and went to bed early. I awoke from slumber to find myself lying on a blanket of rose petals in the castle courtyard at Warkworth. Strangers milled around, but they paid no heed to me or to the music that played. I recognized the lilting Celtic melody I had danced to at Tattershall and looked around for minstrels, but saw none. When I stood up, red and white petals rained down on me. I raised my eyes to the sky, but there was no sky, just turrets. Then, in a blinding flash of light, John appeared in the castle gateway, resplendent in armor and surrounded by a retinue of gorgeously appareled knights, his banner of the griffin flowing in the wind. My heart thundering in my breast, I hid behind a stone pillar before he could see me, for he rode not Saladin but King Edward's ebony charger, and he seemed somehow changed. As he entered the courtyard, a mist began to gather at his feet, and his charger reared in terror, neighing fiercely. I found it strange that John smiled at this. He soothed the restless horse, but so gently and with such grace that he almost seemed to be dancing with the beast. Then he looked in my direction, as if he knew I was watching, and threw me a red rose. I slipped quickly back behind the stone pillar with my pulse racing. After a moment, I dared to look again, but there was no one there, just impenetrable mist, and through the mist I saw a red rose lying at my feet. The castle courtyard stood empty. Only the music played. . . .

I opened my eyes. I lay in bed. It was dark outside. *Just a bad dream,* I thought. I inhaled a long breath and lifted my eyes to the night, wondering what the morrow would bring.

*   *   *

BEFORE THE END OF SEPTEMBER, ANOTHER RE-
bellion arose in the North. King Edward's new Earl of Northumberland, Henry Percy, did nothing to crush it. When Edward
received no response from John, he marched north to stamp it
out himself. Warwick took the opportunity to land in Plymouth,
where men rallied to his standard. The news of his landing reached
Edward at York. He immediately sent a summons to John, ordering
him to meet him in Doncaster with the portion of the royal army
under his command.

I was picking apples in the orchard when the messenger rode
up. Leaving my children and the servants, I hurried to him. The
man knelt on one knee. "Marchioness Montagu, I bring you a missive from your lord husband, the marquess." The man was avoiding
my eyes. I took what he handed me, prepared to accept whatever
came. "Tell Cook to prepare you a good meal. And make yourself
comfortable before the fire in the kitchen. It promises to be a cold
evening."

I watched him leave, with a calmness of spirit that baffled me,
for I knew the tidings he brought had to be cruel. And they were.
Near the town of Doncaster, John had halted his march and addressed his troops. They all knew, he said, that he had always been
loyal to Edward, even against his own brothers and his kin. But the
king had deprived him of the earldom of Northumberland and
given it to Percy, whose father and brothers had died fighting for
Lancaster. "I told them King Edward left me a pauper, with only
a magpie's nest to maintain my estate," he wrote. "And I left it to
them to make their own decision, whether to follow me or leave.
The men did not hesitate. Almost to a man a great shout went up.
'A Warwick!' they cried. 'A Montagu!'"

So the army would follow their commander. It did not surprise
me. I remembered the almost reverent way Agnes's relative had
spoken of John. "There's nothing we woudna do for him, m'lady,"
the tough old soldier had said. "We'd march to the ends of the
world for him, m'lady, every last one of us." The wind whipped my

skirts around me as I folded the missive and went in search of the messenger. I found him enjoying a piece of apple pie and flirting with Cook. He rose, chewing briskly and gulping a swallow of food before bending down on a knee.

I motioned him to rise. "When did you leave my lord husband?" I demanded.

"Two days ago at Doncaster, m'lady."

"Did my lord husband seize the king?"

He colored and bowed his head. "Nay, m'lady . . ."

There was something he wasn't telling me. But I'd find out what it was. "What happened, then?"

"The king got away, m'lady. With Richard of Gloucester, and his friend Lord Hastings, and—"

"How large an army did he have with him?"

"A small band of men, not many . . . Not more than a hundred, I'd say, m'lady."

"So how did he get away?"

"He was warned, m'lady. . . . He got away in the night."

"Warned?"

"Aye, m'lady."

I waited. The man shifted his weight nervously from one foot to the other.

"Where was he when he was warned?"

"Asleep in a cottage. But he jumped out the window and fled." Clearly my questions were making the man miserable.

"Come with me," I commanded.

He fell into step behind me. I went outside, a safe distance from the house, where no one could hear us. "How do you know this?"

Even in the dimness of the falling dusk, I saw that he had turned crimson. "I d-don't know anything, m'lady," he stuttered.

I took a step closer. "You can tell me. The secret is safe with me. Surely you realize that?"

After a hesitation, he said, "But the marquess said not to tell a soul—"

"You warned King Edward, didn't you?"

The man drew an audible breath. He nodded. "Me . . . and Carlisle, the minstrel . . . The marquess sent us to warn the king."

"Did you give pursuit?"

He hung his head again. "Nay, my lady . . . no pursuit."

So that's how it was. Edward had gone into exile, like so many others had done before him during these wretched wars. With his enormous height, he was an easy quarry, and if John had wanted, he could have easily caught up with him. But he hadn't.

I shut my eyes on a breath. *So be it.*

More rumors came to us, most of them confirmed by the messengers and missives John sent me. Elizabeth Woodville had gone into sanctuary at Westminster and given birth to a son she named Edward for his father. Marguerite was still in France, awaiting fair winds; she was expected to sail for England shortly. Warwick had taken London, reinstated dear Henry as king, and was securing the city for Lancaster. The people seemed to accept all this in stride, and why not? First they had Henry, who was weak and let his avaricious, power-hungry favorites loot the land. Then they had Edward, who was strong and promised them better. But he, too, had let his greedy, power-hungry favorites plunder the land. So what had changed? All those promises of peace and plenty to the people had not the weight of a handful of salt.

Now John was back in London, helping to depose a king. *Yet again.* I clutched John's letter tightly as I read. "And Warwick is determined that no revenge be taken against anyone, and wishes to ensure that law and order prevails and that bloodletting is prevented," he wrote. "With one exception. Your uncle of Worcester has been captured hiding in Weybridge Forest and is to be tried before the specially appointed constable—John de Vere, Earl of Oxford, whose father and brother your uncle sent to their deaths. His trial is set for the fifteenth day of October, and there is no doubt about the verdict."

"Geoffrey!" I called, running from the alcove where I had been reading John's letter. "Ursula! Hurry! I must leave for London immediately!"

Twenty-six

EXECUTION, 1470

THE JOURNEY TO LONDON WAS AGONIZING. RID-
ing hard through blustery winds, heavy rain, and dense fog, we
stopped only as long as necessary to rest our horses, for I feared
I would be too late to bid my uncle farewell if we lingered. Had
John been at the Erber, I would have stopped to change my travel-
stained clothes and see him for a moment. But he was in the West
Country on a mission, and so I went directly to Westminster Palace,
where my uncle was imprisoned. It was the sixteenth of October,
the day after his trial. He had been found guilty and was to be executed the following day.

To Warwick's credit, he hadn't committed my uncle to a dungeon, but installed him instead in a well-appointed chamber.
Though the window was barred, it looked out on a circle of garden
in the inner court. My uncle was reading a manuscript. He glanced
up when I entered amid the jangling of the jailor's keys and the
noise of the bolt sliding back.

"Dear child," he said, rising to greet me. His tone held as much delight as if I had come to take wine with him and discuss Latin poetry. He laid his manuscript back down on the table. "Ovid," he confirmed, wiping away a tear at the corner of his eye. "*Tristia* . . . beautiful, lyrical . . . He wrote it during his period of exile from Rome. Well it illustrates his sadness and desolation, for he pined terribly for Rome and his third wife, you know." My uncle's gaze lingered fondly on the manuscript, as though it were a living soul. I waited, but he remained lost in thought. I wondered if he was remembering his dead wife, whom he had loved deeply and missed all these years. He seemed almost to have forgotten I was there.

"Thank you, my dear uncle," I began, "for the kindness and affection you have ever shown me—for reading to me on your knee when I was little . . . for teaching me about the great masters . . . for comforting me when my mother died. But most of all, thank you for helping me to wed John. Without your intercession, Marguerite would never have given her assent."

"Dear child, love is all that matters," he said. He opened his arms wide, and I walked into them. He held me close. "Your aunt Elizabeth brought me love. I had her with me for only a year, and she died giving birth to our dead child. But she lives on in my heart with special remembrance, even after all this time."

The knowledge struck me with sudden force that this man who held me was my last living relative, the only one left of my childhood. A fit of sobbing seized me. I clung to him, smothering my face in his velvet sleeve.

"Nay . . . what are these tears? There's no need for tears, sweet Isobel," my uncle soothed, gently dabbing at my eyes with his handkerchief. "I meet my Maker with a conscience that is clear."

I swallowed hard and stepped back to gaze at him. "But, Uncle . . . the men you sentenced to . . . to that terrible death . . . Do they not weigh on your heart?" I asked, giving voice to the nightmare I carried within me.

"My dear, you understand nothing of the world. 'Tis the higher good that matters, and to achieve it, no means can be ruled out. Even cruelty has its uses. I learned that in Transylvania. Dracula impaled hundreds of Turkish prisoners alive and hewed others into small pieces. Muhammad the Second, that fierce conqueror of Byzantium, is said to have turned pale when he learned of it. He never troubled Dracula after that. Leniency leads only to anarchy. . . . The suffering of those men was necessary to bring England peace."

"But we have no peace, Uncle."

"It will come, child. Have faith in God. . . . May I ask for your prayers for my soul?"

"I shall pray for your repose to the end of my days, Uncle."

"I give you my blessing, dear Isobel, my sister's only child. . . . How proud of you she would have been! Farewell, my beloved girl."

The jailor jangled his keys. I flung my arms around my uncle's neck and hugged him tight, sobbing. Then, from the door, I looked back at him one last time. He gave me a smile and raised his hand in farewell with as much emotion as if he were leaving on a short journey to his estates. He turned back to his manuscript.

My breath caught in my throat. Not even his enemies could deny that my uncle was a brave man.

The day of his execution, the seventeenth of October, dawned bleak and rainy. Hundreds of church bells tolled for Terce as I waited with Geoffrey in the outer court at Westminster for my uncle of Worcester to appear. He was to be led on foot from the palace to the scaffold at the Tower, and I needed to be with him. I wanted him to know that he wasn't alone in the midst of his enemies, that I was with him to the last.

He emerged from the keep, his hands bound before him.

"Uncle!" I cried, running to him. His eyes lit when he saw me, and he paused, but his guards pushed him on. He was ringed by at least fifty men-at-arms, so I followed behind him as closely as I could. The great palace gates clanged open, and I heard a clamoring, but I couldn't see past the guards. As I passed through the gates, the scene revealed itself.

Crowds teemed in the streets. I looked at Geoffrey, bewildered. "They've been gathering since cock's crow!" he shouted, leaning close so I could hear, for a great roar went up when they caught sight of my uncle. All at once, I felt myself being thrown hither and thither, and I realized the rabble had charged us. They jostled and called out as if this were a feast day, but theirs was an evil joy. "Butcher of England!" they cried. "Butcher of England!"

With dark, angry faces, they pushed forward. My uncle disappeared into the midst of the bobbing crowd so that I no longer glimpsed him. The mass of humanity around me jeered louder, shoved harder, and jerked me so wildly that my hair came unbraided beneath my cloak and fell around me as if whipped by a wind. Borne along on their frenzied current, I became separated from Geoffrey. "Lady!" he called. "Lady!"

"Geoffrey!" I cried, reaching for the hand he outstretched above the crowd, but it soon receded from sight like that of a drowning sailor's in heavy seas. I was carried for an endless distance, and more people swarmed toward the massive mob, pouring from doorways and alleyways. A woman's voice shrilled, "Beheadin's too good for 'im! 'E should be drawn apart by wild dogs, that un!" Someone else answered loudly, clearly, "Aye! No mercy for 'im—'e gave none to those poor souls, did 'e? Let 'im scream like they did—let 'im be torn apart!"

The crowd took up the evil refrain. "Tear 'im apart! Tear 'im apart!" they cried, and, "No mercy! No mercy!" Then, abruptly, as if the throng were a single beast with one mind, the words altered and a single grotesque chant thundered in the air. "Feed 'is black heart to the dogs! Feed 'is black ..." I wanted to block my ears from the ugly clamor but could not. The men-at-arms around my uncle shouted, "Keep away, keep away!" and shoved the raging mob back, brandishing their swords to protect him.

I looked around me in horror. I was alone with these mad people. The multitude surged forward, taking me with them. "Let us at 'im!" they screamed. I was struck dumb with terror; I could no longer breathe. There was no air; they kept pressing on me. Soon I'd fall, and they'd trample me. *Trample me, and tear out my uncle's heart!* We were at the Fleet prison now. Dimly I became aware of a different chorus of voices, punctuated by cries and screams of pain. The crowd fell back; some ran away. I looked around in confusion; then I saw the men-at-arms. The furious mob had been cheated of its prey by a contingent of prison guards. They howled their curses and shook their fists, but gradually the dreadful milling eased and the crowd dispersed. Gulping air, I pushed my way through the mass of people and stumbled over to a tavern. I leaned against its redbrick front and looked up to see the last of the men disappear into the safety of the prison. The great doors clanged shut.

My uncle was safe. *At least for one more night.* I drew a long, deep breath and shut my eyes.

AT THE ERBER, I SAT IN MY BEDCHAMBER, GAZ-ing at the river. Small ships passed to and fro, ferrying passengers and cargo up and down the Thames. A wedding party glided by in a vessel festooned with ribbons, and music floated to me from their minstrels. I watched the young bride and groom sitting close together, laughing with their guests, and in spite of myself, I smiled, remembering my own wedding day, my great happiness. . . .

Aye, life goes on, I thought.

Even for my uncle. In his youth he'd known love. When that love was lost, he'd found pleasure and renown in the pursuit of knowledge. He'd mingled with the rich, the powerful, and the lowborn alike; kings, popes, and monks all had called him friend and held him in esteem for his great mind and his many scholarly achievements—for the many books he'd written and the transla-tions he'd made of ancient poetry into Latin from the inaccessible Greek. . . . He'd seen the world . . . the gray fortresses of Europe, the crusader castles of Jerusalem, the glittering, white-marbled city of Venice, which had so enthralled him. . . . He'd visited all the shrines: the thumb of Constantine, the body of St. Helena, a por-tion of the True Cross. . . .

Aye, my uncle had known the powerful, and seen and done great things, but more important, he had always been a deeply pious man. Surely God would show mercy.

Thus consoling myself, I went to bed on that last night of my uncle's life, but my sleep was fitful. The next morning I found my-self trembling as Ursula dressed me. When she was done, I looked fearfully at the door, dreading what lay ahead, unable to force myself toward it.

"Lady, dear, this day will be different," Ursula said gently, a hand around my shoulder. "My lord of Warwick himself has made the arrangements. You . . . and my lord of Worcester are . . . protected."

Biting my lip to suppress my emotion, I managed a nod. Her words made strange sense. She knew that my uncle would be taken to the Tower in a litter with the curtains drawn. He would not be insulted and jostled by a rampaging mob, since Warwick had ordered a curfew. No one was allowed into the streets of London without a special permit, on pain of death.

Surrounded by an escort of a dozen guards, I rode through the empty streets to await my uncle's arrival at the Tower, the clip-clop of Rose's hooves echoing on the cobbles. It was a warm, sunny day; yet the very emptiness of the streets seemed menacing. The frenzied crowd, now mute, pressed on me from the windows, rooftops, and balconies; a thousand pairs of eyes watched me steadily. We reached the Tower and dismounted in the courtyard. A man-at-arms escorted me to the circle of green, but not until I saw the platform did realization strike me with full force.

Only two benches had been set up before the scaffold, and no one else had yet arrived. As Constable of England, the Earl of Oxford would take the first seat, and Warwick the one next to him. I had been assigned the third seat, and it was there that I collapsed onto the velvet cushion, thankful to be alone. I needed time to compose myself before the other witnesses arrived. Along a side wall, a line of monks from Canterbury Cathedral stood singing the chants my uncle loved. These monks were his friends, the recipients of his great generosity, with whom he had idled away many an hour discoursing on the Holy Book.

The sky was icy blue, unmarred by clouds. Perched along the walls and on narrow ledges, ravens gave vent to bursts of raucous cawing, as if to demand we make haste so they might dine. I focused on the chant of the monks so that I would not hear them. *How did we get here from there?* I asked the sky, my sight blurred by tears.

Slowly the other witnesses arrived. They were a motley crew of nobly born Yorkists and Lancastrians, either distantly related to my uncle by marriage or whose families had suffered at his hands. The relatives nodded to me as they passed; the others went by without acknowledgment, though the Earl of Oxford gave me a civil bow before he sat down. Warwick entered, flourished me a bow and a smile, and dropped onto his velvet cushion. The monks ended their song. A silence fell.

The hooded executioner clad all in black made his entrance. Mounting the scaffold heavily, his footsteps resounded in my ears, sending panic to my throat. I must have gasped, for Warwick whispered, "Courage, Isobel." The executioner took up his stance on the side of the platform and faced us with legs apart, hands on the handle of his axe, the blade resting on the straw. My uncle appeared between two men-at-arms, and my heart jumped in my breast. He climbed the steps with quiet dignity. Giving the executioner a smile, he put out his bound hands to him, and the man sliced through the cords with a dagger. No one moved or made a sound as my uncle came forward to address us for the last time. I felt such a rush of emotion that I grew faint. But, girding myself with resolve, I forced back the tears that stood in my eyes. He reached the edge of the platform. I smiled at him and was rewarded with a smile in return.

I didn't hear all that my uncle said, for a fog had fallen around me and my mind had gone numb. I saw his mouth moving, and fragments of his words penetrated my consciousness. ". . . accused of judging by the law of Padua, not of England, but . . . leniency a weakness . . . always wished for peace, not war . . . striven to do my duty to England, to my king, to God . . ." Through the cloud that engulfed me, I became aware that a silence had fallen. I roused myself and tried to concentrate. My uncle was moving to the block. He took off his jacket and handed it to the executioner, who laid it down behind him. He removed his collar and passed it to the man. The cold that seized me grew more chill, and by the time my uncle drew out a gold noble from inside his shirt pocket and handed it to the executioner, I was shivering uncontrollably. The executioner murmured his thanks. My uncle should have knelt now, but he was not yet finished. "One more thing," he said to the executioner in a clear, calm voice. "Kindly strike off my head with three blows of the axe, in honor of the Trinity."

A gasp resounded in the circle of green. I swallowed hard on my tight throat and dug my nails into my palms. The executioner, taken aback at this request, hesitated a moment before nodding assent, and I saw that his own eyes had widened beneath his black hood.

With a glance up at the sky, my uncle made the sign of the cross and said, *"In nomine Patris, et Filii, et Spiritus Sancti, in manus tuas, Domine, commendo spiritum meum." In the name of the Father, the Son, and the Holy Ghost, into Your hands I commend my spirit.* He knelt before the block and laid his neck down on the wood. After a moment's delay, he swept his arms up and out to his sides in a swift motion that signaled acceptance of his fate. The voices of the monks rose in Latin chant, filling the bright air with the darkness of death. *"Sancta Maria, Mater Dei, ora pro nobis peccatoribus, nunc et in hora mortis nostrae—"*

Bowing my head so I would not see what was to come, I echoed their words under my breath. *Holy Mary, Mother of God, pray for us sinners now and at the hour of our death—*

The axe fell. Though I had braced myself for the blow, I knew I would never forget the sound of my uncle's voice and his last word on this earth.

"Jesu—" he uttered, at the first cut.

JOHN RETURNED TO LONDON THE FOLLOWING week. Our reunion was bittersweet. To hear his voice, to feel his arms around me, to touch his form as he slept beside me brought profound joy, but my stomach still churned from the horror of that morning on Tower Hill, and the image of my uncle's death lingered, casting the shadow of guilt over my happiness. Before we left, John took me to St. Paul's to make an offering and pray for the repose of my uncle's soul.

As I made my way up to the altar, leaning heavily on John's arm, my gaze fell on the bank of candles by the side chantry where years ago Somerset had accosted us. For fear of him, that same day, I had written my uncle in Ireland, pleading desperately for his help. And he had granted it. Now Somerset was dead. And my uncle was dead. How much had changed! How much remained the same. . . .

Flooded with sorrow, I knelt before the altar and prayed for my uncle—and I prayed, too, for Somerset.

One great good had come of Warwick's capture of England. He emptied the prisons, and Ursula's father, Sir Thomas Malory, was released from his cell in Southwark, where he had spent the last four years. He had repeatedly been kept from trial by his foe, Elizabeth Woodville, who feared that Warwick might tamper with jurors and witnesses to Malory's benefit, or that Malory might succeed in proving his innocence.

As church bells tolled the hour of Vespers and nightfall descended on the river, we gathered together in the solar for a cup of malmsey at the Erber. Old Malory, now seventy and bent with age, white-haired and frail, was overjoyed by his freedom.

"Ten years I've spent in prison, under two queens. Not many can boast of that!" He gave an audible sigh and sipped his wine, licking his lips after each taste, savoring each precious drop. "You cannot know how good it is to be free until you've been enclosed by three stone walls and a grate for a few years. . . . Nevertheless, even prison has its uses when you're a maker of tales as I am."

"How is that?" I asked, intrigued.

"You see, each time I had to appear for a trial, I made the journey from Southwark to the King's Bench in Westminster by barge along the Thames, boarding the boat at the bridge. My journeys were frequent enough to fix the landscape in my mind—" He tapped his head. "So when I later retold the story of the abduction of Queen Guinevere, one of the details I invented was that Sir Lancelot, in his haste to rescue the queen, rode into the Thames at the bridge and swam his horse to the south bank, before disappearing into the Surrey countryside."

"That was in the good old days, when knights rescued their ladies." John grinned, placing an arm around my shoulders. "Nowadays damsels rescue their knights, don't they, Isobel?" He raised his cup in a toast to me before he drank. "How things change."

Sir Thomas had a thoughtful expression as he regarded us. "Perhaps one day I shall tell your tale of love, for it is quite a story of courage—that is, if I get thrown into prison again by another French—or half-French—queen, God forfend! But first I have some living to do . . . and some business to attend. My lady wife has written me that a dastardly local brewer hasn't paid her the money he owes, using the law to back his right to avoid payment. In King Arthur's time, the law was used for right, but nowadays . . ." His voice died away. In a wistful tone, he added, "Ah, the law . . . what troubles would be vanquished if the law functioned as King Arthur intended. . . . What sorrows eased, what wrongs righted—how greatly it would content mankind and benefit the cause of peace!"

Toying with his wine cup, John said, "I've heard the same words from young Dickon of Gloucester. When he was a boy, he revered his brother Edward. . . . He believed Edward would bring justice to England and right all the wrongs of the land, just as Arthur had done a thousand years ago."

"Well he might have. Had he not wed his witch. But he fell into Vivien's clutches—" Malory quoted from his tales of Arthur's court, his voice as melodious as a troubadour's song. " '*She paused, she turned away, she hung her head, the snake of gold slid from her hair, the braid slipt and uncoiled itself, she wept afresh, and the dark wood grew darker toward the storm.*' "

"Elizabeth Woodville," I said. "Indeed, 'tis how they met, she and Edward. . . . Elizabeth waylaid the king in a wood, knelt down before him, and pleaded with tears in her eyes for the return of her lands, and as she did so, she let slip the coil from her hair so that her gilt tresses fell loose around her to mesmerize the young king."

" 'Tis where I found my inspiration for those words," Malory replied. He turned to John. "There is also a line or two there for you, my lord." His rich voice came again. " '*From mine own earldom*

foully ousted me . . .'" A hush fell, and Malory said, "Nor did I forget
His Grace, King Edward, and the sorceress he wed. . . ."

> *He let his wisdom go. . . .*
> *Then crying "I have made his glory mine,"*
> *And shrieking out "O fool!" the harlot leapt*
> *Adown the forest, and the thicket closed*
> *Behind her, and the forest echoed "fool."*

A dark silence descended over the table. The thought in all our
minds seemed to throb aloud. *And here we are: She has wrought the
storm; all this has come to pass.*

John broke the dread thoughts that enveloped us. With a slap
to his knees, he rose. "Best we retire. We have a hard day's journey
come the morrow, you to Warwickshire to see your lady wife, and
we to Seaton Delaval."

We came to our feet and bid one another good night.

Though winter had thrown its dull gray mantle over the world,
I felt the warmth of the sun's rays, for John was at my side. Every so
often as we rode together, he turned to look at me and he reached
for my hand, and I was reminded of our first journey north together, to Raby, when we were betrothed. That his eyes still shone
with the light of love after so many years made me rejoice.

We celebrated Yuletide of the year 1470 with lavish festivities,
since Warwick had made certain money was no problem for us
any longer and sent us many coffers laden with gold. The halls of
Middleham, where we journeyed for the celebrations, rang with
drinking and song, all the louder and merrier to drown out the
memories and the fears that burdened our hearts. For Warwick,
who held all the cares of the kingdom in his hands as well as the
charge of the seas where he was admiral, was deeply disturbed that
Marguerite had not yet seen fit to sail for England. It was clear that
she did not trust him, and though she had made peace with him,
there had been no forgiveness. His strong fist and vigilance kept
discontent from exploding into open rebellion, but the absence
of a sovereign made his task of ruling the land far more difficult.

Twice he went down to Coventry to meet her, and twice she did not come.

John had charge of the northern coast and spent much time at Bamburgh Castle. The memory of him as he had been that evening on the bluff still flooded me from time to time, and it took all my resolve to banish the image of his anger, the look in his eyes when he had blamed me for what my uncle had done. *In last year's nest, there are no eggs,* I'd remind myself with his words, and banish those memories as I had done many others, sealing them away in my mind as bees sealed away intruders in their hives, for time was precious and seeping away, and we did not know how much more we had. What good did it do to poison present joy with past memories? We had to go forward. Aye, John was at Bamburgh, and, aye, he had not come home to visit for two months, but it was not because of anything I had done or that he held against me; those days were past. It was because the land was boiling like a pot of porridge about to explode, and needed careful tending.

Then, one rainy March day, I heard the distant gallop of horses' hooves. Peering into the misty horizon from my bedchamber, I thought I made out the emblem of John's griffin among the riders. I ran down the worn wood steps to the court, and waited in the drizzle.

John rode through the gates and cantered up on Saladin. He dismounted. Behind him, Tom helped the pup, Roland, down from the cart in which he rode. I rushed to John's side and took his arm, but I saw immediately that he did not wish to speak. Leaving Geoffrey to take care of John's escort, I led him up to our room. He sat down on the cushions by the fire and gave me a weary look. I joined him on the floor.

"What is it, my sweet lord?" I asked. "What has happened?"

He let out a sigh. "I come from Pontefract and can only stay a night, Isobel. . . . Edward has landed at Ravenspur and is marching to York to raise an army. . . . I leave tomorrow to join forces with Warwick, who is coming north from London to fight Edward."

"Pontefract?" I whispered in my confusion. If John had been at Pontefract when Edward landed at Ravenspur, why did he not give battle? Ravenspur stood a mere stone's throw away. "Raising an army?" I said. "So he did not come with one?"

"Nay, he came with less than a thousand men."

But, my mind cried out, *you had six thousand at Pontefract, John! Why did you not give battle when he landed? Why did you not give battle before he went to York?*

My thoughts must have been standing clear in my eyes, for he read them well.

"Dickon was with him, Isobel . . . and even if he had not been, I couldn't bring myself to fall on their little party. We outnumbered them three to one." He turned stricken eyes on me. "My father and Thomas were outnumbered three to one. . . . Clifford rode out from the walls of Pontefract to slaughter them. I'd be no better than Clifford." He dropped his head into his hands.

I took his hands in my own. "Hush, hush, my beloved. . . . You did the right thing. . . . You have always done the right thing, John. There was naught else you could have done." I bent down and kissed his tawny hair, now threaded with silver, for he would be forty in June. "Come, we have no time to waste. Let us forget all else except our love." I drew him into my arms and to our bed.

It was dark when we awoke, and the supper horn sounded soon thereafter. Wine flowed at dinner, and the laughter in the hall reached the heavens. John did not tear his eyes from me, as if he strove to memorize every line, every feature, the shape of each movement. It broke my heart to see him so aggrieved.

"I wish I could dance for you now as I did that night at Doncaster, my beloved," I said.

"A dance, aye . . ." Turning, he summoned a varlet and whispered to him. The man disappeared, only to emerge again in the minstrels' gallery. There was a lull in the music before the musicians picked up their instruments and strummed their chords. It was the melody of our first dance together at Tattershall Castle, a wild, lilting tune that had always summoned for me something of the vast, lonely moors. He rose to his feet and gave me a small bow.

"Lady Isobel, may I have the honor of this dance?" he said in his resonant voice, speaking the words I had heard from him on the night we'd met. From that moment on, I had loved his voice, touched with the accent of the North. The breath went out of me. I rose and gave him my hand. He led me to the dance floor and we took our places. Other dancers joined us, forming a row behind us. We moved a small step to the side, forward three steps, back two, and gave a hop, but I barely knew what I was doing. His eyes held mine, and I could not look away. We reversed the sequence, parted from one another with a step, and drew back together again, and I felt the movement of our breath in perfect rhythm.

The walls of the room receded as the other dancers faded into oblivion, and there was only he and I in all the world, and the music, and a fiery wind beneath my feet sweeping me forward, sweeping me back. He knelt, and slowly I circled him, my hand never leaving his, his eyes never leaving mine. I turned and circled in the opposite direction, engulfed in remembrance of our youth, of our time of roses, our time of hope. My blood smoldered as the past lived again in my heart, and I felt once more the bruising kisses I had known, remembered with tenderness the children I had borne and the sweet moments I had spent beside the fire with the husband who had been my joy on this earth.

The music rose in tempo, and again I was galloping wildly with him across the moors, returning to a castle scented with cinnamon loaves, laughing in the embrace of those we had cherished, long dead, who now rose again to greet us, smiling welcome. I was overwhelmed by the music, by the memories, by my beloved. I knew I would never forget a single detail of his face. He came to his feet and took his turn. I stood still as he passed around me. We moved forward a double step, back one. . . . I remembered the time spent waiting, waiting, not knowing, yearning . . . the time at Bamburgh of love and pain, and forgiveness. . . .

We danced palm to palm, face-to-face, in slow and perfect harmony, first in one direction, then the other, and we were two halves of a circle spinning together in eternity, spinning, spinning. . . . The melody filled all the air, and I could not draw my eyes away from his; I could not move my hand from his. A fiery wind had borne me from Earth back to that magical place where rose petals swirled around me and flowers of fire glimmered in the night, and I never, ever wanted to leave, never wanted the dance to end, never wanted to return to the world I now knew too well.

But end it did, suddenly and with a clash of cymbals. We breathed in unison as the notes quivered into silence. The song was over. The world had stopped spinning, and the time had come when we two must part to separate paths. *Now, just as we had done then.*

But there was still the night; we still had the night. In our room, we sat on the bed after our lovemaking, and John cut a lock of my hair with his dagger. " 'Tis soft as angel's hair," he whispered, taking the locks to his lips.

"How would you know?" I laughed. "In any case, my sweet lord, I keep telling you—angels have golden hair, not chestnut."

"How would you know?" he demanded with a grin, throwing my own words back at me. "I never saw an angel that had golden hair, only chestnut."

I kissed him again, and we made love once more, my being filled with joy and my heart seared with anguish.

MORNING BROKE TOO SOON. THE CHILDREN stood beside me as we bid John farewell. He was in full armor and only his visor stood open, for the journey to London was fraught with peril. In my soul, I knew why he had gone to such great lengths to see me. As he walked to Saladin, my control broke at last, and choking sobs escaped from my throat. I ran to him and threw my arms around his neck to hold him back. The wind whipped my hair against his armor as I clung to him, refusing to let go. Beneath his open visor, I saw his eyes, and in my heart I let out a silent scream.

"No!" I cried, pounding his armored chest with both my fists. "No, no . . . no!" I railed. Two men-at-arms stepped forward and gently pried me from him. John turned back to Saladin, and Tom Gower helped him mount his warhorse. From a great height, John gazed down at me as I fought my sobs. Then he nodded to me, slowly, tenderly, a final farewell, and turned his stallion south. His men fell behind him, silent, somber.

"Farewell, my love!" I cried out, running after him. "Till we meet again—" *Meet again, meet again . . .*

I watched them ride away, and I began to tremble, and the trembling of my body built into an uncontrollable shaking, and the last that I felt was Ursula's arms around my shoulders, the last that I heard was the pitiful wailing of my children, and the last that I saw, as the ground rose up to meet me, were shards of sunlight striking his armor like the blows of a sword, before he vanished into the darkness before my eyes.

Twenty-seven

BARNET, 1471

WARWICK HAD BEEN FIRST ASTOUNDED, THEN FU-
rious, when he heard that John had let Edward and Dickon pass
at Pontefract. In the Lancastrian camp, there were murmurings of
treason. But I understood John's anguish. There was nothing else—
nothing, nothing he could have done! And, as I seemed to have
done all my life, there was nothing else for me but to await the tidings that would surely be brought. With the impending battle between Lancaster and York preying on my mind, the days stretched
before me like a stormy sea, and to bear them I submerged myself
in work, for in work there was a mindless solidity that kept painful
thoughts at bay.

Although there was less need now than ever before to keep
expenses down, from force of habit I went over the household accounts minutely with the steward, examining carefully the daily
purchases of victuals and consumption, the number of meals served,
the cost of the youths we kept for running errands and taking messages, as if by such pretense I could summon back the days of old,

where, if there had been troubles, there had also been hope. Just as I had done in days of yore, I questioned the expenses and suggested ways to cut back. As twilight fell over the world, I retired to my prie-dieu to pray for John, and if weariness assailed me, or desolation overwhelmed me, I reminded myself of my blessings and thanked God for the precious moments that had been mine. And so the days passed. Then, one cold day in April, a week before my wedding anniversary, when the snow still stood only half melted, I witnessed a lone rider galloping up the path.

"I pray you," I said to Agnes, who was dusting the room, "bring him to me in the solar."

"Aye, me lady."

Crossing myself, I murmured a prayer and braced myself. Removing John's old cloak from the peg where it hung, I headed down to the solar. Seating myself carefully, I gathered the cloak to me and forced my trembling fingers to push the darning needle through the cloth as I had done so often before in times of distress.

"My lady."

I glanced up. Tom Gower stood at the threshold of the room. I felt the cloak slip from my fingers, and I rose from my chair with difficulty, a hand on the armrest to steady my legs. He stepped forward, and I saw that he held a missive. I was mistaken! *He has not come to bring me tidings of death,* I thought, *but merely word from John!* I gave him a wide smile.

"Tom, dear Tom . . . rise, I pray you. For a moment, I thought— no, pay no heed to what I thought—" I took John's letter from him and held it to my bosom, still smiling. Then I realized that Tom had not returned my smile, and that his face remained as pale and grave as that cold moment when I had first heard his voice. "Tom . . . how goes the war for the Lancastrians?"

He hesitated before he replied. "I know not, my lady. I dressed my lord the marquess in his armor, then he bade me leave him ere the battle started. To bring you this missive . . ."

Why? The thought stabbed me with the thrust of a dagger. *Gower should be fighting at his side.*

"And this—"

I came out of my thoughts to find Gower reaching inside his doublet. As he fumbled for what he had placed there for safekeeping, I saw that his fingers were stiff and he moved them with difficulty. When I looked at his face, I knew there was something he kept from me. He took out a velvet pouch and offered it to me. Inside lay the ring given to John years earlier by young Dickon of Gloucester when he'd first come to Middleham. I felt the crushing stab of pain in my breast. It was John who had taught Dickon how to wield the weapons of war. Now the two cousins found themselves on opposing sides of York and Lancaster, as each fought for his brother.

I gazed at the stone, acutely aware of the message John was sending me. *If disaster befalls, take this ring to Dickon.* By the return of the ring to its owner, the debt Dickon owed John would be redeemed. I felt that I stood outside myself, looking down on the scene from high above. In the fading light of day, the stone, dark blue like John's eyes, twinkled with the same light I had seen so many times in his.

My heart was beating hard. I turned away, struggling for composure. *The time has come to repay my own debt—a debt to Heaven for granting my prayer years ago.* I was fifteen then, orphaned and alone in the world, when I faced a choice between the taking of vows or the taking of a husband. I had left the nunnery with Sœur Madeleine, seeking a match at court. Yet I knew how the world was made, what little chance I stood of finding love in an arranged marriage. On that evening at Tattershall Castle, my heart breaking with loneliness, I had gazed up at Heaven and made a plea . . . and a vow:

Send me love, and if you send me love, you may send great sorrows, and my heart will be lifted to you in gratitude. . . . Allow me love, and you may allow me great griefs, and never shall you hear me complain, no matter what happens, no matter what losses, what pain, what anguish is my portion. I shall bear all . . . if you send me love.

That night Heaven had answered by sending me John. Then Heaven had swept away every impediment that kept us apart. Against great odds, we had fulfilled our love and found a life together.

I raised my head and looked at Gower. "You've had a long journey, Tom. Tell the cook to prepare you the best meal we can offer, and get rest. . . ."

In spite of myself, tears stung my eyes and my lips trembled. I turned away, and heard his footsteps echo down the hall as he left. Clutching John's letter, I set out for a little bench on the edge of the woods, safe from prying eyes, dimly aware that John's pup trailed after me.

My beloved Isobel,

Tomorrow we give battle. Lest I be unable to write you again, I send you this missive for when I am no more.

Isobel, you have been the deepest love of my heart. Memories of the joys we have known together abound this night, and I feel blessed by Almighty God that I have been allowed such happiness. I know not why, but somehow you feel very close to me at this moment, as if you will step out of the shadows at any instant, and smile for me the smile I have loved since my first glimpse of you at Tattershall Castle.

You will find it strange when I tell you that, as I write you, I can almost hear the music of the dance we danced together that night, and I see your eyes sparkling like jewels amidst the candle-light, blinding me—oh, Isobel, how I have loved thee these fourteen years! What comfort you have brought me through all life's troubles! In a fortnight comes the anniversary of our wedding day, and if I must leave you now, I go with a heart grateful to Heaven for the love and the joy it has seen fit to bestow on me. Yet how fleeting and how few those precious moments seem as I look back—like a handful of gold dust scattered into the darkness, visible one moment, gone the next. If only our hourglass had not emptied so soon, and we could live on together to see our George grown to honorable knighthood!

Alas, Isobel, I have a sense that the last night's candle has been lit. If tomorrow should prove me right, tell the children how much I love them, and never forget how much I have loved you. And know that when my last breath escapes me on the battlefield, it will whisper your name.

Forgive my many faults and the many pains I have caused you. How thoughtless and how foolish I have sometimes been! But, oh, Isobel, if the dead can return and visit those they love, I shall be with you always, always! And when the soft breeze caresses your cheek, it shall be my breath, or when the cool air touches your throbbing temple, it shall be my spirit passing by.

Isobel, my angel, do not mourn my death. Think I am away, and wait for me. For we shall meet again.

Written under my seal this night of the fourteenth of April, Easter Sunday, in the year of Our Lord fourteen hundred and seventy-one, at Barnet.

As if in afterthought, John had added a postscript beneath his signature in a shaky hand: *God keep you, my angel. Until we meet again.*

THE WORLD WENT SUDDENLY VERY QUIET. I HAD bartered with the Fates for my destiny that day, and the Fates had listened and granted what I had asked. However dark the shadows now, I had to remember how fortunate I was to know a love that few are ever given, a love that dazzled my life with its light as the sun warms and bedazzles the earth. The glory of that love will dry the tears, as it always has, for love transcends all things, even time . . . even death. I regret nothing.

Nothing.

Yet I could not crush the hope in my breast of a good outcome. Battle did not have to mean the end; if God ordained differently, we might still have time together.

So ran my thoughts as I sat on the bench, reading and rereading John's letter, Roland at my feet, the wind sweeping the sighing poplars, rustling the leaves of elm and beech, stirring the spruce and larch. The sun set and the birds grew silent, as hymns drifted across the hills. Words and phrases rang in my mind with old familiarity, and suddenly I realized that John had echoed my thoughts, almost as if he had known of my secret pact with Heaven. . . . *I feel so grateful to God . . . allowed such happiness . . . a heart grateful to Heaven for the love and the joy it has seen fit to bestow . . .*

Was it coincidence or something more? I fixed my gaze on the dimming sky. *John, wherever you are, I hear you. . . . I hear you, my love. . . . Godspeed you back into my arms. . . .*

THREE DAYS LATER, AS I WORKED IN THE GARDEN with the children, making a game of gathering twigs for firewood, as Roland yapped and ran around with his ears flapping, I paused to stretch my aching back, and my glance fell on three horsemen galloping up to the house. I dropped the basket of twigs I carried, and ran to meet them.

As I neared them, however, my steps slowed. I knew from their expressions that they bore ill tidings. The thought struck me that no matter how prepared we think we are for loss, never are we truly ready.

Two of the men were wounded, and they dismounted with difficulty. Holding myself stiffly erect, I listened to their report, but I was having trouble with my hearing, and their words kept fading in and out.

"Battle . . . Barnet . . . king's brother Clarence . . . treason . . . abandoned Warwick's side . . . joined Edward . . . furious battle . . . thick fog . . . confusion . . . friend slew friend . . . York prevailed . . . Warwick . . . fled . . . slain . . . The Marquess of Montagu fell in the thickest press of his enemies, fighting valiantly to the end."

The words echoed around me like the howling of the wind: *The Marquess of Montagu fell in the thickest press of his enemies, fighting valiantly to the end. To the end to the end—*

Behind me, I heard my children shriek with delight as they chased one another with their twigs.

I opened my eyes to find myself in bed, tended by Ursula. Tears swam in her eyes. I grabbed her sleeve, tried to rise, to form a question, but she gently pushed me back.

"Nay, Isobel, dear, hush now. . . ." she whispered. "Hush, dear Isobel. . . ."

I fixed my gaze on a patch of sky visible through the window. I must have passed out when I was given the news of Barnet. Remembering my vow, I blinked back the tears that threatened, and forced my lips to curve into the semblance of a smile—

I am the most fortunate of women. . . . Thank you, Heaven. . . . Thank you, John. . . .

AS SOON AS I REGAINED MY STRENGTH, I TRAV-eled to the Scots border near Bamburgh with Tom Gower to see young Dickon, now the most important man in the kingdom besides the king himself. I had a request, and it could not wait, as it concerned a matter of the utmost urgency. As Gower knelt before Duke Richard in the Gloucester tent, I returned the ring Dickon as a boy had given John. Not trusting myself to speak, I did not say much but let Gower speak for me.

"My lord duke," Gower said, "on the eve of the Battle of Barnet, my lord gave me this ring and said I should take it to my lady if anything . . . if anything happened to him. He told me to have my lady bring you the ring . . . and you would understand."

The young duke took the ring and stared down at the stone for a long moment. When he looked up again, his eyes were moist.

"Do you know how I came to give him this ring, Lady Isobel?" he asked me softly.

I shook my head. "He . . . never spoke of it, Your Grace, though he wore it . . . to the end."

"It was at Barnard's Castle. I was nine years old. I had failed a tournament and was ashamed, for John had come all the way from the Scots border to Barnard to watch me tilt, and I was hiding from him—hiding from Lancelot, the bravest knight Christendom ever knew. . . . But he wouldn't leave until he found me. We sat together on a bluff overlooking the thundering River Tees, and he told me something I have never forgotten: *In last year's nest, there are no eggs.* . . . My cousin John was right, my lady. We cannot look back, only forward. He said something else. Something that seems even more important now than it did then. . . . He said that if we let honor and conscience guide our lives, we shall face God without shame when the time comes, and that is the best any man can do."

I swallowed on my tight throat and dropped my lids, for tears had begun to sting. I felt the young duke take my trembling hand. And then I found out what Gower had kept from me that day when he had brought me John's letter.

"Lady Isobel, those who call John a traitor do not understand' as I do. 'Tis true that he wore the king's colors beneath his armor, but he did so not because he was a traitor to his brother Warwick or to Lancaster. He fought beneath his brother's banner and died wearing the colors of his king because, as a man of honor and integrity, he could not live with his torn loyalties. John went to his death determined to remain true to both whom he loved, to the end, as best he could. It is my firm belief that John stands before God without shame this day, Marchioness Montagu."

Unable to speak, blinded by tears, I kept my head down. Gower had dressed John for battle. He had known there was no hope when he'd delivered John's missive.

"Dear lady," Dickon said, "whatever it is you wish to ask, know that if it lies within my power, it is already granted."

I recovered my composure and found the words, "Your Grace . . . I request the wardship of my son, George. He is . . . he is the light of my heart now. . . . It would be difficult . . . difficult . . . to give him up."

I saw the young duke swallow. Then he said, "Marchioness, I shall have the papers signed forthwith and delivered to you at Seaton Delaval within the week."

"Thank you, my lord." As I left the tent, I was swept by an impulse I could not suppress. Turning, I said, "There is much about you that reminds me of my John, Your Grace. He loved you truly."

The young duke didn't reply. He merely gave me a taut nod of acknowledgment, but I saw that the corners of his mouth worked with emotion. I knew he had loved Warwick's daughter Anne since childhood and had been unable, as yet, to surmount the obstacles that kept them apart, even though her husband, Edward of Lancaster, lay dead on the field of Tewkesbury. Silently, in my heart, I blew him a kiss and wished him love.

For love is all there is.

Epilogue

1476

ON THE THIRD OF MAY, TWO DAYS AFTER MAY Day and my fourth wedding anniversary to William Norris, I left for Bisham with Ursula, Geoffrey, and Gower.

"Are you sure you will be all right, Isobel?"

William's eyes rested on me with heartrending tenderness and concern. From astride my horse, I gave my husband a smile of reassurance.

"I am fine, William. . . . I will be fine." I bent down and laid my hand gently on his cheek. "You worry too much. I'll send word from Bisham when I arrive."

He nodded and stepped back reluctantly. I spurred Rose. Ursula, Tom, and Geoffrey fell into a canter beside me. I waved until William was out of sight; then, with the need for pretense gone, I sagged in my saddle and pressed my hand to my brow to steady my dizzy head. Since the birth of my dead child the previous year, I had been ailing. I knew my heart was giving out at last. A few weeks ago, I could barely stand; soon I would be unable to sit

erect. It had begun with fatigue that had descended on me after
Barnet and worsened. Now there was bruising that did not heal.
My body told me I had not long to live, and I wished to die in
Bisham.

John lay buried in Bisham.

For centuries Bisham Priory had been the final resting place
of the Neville family, and it was to Bisham that John had been
brought after the Battle of Barnet to be buried with his brother
Thomas, and his father and mother, and with Warwick, who had
died with him. His brother Archbishop George, who had gone
over to Edward before the battle, had dabbled in treason against
King Edward soon after Barnet, and spent years imprisoned in the
fortress of Hammes in Calais. His confinement under such harsh
conditions had broken his health. Dickon of Gloucester had finally
procured his release, but George had died last month, after only
two years of freedom. He was buried at York Cathedral, the only
Neville not to lie at Bisham Priory.

"Are you sure you're all right, dear lady Isobel?" Ursula asked.

I gazed at my beloved friend, my mind crowded with memories. Her father, Sir Thomas Malory, was another who had died
at Barnet. In those early days after that terrible battle in the fog,
Ursula had comforted me in my grief at John's death and never
breathed a word about her own loss. *So many deaths, so much sorrow . . . To how many was it given to enjoy long life and die in their own
bed, untouched by war?* No one I knew. Maybe one day my children's
children might be blessed with such a world, but that time was not
ours. Soon after Barnet came the Battle of Tewkesbury. York had
triumphed there, too, and dear King Henry had died at the Tower
the following night. Murdered, it was said, by King Edward.

"Now, Ursula, don't you start," I scolded gently. "I'm fine. 'Tis
a fine May day. The sun is shining, the birds are singing, and the
woods are beautiful. What more can I ask? See the blossoms . . ."
I reached up and plucked a flower from a wild cherry tree as we
passed beneath a bough bent low and bright with blossom. On
such a day nineteen years ago, John and I were wed at Raby Castle,
and I wore cherry blossoms in my hair. *Sorrows, aye, but happiness*

too. Such happiness . . . If the road I had trodden had been scattered with thorns, it had also been richly petaled with roses.

After Barnet, I had been determined to dwell not on the sorrow but on the happiness that had been mine, for the specter of Countess Alice had haunted me from the day I received news of John's death. With my weak heart, it would have been a small matter to give in to my grief, but my children were still so young. They needed me, and I had made the vow to Heaven. It proved a good decision. The love I had known, even as it faded into memory, had sustained me. I fingered my jeweled saddle. The gilt was gone now, the leather thin and cracked, but the ruby still sparkled with brilliance, just as it had that day I went to meet John in the saddle shop.

"My lady, pray be truthful," Ursula said in a plaintive voice.

I turned my gaze on her. I couldn't fool Ursula; she knew me too well; and in any case I remained in her debt. Through maidenhood, marriage, motherhood, and widowhood, she had stood by me, this dear friend, and held my hand, and mourned with me, and celebrated with me.

"I need to go to Bisham," I whispered, so Geoffrey and Tom wouldn't hear. " 'Tis time, Ursula. . . ."

She didn't reply right away, and when she did, I saw that tears stood in her eyes. I had caught tears in her eyes too often of late, and I couldn't help an inward sigh. It is always harder on those who are left behind.

"Aye, my dear Isobel," she said in a barely audible voice, "I know about your heart . . . but it has been so for years. I hoped to be told I was wrong."

I reached out and patted her hand. "Do not grieve for me, Ursula, beloved friend. I am at peace."

I inhaled the lovely, scented air, admiring the ever-changing scenery, for the tender green of springtime brightened the landscape. Even the animals rejoiced. Dappled sunlight lit the woods, the world resounded with birdsong, and the forests quickened with the footsteps of fox and deer. In the fields, newborn lambs and calves struggled to stand. We trotted along the winding path in silence, twigs and branches crackling around us as squirrels chased one another around the trees.

I had a sudden sense of time propelled backward—at fifteen, I had journeyed south along this same road, seeking my future, and after John's death, I had again faced the same choice: to wed again or enter a nunnery. I thought of Sœur Madeleine. She had died soon after I last saw her in London when I was betrothed to John, but I had been so much more fortunate than dear Sœur Madeleine. I had living children. Life had taken from me too, but, oh, how much it had given in return!

The image of Marguerite as she had been when I visited her in captivity flashed into my mind. I willed it gone, for it dredged up great sorrow of what might have been. After her son's death at Tewkesbury, fire and joy had deserted her. Bereft, crushed by the misfortune, she sat all day in a chair, a vacant look in her eyes as she gazed back at the past, and that was the way I had found her when I visited Wallingford Castle. Though she knew me and was able to speak, she had become an empty shell, a repository of memories. I thought of Countess Alice. What Marguerite had dealt to others had come back to her, but where lay comfort in that? More than any of us, she had written her own story; yet she could not wash it out with all her tears, return to her victims what she had torn from them, and by so doing, save herself. . . .

After John's death, I was sorely tempted to choose the peaceful cloister where I might return to the past and be with him, if only in my thoughts, but, then, what would become of the children? They would be given over to a guardian who would one day sell their marriage to the highest bidder—and what if that guardian were the Woodville queen? I could not abandon my precious girls to such a fate. For in many ways, Elizabeth Woodville had proven herself more vile and hateful than Marguerite, so much so that Warwick's parting words to Edward had held a dire warning: *"Your queen is a woman so reviled throughout the land that no blood of her ilk will be permitted to mount the throne of England!"* A dread prophecy, for kings were not cast out without a heavy price paid in blood, as our lives bore testament.

After Barnet, William Norris came to pay his respects to me at Seaton Delaval. He told me he loved me—'tis why he had never wed, he said. He knew I didn't love him, but he claimed that mattered not. If I would marry him, he vowed I'd never regret it. And I never had. He was a good man, William, and well I knew the pain of love denied, for I remembered those days after Tattershall as clearly as if they had transpired yesterday instead of years ago.

We were married a year later, on May Day after the first anniversary of John's death. May the Blessed Lord forgive me, but during my wedding service with William, I silently renewed my own vows to John and reminded him, wherever he was, why I was doing this, and of what he had often said when he walked this earth with me: "In last year's nest, there are no eggs."

We must go forward, my dearest love, and do our best for those who need us, I whispered in my heart. Ever mindful of his last words to me, I added, *Until we meet again.*

As we journeyed over the lovely meadows and fields blooming with wildflowers, I thought about William. I felt badly leaving him without a proper farewell, knowing I would never be back, but I did it for his sake. It would have distressed him too much to know how ill I really was . . . so ill, I wasn't certain I'd make it to Bisham alive. The sickness sapped my strength daily.

The knowledge that I had done my best for William gave me comfort now. I had cared for him tenderly, and if I could never replace the one to whom I had given my heart at Tattershall Castle, at least I had made certain that William had never felt unloved, by word or deed. I also found comfort in the knowledge that this good and honorable man would see to it that my girls made suitable—perhaps even happy—marriages. But he was not powerful enough to protect my eleven-year-old George from those who would seek his wardship for the few pounds of inheritance he held. To safeguard my precious son from the Woodvilles, I had to seek out the highest reaches of power. Fortunately I was not left friendless. John's niece, Warwick's daughter Anne, had wed at last her childhood sweetheart, Richard, Duke of Gloucester. Now I could die in peace, leaving my George in their loving care, where he would be safe.

A smile came to me as I thought about my beautiful son. For certain he would be romping somewhere with Roland now. The two were as inseparable as John and Rufus had been.

As soon as I arrived in Bisham, I wrote William as I had promised. Then I wrote Nan. She now lived with her daughter Anne at Middleham, since she had no residence of her own and was a virtual pauper. For she had been deprived of her worldly possessions by her dreadful son-in-law, the traitor Clarence, Dickon's greedy brother, who had gone over to Edward just before Barnet. He would come to no good end, of that I had no doubt.

When my letter was safely on its way to Anne and her mother, I took to my bed. For sleep, I had great need, but for food, none. That was most unusual, for I had always enjoyed a good appetite, but I knew I had to preserve my strength, and so I forced myself to take broth every day. Thus I waited, inquiring each day whether my Anne and her mother had arrived, and when I was told that they had not yet come, I drank my broth and closed my eyes, and fell asleep again until the next day.

Finally, on the twentieth of May, Anne and her mother arrived at Bisham. I was deeply grateful to have lived long enough to see them again, for little Anne's voice stirred memories, and I was reminded of the happy three-year-old child who used to call out after me each time I left her castle.

Fighting a terrible weariness, I tried to open my eyes and welcome them, but my lids proved simply too heavy this morning. The physician's voice droned on at my bedside. Thinking I didn't comprehend, he didn't trouble to lower his voice, and I heard every word. " 'Tis her heart. 'Tis very weak. At thirty-five she is not truly old, and certainly she is strong enough to recover, but she seems to have lost the will to live."

"Does Norris know?" the countess asked softly.

"We have sent him word in London. He is on his way, my lady." Ursula's voice. *Dear Ursula. How glad I am that she found love!*

"She is so lovely . . . and she looks so young, Mother," said a gentle voice I had trouble identifying. Then I realized it had to be little Anne. With great effort, I willed my eyes open.

"Dear Anne . . . you've grown . . . sweet child. . . ." Then, depleted by my excitement and the effort it had taken to get out the words, my lids closed again on me. I heard murmurings and suddenly realized the error I had made. I forced my eyes open once more. "Forgive me . . . Your Grace. . . . I forgot you . . . are grown . . . and a duchess now. . . ."

A hand stroked my hair with a tender touch, soothing my spirit.

"Aunt Isobel, it is just me, just your little Anne," she whispered. "Aye, I am grown, and I have a son of my own now, like you. . . ."

How could I have forgotten why I wished to see her—why I so desperately needed her here at Bisham, why I had written as soon as I had arrived and asked her to come? If I died before I spoke to her about George, how would my soul ever find repose? My lids felt like stones on my eyes, and my arms lay like boulders beside me, but I heaved up the stones and found the strength to seize her hand, even more to raise myself on an elbow. "George—don't let them get my George—" I panted. My breath caught again, but fear made me labor hard. I devoured another intake of air into my lungs and tightened my grasp of her hand—she had to understand, I had to make her understand how important it was, what was at stake! "Take him with you—raise him as a Neville—" I forced more air into my body. "Don't leave my George to their mercy, I pray you!" My strength left me. I could no longer hold up the stones and boulders that oppressed me. I collapsed on the pillow and closed my eyes, heaving for breath.

"Aunt Isobel, you need have no fear. We shall get his wardship and raise George with us at Middleham. He shall have every benefit we can possibly provide him. He shall know what a noble and honorable knight his father was—"

I heard muffled sobs in the background, and I knew they cried for me, but I had been given what I had asked for, what I had so desperately needed, both at the beginning of my journey at fifteen and now, at its end, and my heart lay content within my breast. I smiled.

A familiar voice reached my ears. "John?" I murmured. *How*

can that be? With great effort, I turned my head and forced my eyes open again.

John stood in the corner of the room, near the chamber door, gazing at me. He wore the same green doublet and high boots he had worn at Tattershall Castle, and he looked so young, so hand-some, just as he had looked on the night of the dance . . . the night of the pavane. . . . Suddenly I felt a burst of energy surge from my heart to my lungs, and I cried out in joy, "Oh, John, my love, is it truly you?"

John smiled. "It is, my angel."

I couldn't help it—I laughed through tears of joy. "I keep tell-ing you, angels have golden hair, as any painter or colored-glass maker will tell you."

"My angels have chestnut hair—don't you know that by now, Isobel?"

"I only know that I am the most fortunate of women, beloved."

"I have been waiting for you. Come, my love, 'tis time for us to be together."

"Oh, John . . . gladly, my dearest love . . . Oh, so gladly!"

The stones that held down my body lifted, and I rose easily from the bed and glided to him. I put my hand into his, and we smiled at one another, bathed with a light beyond my understanding. Behind me I heard sobbing, louder now, and I looked back.

Tears streaming down her cheeks, the young duchess folded my hands across my chest, while her mother and Ursula sobbed un-controllably. I wanted to tell them it was all right, that I was happy, that all was well, but I knew they wouldn't hear me.

So I blew them a gentle kiss farewell and turned back to John.

Author's Note

THIS NOVEL IS THE FIRST FICTIONAL EXPLORA-
tion of the very troubled period of English history that led up to
the change of dynasty in the Wars of the Roses. Of Isobel virtu-
ally nothing has survived, while the Kingmaker's brother, Sir John
Neville, flits through the accounts of contemporary chroniclers and
the pages of historical texts, making and changing history, but leaving behind few of his thoughts. In his *Memoires*, the great statesman
Philippe de Commines, who knew Sir John Neville personally, calls
him *"un très vaillant chevalier."* No biography of him exists as of this
date, but his actions are well documented and give us glimpses into
the man he was. Handwriting analysis has also provided valuable
insights into his character.

Isobel and John's love story is based on the known facts. Sir
John Neville did pay the incredible sum of one thousand pounds
to marry sixteen-year-old Lady Isobel Ingoldesthorpe of the Lan-
castrian camp. As to the ambushes laid by Lancastrians against the
Yorkist leaders, these are recorded by several contemporary sources.
In each case, the Yorkists were forewarned by an unknown source.
Here, I brought my own motivations and interpretation to the
story, but I trust they are legitimate and might have happened as I
have depicted. I plead dramatic license for the date given for King
Henry VI's "love day," which took place on March 25, 1458.

The identity of Sir Thomas Malory remains in dispute, and all
that is known for certain is what he himself says in his book—

namely, that he was a knight and a prisoner who finished his tales of King Arthur's court between March 1469 and March 1470. I have used P. J. Fields's identification for the writer of *Morte d'Arthur* as Sir Thomas Malory of Newbold Revel, who spent ten years or more in captivity without trial, but Malory's identification as a Yorkist who died in Warwick's cause is entirely mine. For the ease of the modern reader, the quotations attributed to Sir Thomas Malory's *Morte d'Arthur* come from Alfred, Lord Tennyson's *Idylls of the King*.

The tombs of John and Isobel at Bisham no longer survive. The abbey was destroyed during the sack of the monasteries in the reign of Henry VIII. That Isobel chose to be buried with John evinces her love and regard for her first husband.

From John and Isobel through their daughter Lucy are descended both President Franklin Delano Roosevelt and Sir Winston Churchill, who, five hundred years later, turned back the dark forces of Nazi tyranny and saved free Europe from Adolf Hitler during World War II.

Please note: The poem attributed to Thomas Neville on page 135 is entitled "The Vision of Viands" by Aniar MacConglinne, Irish, twelfth century.

Sir John Neville's letter to Isobel on pages 381–82 draws from a letter written by Major Sullivan Ballou to his wife, Sarah, on July 14, 1861, during the American Civil War.

Throughout this novel, the Percy family name has been pluralized to "Percies" so as to be consistent with the version used by all historians in the numerous historical texts and articles on this family and in this period; see, for example, Ralph A. Griffiths, "Local Rivalries and National Politics: The Percies, the Nevilles, and the Duke of Exeter, 1452–55," *Speculum* 43, no. 4, October 1968.

For those readers interested in pursuing further reading, an abbreviated reading list relevant to the portrayal of events in this book is provided below. A more complete bibliography follows.

Field, P. J. C. *The Life and Times of Sir Thomas Malory.* Rochester, NY: Boydell and Brewer Ltd., 1999.

Flenley, Ralph, ed. *Six Town Chronicles of England.* Oxford: Clarendon Press, 1911.

Gairdner, James. *The Historical Collections of a Citizen of London in the Fifteenth Century (Containing William Gregory's Chronicle of London).* London: Camden Society Publications, new series 17, 1876.

Griffiths, Ralph A. "Local Rivalries and National Politics: The Percies, the Nevilles, and the Duke of Exeter, 1452–55." *Speculum* 43, no. 4 (1968): 589–632.

———, *The Reign of King Henry VI.* Thrupp, England: Sutton Publishing Ltd., 1998.

Johnson, P. A. *Duke Richard of York 1411–1460.* New York: Oxford University Press, 1988.

MacGibbon, David. *Elizabeth Woodville.* London: Arthur Barker Ltd., 1938.

Maurer, Helen. *Margaret of Anjou.* Rochester, New York: Boydell Press, 2003.

Mitchell, R. J. *John Tiptoft, Earl of Worcester.* London: Longmans, Green and Co., 1938.

Ramsey, James Henry. *Lancaster and York: A Century of English History.* Oxford: Clarendon Press, 1892.

Scofield, Cora. *The Life and Reign of Edward IV.* London: Longmans, Green and Co., 1923.

Storey, R. L. *End of the House of Lancaster.* New York: Stein and Day, 1967.

Historical Figures

Henry VI: England's mad, meek, good-hearted Lancastrian king, content to live a monk's chaste life of prayer. His marriage to Marguerite d'Anjou seals his fate.

Marguerite d'Anjou: England's fiery French queen. Wed at fifteen to mad King Henry VI of Lancaster, lonely in a foreign land. All her love and future hopes dwell in Edward, her only child. For him she will fight to the death.

Somerset: The king's cousin of the House of Lancaster. Young, rash, and violent. His charm captures the heart of a queen, but not the heart of the one he loves.

York: The king's cousin of the House of York. Prudent, able, and beloved by the people for his compassion and dedication to justice. The queen's enmity and mismanagement of the realm force him to remember he owns a better title to the throne than do her husband, King Henry, or her son, Edward.

Salisbury: Cousin to King Henry and brother-in-law to York, he stands with York when no one else dares.

Warwick: Salisbury's son. Ambitious, flamboyant, brave, and dashing, he wins the admiration of England and the enmity of two queens.

Edward of March: York's golden warrior son, who wrestles the throne from the House of Lancaster. Irresistibly charming, brilliant, and courageous. England's future seems bright under King Edward IV until he reveals his secret marriage to the lowborn beauty Elizabeth Woodville.

Elizabeth Woodville: Edward's ambitious and detested Yorkist queen. Gilt haired, cunning, and vindictive, she has a heart as dark as her face is fair.

John Tiptoft, Earl of Worcester: Isobel's uncle. Renowned scholar and man of piety, he leaves England to avoid taking sides and returns a hardened admirer of Vlad Dracula, Prince of Transylvania.

Sir Thomas Malory: A knight. His experiences color the tales of King Arthur's court that he writes as he languishes in prison first under Lancaster's queen, then under York's.

Ursula: Malory's daughter, friend to Isobel.

John: Warwick's younger brother. A valiant, true, and honorable Yorkist knight, he falls in love with Isobel, the ward of his father's mortal foe, Marguerite d'Anjou.

Isobel: Ward of the Lancastrian queen Marguerite d'Anjou. In love with John, a Yorkist knight.

Bibliography

The following is an addendum to the reading list given in the author's note.

Nonfiction

Armstrong, C. A. J. *England, France, and Burgundy in the Fifteenth Century*. London: Hambledon Press, 1983.

Barber, Richard. *The Paston Letters*. London: The Folio Society, 1981.

Bennet, H. S. *The Pastons and their England*. Cambridge: Cambridge University Press, 1990.

Chrimes, S. B., C. D. Ross, and R. A. Griffiths, eds. *Fifteenth-Century England, 1399–1509: Studies in Politics and Society*, 2nd ed. New York: Alan Sutton Publishing, 1997.

de Commynes, Philippe. *The Universal Spider: The Life of Louis XI*. Trans. and ed. Paul Murray Kendall. London: The Folio Society, 1973.

Hicks, Michael A. *False Fleeting Perjur'd Clarence: George, Duke of Clarence*. London: Alan Sutton Publishing, 1980.

———, *Richard III and His Rivals: Magnates and Their Motives*. London: Hambledon Press, 1991.

———, *Who's Who in Late Medieval England 1272–1485*. London: Shepheard-Walwyn, 1991.

Kendall, Paul Murray. *Richard the Third*. New York: W. W. Norton & Company, 1956.

Miller, Michael D. *Wars of the Roses*. http://www.warsoftheroses.co.uk.

Myers, A. R. *England in the Late Middle Ages*. London: Penguin Books, 1952.

———, *English Historical Documents*. London: Eyre & Spottiswoode, 1969.

Rawcliffe, Carole. *The Staffords, Earls of Stafford and Dukes of Buckingham, 1394–1521*. Cambridge: Cambridge University Press, 1978.

Richardson, Geoffrey. *The Hollow Crowns*. Shipley, England: Baildon Books, 1996.

———, *The Lordly Ones: A History of the Neville Family*. Shipley, England: Baildon Books, 1998.

———, *The Popinjays: A History of the Woodville Family*. Shipley, England: Baildon Books, 2000.

———, *A Pride of Bastards: A History of the Beaufort Family*. Shipley, England: Baildon Books, 2002.

Storey, R. L. *The Reign of Henry VII*. New York: Walker and Company, 1968.

Stowe's Survey of London. Intro. by H. B. Wheatley. New York: Everyman's Library, 1970.

Woodhouse, R. I. *The Life of John Morton, Archbishop of Canterbury*. London: Longman, 1895.

Nonfiction: Medieval Life

Aldred, David. *Castles and Cathedrals: The Architecture of Power*. Cambridge: Cambridge University Press, 1993.

Bayard, Tania. *Sweet Herbs and Sundry Flowers for the Medieval Gardens and the Gardens of the Cloisters*. New York: The Metropolitan Museum of Art, 1997.

Bishop, Morris. *The Middle Ages*. Boston: American Heritage Library/Houghton Mifflin, 1987.

Black, Maggie. *The Medieval Cookbook*. London: British Museum Press, 1992.

Carey, John, ed. *Eyewitness to History*. New York: Avon Books, 1987.

Coghlan, Ronan. *The Illustrated Encyclopedia of Arthurian Legends*. New York: Barnes & Noble Books, 1993.

Dyer, Christopher. *Standards of Living in the Later Middle Ages*. Cambridge: Cambridge University Press, 1989.

Englebert, Omer. *The Lives of the Saints*. New York: Barnes & Noble Books, 1994.

Freeman, Margaret B. *Herbs for the Medieval Household*. New York: The Metropolitan Museum of Art, 1971.

Gascoigne, Christina. *Castles of Britain*. New York: Thames and Hudson, 1980.

Gies, Frances, and Joseph Gies. *Life in a Medieval Castle*. New York: Harper & Row, 1974.

———, *Life in a Medieval City*. New York: HarperCollins, 1981.

————, *Life in a Medieval Village*. New York: Harper & Row, 1990.

————, *Women in the Middle Ages*. New York: HarperCollins, 1980.

Gill, D. M. *Illuminated Manuscripts: The Exquisite Art of the Medieval Manuscript*. New York: Barnes & Noble Books, 1996.

Hanawalt, Barbara A. *Growing Up in Medieval London: The Experience of Childhood in History*. New York: Oxford University Press, 1993.

Harpur, James, and Elizabeth Hallam. *Revelations: The Medieval World*. New York: Henry Holt, 1995.

Heller, Julek, and Deirdre Headon. *Knights*. New York: Schocken Books, 1982.

Herriot, James. *James Herriot's Yorkshire*. New York: St. Martin's Press, 1979.

Hopkins, Andrea. *Knights: The Complete Story of the Age of Chivalry from Historical Fact to Tales of Romance and Poetry*. London: Quarto Publishing, 1990.

Howarth, Sarah. *The Middle Ages*. New York: Penguin Books, 1993.

Images of Britain. Stamford, CT: Longmeadow Press, 1990.

Kendall, Paul Murray. *The Yorkist Age: Daily Life During the Wars of the Roses*. New York: W.W. Norton & Company, 1970.

Maynard, Christopher. *Days of the Knights: A Tale of Castles and Battles*. London: DK Publishing Inc., 1998.

Price, Mary. *Medieval Amusements*. New York: Longman Group Ltd., 1988.

Reader's Digest. *Everyday Life through the Ages*. London: Reader's Digest, 1992.

Reeves, A. Compton. *Delights of Life in Fifteenth-Century England*. New Orleans: Richard III Society, Inc., 1989.

Ross, James Bruce, and Mary Martin McLaughlin. *The Portable Medieval Reader*. New York: Penguin Books, 1977. (Includes "The Vision of Viands.")

Rowling, Marjorie. *Life in Medieval Times*. New York: Berkley Publishing Group, 1979.

Ruby, Jennifer. *Costume in Context: Medieval Times*. London: B. T. Batsford Ltd., 1993.

Swabey, Ffiona. *Medieval Gentlewoman: Life in a Gentry Household in the Later Middle Ages*. New York: Routledge, 1999.

Turnbull, Stephen. *The Book of the Medieval Knight*. London: Arms and Armour Press, 1995.

Ward, Jennifer C. *English Noblewomen in the Later Middle Ages*. London: Longman Publishing Group, 1992.

Willett, C., and Phillis Cunnington. *The History of Underclothes*. New York: Dover Publications, 1992.

Fiction

Bulwer-Lytton, Sir Edward. *Last of the Barons*. New York: R. Worthington, 1884.

Chaucer, Geoffrey. *The Canterbury Tales*. New York: Bantam, 1981.

de Pizan, Christine. *The Book of the Duke of True Lovers*. Trans. Thelmas Fenster. New York: Persea Books, 1991.

Geoffrey of Monmouth. *The History of the Kings of Britain*. Trans. Lewis Thorpe. New York: Penguin Classics, 1977.

Langland, William. *The Visions of Piers Plowman*. Ed. A.V. C. Schmidt. Rutland, VT: Charles E. Tuttle, 1995.

Malory, Sir Thomas. *Le Morte d'Arthur*. Edited by Janet Cowen. 2 vols. New York: Penguin Classics, 1970.

Tennyson, Lord Alfred. *Idylls of the King*. New York: Signet Classics, 2003.